EXILE

Also by Shannon Messenger

Keeper of the Lost Cities

Let the Sky Fall

KEEPER
OF THE LOST CITIES

EXILE

SHANNON MESSENGER

Aladdin

New York London Toronto Sydney New Delhi

For Liesa Abrams Mignogna,
editor extraordinaire,
(and likely the REAL Batgirl)

ALADDIN

An imprint of Simon & Schuster Children's Publishing Division
1230 Avenue of the Americas, New York, NY 10020
First Aladdin hardcover edition October 2013
Copyright © 2013 by Shannon Messenger
All rights reserved, including the right of reproduction
in whole or in part in any form.
ALADDIN is a trademark of Simon & Schuster, Inc., and related logo
is a registered trademark of Simon & Schuster, Inc.
For information about special discounts for bulk purchases,
please contact Simon & Schuster Special Sales
at 1-866-506-1949 or business@simonandschuster.com.
The Simon & Schuster Speakers Bureau can bring authors to your live event.
For more information or to book an event contact
the Simon & Schuster Speakers Bureau at 1-866-248-3049
or visit our website at www.simonspeakers.com.
Designed by Karin Paprocki
The text of this book was set in Scala.
Manufactured in the United States of America 1016 FFG
6 8 10 9 7 5
This book has been cataloged with the Library of Congress.
ISBN 978-1-4424-4596-3
ISBN 978-1-4424-4598-7 (eBook)

PREFACE

SOPHIE'S HANDS SHOOK AS SHE LIFTED the tiny green bottle.

One swallow held life *and* death—and not just for her.

For Prentice.

For Alden.

Her eyes focused on the clear, sloshy liquid as she removed the crystal stopper and pressed the bottle to her lips. All she had to do was tip the poison down her throat.

But could she?

Could she give up everything to set things right?

Could she live with the guilt, otherwise?

The choice was hers this time.

No more notes.

No more clues.

She'd followed them to this point, and now it came down to her.

She wasn't the Black Swan's puppet anymore.

She was broken.

All she had left was trust.

ONE

I STILL CAN'T BELIEVE WE'RE TRACKING Bigfoot," Sophie whispered as she stared at the giant footprint in the muddy soil. Each massive toe was as wide as her arm, and the print formed a deep, mucky puddle.

Dex laughed, flashing two perfect dimples as he stood on his tiptoes to examine a scuff in the bark of a nearby tree. "Do humans really think there's a giant hairy ape-man running around trying to eat them?"

Sophie turned away, pulling her blond hair around her face to hide her flushing cheeks. "Pretty crazy, right?"

Almost a year had passed since she'd found out she was an elf and moved to the Lost Cities, but she still slipped sometimes and sounded like a human. She *knew* sasquatch were really just tall green shaggy creatures with beady eyes and beaklike noses—she'd even worked with them in the pastures at Havenfield, the enormous estate and animal preserve she now called home. But a lifetime of human teaching was difficult to forget. Especially with a photographic memory.

Thunder cracked overhead and Sophie jumped.

"I don't like this place," Dex mumbled, his periwinkle eyes scanning the tree line as he moved closer to Sophie. The damp, heavy air made his light blue tunic stick to his skinny arms, and his gray pants were caked with mud. "Let's find this thing and get out of here."

Sophie agreed. The murky forest was so dense and wild. It felt like a place time had forgotten.

The thick ferns in front of them rustled and a brawny gray arm grabbed Sophie from behind. Her feet dangled above the ground, and she got a face full of musky goblin sweat as her bare-chested bodyguard shoved Dex behind him, drew his curved sword from the scabbard at his side, and pointed it at the tall blond elf in a dark green tunic who stumbled out of the wall of leaves.

"Easy there, Sandor," Grady said, backing away from the glinting point of the black blade. "It's just me."

"Sorry." Sandor's high-pitched voice always reminded Sophie of a chipmunk. He dipped a slight bow as he lowered his weapon. "I didn't recognize your scent."

"That's probably because I just spent twenty minutes crawling around a sasquatch den." Grady sniffed his sleeve and coughed. "Whew—Edaline is not going to be happy with me when I get home."

Dex laughed, but Sophie was too busy trying to wriggle free from Sandor's viselike hold.

"You can put me down now!" As soon as her feet touched the ground she huffed away, glaring at Sandor and struggling to remove the giant wedgie he'd given her. "Any sign of the sasquatch?"

"The den's been empty for a while. And I'm guessing you guys haven't had much luck picking up the trail?"

Dex pointed to the scratch he'd been examining in the bark. "Looks like it climbed this tree and traveled in the branches from here on out. No way to tell which way it went."

Sandor sniffed the air with his wide, flat nose. "I should take Miss Foster home. She's been in the open for far too long."

"I'm fine! We're in the middle of a forest and no one besides the Council knows we're here. You didn't even have to come."

"I go where you go," Sandor said firmly, sheathing his sword and running his hands down the pockets lining his black military-style pants to check his other weapons. "I take my charge very seriously."

"Obviously," Sophie grumbled. She knew Sandor was only trying to protect her, but she hated having him around. He was a seven-foot-tall constant reminder that the kidnappers she and Dex had narrowly escaped were still out there somewhere, waiting for the right time to make their next move. . . .

Plus, it was humiliating being followed by an ultraparanoid goblin all the time. She'd been hoping she'd be done with the bodyguard thing by the time school started again. But with less than two weeks left on her vacation and the Council hitting dead ends on all their leads, it looked like her burly, slightly alien-looking shadow was coming with her to Foxfire.

She'd tried convincing Alden he could just keep track of her with the crystal registry pendant latched around her neck, but he'd reminded her that the kidnappers had no problem tearing it off the last time. And even though this one had extra cords woven into the choker and a few other added security measures, he refused to put her life in the hands of an inanimate accessory.

She repressed a sigh.

"We need Sophie here with us," Grady told Sandor as he pulled Sophie into a quick, reassuring hug. "Are you picking up anything?" he asked her.

"Not nearby. But I can try widening my range." She moved away from him and closed her eyes, placing her hands over her temples to focus her concentration.

Sophie was the only Telepath who could track thoughts to their exact location—and the only one who could read the minds of animals. If she could feel the sasquatch's thoughts, she would be able to follow them straight to wherever it was hiding. All she had to do was *listen*.

Her concentration spread like an invisible veil across the scenery, and the chirping and creaking sounds of the forest faded to a low hum as the "voices" filled her mind. The melodic thoughts of the birds in the trees. The hushed thoughts of the rodents in the ground. Farther away in a small meadow were the calm thoughts of a doe and her fawn. And farther still, in the thicker parts of the underbrush, were the stealthy thoughts of a large cougar, stalking its prey.

But no trace of the heavy, thundering thoughts of a sasquatch.

She pushed her focus toward the snowcapped mountains. The stretch was longer than most Telepaths could handle, but she'd reached much farther when she was calling for rescue from her captors—and she'd been half-drugged at the time. So she was surprised when her body started to shake from the strain.

"It's okay, Sophie," Grady told her, squeezing her shoulder. "We'll find it another way."

No.

This was why Grady had brought her along for this rescue, despite Sandor's numerous concerns for her safety. He'd already tried three other times to capture the beast, and came home empty-handed. He was counting on her.

She tugged out a loose eyelash—her nervous habit—as she pushed her mind as far as she could go. Spots of light flashed across her vision, each one paired with a stab of pain that ripped her breath away. But the misery was worth it when she caught the vaguest whisper of a thought. A fuzzy image of river with mossy green rocks and white, trickling water. It felt softer than the sasquatch thoughts she'd touched when she practiced at Havenfield, but the thought was definitely too complex to belong to any of the normal forest animals.

"It's that way," Sophie said, pointing north before she took off through the trees. She was glad she'd worn lightweight boots instead of the flat, dressy shoes she was usually supposed to wear, even with her plain tan tunic and brown pants.

Dex sprinted to catch up with her, and his messy strawberry blond hair bounced as he matched her pace. "I still don't understand how you do that."

"You're not a Telepath. I have no idea how you do any of the things Technopaths do."

"Shhhhh, they'll hear you!"

Dex had made her promise not to tell anyone about his newly discovered talent. Dame Alina—Foxfire's principal—wouldn't allow him to take ability detecting if she knew he'd already manifested, and Dex kept hoping he'd trigger a "better" talent, even though it was incredibly rare to have more than one ability.

"You're being dumb," Sophie told him. "Technopathy is cool."

"Easy for you to say. It's not fair you get to be a Telepath *and* an Inflictor."

Sophie cringed at the last word.

If it were up to her, she'd drop the dangerous ability in a heartbeat. But talents couldn't be switched off once they'd been triggered. She'd checked. A lot.

Sophie's muscles burned as the ground became steeper and the cold drizzly air stung her lungs—but it felt good to run. Ever since the kidnapping everyone kept her closed in, trying to keep her away from danger. All it really meant was that she was the one being held prisoner while the bad guys ran free.

The thought spurred her legs faster, like if she just pushed herself harder, she could get far enough from her problems to make them disappear. Or at least far enough from Sandor— though the goblin was surprisingly agile for his bulky size. She'd never been able to ditch him, and she'd tried *many* times over the last few weeks.

The path grew narrower as they moved toward the mountains, and after several more minutes of climbing, it curved west and ended in a gurgling stream. White puffs of mist hovered above the rocks, giving the water a ghostly feel as it snaked up the rocky foothills.

Sophie paused to catch her breath, and Dex bent to stretch his legs. Grady and Sandor caught up as she was checking on the sasquatch's location.

"You're supposed to stay by my side," Sandor complained.

Sophie ignored him, pointing toward the snowcapped mountains. "It's up there."

The thoughts felt sharper now, filling her mind with a

shockingly vivid scene. Every tiny leaf on the lacy ferns was crystal clear, and she could almost feel the cool water splashing against her skin and the breeze tickling her cheeks. But the really strange part was the warm calm that wrapped around her consciousness. She'd never experienced a thought as such a pure emotion before—especially from a creature so far away.

"No more separating," Grady ordered as they started to follow the stream higher up the mountain. "I'm not familiar with this part of the forest."

Sophie wasn't surprised. The trees and ferns were so thick she was sure no one—human or elf—had set foot there in a very long time.

Squishy green moss coated the ground, muffling their footsteps. It was also slick, and the third time Sophie slipped, Dex grabbed her arm and didn't let go. The warmth of his hand sank through the fabric of her sleeve and she felt like she should pull away. But he was steadying her balance, which made it easier for her to concentrate on what the sasquatch was thinking.

The beast must have been eating, because a satisfied feeling settled into the pit of Sophie's stomach, like she'd just had an extra helping of mallowmelt.

She hurried forward—afraid it would move on now that it was full—and accidentally stepped on a fallen branch.

Craaaaaaaaaaaaaaaack!

Goose bumps erupted all over her body, and even though she

knew the emotion wasn't hers, Sophie couldn't ignore the shivering terror. She had no idea what that meant—but she didn't have time to think about it. From the images flashing through her head she could tell the sasquatch had started to flee.

She jerked her arm out of Dex's grip and took off after it.

The beast ran so fast its thoughts turned to a blur. Sophie concentrated on channeling energy from her core into her legs, but even with the extra strength she could still feel the sasquatch pulling farther ahead. It was going to get away—unless she found a way to boost her speed.

A brain push.

She hadn't been thrilled when she'd learned that she could perform the incredibly rare telepathy skill. But as she shoved the warm energy humming in the back of her mind into her legs and felt her muscles surge with a tremendous burst of power, she was suddenly grateful for the strange ways her brain worked—even if it did make her headache worse. Her feet barely touched the ground as she raced over the soggy soil, leaving Dex, Sandor, and Grady far behind.

The sasquatch's thoughts turned clearer again.

She was catching up.

The extra energy didn't last as long as she'd expected, though, and as her strength drained she found herself barely able to stumble forward.

It's okay, she transmitted, desperately shoving the words into the creature's mind. *I'm not going to hurt you.*

The sasquatch froze.

Its thoughts were a jumbled mix of emotions, and Sophie couldn't make sense out of any of them. But she took advantage of its momentary stillness, rallying the last of her energy to fumble toward a narrow opening in the thick wall of foliage. She could feel the sasquatch on the other side of the trees.

Waiting for the others would be the safer thing to do—but who knew how much longer the creature would wait around? And the creature felt calm at the moment. Curious.

Three deep breaths spurred her courage. Then Sophie padded into the clearing.

TWO

OPHIE'S GASP ECHOED OFF THE CIRCLE of trees, and she blinked to make sure her eyes were working.

A few feet in front of her stood a shimmering pale horse with outstretched feathered wings. It wasn't a pegasus—she knew from the books she'd studied at Havenfield that those were smaller and huskier, with deep blue spots and midnight blue manes. This horse had wavy silver hair that trailed up its neck and parted around a horn of swirled white and silver that jutted from its forehead like a unicorn. But the unicorns she'd seen didn't have wings.

"What are you?" Sophie whispered as she stared into the horse's deep brown eyes. Usually she thought brown eyes were flat and boring—especially her own—but these had glinting flecks of gold, and gazed back at her so intently she couldn't look away.

The horse whinnied.

"It's okay. I won't hurt you." She transmitted images of herself caring for other animals.

The horse stamped its hooves and nickered, but stayed put, eyeing Sophie warily.

Sophie focused on its thoughts, searching for anything she could use to make it trust her. The complexity of its mind was shocking. She could feel rapid observations and quick calculations, just like when she was reading an elvin mind. And the emotions were so intense. Now she knew how Empaths must feel—and she was glad she wasn't one of them. It was hard to know which feelings were hers.

"*There* you are!" Dex said, stomping into the clearing. His jaw fell open as the horse whinnied and took to the sky.

"It's okay," Sophie called. "He's a friend."

Friend.

As soon as she transmitted the word, the horse froze, hovering above them. Dozens of images flashed through Sophie's head. Then a new emotion nearly choked her. Her eyes burned and her heart ached, and it took her a second to translate the feeling.

"You're lonely?" Sophie whispered.

"That's not a sasquatch," Dex mumbled.

"Yeah, I caught that," Sophie told him. "Do you know what it is?"

"An alicorn," Grady murmured behind her, triggering a new wave of panic from the flying horse.

Another friend, Sophie transmitted as it soared higher into the clouds.

Grady was actually more than a friend. He was her adopted father. But for some reason she had a hard time calling him that—even with her adoption being final now.

It's okay, she promised the alicorn. *No one is going to hurt you.*

The alicorn whinnied, its mind focused on Sandor—and the weapon at Sandor's side.

"Sandor, you're scaring it. You need to get back."

Sandor didn't budge.

"Please," Grady told him. "We *can't* lose this creature. You know how essential it is to our world."

Sandor sighed and stomped out of the clearing, grumbling about it being *impossible* to do his job.

"This horse is really that important?" Sophie asked, squinting at the sky.

"Uh, yeah." Dex's voice was annoyingly smug. "They've only found one—ever. The Council's been searching for another for centuries."

"Millennia," Grady corrected. "Throughout our time on this planet we've worked to discover all of its secrets. And then by accident, really, a magnificent alicorn stumbled into our lives, proving the earth still had a few tricks up its sleeves. We've been trying to find another ever since. We can't let it slip away. Can you call it down to us, Sophie?"

The pressure of his request sat heavy on her shoulders as she promised to try.

Safe, she transmitted to the terrified creature, adding images of her caring for other animals to try and reinforce the word. Then she sent a picture of the alicorn standing next to her in the clearing. *Come down.*

When the alicorn didn't respond she added an image of how she would look if she were stroking the alicorn's shimmering mane.

A rush of loneliness poured over her again—stronger this time. An ancient-feeling ache. Then the alicorn circled once more and landed just out of Sophie's reach.

"Incredible," Grady breathed.

"Good girl," Sophie whispered.

"Girl?" Dex asked.

Sophie nodded, wondering how she knew that. It almost felt like the alicorn had told her. . . .

"The alicorn at the Sanctuary is male!" Grady said, snapping her out of her musings. "This is the find of a lifetime, Sophie!"

Sophie grinned, imagining the look on Councillor Bronte's face when he heard the news. He despised her human upbringing and her connection to the Black Swan—a secret group of rebels who seemed to be behind every mystery in Sophie's past—and was always trying to prove she didn't belong in their world.

"Um . . . not to kill everyone's excitement here," Dex interrupted, "but how are we going to get her home?"

Grady's smile faded. "That's a good question. The sasquatch harness won't fit—and even if I dashed home, it's not like we have an alicorn restraint."

"Maybe we don't need one." Sophie stared into the alicorn's unblinking eyes and transmitted *friend* again. Then she reached out her hand and took a slow step forward.

"Careful," Grady warned when the alicorn whinnied.

"Easy, girl," Sophie whispered, not breaking eye contact as she took another step.

Calm.

She sent a flood of images of her petting different animals, trying to communicate what she was about to do.

The alicorn processed each scene, focusing on Sophie. She nickered.

Sophie hoped that meant "Go ahead." She held her breath and closed the last space between them.

Her fingers brushed the smooth, cool fur on the bridge of the alicorn's nose. The shimmering horse snorted, but didn't back away.

"Good girl," Sophie said, tracing her fingers up toward the horn. She fingered the strands of silvery mane, surprised at how cold they were, like threads of ice.

The alicorn released what sounded like a soft sigh. Then she nuzzled Sophie's shoulder. Sophie giggled as the wet nostrils tickled her neck.

"She likes you," Grady whispered.

"Is that true, girl? Do you like me?"

A shiver streaked down Sophie's spine as something tickled her consciousness. The longer it bounced around her mind, the more it took shape, until it formed a single word.

Friend.

"What's wrong?" Grady asked as Sophie took a step away, shaking her head.

"Sorry—I'm just not used to how powerful her mind is." She stroked the horse's gleaming cheek, trying to make sense of what just happened.

Had the alicorn learned a word from her? Was that possible?

"Think she'll let me touch her?" Grady asked, taking a cautious step forward.

The alicorn reared and flapped her wings.

Grady backed off. "That's going to be a problem."

In order to light leap with the alicorn, someone would need to keep physical contact with her to form a connection between them.

"I can leap her—" Sophie offered.

"Absolutely not!" Grady's shout made the alicorn whinny, and he lowered his tone to a whisper before he added, "That's far too dangerous."

"I can handle it," Sophie insisted. All the excitement had erased both her headache and her weariness from the brain push.

"Um, remember what happened last time?" Dex interrupted.

Sophie glared at him, stunned he was siding with Grady on this.

"Hey, don't look at me like that. You almost faded away."

His voice caught as he said the last part, and Sophie couldn't help wondering how much Dex had seen that day. She'd thought he was unconscious when she made the nearly fatal leap to escape the kidnappers. But apparently he'd watched the light pull her away—or at least that's what Elwin had told her. She and Dex had never talked about what happened. All Sophie remembered was warmth and flashing colors and a pull so irresistible she'd been ready to follow it anywhere—and very nearly had.

She'd *never* forget the agony of drawing herself back together. And now whenever she leaped, she felt slightly dizzy. But the dizziness only lasted a few seconds, and in all the times Elwin had tested her since she'd recovered, he'd never found anything wrong. Plus, all of that happened before she knew how to use her enhanced concentration. Before she even knew her concentration had been enhanced. Not to mention, the kidnappers had taken her nexus.

She cupped the sleek black cuff on her wrist, fingering the sparkly teal jewel set into the center, surrounded by swirling lines of diamonds. The nexus put a force field around her, making it impossible for her to lose even a single particle of herself during a leap. Which meant she could use *her* concentration to protect the alicorn and leap them both home safely.

It made sense in her head—but she couldn't fight off a tiny quiver at the idea of another risky leap.

"We don't have any other options," Sophie said, as much for herself as to convince Grady and Dex. "Unless there's something I'm missing?"

When no one had any other suggestions, she took a deep breath and imagined her concentration covering the glittering horse like a protective seal. Her headache returned and she had to channel the last of her core energy to cover such a large creature, but she scraped together enough strength to feel a firm grip.

She could do this.

Before she could change her mind, she placed one hand on the alicorn's cheek and used the other to grab the pendant hanging from a long chain around her neck. She held the crystal up, and light hit the single facet cut into the stone, refracting toward the ground.

"Sophie, don't you—" Grady started to say, but he was too late.

She stepped into the light, letting the warmth swell under her skin like thousands of tickling feathers as the simmering rush swept her and the alicorn away.

THREE

THE LUSH PASTURES OF HAVENFIELD glittered into focus as Sophie's body re-formed on the wide, flower-lined path that cut through the main grounds. Her legs held strong beneath her, but the dizziness was almost overwhelming, and rainbow flecks of light obscured her vision, like she was seeing the world through a kaleidoscope. She wobbled, wishing she had something to hold on to as the alicorn screamed with terror and took off into the sunset-streaked sky.

Sophie stumbled after her, but she'd only made it a few steps before strong hands grabbed her by the shoulders and spun her around.

"What were you thinking?" Grady's arms shook as he held her tight, but Sophie was more worried about the blurry gray blob looming behind him. Even through the swirling colors she could make out Sandor's furious glare.

"I'm fine, I promise," she said, gulping down air and willing the words to be true.

The winged horse whinnied and the wave of panic helped Sophie focus. "I have to calm her down before she flies away."

Grady's grip on her shoulders tightened for a second. Then he shook his head and released her. "We'll continue this conversation later."

She was sure they would, and she didn't have time to worry about it. Her head was finally clearing—and just in time. Verdi, their resident T. rex—who *still* hadn't adapted to her vegetarian diet—was roaring, like she was craving a glittering-horsey snack.

The alicorn veered away from the neon-green-feathered dinosaur, heading toward the Grove, a lush orchard of bulbous, twisted trees. Several squat brown gnomes streamed from the arched green doors in the trunks, their huge gray eyes staring at the alicorn as she circled overhead.

"Help—I need something to lure her down," Sophie called as she raced past them, though several gnomes had already taken off toward the row of golden silos that lined the farthest cliffs. The gnomes weren't servants—they lived with the elves by choice—and they were masters when it came to plants and animals. Hopefully, they knew some treat an alicorn wouldn't be able to resist.

"Boy, are you in trouble," Dex said as he caught up with Sophie. "You'll be lucky if Grady and Edaline let you out of the house before you turn two hundred and fifty."

"Not helping, Dex."

Please come back, she transmitted when the horse flitted even higher. *Friend.*

"Try these," Grady said behind her, holding out a handful of twisted, pale blue stalks.

A spicy, cinnamonlike scent tickled Sophie's nose as she took them and held them toward the sky. "Come down, girl," she called, sending images of the alicorn feasting on the slender twigs. *I have treats.*

Curiosity wove through Sophie's emotions.

Treats! Sophie repeated.

The alicorn whinnied and circled lower, but didn't land. Sophie kept repeating her promise of treats and waving them in the air until finally, after three more rotations, the alicorn slowly touched down a few feet away, prodding the ground with her gleaming hooves.

Sophie smiled and held out the stalks. "Here, girl."

The winged horse studied Sophie with her enormous brown eyes. Then she lunged forward, and her wet, square-toothed snout chomped the tops of the treats straight from Sophie's hand. Sophie barely had time to get her fingers out of the way before the alicorn gobbled the rest.

"Ew," Dex complained, plugging his nose. "Who knew sparkly horses had such bad breath?"

"It's nothing on Iggy breath," Sophie reminded him. Her pet imp might only be a palm-size furball, but every time he opened his mouth it was like standing near a mountain of rotting eggs and dirty diapers. "I think we're going to need more of these," she added when the alicorn's rough purple tongue started licking her palm.

"Already on its way." Grady pointed to a gnome stumbling toward them with a bundle of the blue stalks almost as tall as he was.

Gnomes looked more like plants than animals, with rough, earthy skin and bright green thumbs. Sophie still got a little startled when she saw their strange features, so she wasn't surprised when the alicorn whinnied and reared back. But the gnome wasn't fazed, flashing a green-toothed grin as he spread the treats in a thin trail leading to an aviary they usually used for pterodactyls. The nervous horse eyed the stalks suspiciously, but after a minute she lowered her head and began munching her way toward the enclosure. She was still feasting on the last of the treats when Grady closed the gate, locking her inside the small dome of interwoven green bamboo stalks.

Panic bloomed inside Sophie's mind as the alicorn tried and failed to spread her wings in her enclosure.

"It's only for a few hours," Grady explained when he caught Sophie's frown. "The gnomes are already working to enclose the Cliffside pasture."

"Wow, really?" Grady and Edaline had vacated the Cliffside pasture not long after Sophie had disappeared, not wanting to go anywhere near the caves where she'd supposedly drowned. After she'd been rescued they'd added a high metal fence all along the cliffs' edges to block anyone from using the path that led to the beach below. Sophie wasn't sure if the complex padlock was meant to keep her in or keep others out, but either way she had no problem staying away from those caves. She never wanted to see them again.

The pasture was a perfect expanse of soft grassy knolls to house a flying horse, though, so she could see why Grady was willing to use it. But enclosing it would be a massive undertaking. Good thing the gnomes were amazingly industrious creatures. They absorbed energy from the sun and needed almost no sleep, so they were always looking for ways to stay busy. If anyone could work such a miracle, it was them.

"Can we at least give her more treats to cheer her up?" The alicorn was staring at her with sad, watery eyes.

"The gnomes are getting her more right now. It's a good thing they harvested a bunch of swizzlespice today."

See, you'll be okay, Sophie told her. *I promise.*

The alicorn looked away.

"She hates me now."

"She'll forgive you." Grady rested his hand on her shoulder and it gave Sophie the courage to turn and face him.

"What about you?" she asked quietly. "Still hate me for leaping her here?"

Grady closed his eyes. "Sophie, nothing you do will ever make me *hate* you. But what you did was very dangerous. If something had happened to you, I'd . . ."

Sophie stared at her feet. "I'm sorry. I really do try to be careful."

"I know. But you can never be careful enough, okay?"

She nodded and he strangled her with a hug.

She caught a whiff of the sasquatch funk in his tunic and pulled away, coughing. "So, what's my punishment?"

"I want Elwin to check you out in the morning, make sure you really are okay."

Sadly, that wasn't a surprise. She'd pretty much set the record for most physician house calls ever—ironic considering how much she hated doctors.

"And you get to bathe the verminion for the next month," Grady added.

Sophie groaned. She swore the giant mutant-hamster-thing had been plotting to destroy her since she'd helped trap it when it arrived at Havenfield. "That's just mean."

"No, that's awesome," Dex corrected.

"Glad you think so, Dex," Grady told him, "'Cause you get to help her."

"Hey—I didn't do anything wrong!"

"I never said you did. But do you really think Sophie will let you just stand there and watch her work?"

He was right. She was totally going to rope Dex into helping her—and he came over almost every day. They were best friends, after all.

But something about the way Grady was smiling at them made Sophie's cheeks feel hot. Dex must've noticed it too, because his face was bright red as he mumbled some excuse about his parents worrying if he wasn't home soon, and quickly leaped out of there.

Grady took Sophie's hand, his smile fading. "I don't think we should tell Edaline about your little adventure, what with tomorrow . . ."

"I'm sorry I scared you."

He gave her a sad smile. "Just don't do it again. Now come on, let's go wash off the sasquatch grime and tell Edaline what we found."

By the time Sophie had showered and changed and fed Iggy his dinner so he wouldn't trash her room—imps could be very troublesome creatures if they were discontent—the sun had set and the gnomes had finished preparing the pasture. Goose bumps prickled Sophie's skin as she made her way to the new enclosure, and even though she tried not to look, her eyes still wandered toward the cliffs, where moonlight glinted off the edge of the iron gate.

She forced herself to look away, focusing on the thick stalks that looked like purple bamboo bent into wide arches, creating a weblike dome over the mile-wide space. More arched stalks had been lined up like dominoes, creating a covered pathway to securely transport the alicorn from one enclosure to another. But the alicorn was nowhere to be seen.

"She's too panicked," Grady explained when Sophie found him at the pterodactyl pen. "The gnomes are afraid to move her right now. She might hurt herself trying to escape."

"You don't have to be afraid, pretty girl," Edaline whispered as she approached the bars, holding swizzlespice. "We're trying to help you."

The alicorn whinnied and bucked.

Edaline backed away, brushing her wavy, amber-colored hair out of her face. "I'm not sure what else to try."

"Think you can calm her down, Sophie?" Grady asked.

"Maybe." Sophie stepped closer, and as soon as the alicorn spotted her she stopped thrashing. The moonlight had turned her opalescent fur to gleaming silver, and her dark eyes glittered like stars.

Friend? Sophie transmitted.

Friend! the alicorn transmitted back, lowering her snout so Sophie could reach through the bars and scratch her cheeks.

"Amazing," Edaline breathed as she smiled for the first time in at least a week. The dark shadows under her turquoise eyes faded, too. "Can you get her to walk to her new pen?"

"I'll try." Sophie transmitted images of the Cliffside enclosure, repeating, *Your new home.* When that didn't seem to help she added a picture of the alicorn grazing inside.

The alicorn processed the image, then replied with one of her own: a dark, starry sky with a glittering silver horse flying free.

"I don't think she wants to stay here," Sophie whispered.

"Well, she has to. She's far too important," Grady reminded her. "Plus, this is the only way to keep her safe. Think about what would happen if humans got their hands on her."

An image of the alicorn strapped to a million creepy medical machines flashed through Sophie's mind, and she shuddered as she transmitted, *It's safe here.*

Safe, the alicorn repeated, but it didn't feel like she really understood the word. Or maybe she didn't care.

Sophie tried a different tactic. *You won't be lonely anymore.*

The alicorn processed that, and after several seconds transmitted back a tentative, *Friend?*

Friend, Sophie told her, sending the image of the enclosure again. *Safe. Let's move you to your new home.*

This time the alicorn didn't argue and Sophie nodded to Grady. He gave the gnomes the signal to open the gates between the pastures.

Calm, Sophie transmitted as the alicorn tensed, but she still felt a surge of panic as the gates slid apart and the alicorn galloped forward, racing through the tunnel at full speed.

Sophie jogged after her with Grady and Edaline right behind, and they all sucked in a breath when the shimmering horse reached her new pasture and spread her wings, flying to the highest part of her dome.

"Well done, Sophie," Grady said, squeezing her shoulders. "What would we do without you?"

She blushed from the praise. "Have you told anyone we found her?"

"I tried to reach Alden, but he was out of range. I'll try him in the morning."

Sophie shivered, even though she wasn't cold. There were only a few places an Imparter—a small silver square that worked a bit like a video phone—would be out of range, and they were all dark, forbidden places. She hated to think Alden was out there, risking his life trying to find her kidnappers.

The alicorn whinnied and landed, snapping her back to the present.

Sophie reached through the purple bars, and after a second the horse trotted close enough for Sophie to stroke her shimmering neck. *I wish I knew what to call you.*

It seemed wrong to call such a breathtaking creature something as boring as "the alicorn." *Do you have a name, pretty girl?*

She didn't actually expect an answer, but a thought prickled her mind anyway. It felt strangely warm and soft, and when she concentrated, it twisted and flipped into a word.

"Silveny?" Sophie whispered.

The alicorn nickered.

"What did you say?" Edaline asked.

Sophie shook her head to clear it. "I think her name is Silveny."

Silveny nickered again.

"Wait—you can speak to her with *words*?" Grady asked.

"Sometimes she repeats the words I transmit—but this didn't feel like that. This was more like she spoke to me in her own language and I translated it."

For a second they both just stared at her. Then Grady laughed. "The wonders of your talents never cease."

Sophie tried to smile, but her stomach turned sour.

Being a Polyglot—able to understand any and all languages—was another talent that had been triggered during her kidnapping. A *third* special ability. She should probably be proud to have so many skills, but she couldn't help worrying about what her abilities meant. And what she'd be expected to do with them.

A haunting voice whispered from her memories: *You're their little puppet.*

"You okay, Sophie?" Edaline asked, a thin worry line between her brows.

"Yeah, just tired." As the words left her mouth she realized they were true. Every part of her ached, and remnants of her headache still pulsed behind her eyes. "I think I'm going to bed."

She could tell Grady and Edaline weren't convinced, but they didn't press the issue. She stroked Silveny's silky nose, promised to see her in the morning, and headed to her bedroom, which took up the entire third floor of Havenfield.

Her room was dark—lit only by the moonlight streaming through the walls of windows. She lingered in the doorway, snapping her fingers and waiting for the crystal stars that dangled from the ceiling to flood the room with light before she went any farther.

Sandor had already done his nightly sweep of her room to check for intruders—but she still scanned every nook and shadow, searching for any sign that someone had been there besides her. Other than a badly chewed shoe—Iggy's handiwork—everything was in its place. Not even a single petal on the flowers woven into her carpet had been touched.

Satisfied, she closed her door, changed into her pajamas, and sank into her enormous canopy bed, stretching her weary muscles as she did. She snuggled her face against Ella, the bright blue stuffed elephant she couldn't sleep without, and snapped her fingers again, switching off the lights. Iggy took his place on her pillow, curling his tiny gray body into a ball and within seconds he was snoring like a chain saw. Sophie scratched his fuzzy tummy, wishing she could fall asleep so easily, and clapped her hands to lower the thick shades across her windows.

She'd hoped to close her eyes and dream of sparkly winged horses flying through a bright blue sky. Instead, black-cloaked figures haunted her mind, snatching her from the shadows and dragging her away in a drugged haze. Sharp bonds sliced her wrists and ankles as someone shouted questions she didn't know the answers to. Then fiery hands seared her skin and ghostly whispers swirled through the blackness.

They would find her.

She would never escape them again.

FOUR

IT WAS ONLY A DREAM, SOPHIE TRIED TO tell herself as she wiped the cold sweat off her forehead. But her skin throbbed from the memory of the pain, and she could still smell the noxiously sweet sedatives that had burned her nose. And that voice . . .

She would *never* forget that voice.

She shivered as she crawled out of bed, tiptoeing across the carpet and pressing her ear against her smooth wooden door. Her racing heart slowed when she heard Sandor's steady breathing on the other side. Deep down she really *was* grateful for his protection. She just wished she didn't need him.

Dex didn't have a bodyguard. He'd simply been in the wrong place at the wrong time, and Sophie still felt horrible about that. *She* was the one they'd been after, because they'd wanted *to see what she could do.*

But . . . what did they think she could do?

The question haunted her more than the nightmares, and she padded to her desk to retrieve the only thing she knew would calm her down.

The silk-wrapped bundle had been tucked safely at the back of the bottom drawer and she didn't remove the cloth until she'd hidden herself under her covers. The cool silver sphere turned warm at her touch, and the word SPYBALL glowed in golden letters, casting a dim light in her little cave of bed sheets.

Sophie closed her eyes, needing a second before saying the names she'd carefully memorized—the names the Council had forbidden her to know.

"Show me Connor, Kate, and Natalie Freeman," she whispered, opening her eyes as the Spyball flashed and three figures came into focus in the center of the orb.

Her mom looked thinner, her sister looked taller, and there were streaks of gray in her dad's hair that Sophie didn't remember him having—but it was *them.* Sitting around a dinner table in some faraway part of the world, eating fettuccini like the perfect happy family. With no idea she even existed.

It was what she'd wanted for them—what she'd begged for. To be erased, so they wouldn't have to miss her in their new lives. But it wasn't easy being forgotten. Especially since she couldn't forget them.

She watched until her eyes blurred with tears. Then she smeared them away and whispered, "Show me Mr. Forkle."

The Spyball turned black and flashed the word she was getting very tired of:

UNKNOWN.

Her grip tightened on the sphere, trying to squeeze it into submission. She knew it wasn't his real name, but part of her kept hoping the Spyball would somehow figure out his real identity. He was her only link to the Black Swan. The one who'd rescued her and Dex when they'd been taken. The one who'd triggered all of her new abilities. He'd even posed as her next-door neighbor when she lived with her human family, and was probably the one who planted the secrets in her head.

He had all the answers she needed.

But *he* didn't want to be found.

She wrapped the Spyball back in the cloth and returned it to its hiding place. The drawer above it held a thick teal book, which she removed next, along with another silk bundle. She sank to the floor, leaning against the side of her desk as she unwrapped the bottle of moonlight. The pale glow made it just bright enough to see, without letting Sandor know she was awake.

Her fingers traced the etched lines of the silver bird on the cover. *A moonlark.*

Seeing it gave her chills every time.

Alden had given her the memory log as a way to chronicle

her dreams and keep track of any memories that weren't hers. But since the kidnapping she'd been using it to conduct her own investigation into the Black Swan. She kept hoping they'd left clues in her memories that would tell her how to find them.

The problem was, she had no idea how to access any of the secret information they'd planted. All the times she'd had "flashes," there'd been something to spark the hidden memory—usually a note or gift the Black Swan had given her. Without anything to trigger the flashback, she was stuck wading through thirteen years of memories—and thanks to her photographic memory she had a *lot* of memories to sort through. But she'd been focusing on two incidents that felt like they had to be key.

The first was when she was five. She'd woken up in the Emergency Room, and the doctors told her she'd fallen and hit her head and her neighbor had called 911. From that moment on she'd been able to read minds. She knew now that Mr. Forkle had triggered her telepathic abilities that day. What she didn't know was why. Five was incredibly young to manifest a special ability, and the talent had made it *much* harder for her to blend in with humans. So why trigger it then? And why couldn't she remember what happened?

The second incident was when she was nine. Again she'd ended up in the hospital, this time for a severe allergic reaction. The human doctors never figured out what caused it, but a few months ago she'd found out the hard way that she was deathly allergic to limbium, a special compound that affected certain areas of the brain. She even had to wear a vial of an antidote Elwin had created in case she accidentally consumed any. Only elves knew how to make limbium, but she knew now that she'd had contact with at least one elf back then without realizing it—and the symptoms of both reactions had been the same. So someone must have given her limbium. But who? And why?

Two blurry spots in her past. Both times when the elves had clearly interfered with her life. That couldn't be a coincidence.

The kidnappers hadn't been able to wipe away her memories—but the Black Swan *made* her. And they'd had no problem planting secret information in her head. So couldn't they take some away?

She needed those memories back. Deep in her subconscious there had to be something left, a clue that could trigger some tiny piece they missed. She just had to find it.

Iggy flitted over to her leg, curling up on the top of her knee as she turned to the first blank page in the memory log.

Come on, brain. Give me something useful this time.

"Still having trouble sleeping?" Elwin asked, squinting through thick iridescent spectacles as he squatted in front of her. The morning sun streamed through the glass walls of the living room, where Sophie sat on the sleek white couch. "Those dark circles are starting to look like bruises."

"I have a lot on my mind."

He lowered his glasses to study her. "Anything you want to talk about?"

Her mind flashed to her dizzy spell the day before, but she looked away and shrugged. She was tired of being tested and watched and fussed over. Besides, if something were wrong with her, Elwin would've found it by now. His glasses could see right down to her cells.

Elwin heaved a sigh as he stood, looking incredibly out of place with his lime green, gremlin-covered tunic in the elegant, pristine room. Havenfield usually had a few books and gadgets strewn about, leaving splashes of color. But Edaline had been on a cleaning rampage, trying to keep herself distracted.

"Look up," Elwin instructed, slipping on his glasses again.

Sophie obeyed, and her eyes caught the light from the cascading crystals of the chandelier in the center of the room. It felt like the colored flash seeped into her brain, making her head throb.

"You all right?" Elwin asked, as she flinched.

"Why? Do you see something?"

Elwin frowned and leaned closer, squinting at her forehead. "No, everything looks normal."

She released a breath she didn't realize she'd been holding.

Everything looked normal.

Everything *was* normal.

She was just tired from the sleepless night.

"You really need to rest," Elwin said, echoing her thoughts. "Maybe you should try some slumberberry tea before bed."

"No sedatives."

"It's just tea—"

"No sedatives." She'd lost weeks of her life to a drugged haze while she was held hostage. She never wanted to feel that way again.

Elwin sank next to her on the plush couch. "Fine. We can let the insomnia go for now. But if you don't start sleeping, we are going to have to come up with a plan. Understood?"

He waited for her to nod.

"Good. And I want to check on you in a couple of weeks. School will have started by then, so just come by my office. I'll have your usual bed ready."

Sophie glared at the ground. Of *course* she had to visit the Healing Center during the first week of school. Her friends would tease her relentlessly about it—especially Keefe.

"Glad you're excited to see me again." Elwin winked as he stood and pulled out his pathfinder.

She opened her mouth to apologize, but a swell of panic surged into her mind and knocked her words away.

"What's wrong?"

"I . . . I don't know. I think something's wrong with Silveny." She stumbled to her feet and raced toward the arched, golden door of Havenfield's main entrance.

Sandor jumped in front of her. "You must stay inside if there's trouble."

A fresh surge of terror poured into her mind, cold and sharp. "But Silveny needs me."

When he didn't budge, she bolted for the back door. Sandor growled, sounding so much like an angry bunny rabbit Sophie couldn't help smiling as she slipped outside and took off through the pastures.

Sandor chased after her, shouting for her to come back as she ran past pens filled with triceratops and wooly mammoths, and one with some sort of enormous beetle-looking creature that must have arrived in the night. The intensity of Silveny's panic increased with every step, and when Sophie crested the final hill, her heart felt like it dropped into the pit of her stomach.

A thick black harness bound the gleaming horse's wings, and three figures in dark hooded capes stood inside her enclosure, dragging Silveny away.

FIVE

S TOP!" SOPHIE SCREAMED AS HER whole body started to shake. Her vision dimmed and blackness clouded her mind—but Sandor grabbed her arm and yanked her behind him, and the jarring motion pulled her out of the frenzy.

"Who goes there?" Sandor demanded.

"I don't answer to you, Goblin," the taller figure called in a dry, snooty voice.

Sandor drew a handful of star-shaped blades from his pockets, a bit like ninja stars, but with longer points and spiraled edges. "You have three seconds to identify yourselves or I will use these—and I assure you my aim is flawless."

"What's going on here?" Grady shouted as he rushed up

behind them. He put one hand protectively on Sophie's shoulder as he squinted at the figures. "Vika? Timkin? Is that you?"

One of the figures tossed her hood back, sweeping her wavy brown hair out of her eyes. "Who else would it be?"

The last of the dark fog cleared from Sophie's mind, leaving traces of a headache.

It wasn't *them*.

Though the Hekses were almost as bad. Especially since Sophie knew who the third figure was even before she swept back her hood, revealing a scowling face and a mass of frizzy brown curls.

"Stina," Sophie grumbled, glaring at the girl who went out of her way to make her life miserable at school. "What are you doing here?"

Stina tugged on Silveny's harness. "We're here to collect the alicorn so it can be *properly* rehabilitated."

Calm, Sophie transmitted as Silveny's panic flooded her mind. *I won't let her take you.*

She was amazed Silveny had even let them get close enough to attach the reins. Clearly she needed to teach the glittering horse how to recognize pure evil.

"I wasn't aware that had been decided," Grady said, tightening his grip on Sophie's shoulder as she tried to step forward.

"Please, you didn't think they'd have *you* rehabilitate the alicorn, did you?" Timkin asked as he jerked Silveny's reins toward him. "A noble creature deserves a *noble* trainer."

"Last I heard, your wife was the only one appointed to the nobility," Grady corrected. "And only as a Regent, not an Emissary."

"Give it time," Timkin growled, yanking Silveny's reins so hard he wrenched the frightened horse's neck.

Regent, Emissary, noble—Sophie didn't care. "You're hurting her!" she screamed as she lunged toward the enclosure.

Sandor blocked her.

"We're doing nothing of the sort," Vika snapped back

"I can feel her pain," Sophie insisted.

Stina laughed her high, wheezy snicker. "Last I checked, empathy wasn't an ability your *creators* gave you."

"Last *I* checked, you hadn't manifested any abilities at all," Sophie spit through gritted teeth. "And I don't have to be an Empath. I can feel her emotions with my mind."

Timkin snorted. "That's impossible."

"If it were coming from anyone else, I'd agree with you," a voice with an unmistakably crisp accent announced. "But you're forgetting how remarkable Sophie is."

Sophie spun around, relieved when she found four figures still glittering from their leap into the pasture. Alden, tall and regal in his dark blue cape, stood beside a beautiful girl Sophie's age with long dark hair. On his other side were two teenage boys, one with dark hair and impossibly teal eyes, and one with carefully disheveled blond hair and his trademark smirk.

Biana and Fitz stared in wonder at Silveny.

Keefe grinned at Sophie. "Yeah, Foster's always doing crazy

things no one can understand. It's how she keeps her sense of mystery."

"Lord Alden," Timkin said, lowering his hood and shaking his black hair as he dipped an exaggerated bow. "An honor, as always."

"No need for ceremony, Timkin." Alden turned to Grady. "I'm sorry to be late. I'd hoped to get here before the Hekses arrived. But Fitz, Keefe, and Biana insisted on seeing the long-lost alicorn, and someone needed time to fix their hair."

"Hey, a guy's gotta look his best for the ladies." Keefe patted the back of his head. "Right, Foster?"

Sophie ignored him—though she could feel her cheeks blushing. She turned to Alden. "Please, you can't let them take Silveny."

"He doesn't answer to you," Stina announced. "He answers to the Council, and I'm sure they've told him to give her to us."

"That was their plan," Alden admitted. "The Heks family has had tremendous success rehabilitating unicorns using their empathic abilities, and it was Vika's grandmother who rehabilitated the alicorn in the Sanctuary. So it seems only logical to let them prepare Silveny."

"But she hates them!"

Silveny whinnied, like she agreed.

"Can you really feel what she's feeling?" Alden asked.

"Yes. Right now she's scared and angry and wants to get away from them."

"She's making that up." Vika dragged Silveny close enough to put her hand on her shimmery neck. "I feel nothing of the sort—and I actually *am* an Empath."

An image flashed into Sophie's mind, and she couldn't help grinning. "Silveny wants to bite your hand."

"You can't possibly know that." But Vika whipped her hand away awfully fast for someone who didn't believe.

Silveny took advantage of her distraction, jerking her harness so hard she knocked Vika and Timkin to the muddy ground of her enclosure. They dropped their reins as they fell, and Silveny galloped toward the opposite end of her pasture, dragging Stina through the mud until she finally let go.

Sophie raced to the purple bars and had just enough time to reach through and unhook the buckle on Silveny's harness before the others caught up. The grateful horse spread her wings and flew to the highest part of her barred dome.

Vika snatched Sophie's wrist with a mud-streaked hand. "You wretched girl! Call her down right now."

"Why do you need my help? Aren't you the expert?"

Keefe snickered. "Ooh, good one, Foster!"

"Shut up," Vika hissed, tightening her grip.

"Unhand her," Sandor growled, and Sophie heard a scrape of metal, like he'd unsheathed his sword.

Vika glared at him for a second, then shoved Sophie back, sending her tumbling into Fitz's arms.

"You okay?" he asked, flashing his movie-star-worthy smile as he steadied her.

She was fairly certain her face was on fire as she pulled away and mumbled, "Yeah. Thanks."

"How exactly are you communicating with the alicorn?" Alden asked her.

"I'm not sure. Sometimes it's just a bunch of images flashing through my mind. Sometimes it feels like she's filling my head with her emotions, making me feel them too. Sometimes it's a word. But it's—"

"A word?" Alden interrupted.

Timkin's laugh was a sharp, ugly bark of sound. "You expect us to believe that?"

"How else would I know her name's Silveny?"

Silveny nickered.

"That could just be a coincidence," Stina argued. "I bet she'd respond to anything. Silvery. Filveny. Zilveny."

Silveny didn't so much as glance at her.

"Silveny," Timkin whispered.

Not only did Silveny nicker, she dive-bombed all three of them, making them drop to the mud to avoid being knocked over.

Alden smiled. "I think that settles that."

Vika tried to wipe the dirt off her face but only succeeded in smearing it more as she stumbled to her feet. "I don't see why this matters. I'm sure the Council's already given the order for us to take her, Alden."

"Doesn't Silveny get any say?" Sophie asked him.

"Of course she doesn't!" Timkin shouted. "Animals live where we tell them to live. They're not *intelligent* creatures."

"Surely I must have misheard you, Timkin," Alden said quietly. "None of us would ever imply a lack of respect for a living being. Especially someone with *noble* aspirations."

Timkin's features bent into thin, angry lines, but he said nothing more than, "Indeed."

Alden nodded. "Then I'm sure you would also agree that if Silveny can communicate her wishes, we should respect them. The question is: What does she want?"

"She wants to stay here," Sophie announced.

Stina rolled her eyes. "Please. She's just making that up so she can keep the alicorn for herself."

"I think the mud streaking your clothes makes it pretty clear how Silveny feels about you," Grady pointed out.

"But we rehabilitated the other alicorn," Vika argued.

"Not you, personally. And that was before we had Sophie," Alden reminded her. "Her unique abilities make her better equipped."

"You can't be serious—"

"I am, I'm afraid. The Council wants Silveny to receive the best care, and since Sophie has a means of communicating with her far beyond your capabilities, Havenfield is the better choice."

Vika's eyes narrowed and she stalked as close to Alden as

the bars of the enclosure would allow. "You can bet the Council will be hearing about this."

"Of course they will. I'll be sending them a full report as soon as I get home. That's part of my job as an Emissary. As is rendering *final* decisions in matters such as this."

"Unbelievable," Timkin muttered as he fished a pathfinder from his muddy cape and held the slender silver wand up to the sunlight. "Trusting that freak of a child. No wonder I'm hearing whispers of the Council's incompetence."

The Hekses leaped away before anyone could respond.

Alden released a long, heavy sigh.

Sophie stared at the ground, wishing there were a hole she could crawl in to hide. Instead, she called Silveny down and stroked her gleaming mane. *Calm. They're gone.*

"Is the unrest getting worse?" Grady asked Alden.

Sophie tugged out an eyelash as Alden hesitated to answer.

Crimes like kidnapping were supposed to be unheard of in the elvin world—as were rebellions and underground groups and conspiracies to burn down the human world. Her and Dex's dramatic escape had been the rude awakening no one wanted, and as the weeks passed with no sign of the culprits, more and more people had begun questioning the Council as leaders.

"We're doing our best to keep it under control," Alden finally replied. "Though if we had another Emissary . . ."

"You know I can't."

"I know. And the alicorn will help tremendously. She could solve *everything*."

Silveny snorted, and Sophie couldn't help wondering how such a stinky creature could be so important.

"I do have some information for you about that other matter," Alden added, leading Grady out of earshot—not that Sophie couldn't have guessed what they were talking about. It always had something to do with her.

"You okay?" Biana asked, coming to stand beside her. "You're not a fr—you're not what they called you. You know that, right?"

Sophie shrugged, not looking at her. She'd been called a freak her whole life. And she couldn't care less what Stina said. But ever since the kidnapping, she'd been hearing it from other people too. Everyone knew about her strange abilities now—and her mysterious connection to the Black Swan—and no one seemed to know what to do with that information.

"Biana's right," Fitz said, dragging her out of her gloomy thoughts. "Don't let what they said get to you."

We all think your talents are awesome.

Sophie was proud of herself for not jumping as Fitz's deep, accented voice filled her head.

Fitz had helped her pull herself back from the light when she was fading, and ever since, he'd become the only Telepath who could transmit thoughts into her mind. He still couldn't hear what she was thinking—something she was eternally grateful for—and she could block him if she wanted to. But she didn't want to.

Though . . . his thoughts did feel strangely wrong. Too loud and too warm, like his transmissions were mixed with a hair dryer whirring in her head. But he probably had to make his thoughts stronger to get past her blocking, and she'd gladly take the slight headache to keep their secret conversations.

Thanks, she transmitted back. *You really don't think it's weird that I can talk to Silveny?*

Are you kidding? I wish you could teach me how to do it.

Sophie smiled. *I can try.*

"Hey—what did I tell you two about secret Telepath conversations?" Keefe asked as he shoved his way between them. "Unless you're talking about *me*, keep it out loud."

Fitz laughed. "Keefe just wishes he could swap secret messages with you."

"Please, I don't need your little mind tricks. I can *feel* Foster's secrets"—he fanned the air around her—"and I feel some pretty *intense* emotions right now."

"Probably because I'm wondering if I should strangle you or beat you with my shoe!"

"The shoe would be funnier," Fitz jumped in.

Sophie smiled. "Might be a bad idea to do it in front of a member of the nobility, though."

"Nah—my dad would understand. I'm pretty sure he dreams about doing the same thing."

Keefe smirked at both of them. "Bring it on."

"I'd be careful if I were you, Keefe," Biana warned. "Remember, Sophie's an *Inflictor*."

Biana said it with a smile, but it still made Sophie want to hide. If she lost her temper, she could seriously hurt some-body—and she had no idea how to control it. She'd almost done it to the Hekses when they were trying to take Silveny. And she'd accidentally incapacitated Sandor the first time she saw him. She'd never forget the way his muscled body collapsed to the floor, writhing in pain.

No one should have the ability to do that to someone. . . .

A strangely soothing warmth filled Sophie's mind, almost like Silveny was trying to comfort her. But a horse couldn't do that—could she?

Sophie stepped closer to the bars, stroking Silveny's velvet nose.

Calm, Silveny transmitted.

Sophie's eyes widened.

"Oh—I almost forgot to show you," Biana said, holding out her wrist and breaking whatever connection Sophie and Silveny had. "Notice anything different?"

"You got your nexus off?"

Biana nodded proudly. "It unlatched yesterday, after I leaped home from shopping with my mom. That's five weeks earlier than Fitz."

"And she won't let me forget it."

Fitz had set some sort of record when his nexus unlatched when he was thirteen. Most kids were fifteen or sixteen before their concentration levels were strong enough to let them safely light leap on their own.

"At least I still beat Keefe," Fitz said, grinning at his friend. "He'll probably be the only one in our grade level still wearing one."

"Hey—only because I'm a year ahead!" Keefe argued.

"Still, don't you turn fifteen soon?" Fitz asked him.

Keefe rolled his eyes. "Not *that* soon. Besides, let's not forget that Foster beat us all. Her level's been full since we latched her new nexus on."

"Yeah, but she doesn't count because Elwin's making her wear it anyway," Biana retorted. "No offense," she added, looking at Sophie.

Sophie shrugged and stared at the full meter on the underside of her nexus. Much as she hated it, Biana was right. After she faded, Elwin had tweaked her latch so that it would only unlock when *he* decided she was ready, and not a second sooner.

Keefe nudged her. "So, you gonna fly us around on your new pet, or what?"

"You think she'd let me do that?"

Sophie's mind filled with an image of her being whisked through the sky on Silveny's back. *Fly?* she transmitted, sending Silveny the same scene.

Fly! Silveny transmitted back. *Fly! Fly! Fly!*

"Only one way to find out," Keefe added.

"Not a chance," Grady said as he and Alden rejoined them. "We don't need to add 'falling from the sky' to Sophie's list of injuries."

Sophie glared at everyone as they laughed.

"You're really lucky, Sophie," Biana added, her eyes stretching wide as Silveny flapped her wings. "She's the most beautiful thing I've ever seen."

"She is, isn't she?"

Keefe groaned. "What is it with girls and sparkles?"

"Sparkles make everything better," Biana informed him, and Sophie had to agree.

"You don't think she's amazing?" Sophie asked him.

"Eh, give me something that shoots fire any day."

"Or stinky gas," Fitz added, elbowing him. "A gulon maybe?"

"I am *definitely* a fan of gulons."

Legend had it that Keefe had been the mastermind behind something called The Great Gulon Incident, but Sophie still had no clue what had actually transpired.

"Yes, well, we can discuss your delinquency another time, Keefe," Alden said, reaching into the pocket of his cape and retrieving his pathfinder. "Sophie and Grady have an important day ahead of them."

"Ooh, are you guys going to Atlantis for the eurypterid races? I hear they sometimes claw their way into the stands and . . ." Keefe's voice trailed off when he noticed the warning look Alden was shooting him. "Oh. Right."

Everyone became very interested in their feet.

Sixteen years ago to the day, Grady and Edaline had lost their only daughter in a tragic fire. And every year on the anniversary of the loss, they went to visit her grave.

"I'm so sorry, my friend," Alden said, moving close enough to squeeze Grady's shoulder.

"Me too," Fitz added quietly, echoed by Biana and Keefe.

Grady looked away, wiping his eyes, but Sophie glanced at her friends, surprised to see how sad they seemed. Death was such a rare occurrence for elves that most of them didn't understand it, or feel the right amount of sympathy. She was about to wonder what brought on the change when a blurry memory flashed through her mind:

A devastated Fitz, holding the small Albertosaurus she'd given him during midterms and telling her he'd been to her funeral.

She'd been so heavily drugged by her kidnappers that she had no idea how much of that was real and how much of it was a delusion she'd created as she desperately tried to call for help. But she did know that for about two weeks, everyone thought she and Dex were dead.

It was strange to imagine her friends mourning for her.

She buried the morbid thought as Biana asked, "Do you want to come over tomorrow?"

"I'm . . . not sure. I'll let you know, okay?"

Biana nodded.

Fitz waved, and Keefe told her to have fun with her sparkly

horse as Alden held his pathfinder to the light. "I'll be thinking of you, my friend," Alden told Grady. "And, Sophie? We'll talk soon."

The light pulled them away before she could ask why.

Grady stood there, staring into space, like he wasn't sure where to go now. Or maybe he wasn't ready.

"You don't have to come today," he told Sophie after a second. "It's not an easy thing to do—"

"I know." She wrapped her arms around him, wishing she could squeeze away the sadness in his voice. "But I *want* to come."

Grady sank into the hug, and an extra second passed before he pulled away, his eyes blinking back tears. He cleared his throat and took her hands. "Well, then, we'd better get ready."

SIX

SOPHIE FIDGETED WITH THE SATIN sash of her emerald green dress and wondered for the tenth time if she should change. It felt wrong to visit a cemetery in something other than black, but Edaline had told her the tradition was to wear green—the color of life.

"You look beautiful," Grady said as he peeked his head around the door to her bedroom.

She smiled. "You don't look too bad yourself."

"Thanks. But I truly hate these things." He tugged at his green velvet cloak as he stepped into her room. "Whoever decided we should wear capes was an idiot."

He didn't have to tell her. She'd hated the capes from the

moment she'd seen her ridiculous school uniform with its stupid elbow-length monstrosity. But capes were the mark of the nobility, and even though Grady and Edaline had tried to separate themselves from that life, the Council would never let Grady fully resign. His ability as a Mesmer was too rare and important.

"Need help with yours?" Grady offered.

Sophie nodded and he grabbed the silky green cape from where she'd left it on her bed. Grady draped it across her shoulders and gathered the ends at the base of her neck. She reached for the blue halcyon clasp she used for school, but Grady stopped her, holding out a yellow-diamond-encrusted eagle soaring with a ruby rose in its talons—identical to the broach securing his own cape.

"The Ruewen crest," Sophie whispered as he pinned it through the thin fabric.

Her Foxfire uniform bore the same seal over her heart, identifying her as part of Grady and Edaline's family—but having him give her the clasp, especially considering the day, made her feel choked up.

Grady cleared his throat. "Are you sure you want to—"

"I'm sure." They'd been doing this for sixteen years. She wasn't going to let them do it alone anymore.

Unless . . .

"Do you not want me to go?"

"We *always* want you with us, Sophie. I'm just afraid you don't realize how hard this will be."

She reached for his hand, twining their fingers together. "I know. But we're family now, right?"

"We definitely are." He pulled her in for a hug, stroking her hair as he whispered, "I love you."

"I love you, too." She thought about adding "Dad" at the end, but the word stuck to her tongue.

"I guess we should probably get going. I've already informed Sandor that he's not coming with us—"

"He's not?"

"Only elves are allowed near the Wanderlings. Even the Councillors leave their bodyguards behind. So he's agreed to entrust you to our care for the next few hours."

"Whoa—I can't believe you got him to agree to that."

"He protested. A *lot*. But I reminded him of what I can do." The seriousness of his tone gave Sophie chills.

She rarely thought about what being a Mesmer really meant for Grady. But total mind control was definitely a powerful thing.

"And, I agreed to carry this, in case I lose my focus," he added quietly, removing a small silver weapon from an inner pocket of his cloak.

Sophie felt all the blood drain from her face. "Where did you get a melder?"

She'd never forget the way Dex had collapsed to the ground, paralyzed and seizing up after the kidnappers blasted him with one. Looking at the palm-size gadget now, it was hard to imagine so much evil coming from a sleek, curved handle connected to a triangle of silver with a single button in the center. She hated seeing it in Grady's hand.

Grady shoved it back into his cloak. "The Council insisted I keep one in the house as a last resort. Don't worry, I have no plans to use it."

She hoped not.

Then again, no one ever *planned* to be attacked.

"Where's Edaline?" she asked, changing the subject before she could relive any more nightmares.

Shadows seeped into his features, and he closed his eyes a second longer than a blink.

"Oh. I'll get her," Sophie offered.

Grady didn't protest as she moved past him and headed down the curved staircase to the second floor. Even with the sunlight streaming through the crystal walls, the hallway leading left seemed to be shrouded in gloom. Sophie hurried to the end, where there were three narrow doors. Doors that were always closed.

The center door was slightly ajar.

"Edaline?" Sophie whispered, not wanting to startle her as she tiptoed into the quiet bedroom.

Sophie had only been in this room once in all the months she'd lived there—and only by accident. But it looked exactly the same. She suspected it had been exactly the same for the last sixteen years, though the room felt dim and dusty—like someone desperately needed to flick on the crystal chandeliers or pull back the faded lacy curtains and let in some light.

Edaline didn't say a word as Sophie crossed the soft carpet and sat next to her on the edge of the canopied bed.

"Grady and I are ready whenever you are." Sophie's voice echoed through the silent room.

Edaline swallowed as she nodded, then turned to face Sophie. She sucked in a breath when she spotted the broach.

"I don't have to wear it if—"

"No." Edaline stopped her from unfastening it. "You *should* wear it. I'm sorry. It just surprised me because it makes you look even more like her."

The words were strange, prickly things, and Sophie never knew what to do when Edaline said them. She knew Edaline meant them as a compliment, but Sophie couldn't help wishing that she didn't have to be the shadow of someone else. Or worrying that the similarity had anything to do with why they adopted her.

She followed Edaline's gaze to the framed photo on the desk across the room.

A carefree Grady and Edaline stood with their arms around a slender blond girl—Jolie, when she was about Sophie's age.

Jolie had Grady's light hair and Edaline's bright turquoise eyes. She was striking and graceful and smiling, with rosy cheeks and gleaming white teeth.

Sophie walked over to the floor-length dressing mirror in the corner and tried to see the resemblance.

"My goodness you have strange eyes," a high-pitched voice announced.

Sophie whipped around. "Who's that?"

"Vertina." Edaline gave a sad smile and made her way over to Sophie. "I guess you've never seen a spectral mirror before?"

Sophie turned back to the mirror, gasping when she noticed a tiny face in the upper left side. A girl with shiny black hair, pale skin, and sapphire blue eyes. She looked like she was about fifteen, and she had that snotty *I am older and cooler than you* glare that Sophie had seen a *lot* of back in the human world when she was stuck as the twelve-year-old high school senior.

"What is it?" Sophie whispered.

"It?" the tiny girl snapped, her pretty face twisting into a scowl. "Who are you calling 'it'? You're the one with the freaky eyes."

"Hey!" Sophie still wasn't totally comfortable being the-only-elf-with-brown-eyes, but she wasn't about to let some mirror-girl insult her.

"Now, now, Vertina," Edaline said, placing a hand on Sophie's shoulder. "That was out of line."

"Sorry." She didn't sound like she meant it, though.

Sophie reached up and touched Vertina's face, half expecting it to feel like warm skin. All she felt was smooth, cold glass.

"Get your smudgy fingers away from me!" Vertina huffed, ducking under Sophie's hand. "It's bad enough I'm up here alone all the time, gathering dust like some common piece of furniture." She turned her tiny face away, her glassy eyes staring somewhere beyond them as she whispered, "I miss Jolie."

"Me too," Edaline said, tears streaming down her cheeks.

Sophie pulled Edaline back, and when they were far enough from the glass for their reflections to disappear, Vertina vanished.

"What was that thing?"

It took Edaline a second to answer. "Spectral mirrors help you get dressed or style your hair."

"Is it alive?"

"Just a clever bit of programming. A novelty that never caught on because people realized they didn't want their mirror to tell them they looked tired or out of fashion. Jolie loved hers, though. They became friends. She even used to come back to visit Vertina on her rest weekends from the elite towers. They were that close." Her voice broke again.

"Come on," Sophie said, leading her toward the door. "Grady's waiting for us."

Edaline wiped her eyes, casting one last glance over her shoulder at the now silent mirror before she followed Sophie out to the hall.

They climbed the stairs to the fourth floor at a crawl. Edaline seemed in no hurry to get where they were going, and scaling the stairs was always a challenge for Sophie, especially in the low heels she'd decided to try. She was thirteen now—seemed like the time to switch to more mature footwear. If only she had the balance to pull them off. She tripped so badly on the last step that she would have fallen if it weren't for Grady's quick reflexes.

"Still getting the hang of walking, huh?" he teased as he caught her with his free arm. His other hand held a red satchel, which he handed to Edaline.

"Hey, I can't be perfect at everything," Sophie retorted with a smile.

"True enough." Grady held her hand as she climbed onto the platform under the glittering chandelier in the center of the cupola. Five hundred intricately faceted crystals hung individually from silver cords, forming a sparkling sphere. The Leapmaster 500.

Edaline fidgeted with the satchel she'd slung over her shoulder and Grady stared at the ceiling, neither seeming ready to give the command.

Sophie cleared her throat. "Where exactly are we going?"

A few seconds passed before Grady whispered, "The Wanderling Woods."

The Leapmaster sprang to life, twisting until a single crystal lowered enough to catch the sunlight streaming through the windows.

Nobody moved toward the beam that refracted to the ground.

Sophie could imagine them standing like this every year—too sad to step forward. But this year she was there to help them.

Slowly, gently, she pulled them into the light.

SEVEN

SOPHIE HAD BEEN IN QUIET PLACES before, but she'd never experienced anything like the silence of the Wanderling Woods. There was no chirping or tweeting. No branches creaking or rustling. It was like all sound—all life—had been sucked out of the scenery, leaving nothing but a thick, almost tangible emptiness.

Even the silver pebbles didn't crunch under her feet as she followed Grady and Edaline down a winding path, which seemed to glow as she moved, shining the way to the narrow gateway ahead. A vine with white star-shaped flowers trailed up two gilded columns to an arched golden sign with looping, intricate letters that spelled out:

Those who wander are not lost.

"I've heard that before," Sophie said, mostly to herself.

She racked her brain, needing to be sure it was her own memory, not something someone put there. An image of a short poem flashed in her mind and she stopped walking. "That's from *The Lord of the Rings*. Well—not exactly. But it's close."

"*The Lord of the Rings*?" Edaline repeated.

"It's a series of human books. And it has elves in it." Elves that had some similarities to what elves really were, now that she thought about it.

"Are the books older?" Grady asked.

"I think Tolkien wrote them during the Nineteen Thirties or Forties."

"That's back before the Human Assistance Program was banned." Grady smiled when her eyebrows shot up. "We used to send members of the nobility in disguise to try to teach humans our ways. The treaties had fallen apart, but we still hoped to guide them, bring them out of the darkness and into a new age of light. In fact, most of the great human innovations of the last few centuries happened under elvin tutelage. Electricity. Penicillin. Chocolate cake. But too many of our gifts backfired, and a few decades ago the problems escalated to a point where the Council had no choice but to terminate the program and ban all human contact."

"What does that have to do with *The Lord of the Rings*?"

"Let's just say there were some who couldn't resist manipulating the legends about elves a bit."

"So . . . you're saying J. R. R. Tolkien met an elf, and that's where he came up with some of the story?"

"I wouldn't be surprised. Though I'm sure he was only told bits and pieces. Do the books talk about the Wanderlings at all?"

"I don't think so."

"Then he didn't know what the statement meant." Grady motioned for her to follow him. Edaline trailed silently behind as they crossed under the arch and entered the woods. "*These are the Wanderlings*," Grady whispered.

It was unlike any forest Sophie had ever seen. The glowing path wound through a sea of carefully arranged trees, each one surrounded by meticulously groomed shrubs. No two trees were alike. Some were short and broad. Others tall and slender. Some had graceful branches that swayed in the silent breeze. Others looked stout and strong. There were leaves in every shape, size, and color. Some had flowers. One even had thorns. And at the base of each tree was a round white stone with a name carved in plain black letters.

Grady led Sophie to the nearest tree, which reminded her of a weeping willow—if weeping willows had red leaves and bloomed with thousands of tiny purple flowers.

"Each Wanderling's seed is coiled with a single hair from the one who's been lost," he explained. "When it sprouts, it absorbs their DNA, taking on some of the attributes of the life they now share. Letting the lost live on."

Those who wander are not lost.

"Cyrah had straight auburn hair," Edaline whispered, running her hand through the swaying red leaves. "And flecks of violet in her eyes."

Soft purple petals showered them, and Sophie caught as many as she could, hating that they would wither on the ground. "Did you know her?"

Grady brushed the bits of flower off his cape. "Not well. She was Prentice's wife."

The petals slipped through Sophie's fingers.

Prentice had been a Keeper for the Black Swan, back before everyone knew they were working against the *real* rebels. Now he lived in Exile, his mind shattered by the memory break that the Council had ordered so they could find out what he was hiding. And the secret he'd refused to tell them was *her.*

Where they hid her.

Why they'd made her.

Who she was.

His wife died not long after his mind was shattered. Lost her concentration during a light leap somehow and faded away before anyone could save her. Leaving Wylie, their only son, orphaned. Sophie had never met him—he was in the elite levels at Foxfire and lived in the secluded elite towers—but she sometimes wondered if he knew she existed. And how he felt about her if he did.

She looked up and a ray of sunlight caught her eyes, sinking into her brain and pulsing with that same headache she kept getting.

"You okay?" Grady asked as she rubbed her temples.

"Sure." She focused on the forest, surprised to realize how many trees there were. There had to be at least a hundred, spread among the meandering hills and carefully manicured bushes. It seemed like a lot, but . . . the Wanderling Woods was the elves' *only* graveyard. Could they really have only lost a hundred elves in all the centuries they'd been alive?

She reached for Grady's and Edaline's hands.

They held on tight and moved slowly down the path, their glassy eyes staring straight ahead. The path twisted through the quiet forest, leading them through patches of shadow and light until they rounded a large bend and entered a small sunlit clearing.

A lump formed in Sophie's throat.

Elevated on a small hill and silhouetted against the sky was a fragile-looking tree with pale bark, dark green leaves, and slender limbs that fanned out toward the sun. Soft yellow leaves draped off the end of each bough like Spanish moss, making the tree elegant and wispy. And large blossoms the exact same blue as Edaline's eyes blanketed the branches, filling the air with a scent like honey and berries and sugar.

The graceful tree blocked the early afternoon sun as they approached. Sophie couldn't take her eyes off the inscription on the white stone marking the grave.

Jolie Lucine Ruewen

Without a word, Edaline opened the satchel she'd been carrying and removed a clear fluted bottle filled with a deep purple liquid.

"A special tonic the gnomes make," Grady explained.

Edaline popped the cork and drizzled the thick syrup along the base of the tree. When the last of the liquid had drained, she smacked the bottle against the tree's trunk. The glass shattered into a million tiny flecks, sprinkling the wet grass. And as the sparkle-coated syrup sank into the ground, a bright green vine sprang from the dark soil and slowly coiled its way up the bark of Jolie's tree. Ruffled purple flowers bloomed along the stem, and every inch of the vine gleamed, like it had been covered in glitter.

Grady wiped his eyes as he took Edaline's hand. "The vine only lasts a few weeks, but it's the best gift we can give her."

"Plus this." Edaline's voice was barely audible as she gently pulled one of the branches down, revealing a silver charm bracelet tucked between the blossoms. She removed a tiny crystal star from her pocket and added it to the already full chain. "We gave her this bracelet when she started Foxfire, and we bought her a new charm every year on the first day of school. She used to wear it every day, but we found it when they gave us her things from the elite towers, so we brought it here, and give her a new charm every time we come."

Sophie bit her lip, wondering if she should say something.

But what?

"I'm so sorry," was all she could come up with.

"It's not your fault," Grady told her, squeezing her shoulder. But something in his tone had darkened.

Edaline started to shake with sobs and Grady pulled her against him, letting her cry on his shoulder.

"I'll give you guys a minute," Sophie whispered, backing away. She'd thought she could help by being there—but nothing would ever make it less painful. And Jolie's loss was *theirs*.

She didn't belong.

She slipped quietly down the path, trying to remember which way would take her to the entrance. She'd wound through the trees for several minutes before she realized she didn't recognize any of them. Turning back didn't help, and as she turned around yet again and still didn't recognize anything, she was forced to admit that she was lost.

And she was alone.

She'd been wishing for solitude since the kidnapping—but standing there by herself in the eerie silence felt *wrong*. Like the woods were holding their breath, waiting for something to happen.

She wasn't about to stick around and find out what it was.

Running now—and cursing herself for wearing the stupid heels—she raced up the nearest hill, hoping she'd be high enough to get her bearings. But two small trees planted side by side at the crest distracted her.

Saplings.

Her blood turned to ice when she read the names carved into the white stone markers.

Sophie Elizabeth Foster

and

Dexter Alvin Dizznee

EIGHT

PAIN SHOT UP HER ARM AS SOPHIE pinched her wrist, and she released the breath she'd been holding.

She wasn't dead.

She wasn't dreaming either—though this had all the makings of a nightmare.

Her eyes studied the trees, focusing on the one that was just slightly taller than the other. The pale trunk was scrawny and weak, but the tree still stood on its own. Golden, star-shaped leaves covered the skinny branches, with deep brown seedpods peppered among them. No flowers. No color. Just a plain, basic tree.

Her tree.

She couldn't help feeling a little disappointed with it—especially compared to Dex's, which had a twisted trunk, spiky, strawberry red leaves, and periwinkle berries. There was something so inherently *Dex* about it. Even without the marker, she could've guessed it was his grave.

She had a *grave*.

A glint of silver at the base of the thickest bough caught her eye and she reached out with shaky hands to unclasp a silver charm bracelet with two charms: an elephant covered in blue diamonds, and some sort of locket etched with intricate swirls.

The scenery blurred as the world started to spin too fast, and she sank to the ground, burying her face between her knees. She counted each breath, trying not to throw up her breakfast all over the grass. Sixty-three breaths had passed before Grady's hushed voice shattered the silence.

"They kept the trees."

Her head snapped up, but her eyes couldn't focus on the two people standing over her. She thought it was the sudden bright light, but then something wet streaked down her cheek.

Grady and Edaline dropped to the ground beside her, strangling her with a hug. Sophie's tears soaked Grady's cape as Edaline rubbed her back.

"We should've warned you," he said through a sigh. "I just didn't want to upset you if they weren't even here."

Sophie tried to make her mouth ask any of the questions

swelling inside her brain, but all she could choke out was, "How did they . . . ?"

Edaline must've known what she meant because she whispered, "We gave them a hair from the silver brush in your room." She swept a strand away from Sophie's cheek. "And we planted the seed at your funeral."

Sophie closed her eyes, but it didn't stop her from imagining them standing on that hill, crying as they placed her seed in the ground. Clinging to each other as they fastened her charm bracelet around the branch, planning to add to it each year.

Was Dex's family there too?

Who else came?

Her mind ran through a list of names and she shook the upsetting thought away. She forced herself to sit up, wiping her runny nose on the back of her hand. "But you know we're alive now. Why are they still here?"

Grady touched the slender trunk of her tree. "Probably because the Wanderlings are living things. Would it be right to kill them, simply because we planted them by mistake?"

"I guess not," she mumbled.

It wasn't the tree's fault the kidnappers tossed her registry pendant into the ocean and tricked everyone into believing she'd drowned. But it still gave her the creeps knowing she had a grave. And not any grave—a tree mixed with her DNA, absorbing tiny parts of her as it grew and changed. Almost like a part of her had been stolen, somehow.

Edaline held Sophie tighter as she shivered and whispered, "I'm so sorry."

They were the same words Sophie had said to them at Jolie's grave. And they helped about as much. But if Grady and Edaline could be strong, so could she.

Her hands curled into fists and something metal cut into her palm. "Oh, I found this." She held out the charm bracelet. "Is it okay if I keep it?"

Edaline covered her mouth and looked away.

Grady cleared his throat. "Of course. We wanted you to have it. In fact, this is good. Just in time for when you start your first full year at Foxfire. We'll have to get you a new charm."

Sophie examined the charms they'd picked, smiling at the tiny blue diamond elephant, which must've been inspired by Ella. The locket turned out to be a small compass rimmed with tiny diamonds. Loopy letters had been engraved on the inside.

"'Let the past be your guide,'" Sophie read aloud.

"What's that?" Edaline asked.

"The inscription on the compass."

"Compass?" Edaline turned pale as Sophie held out the charm. "We didn't add that charm."

Sophie felt her jaw drop as Grady snatched the bracelet and squinted at the inscription. "All I see is a jumble of old runes. You're sure you see a message?"

He handed the bracelet back, and Sophie had to remind herself to breathe as she checked the inscription, which still read the same way. When she closed the locket and looked closer at the etchings, she understood why. Mixed in with the intricate swirls was a black curl with a pointed end, like the curve of a bird's neck, ending in a beak.

The sign of the swan.

NINE

I T'S ABOUT TIME," SOPHIE WHISPERED, EVEN though her hands were shaking.

She'd been waiting for the Black Swan to make contact ever since they'd revealed themselves with her rescue. Maybe they were finally going to explain why they'd made her and what they wanted her to do.

It did feel strange knowing they were still watching her, though—still planting messages and clues in the shadows, waiting for her to find them.

She glanced over her shoulder, half expecting to see a face peeking through the trees. But the woods were as silent and empty as ever.

Sophie studied the inscription again, which must've been

written in their special cipher runes—the only runes she could read, thanks to the way the Black Swan trained her brain.

"I thought you knew the Black Swan's code?" She'd seen Grady looking through scrolls with cipher runes tucked in the margins.

"Only a few scattered phrases." His voice had turned dark. Angry, almost. "What does it say again?"

"Let the past be your guide." She moved the compass in every direction and the arrow always pointed north, just like it was supposed to. So the clue had to be the message itself.

Couldn't they just say, *Meet us here and we'll explain everything?* Was that really so much to ask?

"Put the charm down, Sophie," Grady ordered, so loud it made her jump.

"What? Why?"

"You're not taking another thing from them. If they want your help, they need to turn themselves in to the Council, face up to their actions—"

"What actions?" Grady had been *strange* about the Black Swan—always getting angry or changing the subject whenever she brought them up or asked about the Council's search to find them. "You're acting like they're the bad guys."

"Grady," Edaline said, stopping him before he could reply. "Today is not the day for this."

Grady sighed, and the pain in his eyes hurt Sophie's heart.

Edaline was right. They were there to mourn their daughter, not talk about the hunt for the Black Swan.

But . . .

"I'm keeping the charm," she mumbled, not looking at Grady.

"It's not safe—"

"It's just a charm, Grady," Edaline interrupted. "What are they going to do, track her with it? They already know where we live."

Sophie risked a glance at Grady, who looked like he wanted to argue. Instead he held out his hand. "Let me see it again."

Sophie hesitated, wondering if he would give it back. She couldn't imagine Grady being unfair like that, though, so she handed it over and Grady held it to the light, squinting at the bracelet from every possible angle.

"I suppose Edaline's right," he said through a sigh. "The charm's not dangerous, but the message *is*. You can do what you want with the compass, but don't you dare let them lead you around with the clue. You're not their puppet."

"I *know*. But they also rescued me," she reminded him for what felt like the hundredth time. "They're trying to help. So whatever this message means, I think we should figure it out."

Grady pinched the bridge of his nose like the conversation was giving him a headache. Several seconds of silence passed before Edaline spoke for him.

"I think we should show it to Alden. See what he thinks we should do."

"Works for me." Sophie stood, dusting the grass off her wrinkled dress and pulling out her Imparter. "Should I hail him and let him know we're coming to Everglen?"

"We can't go right now," Edaline said quietly. "We still have to visit Brant. But maybe it's better if you don't—"

"No, I'm coming with you." All the information overload had made her forget there was another part to Grady and Edaline's annual mourning tradition.

Visiting Jolie's fiancé.

Grady and Edaline shared a look before Edaline reached for Sophie's hand. "Are you sure? Seeing Brant is the most upsetting part of this whole process."

More upsetting than visiting their daughter's grave?

"Brant's not himself anymore," Grady said, like he knew what she was thinking. "It's not easy to see him so . . . broken."

His face was as haunted as his tone, and Edaline looked just as pale.

"I go where you go," she told them, sounding like Sandor—minus the squeaky voice. She hadn't been much help to them at Jolie's grave, but she wasn't letting them do this alone. Not anymore.

Not ever again.

"An elf lives *here*?" Sophie couldn't help asking as the scenery came into focus.

Everything she'd seen in the elvin world was enormous and

made of jewels or crystal or glass, with elaborate architecture and gold or silver accents.

The square, windowless stone structure in front of them looked more like it belonged to a human. A poor, reclusive human, with ugly taste in houses.

Edaline fidgeted with the velvet satchel clutched in her white-knuckled hands. "We had to move Brant somewhere he felt safe."

The house didn't look "safe." It looked cold and bleak. Even the land around it was nothing but jagged rocks and dark, dusty soil.

"Brant's afraid of fire now, as I'm sure you can understand," Grady said quietly. "He couldn't sleep until we found him somewhere that wouldn't burn. All his furnishings are fireproof—we even have his clothes specially made."

"What about his family? Don't they help you guys take care of him?"

Grady shifted uncomfortably, and Edaline's eyes dropped to the ground.

"It's . . . dangerous for them—not that *Brant's* dangerous. He barely moves. Just stares at the wall, mumbling to himself. But the guilt . . ." Edaline's voice cracked, and she cleared her throat before she whispered, "The guilt could break them apart."

Grady took Edaline's hand. "There's a reason violence and cruelty are unheard of in our world, Sophie. Our minds aren't capable of processing the guilt that comes with such atrocities—or they aren't supposed to be, at least. It's why no one suspected kidnapping when you and Dex vanished. Why no one wanted to believe that the Everblaze was burning. Because if one of us were to do something like that, the guilt would splinter our minds and let the darkness seep through the cracks."

"But why would Brant's parents feel guilty?" Alden had told her the fire was an accident.

"They *shouldn't*. But guilt is an insidious thing—especially mixed with severe grief. It slips inside, casting doubt, making you wonder if there was anything you could have done, anything that would have changed . . ." Grady stared into the distance, and Sophie wondered if Brant's parents weren't the only ones wrestling with guilt.

"It wasn't your fault," she said quietly.

"I know." The anger in his tone was unmistakable, and he didn't look at her as he walked away. But he'd only gone a few steps when he spun back to face her. "Before we go inside, you have to promise that you will not—under *any* circumstances— try to read Brant's mind."

"I know the rules of telepathy." Telepaths had their own code of ethics to follow, rule number one of which was *Never read a mind without permission.*

"It's more than that. Brant's sanity *cracked* during the fire. Watching the house burn, knowing Jolie was inside, knowing he couldn't save her—it was too much." Grady's voice vanished for a second and he had to swallow to bring it back. "The trauma and guilt broke part of him. He's not completely catatonic, like someone whose sanity is *shattered*. But reading Brant's mind is *extremely* dangerous. Promise me you will *not* open your mind to his thoughts."

"I promise."

He stared her down, like he was searching for the truth in her words. Then he nodded, turned back toward the gray stone house, and climbed the steps to the thick metal door. Icy wind stung Sophie's cheeks as she and Edaline followed. When they'd joined his side, Grady pulled the chain that hung above them, and a low chime rumbled through the house. Followed by an endless silence.

They stood there so long Sophie started to wonder if Brant was actually home.

Then a deep voice called, "Come in."

TEN

DON'T STARE AT HIS SCARS.

Sophie repeated the command over and over, ordering herself to obey. She tried to focus on the gray walls with the glowing blue crystals set among the stones, or the four metal chairs—the only furniture in the room—that were bolted to the ground by large silver springs. But her eyes always returned to the warped, puckered dents on Brant's chin, or the red splotches and thin white lines that twisted and tangled their way up half of his cheek.

He hacked a wheezing cough, covering his ruined mouth with a hand that was red and raw. "You brought a new person," he rasped when his throat had cleared.

Grady wrapped an arm across her shoulders and Sophie was surprised to feel that he was trembling. "Yes, this is Sophie. She lives with us at Havenfield, now."

Brant smiled, making his lip fold into the mottled lumps of flesh around it. Sophie dropped her eyes to the yellow-orange shirt he wore, with long floppy sleeves and a tie around the middle. It looked a bit like a bathrobe.

Brant coughed again. "How very . . . unexpected." Before anyone could reply, he pointed to the satchel Edaline clutched against her stomach. "Is that for me?"

Edaline crossed the room to where Brant sat and placed the satchel in his lap. "You know I never forget."

The fabric shredded as he tore into the sack the way a small child might rip open a present, revealing a round silver box. "Custard bursts!"

Edaline smiled. "Chocolate, butterscotch, and lushberry. I made them this morning."

Brant pried open the lid, pulled out a square purple puff that looked a bit like a colored marshmallow and took a bite. Pink juice dribbled down the scar on his chin as he smacked his lips and stuffed the rest in his mouth. "Aren't custard bursts the best thing you've ever tasted?" he asked Sophie, spitting bits of crumbs.

Sophie had never heard of them, but she didn't want to admit it so she just said, "Yeah."

His smile faded to a frown. "You've never tried one, have you?"

"No—I—" Sophie started, but Edaline cut her off.

"I only make them once a year."

Brant didn't say anything—and he definitely didn't offer her one—as he closed the tin and tucked it back in the shreds of the bag. Sophie stared at her feet, counting the blisters peeking around the edges of her shoes. Seven separate welts had already formed—and she was sure there were more to come. But they stung less than knowing Edaline had a special treat she'd never shared with her.

Brant hacked another wheezing cough, shattering the silence.

"Are you sick?" Edaline asked.

"Don't!" He shouted as she reached out like she wanted to check his forehead for fever. He curled his knees into his chest and wrapped his arms around his legs, forming an impenetrable ball. "I'm fine."

His voice sounded hoarse, though.

"Sit," he ordered, motioning to the three empty chairs. "Tell me what's happened over the last year. Clearly, there have been some *changes*."

Sophie sank into a springy chair, surprised to discover it was actually comfortable. The metal was soft somehow, molding to her body like a cushion would—but it was cold. Or maybe the chill had more to do with the way Brant's pale eyes had focused on her again. They were more of a gray than a blue, and they were framed with thick lashes the same jet black as his hair.

She realized then that Brant should have been good-looking. But the fire had ruined him.

Don't stare at his scars.

"I've seen you before," he murmured, still studying Sophie.

"You have?"

He nodded as his eyes traced every inch of her face, finally settling on her neck.

His metal tin of custard bursts clanged against the ground as he lunged for her.

Sophie shrieked and tried to block him, but he pinned her shoulders to her chair with one arm while his other hand tore at her cape.

"That's mine!" he shouted as Grady yanked him away and tossed him to the far side of the room.

"What's gotten into you?" Grady yelled as Brant cowered in the corner, murmuring, "Mine," to his fist.

Edaline rushed to Sophie, checking her for injuries. "Are you all right?"

Sophie nodded, not quite able to speak yet. She kept one eye on Brant as she adjusted her clothes, frowning when she noticed something missing. "He stole my family crest."

Brant kissed his fisted palm, and Sophie noticed the tiniest speck of yellow sparkle peeking between his fingers. "Mine," he said, laughing this time.

"I . . . guess he recognized Jolie's pin," Edaline mumbled, her eyes turning watery.

"Brant, give it back," Grady ordered, stalking toward him.

"It's okay, he can keep it," Sophie told Grady as he grabbed Brant's hand and Brant screamed and tried to shove him away. She seemed to be making everything worse by being there—and she didn't want that. Besides, Brant had known and loved Jolie in a way she never could. Jolie's pin belonged to him much more than it ever would to her.

"Mine!" Brant shouted, laughing and kissing the jeweled bird before he slipped it into the pocket of his long cloak. His whole body relaxed when his treasure was safely tucked away and his face twisted into an ugly smile.

Edaline straightened up. "Maybe we should go—"

"No!" Brant shouted, coughing and shaking his head. When he met Sophie's eyes he seemed calm again. "Stay."

"Really, I'm fine," Sophie promised, and after hesitating a second, Grady helped Brant settle back into his chair and handed him his tin of custard bursts.

Edaline stayed next to Sophie, playing bodyguard.

Brant coughed again, dry and hoarse.

"Want me to conjure you some tea?" Edaline offered.

"*Nothing hot!*" He dragged out the last word into a desperate wail. Then the wail turned into a crackling laugh and he rocked back and forth, rubbing his ruined chin.

Grady launched into a long update on everything that had happened over the last year, but Sophie couldn't tell if Brant was actually listening. Mostly he stared at her with his damaged face, which made her want to look anywhere but at him, and yet he held her gaze like a tractor beam.

Edaline finally broke their awkward staring contest when she mentioned Silveny.

Brant's tin of custard bursts crashed to the ground again, and Sophie braced for another attack as Edaline jumped in front of her. But he simply stood, his eyes darting between the three of them. "You found another alicorn? A female?"

Grady moved to Sophie's side, taking her hand. "Sophie was the one who picked up Silveny's thoughts in the forest and helped us bring her home. She'll be the one rehabilitating her too."

Brant walked toward the wall, gazing at the smooth stones like someone might gaze out the window. "So the timeline will be reset." He spun back toward them, his gray eyes sparkling as they met Sophie's. "It's a turning point. In our ever-changing world."

"Uh . . . sure."

The room fell into silence and Sophie started to squirm, wondering how much longer they'd have to sit there in the cold, unsettling room with the cold, unsettling elf.

Fortunately, Brant made it easy on them.

"I'm tired now," he mumbled, dropping to the hard floor and curling up like a baby. "I need to rest."

Sophie expected Grady and Edaline to help him to his bed. Instead they got up and crouched beside him, squeezing his shoulder and telling him to sleep well.

"See you next year," Brant murmured through a yawn. He patted Jolie's pin in his pocket, like he needed to make sure it was there before he closed his eyes.

By the time they made it to the door, Brant was already snoring.

"You sure you're okay?" Grady asked for the third time as they climbed the steps to their bedrooms at Havenfield.

Sophie forced a smile, hating that she'd gone to *support* them, and somehow ended up worrying them more. "It *was* hard, like you said it would be. But I'm fine, I promise. I just want to go to bed."

"You're not going up there to try and figure out the Black Swan's clue, are you?" Grady folded his arms across his chest.

The sun was barely setting, and none of them had eaten dinner, but Sophie was ready for the emotional day to be over. "They waited more than three weeks to contact me—they can wait another night."

She leaned in to hug them good night, but Edaline pulled away. She closed her eyes and snapped her fingers and a small plate filled with four pink puffy squares appeared in her hand. Sophie jumped back a step—she wasn't sure she'd *ever* get used to Edaline's ability to pull things out of thin air—as Edaline held out the plate to her.

"I made these chocolate-cherry custard bursts for you. I guess I should've given them to you earlier. . . ."

"Thank you," Sophie said, filling the silence when Edaline's voice trailed off.

She picked up a piece, surprised when it felt smooth like a hard candy. But it was like biting into a sweet, sticky cloud filled with a fudgy chocolate cream and cherry goo. She had to slurp so it wouldn't run down her chin.

She'd thought nothing could ever taste better than mallowmelt—but now she wasn't sure.

Grady and Edaline laughed as she stuffed the rest of it into her mouth, puffing out her cheeks.

"They were Jolie's favorite too," Edaline whispered. "I guess that's why I don't like to make them—but if you like them, I can do it more often."

Sophie could've eaten a thousand of them, and she was sure she'd crave them every day. But . . .

She held up the plate to show the three she had left. "These are enough."

Edaline wrapped her arms around her. "We'll see."

They kissed her good night and Sophie climbed the last flight of stairs, nodding to Sandor when she reached her bedroom door.

"All is well," he assured her as his eyes lingered on her shoulder, like he could somehow see the bruise that was forming from where Brant restrained her. She swore goblins had a sixth sense for injuries. But he didn't ask. Just stepped aside to let her pass.

As soon as she set foot in her room, low music started playing. Human music. An old song she'd listened to hundreds of times growing up.

"Dex stopped by," Sandor explained behind her. "He left something to cheer you up."

"Oh."

Part of her had hoped the Black Swan was making contact again. But when she spotted Iggy's cage—which had been moved from its small table against the wall of windows to the center of her bed—she forgot her disappointment.

Iggy—or she assumed it was Iggy—was now a puff of pink frizzy curls. Dex must've fed the tiny imp one of his special hair-growing elixirs, which Iggy didn't seem to mind at all. He was having a lot of fun chasing his pink ringlets around and around. Her iPod had been propped against the cage, and when the song ended, Dex's face filled the screen.

"Hey, Sophie," he said, flashing his dimpled grin. "I thought you might need a laugh after today, since I'm sure it wasn't easy." He looked down, biting his lip before he added, "My mom told me this morning that we might have trees there. Did you see them? That's . . . kind of weird, don't you think? I mean—well, never mind. I guess you'll tell me about it if you saw them. And here's hoping mine captured my stunning good looks." He smiled again, though it looked a little sad. "Anyway, since school is starting soon, my mom wants me to stay home a little more—and my dad needs me to help him at the store—so I guess you're on your own with the verminion for the next few days. Try not to let it eat you!"

He gave a goofy wave before the screen went black and Sophie picked up the iPod, trying to figure out how he'd pulled off the trick. Dex was crazy for thinking technopathy wasn't cool.

She set her custard bursts on her desk to finish later, changed into her pajamas, and pulled her puffy pink imp out of his cage, placing him on her pillow before she settled into bed. His fur felt softer than normal, and when she rumpled it he started making his squeaky sound that reminded her of a purr.

Iggy curled into a ball as she lowered the drapes, and within a few seconds he was asleep. But it wasn't his motorboat snoring that filled her mind as she closed her eyes.

It was Brant's raspy, haunting voice repeating over and over.

I've seen you before.

He never told her where.

ELEVEN

OME. FRIEND.

The strange whisper dragged Sophie back to consciousness, and she was grateful for it. Brant's scarred, twisted face had joined her nightmares, and she could practically feel him pinning her against the chair—but instead of taking her pin he took her hand as he laughed and screamed, "Mine!"

At least she'd figured out why he said he'd seen her before. She must've reminded him of Jolie, which felt . . . strange.

Come. Friend.

Sophie shook her head, realizing where the whispers were coming from. *Silveny?*

Friend! the alicorn replied, louder this time and mixed with a rush of excitement.

Sophie stumbled to her feet, knocking Iggy to the floor with a startled squeak.

"Sorry," she whispered as he shook his paws at her, making his pink curls bounce. Sophie grabbed the first pants and tunic she found and threw them on, but couldn't tie the shirt's sash. Her hands were shaking too hard.

How could she hear Silveny if she wasn't listening for her?

The day before, she'd assumed Silveny's emotions had been so intense that it had made her subconsciously open up her mind. But now each repetition pounded into her brain like a stone, and when she tried to shield, all it did was muffle the noise.

Come! Friend! Come! Friend! Come! Friend! Come! Friend! Come! Friend!

"What's wrong, Miss Foster?" Sandor asked as she hopped out her bedroom door, still putting on her other boot.

"I don't know," she admitted, beelining for the stairs.

Edaline sat at the table in the dimly lit kitchen, her shadowed eyes looking like she hadn't slept at all. She jumped when Sophie rushed toward the door, nearly spilling her tea. "Are you okay?"

"I think so." Sophie slipped outside, racing toward Silveny's pasture.

Sandor caught up with her, grabbing her arm to stop her. "You really love to make my job difficult, don't you?" he asked as he scanned the scenery.

"Sorry, I'm just trying to check on Silveny."

Sandor sighed and drew his weapon. "Stay behind me."

He moved slow and soldierlike as he led her forward, trying to keep his eyes on everything at once. But when Silveny's enclosure came into view, the glittering horse was alone, circling the highest part of her dome, still transmitting *Come! Friend!* over and over. As soon as she spotted Sophie, she swooped down and trotted to the bars, shoving her nose through and snuffling.

Sophie gagged. Alicorn morning breath almost rivaled Iggy breath.

"What's wrong, girl?" Sophie asked as Sandor put his weapon away.

Cold emptiness rushed through her mind, sinking into her heart. *You're lonely?* she asked.

Lonely, Silveny repeated. *Friend.*

"Everything okay?" Grady called, jogging up behind them. His hair was tousled and he was wearing something that looked part bathrobe, part trench coat, which made Sophie realize how early it was. The sun was just beginning to streak the purple sky with hints of orange and pink. "Did something happen?" he asked.

"No, everything's fine. Silveny was just calling me. She can transmit straight into my brain somehow—and I can't block her. How is that possible?"

"I have no idea." He yawned, rubbing the sleep out of his eyes.

"I guess you'll have to ask Tiergan about it when Foxfire starts."

Sophie nodded, trying to stay as calm as Grady. But she didn't like feeling other voices in her head. It was worrying enough that Fitz could do it. Now Silveny could too?

Wasn't her mind designed to be *impenetrable?*

How are you doing this? she transmitted, stroking Silveny's velvety nose.

Friend! Lonely! was the only reply.

Sophie sighed. "Do you think we should move her to the Sanctuary so she can be with the other alicorn? She's already on a vegetarian diet."

"Readying a creature for relocation takes much more than changing what they eat. They need to be so well adjusted to captivity that they no longer have any desire to leave. Plus, the Sanctuary is a very delicate ecosystem. Introducing an animal too early could destroy the careful balance we work so hard to maintain. We need to test her to make sure she's not carrying any diseases, and we need to make sure she isn't aggressive with other animals. And, most important, she needs to be willing to trust people other than you."

Grady stepped closer and Silveny reared back.

Sophie frowned. Silveny had let the Hekses get close to her—though that had probably made it worse, since they'd restrained her in that terrible harness.

"Sorry, girl," Sophie said, rubbing Silveny's cheek. "You'll have to stay with me for a little while longer."

A new feeling poured through Sophie's mind, one that made her feet itch to run.

"I think she's restless. Maybe we need to let her out of her enclosure."

Silveny whinnied, like she agreed.

Grady shook his head. "We can't risk that she'll fly away."

"I don't think she will."

"We still can't chance it. The Council has trusted you—trusted *us*—with a tremendous responsibility by leaving Silveny in our care. She's incredibly important to our world."

Sophie stroked Silveny's chin. "I just hate seeing her locked up."

Almost as much as she hated Silveny's incessant transmissions.

Silveny, please. Quiet. She tried to think of an image to explain silence—but how did a picture convey the absence of sound?

It didn't matter. Silveny was insistent, stamping her hooves and transmitting her commands.

"We have to do something to calm her down. She's giving me a migraine."

"Why don't you go in the enclosure with her?"

Sophie doubted it would be enough, but it was better than nothing.

Treat? she asked Silveny as she grabbed a fistful of swizzle-spice from the nearby pile.

She threw the stalks as far as she could, and when Silveny

trotted after them, Grady unlocked the gate and she rushed inside. By the time the distracted horse realized what happened, the gate was safely latched again.

"Now what?" Sophie whispered as Silveny eyed her, sniffing the air for more treats.

"You're the one who has the special connection to her."

Yes, but having a connection didn't mean she knew how to entertain a large glittery horse. She couldn't exactly play fetch.

She settled for calling Silveny to her side and rubbing her shimmering fur until her mood mellowed.

"It's so strange that you can use your telepathy on her," Grady murmured. "I just tried mesmerizing her and it had no effect at all. I wonder what they did to your mind to make it work that way."

Sophie cringed.

"Sorry. I didn't mean it like that."

"It's okay. I know I'm a freak."

"You're *not* a freak, Sophie."

"Come on, everyone thinks it."

"Not me."

"Right. Sure." She pulled her hair around her face, wishing she could hide.

"I know it's hard—"

"Do you?"

Silveny whinnied at the shouted question, and Sophie reached for her. *Sorry. Calm.*

Calm, Silveny repeated, filling Sophie's mind with warmth again.

"I do," Grady said quietly, and the sadness in his tone made Sophie turn to look at him. "It's not exactly easy being a Mesmer."

Now he had her attention. When she'd first met Grady, he went out of his way to avoid telling her what his ability was. But she'd thought that was because the Council was always pressuring him about it—not because he didn't like it.

"Kids at school didn't trust me after I manifested. Told me they didn't want me messing with their minds. Others would lie to get out of detention and say I *made* them do whatever they got caught doing. And when I got awards or praise, they'd claim I used my ability to cheat. Even Edaline's parents teased me when we got engaged. Said they should find a way to make sure I hadn't mesmerized her into marrying me. They meant it as a joke, but . . ."

Sophie felt the same way when people teased her about being an Inflictor—even when they were just having fun.

"Being powerful worries people, Sophie. It's unfair and it hurts, but can't you understand why it happens?"

She kicked the ground. She could, but that didn't mean she liked it.

"You've had a huge burden dumped on you. Trust me—no one understands that better than me. I wish I could make it easier, but I can't. Except to tell you the same thing my parents told me when I would get so angry I wanted to throw stuff. They'd say, 'Someday your ability will do big things, and the world will be grateful we have you.'"

The words should've been comforting—and they were. Except . . .

What if she really was someone's *puppet*? Could she be programmed to do certain things?

Bad things?

"So, do you think Silveny will let you sit on her back?" Grady asked.

"Huh?"

"If you're going to be working with her, you're going to need to learn how to ride her."

Sophie had a feeling he was just trying to distract her and cheer her up—but it would be fun to ride an alicorn.

Then again, she was suddenly realizing how very large Silveny was, and how very high off the ground her back was. "How do I even get up there?"

"Can you get her to kneel down?"

"Maybe."

Kneel, she transmitted, sending Silveny an image of the position she meant. She had to repeat it three times before Silveny lowered her head and bent her front legs.

"Amazing! Now just make sure she's calm, and climb on."

Sophie stared at the crouched horse. "What if I fall?"

"We have Elwin on standby."

"Very funny."

"Come on, aren't you always saying we worry too much and never let you take any risks? Well, here's your risk."

It was strange to have Grady so relaxed about her safety. Though, he *did* regularly ride around on mammoths and dinosaurs, so this wasn't exactly out of the ordinary. But he never had *her* do those things.

Of course, Silveny was a glittering winged horse, not a *Tyrannosaurus rex.* So she sucked in a breath for extra courage, sent Silveny images of what she was about to do, and slowly stretched one leg over the horse's neck. Silveny raised her head as she straightened, sliding Sophie down to the dip in her back just behind her wings.

Fly? Silveny asked—and before Sophie could respond, the excited horse flapped her enormous wings and launched into the sky.

Sophie screamed as the whipping wind made her eyes water.

Grady shouted things like "squeeze your legs" and "wrap your arms around Silveny's neck"—but those required *moving.*

Moving was so not going to be possible.

After what felt like an hour, but was probably only a few seconds, Sophie managed to get a white-knuckled grip on Silveny's mane, coiling the ends around her wrists for extra support. With her panic at a slightly more manageable level, she realized they were circling the top of the domed enclosure.

Silveny was flying low enough to avoid the thick purple bars, but Sophie ducked anyway.

"Here, Silveny," Grady called, running into the enclosure and holding out a handful of swizzlespice. "Come down for a treat."

Silveny ignored him. Apparently, terrifying her only friend was better than snacks.

"Order her to land," Sandor called.

"Working on it!" Sophie shouted back.

She took a deep breath, forcing her mind to relax as she transmitted images of them standing on the ground. *Down.*

Silveny nickered. *Fly.*

Down.

Fly.

Down!

Fly!

DOWN!

FLY!

Silveny's mood turned giddy over this new game and Sophie wondered just how much trouble she'd be in if she strangled the obnoxious horse once they were back on solid ground.

Silveny veered to the left, sending Sophie flailing right. Grady and Sandor gasped, but before Sophie lost her balance Silveny's wing tipped her back into place. When the same thing happened three more times, Sophie realized what Silveny was trying to tell her.

You want me to trust you?

Trust, Silveny repeated, though Sophie wondered if she *really* grasped the concept. Especially since she started flying faster, with more twists and turns than any roller coaster would ever—could ever—have.

Easy! she ordered, sending images of straight, slow flying.

"Don't panic, Sophie." Grady called. "I'm going to get you down!"

Sophie glanced below, where a group of gnomes had entered the enclosure and were helping him uncoil a thick silver lasso.

"Don't!" she screamed, imagining Silveny turning bucking bronco in the air.

"It's okay, I know what I'm doing."

Somehow she doubted that. "I can get her to come down on my own."

"You've got one more minute!" he shouted back. "Then I'm dragging you down."

Being hog-tied to a terrified alicorn and yanked from the sky was definitely not on Sophie's Things I Want To Do list.

Silveny, please. Take. Me. Down!

She transmitted more images of her standing on the ground, all of which Silveny ignored.

Scared, Sophie said, trying a different tactic. But Silveny didn't seem to understand the concept, flipping them in a series of loops.

"Hang on," Grady called, and Sophie heard the unmistakable swish of a rope slicing through the air.

Take us down! The transmission mixed with so much fear and panic it felt like a cold blast when it left her mind.

Silveny screeched, tucked her wings, and dropped from the sky like a missile.

Sophie squealed and braced for impact. But at the last possible second Silveny leveled off and touched down, stopping so abruptly it sent Sophie tumbling forward.

By some miracle she managed to land on her feet, but her legs were shaking and her head was spinning so fast, she stumbled and collapsed.

Right into a pile of alicorn manure.

TWELVE

THIS IS WHO WE'RE TRUSTING WITH the most important creature on our planet?" a sharp voice barked as Sophie flailed in the stinky waste—which was surprisingly glittery. Apparently, she'd found the one thing sparkles *didn't* make better.

And if she weren't already nauseous from the wild flight and the gagging smell of manure, the sound of that voice would've done it.

Sophie wiped the shimmering poop off her cheek as she stood to face not just Bronte—a smallish elf with cropped brown hair and features as sharp as his voice—but the entire elvin Council in full regal garb, standing just outside the enclosure.

Sophie dipped an ungraceful curtsy and stared at their circlets, each encrusted with different-colored jewels to match their elegant capes. She tried to remember their names, but it was hard when they weren't in front of their conveniently labeled thrones in Tribunal Hall. She could only recognize five of them.

Two goblin bodyguards flanked the group on each side, and next to the closest one stood Alden, his lips twitching with the smile he was fighting back.

"Yes, Bronte," Alden said, offering Sophie a silky handkerchief from a pocket in his navy blue cape. "And Sophie is more than worthy of the task. Though clearly we've caught her in the middle of some excitement."

Sophie's face burned as she moved closer and reached through the purple bars to accept the handkerchief. The stench followed her with every step, and all the silky cloth did was smear the filth more.

"So, you can fly with Silveny?" Alden asked, a hint of awe in his voice.

"Apparently," Grady answered for her as he exited the enclosure and approached the Councillors. He inclined his head in a slight bow. "To what do we owe this honor?"

"I know we come unannounced," Councillor Emery—the spokesman for the Council—said in his deep, booming voice. His eyes were the same shade as the sapphires covering his circlet and his shoulder-length hair was almost as dark as his skin.

"We were eager to see this remarkable discovery for ourselves."

The others murmured in agreement, their eyes glued to Silveny, who was preening the feathers on her glistening wings, looking gleaming and majestic and without a single fleck of poop on her anywhere. Sophie started plotting revenge.

"Can you really communicate with her?" Kenric asked. With his vivid red hair and wide shoulders he was the easiest to recognize—and one of Sophie's favorite members of the Council, thanks to his warm smile.

"Not only can they communicate," Grady answered for her, "but Sophie discovered this morning that Silveny can transmit to her—even when she's trying to block her."

Several Councillors gasped.

Alden frowned. "Most curious."

"Indeed," Councillor Terik said, sweeping back his wavy brown hair. Sophie remembered him from their private consultation a few months back. He was a Descryer—able to sense and interpret potential—and the Council had ordered him to take a reading of her. Unfortunately, all he'd felt was "something strong" and hadn't been able to translate what it meant.

"How did you find her?" he asked, his cobalt blue eyes focused so intently on Sophie she felt like he was trying to take another reading.

"It was kind of an accident," she admitted. She explained how she'd followed Silveny's thoughts, assuming they came from the sasquatch.

Silveny trotted to her side as she spoke, and Sophie pretended not to see her, not ready to forgive her for the manure situation.

"Incredible," Councillor Terik breathed as Silveny nudged Sophie, refusing to be ignored. "Our long-lost elf, and the most searched-for creature on the planet, stumbling across each other in the middle of a forest in the Forbidden Cities. It's almost impossible to believe there were no other forces at play. Especially when you consider the unique connection the two appear to have. It seems unlikely that it happened purely by chance."

Councillor Emery cleared his throat. "Are you implying that someone *intended* for Sophie to find the alicorn?"

His words seemed to swell in Sophie's mind.

She stared into Silveny's watery brown eyes. Eyes that were almost the same color as hers. Eyes that stared back at her with an intensity and intelligence like no other animal she'd ever encountered. Eyes that belonged to an animal who could break through her mental blocking in ways even elves couldn't.

Had she been *led* by the Black Swan specifically to find her?

"It's impossible," Oralie's fragile voice announced, shattering the silence everyone had fallen into. The blond beauty in a cape and circlet the same soft pink as her rosy cheeks shook her head as she stepped forward and added, "No one could orchestrate such a feat. Not even the Black Swan."

"Oralie's right," Kenric agreed. "We've been searching for another alicorn for decades."

"Centuries," Alden corrected. "Without even the slightest hint that another might exist. Are you suggesting the Black Swan has been *hiding* Silveny all this time, risking that the other alicorn would expire before they could reproduce?"

"When you put it that way, it does sound rather absurd," Councillor Terik admitted. "But surely you can agree that it's a stunning coincidence. Especially considering that this completely resets the timeline."

"What does that mean?" Sophie asked, squirming as all eyes turned back to her.

"Hasn't anyone educated this child in the fundamental principles of our world?" Bronte shook his head so dramatically that his Ancient ears wiggled.

Elvin ears turned pointy as they aged, which meant prominent points like Bronte's were a sign of wisdom and experience. But to Sophie they looked far too much like the cheap costume ears she used to see humans wear when they pretended to be elves. Usually paired with tights and shoes with bells on the toes.

"Councillor Terik was referring to the Timeline to Extinction," Alden said, reminding Sophie that there were more important things to think about than pointy ears. "With only one alicorn in our care, and no guarantee that we'd ever find another, we've been facing the very real possibility that this majestic species would someday go extinct."

He whispered the last word, like it was too horrible to say

at full volume. The elves believed that every creature on earth existed for a reason, and to let one die off would cause irreversible damage to the planet's delicate balance. That was why they'd built the Sanctuary and worked so hard to protect and conserve the creatures humans thought were either myths or lost.

"But now all of that has changed," Councillor Terik added quietly. "*Everything* has changed."

"Indeed it has," Councillor Emery agreed. "And it couldn't have happened at a better time. This is exactly the kind of discovery that will restore calm and order to our world. The symbol of hope and stability we've been waiting for."

Silveny nudged Sophie again, filling the air with her rancid breath. Sophie couldn't believe such a stinky, stubborn creature was so important.

"All the more reason why the alicorn's care should be entrusted to experts. Look at her!"

Sophie's cheeks flamed as Bronte pointed a bony finger at her sparkly poop-covered clothes.

"We are looking," Councillor Emery replied. "The alicorn trusts her completely."

"And Edaline and I are here to help her," Grady added. "We have years of experience."

Bronte snorted. "Two of our world's most scandalous misfits—oh yes, I feel *much* better. Need I remind you that mere months ago the Ruewen name was uttered only with ridicule and scorn? How many years have you isolated your-self at this estate—letting the rumors spread of your mad-ness without bothering to deny them?" He turned to face the Councillors. "And how can we forget the day he stood before us and dared to accuse us of neglectful rulership before renouncing his title as Emissary? What right does he have to demand our trust—especially now, when our every decision is being scrutinized by a disconcerted public?"

Sophie fidgeted in the deafening silence that followed.

She'd known that most of the elves had thought Grady and Edaline were weird—she'd heard plenty of gossip when she was first assigned to live with them. But they'd pulled away from everyone because they'd lost their *only daughter*—and had to care for Brant—in a world where almost no one knew how to relate to their grief.

Couldn't the Council understand that?

"Things have changed, Bronte," Alden said quietly. "We've all seen the transformation in Grady and Edaline since Sophie came to live with them. And with—"

"Oh, we have, have we?" Bronte interrupted. "Granted, they leave the house a bit more—though several of those times were merely to attend Miss Foster's Tribunals."

Sophie cringed at the word.

"But they still avoid participating in regular society. And hasn't Grady repeatedly turned down our request that he return to his position as Emissary—a position that would greatly aid in our efforts to stop the organization that seeks to harm a member of his own family?"

Another moment of awkward silence passed, and this time Councillor Emery rubbed his temples, probably moderating telepathic discussions between the Councillors. Sophie had a feeling she knew what questions they must be asking. The same ones she'd been trying not to ask herself these last few weeks.

Why *wouldn't* Grady become an Emissary again?

Didn't he *want* to help them catch her kidnappers?

"Bronte does raise an interesting point, Grady," Councillor Emery finally said. "It would do much to instill public confidence in our decision to let Sophie rehabilitate the alicorn if you reclaim your title as Emissary. Would you be willing to accept the appointment?"

Say yes, Sophie thought, wishing she could transmit the words but not daring to interfere. *Please say yes.*

Maybe if Grady had looked in her eyes, he would've seen the hope she was hiding. But he didn't look at her—or anyone—as he folded his arms and said the word that felt like a slap to Sophie's heart.

"*No.*"

THIRTEEN

HY NOT?"

It took Sophie a second to realize the question had come from her, and another after that to decide she wasn't sorry for asking.

Grady shook his head, his eyes pleading with her to drop it. But she wasn't letting him off that easy.

"Why don't you want to help the Council?"

"It's not that I don't want to help them, Sophie. It's just . . . complicated."

"Doesn't seem complicated to me," she grumbled.

Bronte laughed—a harsh, crackly sound. "For once Miss Foster and I are in agreement. I would very much like to understand what's so complicated about using your talents to serve our world. Isn't that the obligation of those gifted with special abilities? To use them to aid the greater good?"

"Grady does a tremendous service for us here at Havenfield," Alden said, when Grady didn't respond. "Need I remind you of how many creatures he and Edaline have successfully rehabilitated?"

Bronte rolled his eyes. "Please—that's a job even someone Talentless could do."

"And yet, not five minutes ago you were arguing that the complexities of caring for Silveny required special expertise, were you not? So which is it?" Alden's voice was calm, but thin lines had crept across his face, betraying his frustration.

Or was it worry?

"Successfully rehabilitating the rarest creature in our world is *quite* different from training a T. rex to eat salad. Not only that, it's an honor and a privilege that should be given to someone *worthy*. I'm sure Timkin Heks wouldn't hesitate to enlist as an Emissary if we called upon him to do so."

"No, I rather suspect that's his entire motivation for offering his services in the first place," Alden said with a rueful smile. "His quest for prominence is hardly a secret."

"His motivation for volunteering is no more selfish than Grady's refusal to be reinstated," Bronte snapped back.

"Selfish? You dare to claim my reasoning is *selfish*?"

Silveny whinnied at Grady's outburst, and Sophie rushed to her side to calm her.

Grady stalked toward Bronte, standing so close their noses practically touched. "You know full well why I resigned—and given recent events, you should understand my objections even more. Havenfield is the best place to house Silveny, and Sophie is the most capable person for the job. If you're too afraid of public scorn to accept that decision, then you deserve every bit of the criticism you're receiving. Transfer the alicorn to the Hekses if you wish—but I will not let you bully me into submission."

"Grady, please," Alden called as Grady stormed away, leaving Sophie behind with the twelve stunned Councillors.

"Insolent fool," Bronte grumbled. "I vote we relocate the alicorn immediately."

Several of the Councillors murmured their agreement and Sophie's heart sank. Silveny may be driving her crazy, but the stubborn horse didn't deserve to be at the mercy of the Hekses. She could remember all too well the feel of Silveny's terror as they jerked her around in that miserable harness.

She reached up and rubbed Silveny's nose, right where the straps had cut in.

"Let's not be hasty," Councillor Emery said, waiting for everyone to quiet before he continued. "Can we really discount Miss Foster's connection to this creature?"

Sophie tried to stand tall as twelve pairs of eyes turned to scrutinize her. Sure, she was young, and new to their world, and still learning how to control her abilities, and currently covered in shimmering manure. But Grady and Alden were right—she could do this. *Way* better than the Hekses could.

Oralie's quiet voice broke the silence. "I think we should let Sophie try. I can feel her determination from here—as well as the bond between her and Silveny. Those advantages are far superior to what little experience the Heks family may have."

"I agree with Oralie," Kenric chimed in.

Bronte snorted. "Of course you do."

To be fair, Kenric did seem to favor the pretty blond Councillor over the others.

"I'm inclined to agree as well," Councillor Emery announced, motivating three of the Councillors whom Sophie didn't know to vote in her favor as well. Which made the vote six to six. Unless someone else changed their mind.

Sophie glanced at Councillor Terik. He was studying her with his intense, almost probing stare, and after what felt like an eternity he said, "I vote that we see what Sophie can do with this creature. If her progress isn't what it should be, we can always reassess."

"So, we have a majority then!" Alden sounded more relieved than pleased.

"For now." Bronte turned to glare at Sophie. "We need the alicorn moved to the Sanctuary as soon as possible. If you don't make *rapid* progress, we'll have no choice but to turn her over to the Hekses."

"I can handle it," Sophie promised.

"We'll see. And be sure to tell your father we'll be monitoring your progress closely."

"He's not my *father*."

A *father* wouldn't refuse to help find her kidnappers. And she didn't want to be the daughter of anyone who would let Silveny suffer at the hands of the Hekses just to avoid working for the Council.

But . . . Grady wasn't callous—especially when it came to animals. There had to be something he wasn't telling her. Something *big*.

"Yes, well, I'm glad that's settled," Alden said, forcing a smile. "The Councillors had been hoping for a demonstration of how you interact with Silveny, Sophie, but I think it would be better to do that another time. Perhaps when there are a few less feces."

Sophie scowled, but several of the Councillors smiled as they reached for their pathfinders, and the tension that had been tangled around them seemed to ease. Even Sandor snickered.

I need to talk to you, she transmitted to Alden, not wanting to tell the entire Council about the charm. *It's about the Black Swan.*

Alden didn't react to her transmissions, but he told the Council, "I'm leaving right now for my next assignment, and will be away for a few days. Perhaps we can regroup then?" A tiny wink at the end told her he meant the last part for her.

Part of her was relieved. Sophie wasn't sure if Alden would make her turn over the charm, and she needed to figure out the clue first.

So she dipped another ungraceful curtsy and watched Alden and the Councillors glitter away. Then she ran for her room, stripped off her soiled outfit, and jumped into a scalding shower. When all trace of sparkles and manure had been scrubbed away, she changed into fresh work clothes and rushed downstairs, vowing to make it very clear to Silveny that there would be no more headache-inducing demands, unexpected flights, or poop-filled landings.

Sophie froze when she spotted Grady sitting with Edaline at the kitchen table.

"Is something wrong, Miss Foster?" Sandor asked as he swerved to avoid crashing into her.

She was trying to decide if she wanted to talk to Grady. But all she said was, "Just checking on Silveny. She's finally quieted down."

"Well, that's good news." Edaline motioned for Sophie to take her usual seat.

Grady hid behind the official-looking scroll he was reading as Sophie sat in the chair across from him.

Edaline snapped her fingers, and a golden muffin with purple splotches appeared on the table. "I made blitzenberry muffins. They were another of Jolie's favorites."

Sophie squeezed Edaline's hand as she reached for the

muffin and took a bite. The tart berries fizzed and popped on her tongue, and the cake was smooth like melted butter. "They're amazing. Thank you."

"Of course." Edaline turned away to wipe her eyes.

Grady still hadn't said a word—and Sophie decided she was done letting him off the hook. "Are you ready to tell me why you won't help the Council?"

He made a sound that was more of a groan than a sigh and set his scroll on the table. "I won't help them," he said, rubbing his temples, "because they don't want to find the kidnappers, Sophie. They want me to help them find the Black Swan."

"And you don't want to find them."

It wasn't a question—but that didn't mean she understood it.

"Not the way the Council wants to, no. They want to reach out as allies. But if the Black Swan were our allies, we wouldn't have to *find* them. If they were on our side, they wouldn't be hiding. They wouldn't be leaving secret messages on charm bracelets in the middle of the Wanderling Woods, using a young, innocent girl like their pup—"

"Grady!" Edaline warned.

"I'm sure they have a good reason for wanting to stay secret," Sophie argued, when Grady stayed quiet. She looked to Edaline to back her up, but Edaline was staring at her cup of tea like it was the most fascinating thing in the entire universe.

Grady crunched the edge of the scroll in his fisted hand.

"Oh, I'm sure they have a reason, Sophie—and it's anything but *good*. They're not to be trusted."

"You keep saying that, but I don't understand. They're the ones who—"

"Rescued you. Yes, I know. You keep saying *that*. And completely forgetting that they left you unconscious on the streets of a Forbidden City with only a few clues to help you find your way back. Why didn't they bring you and Dex safely back to our world?"

"He said he couldn't risk being discovered."

"What do they have to hide? And how did they know where you were?"

"I don't know," she mumbled, squishing a piece of her muffin into a sticky blob. The tiny berries stained her fingers purple. "I don't know anything about them. No one tells me anything."

"You know everything you need to know."

"Obviously not! There has to be a reason why you're so convinced the Black Swan is evil. If you want me to believe you, you need to tell me."

"You don't want to know," he said as he stood to leave.

Sophie grabbed his arm. "Actually, I do."

The room seemed to hold its breath as he stared at her fingers on his skin, and his mouth formed three different words before he said, "Fine."

"Grady!" Edaline knocked her teacup as she stood, sending it crashing to the floor.

"She deserves to know."

Edaline shook her head, but she didn't argue as she stepped over the mess and faced the wall of windows.

Grady bent and picked up one of the larger shards of glass, staring at the jagged edges.

"I know we can't trust the Black Swan," he whispered, "because the Black Swan murdered Jolie."

FOURTEEN

UT . . . IT WAS AN ACCIDENT," SOPHIE mumbled, surprised to realize she was suddenly standing.

A *terrible accident*—that's what Alden had called it. She could still remember the sadness in his voice, the way Della had turned away, trying not to cry. Neither of them had shown any sign that they suspected murder.

"It was no accident." Grady's voice was dark and hard.

"How do you—what did they—have you—" There were too many words and questions crashing around inside her head. She didn't know which one to go with.

Or maybe she did.

"Why?"

"Why what?"

"Why would they do that?"

The Black Swan were elusive and secretive—but they'd also stationed someone to keep constant watch over her when she was living with humans. They went to great lengths to make sure she had everything she needed to stop the Everblaze from killing any more innocent people. And they were the only ones who didn't believe that she and Dex were dead, coming to their rescue in the nick of time.

Murderers didn't do things like that.

Edaline gazed blankly into the pastures as she whispered, "I know this is hard to hear, Sophie. It's hard for us, too."

"It just . . . doesn't make sense."

"You think I'm lying?" Grady snapped.

"Of course not. But could there be a misunderstanding?"

"Trust me—there was no mistake."

"Then why? Why would they kill . . ."

She couldn't even say it.

"To punish me. Or scare me into submission. I'm still not sure which." Grady stalked to the windows, but he didn't stand near Edaline, and she didn't step closer to him. "They'd been trying to recruit me for months. Slipping me notes to convince me to join their forces."

"Why would they—"

"Because I'm a Mesmer, Sophie. Think of how much easier it would be if they had my power in their arsenal. I could make anyone do anything they needed. I could mesmerize the entire Council if I wanted to, make them sign any law into effect. I could make them all jump off a cliff if I felt like it."

Sophie couldn't hide her shudder.

She'd thought inflicting was a terrifying ability, but the things Grady could do were a whole other realm of horrifying. She was amazed the Council didn't forbid him from using his power. But they only did that after something went wrong, like when they forbade pyrokinesis after several elves died trying to spark Everblaze.

"The Black Swan would've done anything to get me on their side. And when I made it very clear that there was nothing they could say to convince me, they sent me one final message. Slipped it into the pocket of my cape—like they wanted me to know they could get to me anywhere. 'You don't know who you're dealing with.' If I'd known what they meant I . . ."

Grady's voice cracked and Edaline moved to his side.

"It wasn't your fault," she whispered, wrapping her arms around his shoulders.

Grady jerked away. "I *know*. It was *their fault*. Three days after I got that note, Jolie died in a fire. A fire that no one ever found the cause of. The Council ruled it an accident, but I knew. The Black Swan was showing me who I was dealing with. What lengths they'd go to."

He slammed his fist against the window so hard it cracked the glass.

Sophie jumped as Sandor grabbed her shoulders, like he was afraid Grady had become a threat. But Grady just stood there watching the hairline fissures spread through the glass.

Sophie watched them too, trying to make her brain connect the pieces Grady just gave her with the things she already knew. How could the same people that made her, protected her—even at the cost of their own sanity—kill an innocent girl, just to punish Grady or scare him into changing his mind? But how else could she explain what Grady was telling her? Could all of those things really be a coincidence?

"Does the Council know about this?" she asked.

"Of course. I told them everything—but it was back when they were still deluding themselves into believing that the Black Swan didn't exist. And murder wasn't something that happened in our world. Alden did what he could to help me investigate, but the Black Swan had covered their tracks well— they're good at skulking in the shadows like cowards! And without proof, the Council treated me like I was some raving madman, broken by the loss of my daughter. Told me to 'let the lost stay at peace.' To 'look forward, not back.' To 'focus on what matters.' *My daughter matters!*"

He swung to punch the window again, but Edaline grabbed his arm. "Please, Grady," she whispered. "Enough."

His arms shook as he fought for control. Then he unclenched his fists and his whole body seemed to droop.

"So that's why you left your job with the Council," Sophie said as Edaline led him back to the table.

Grady sank into a chair and Edaline crouched beside him, examining his knuckles. "If they wouldn't help me, why should I help them? Besides, I wanted no part of such a blind, incompetent organization—and I want even less to do with them now. I want nothing to do with anyone connected to the Black Swan."

"Grady," Edaline warned as Sophie clutched her stomach like she'd been punched.

She would always be connected to the Black Swan.

Always.

"Sophie," Grady called as she turned and ran. But she couldn't stop, couldn't speak, couldn't do anything except race upstairs, shut herself in her bedroom, and collapse on the bed.

If Grady was right—if the Black Swan did what he'd said . . .

She heard Edaline's quiet knock, but she couldn't make herself answer.

Edaline came in anyway and wrapped her in a hug. "Grady didn't mean *you*, Sophie." She rubbed Sophie's back, tracing slow, gentle circles. "He loses himself sometimes. Lets the anger take control. I used to try to make him put those feelings behind him, just like he'd try to help me stop holding on to some part of her like it could bring her back. But it's different from that. He *has* to stay angry. If he doesn't blame *them*, he might start to blame himself, and if he did . . ."

She didn't finish, but Sophie knew. She remembered what Grady had told her about Brant's parents.

About *guilt*.

"So you don't think Grady's right?" Sophie whispered.

She couldn't breathe as she waited for Edaline's answer, and her lungs were burning by the time Edaline squeezed her hand and said, "I don't know what to believe. But I do know it has nothing to do with you."

"But the Black Swan *made* me."

"Who *they* are has nothing to do with who *you* are. Grady and I have known that from the moment Alden asked us to take you in. Don't you ever let anything make you think otherwise."

Sophie wanted to believe that—more than anything. And maybe it would be true if she were normal.

But she wasn't normal.

She was the Black Swan's "creation." They'd twisted and tweaked her DNA, designing her specifically for *something*.

And if the Black Swan were murderers . . .

"Please try to let this go, Sophie. Grady's just having a hard day. In fact, why don't you go do something fun to take your mind off things? Where's Dex today?"

"He has to help his dad at the store."

"Well, then why don't you go visit him there? I'm sure Kesler would let him take a break. Or you could stay there and put your fabulous alchemy skills to use. Maybe you'll be the one to finally burn down that ugly store."

Sophie couldn't help smiling—though sadly, given her general patheticness when it came to alchemy, there was a very good chance she really would start a fire. She'd almost burned down Foxfire several times.

And Edaline did have a good idea about visiting Dex—but not for the reason she was saying. Sophie couldn't let this go. She needed to know the truth about the Black Swan. And Dex was the only other person who'd met one of them.

It was time for her and Dex to have the conversation they'd been carefully avoiding. Whether they were ready for it or not.

FIFTEEN

YOU'D THINK THEY'D NEVER SEEN A goblin before," Sophie muttered to Sandor as the crowds of pedestrians gawked at them.

Mysterium was a working-class city, packed with elves in simple tunics and pants making their way down the narrow sidewalks to the vendor carts or to plain, identical buildings. Sandor—with his giant body and giant muscles and giant sword—might as well have been wrapped in neon lights.

"I hate to break it to you, Miss Foster, but they're not staring at me."

Sophie opened her mouth to argue, but stopped when she realized Sandor was right.

She was used to getting stares and whispers. In fact, the first time she'd come to Mysterium, she and Edaline had created quite the spectacle, between their noble gowns and Edaline's antisocial reputation.

But this time there was fear in their eyes.

"That's the girl who was taken," someone whispered.

Words like "trouble" and "menace" quickly followed.

A mother even grabbed her children's arms, like she feared being near Sophie might somehow get them taken too.

Sophie wanted to be annoyed, but . . . that *was* what happened to Dex.

Sandor moved in front of her as Sophie ducked her head and picked up her pace, and they didn't stop until they'd reached Slurps and Burps, the only unique building in the entire city with its topsy-turvy structure and rainbow paint job. The door belched as they entered, and a plume of purple smoke greeted them with the stench of old pickled cabbage.

"I *told* you not to add the savoyola until the flame turned blue!"

"No, you said red!"

"Red heat makes it curdle and combust!"

"I *know*."

"Then why did you add it?"

"Because you told me to!"

Despite the gag-inducing stench, Sophie smiled as she and Sandor wove through the maze of shelves filled with tiny vials and bottles. When they finally reached the back laboratory, the scene was even more chaotic than she'd imagined.

Thick pink slime covered everything—the lab table, the ceiling, and especially the tall slender man who looked even more like his son with the vibrant goo coating both of their faces.

"You look like when I smacked you with that splotcher," Sophie told Dex, grinning as he tried to smear away the pink sludge from his cheeks. Splotching was a type of telekinesis duel, and she had easily defeated him and left him splattered with hot pink splotcher slime.

Kesler swatted at the tiny flames that had caught on the bottom of his white lab coat. "Sorry, we didn't hear you come in. How can I help you, Sophie?"

"I needed to talk to Dex, but maybe I should come back later. . . ."

"No—don't go," Dex blurted. "I mean, um, I could use a break. Let me just clean up real quick."

He raced toward the storage room, nearly slipping in a pink puddle as he ran.

Kesler shook his head. "I think your alchemy skills are rubbing off on him, Sophie."

"*It wasn't my fault!*" Dex shouted from the other side of the wall.

Kesler mouthed, *Yes it was,* before he said, "Well, I'd better get this mess taken care of. Feel free to wander around. I'm sure we have at least a *few* elixirs Edaline isn't keeping on hand in case you have another one of your incidents."

Sophie wasn't so sure. She'd seen Edaline's medicine collection. It was getting out of control.

Still, the Dizznees made a *lot* of elixirs, most with names like Buff Stuff and Curley-Dew and Fuzzy Fizz. Kesler liked to keep things as ridiculous as possible—his small way of rebelling against the stuffy nobles who frequented his store. But that didn't mean his concoctions weren't seriously powerful. Slurps and Burps had an elixir or balm for almost every problem or ailment anyone could ever have. Which was why the store was so cluttered with shelves. Sandor was struggling to maneuver his bulky frame through the aisles without knocking things over.

A blue bottle caught Sophie's eye as she browsed.

"What's Fade Fuel?" she asked, picking up the delicate flask. Clear liquid sloshed inside, and the glass felt warm to the touch.

"Helps you regenerate faster if you fade during a leap," Kesler called.

Her grip tightened on the vial. Maybe it could ease the strange headaches and dizziness she kept getting.

"Better put that away," Kesler said behind her, startling her so much she nearly dropped the bottle. He took it from her, holding it up to the light until the bottle glowed. "This would've made Elwin's job a lot easier when he was trying to bring you back. But it has limbium in it."

Just the word made her skin itch and her stomach heave.

Kesler frowned as he set the bottle back on the shelf. "I helped him make a version without the limbium, but it was hardly the same. Good thing you're such a fighter."

"Yeah," Sophie mumbled, not quite sure what to say. "What exactly does limbium do?"

"Many things, depending on what you mix it with. Mainly it affects the limbic system."

A diagram from one of her old human science books filled Sophie's memory. "That's the emotional center of the brain, isn't it?"

"And the center of behavior, long-term memory, and motivation. It's also the root point of any special ability. Not something to be tampered with lightly. Which is why we put it in *very* few elixirs—and only use a drop. Though in your case that's still a fatal amount. . . ."

She rubbed her arms, remembering the burning hives she'd gotten within moments of drinking the elixir Dex had given her. Had it really only had a drop?

"Why were you asking?" Kesler asked. "Are you still feeling side effects from the leap?"

Sophie hoped he didn't notice her slight hesitation before she said, "How could I be? Grady and Edaline make Elwin check me like once a week."

"That's not actually an answer," he pointed out.

She had to fight the urge to tug out an eyelash. "I'm fine."

And she *was* fine.

Once again she reminded herself of how very many times Elwin had checked her. She probably just needed more sleep.

Kesler didn't look convinced, though, so she added, "I've just been having a lot of nightmares. But there's no elixir for that."

"Not unless you want a sedative," Kesler agreed.

"Thanks, I'll pass."

"Yeah, I'm with you on that," Dex said as he joined them. He'd changed to a blue tunic and washed away most of the pink slime, but there was still a small patch near his left ear. "I've had enough sedatives to last five lifetimes."

Kesler coughed—but it sounded more like a choke. He cleared his throat after a second and whispered, "I'd better get back to cleaning up. Dex, why don't you take Sophie up to your lab?"

"You have a *lab*?"

"Yes—and he uses it to make all kinds of elixirs he *shouldn't*."

Sophie smiled. She'd seen one of Dex's special elixirs in action last year when he'd turned Stina bald. She'd just never pictured him with a *lab*. She'd still never seen his room. He always came over to Havenfield.

"It's this way," Dex said, leading her to a door labeled SUPPLIES.

Sandor tried to follow them inside, but the cramped aisles of glass shelves in the storeroom were definitely not spaced far enough apart to fit a bulky goblin. After a few steps he sighed and scanned the room. "I suppose I can keep watch from here."

Sophie's smile widened. She'd been trying to figure out how to get some alone time with Dex. Now she just had to figure out how to bring up the subject they'd both been oh-so-carefully avoiding for the last few weeks. . . .

Dex led her up an iron stairway, clapping his hands when they reached the top. A string of dangling spheres lit up, illuminating a small room under a nook in the store's crooked roof. The only furniture was a lab table and chair surrounded by a curved wall of shelves, all of which were surprisingly organized. Sophie had expected all sorts or crazy bubbling beakers and flasks, but all of Dex's alchemy equipment had been shoved to the corner of the table, replaced with tiny circuits and wires and pieces of gadgets.

"Practicing with your ability?" she asked, glad to see that he wasn't letting his talent completely go to waste.

"Just until I manifest something else."

"You're so weird."

"That's why you like me." He grinned and motioned for her to take the room's only chair. Then he leaned against the table, grabbing a piece of gadget and fiddling with the wires as he asked, "So, what's up—and don't say 'nothing.' I know you better than that."

All useful words seemed to vanish from her mind. "I, um . . . I was just wondering—hey, is that the card I gave you?" She pointed to a blue notecard standing up in the center of his desk.

Dex's cheeks flushed as he snatched the card and set it on the highest shelf he could reach. "Stop stalling."

Sophie pulled at the sleeves of her gray-striped tunic. "Okay. Fine. I . . . need to know what you remember."

She didn't say any more, but she didn't need to. Dex scooted away, folding his arms across his chest. Seconds stretched into minutes—though they felt like hours—before he finally mumbled, "Why? Did something happen?"

"Sort of. Grady told me something and I'm trying to figure out if it's true. I'd tell you more, but it's not my secret," she added when Dex's eyes narrowed. "Grady barely agreed to tell *me*."

Part of her wished he hadn't.

Dex twisted the wires on the gadget tighter. "You can trust me, you know."

"I do trust you, Dex. That's why I need to know what you remember—if you even remember anything."

"Oh, I remember."

The shudder in his voice made her mouth taste sour.

"You really want to know?" he asked.

No.

Not really.

But she nodded anyway.

Dex nodded too. Then he sank to the floor, making all the

vials rattle as he leaned against the shelves. "I only remember pieces. Hearing you scream when we were in the cave. The rotten candy smell of the drugs. Your face as you watched them take me. I remember that part really clearly because you didn't look scared."

"I didn't?"

"No. You looked angry—and I knew it meant you were going to fight. So I told myself I had to fight too. As hard as I could. Then everything was black and I couldn't tell if I was asleep or awake. But the pain felt real so I'm guessing the whispers were real."

Sophie hugged herself, trying not to tremble as her own memories rushed back. "Whispers?"

"Jumbled sounds, mostly. But sometimes it sounded like they were saying, 'He's useless.'"

He twisted the piece of gadget so tight the wires snapped.

Sophie got up and sat beside him. "You're not useless, Dex."

"I was to them."

"That's a good thing."

"I guess." He pulled at the broken bits of wire. "The hardest parts were the times the drugs faded. Lying there, not knowing where you were. I tried to get up once, but they had my feet tied. And they did this . . ."

He leaned over, lifting the side of his tunic and revealing a faint red oval, about the size of a fingerprint, just below his ribs.

"Is that . . ."—Sophie leaned closer, squinting at the mark— "They burned you?"

She'd thought they'd only done that to her, but there was the proof, right on Dex's skin. She didn't realize she'd reached out to touch it until Dex jumped.

"Sorry," she mumbled, whipping her finger away. But not before she'd felt the coarse puckers of the scar.

He cleared his throat. "They told me they'd do it to you if I moved again. So I didn't move. I barely let myself breathe."

His words felt heavy.

Or maybe that was her guilt.

"Dex, I—"

"Don't. It wasn't your fault, okay?"

He glared at her until she nodded, but her eyes still burned with the tears she was fighting.

"It's okay, Sophie. *They* did it—not you. And you had it way worse than I did."

She rubbed her wrists, wondering how red and blistered they'd been after her interrogation. She'd been blindfolded, and after she was rescued there was no trace of the burns. If she didn't remember the pain, it would be like it never happened. But Dex . . .

"Elwin couldn't heal the wound?" she whispered.

"He said the burn had been there for too many days. He offered to try yeti pee to see if it would help, but I told him thanks, I'll pass. Save it for the next time Sophie tries to blow up the school."

Sophie forced herself to smile at his joke, but inside she felt like she was breaking.

Dex had a *permanent* scar.

Just like Brant.

Brant's haunted face filled her mind and she remembered Edaline's warning about guilt.

She buried her own feelings as deep as they would go. She couldn't let herself end up like *him*.

"Anyway, that's all I remember," Dex said quietly. "Well, until we were rescued, and all I remember about that is realizing I was being carried and being too scared to move in case it was the kidnappers. But it turned out to be the good guys."

"The good guys," Sophie repeated. She could taste the words on her tongue, but she couldn't tell if they were true. "You really think the Black Swan are good?"

"They rescued us, didn't they?"

"Yeah, and left us on the street with no nexus, no protection, and no way home except a note with a vague clue." The bitterness in her voice surprised her. Maybe she agreed with Grady more than she wanted to admit.

Dex shrugged. "He knew you'd figure it out."

"Maybe the clue. But how could he know that I'd figure out how to use my new abilities to get us home safely? I *barely* did."

"I guess he believed in you."

Sophie snorted.

"What? I'm serious. I mean, it's all kind of a blur, but I

do remember that after he made me choke down that awful sludge, he set my head back on the ground, and then I heard him mumble, 'You can do this, Sophie.' Said it over and over."

"I don't remember that."

"Maybe you were already out. I don't know. But I know he said it. It was what helped me calm down as the drugs pulled me under. Because I knew he was right."

Dex blushed as he said the last part, but Sophie was more focused on the image filling her mind.

Mr. Forkle—grumpy, bloated Mr. Forkle—whispering, "You can do this, Sophie," over and over.

It was a tiny thing, really. Just a small bit of encouragement.

But it meant something.

It meant everything.

SIXTEEN

R. FORKLE *CARED*.

He may have left them alone and unconscious on the streets of a Forbidden City, but he truly believed Sophie would be able to get them home safe. And that's exactly what she'd done—even if things hadn't gone *quite* according to plan.

"Does that answer your question?" Dex asked, breaking the silence.

"Yeah. It actually does."

Grady was wrong about the Black Swan.

Whatever reasons they had for staying secret, it couldn't be because they were murderers.

Murderers didn't *care*.

She had a feeling Grady would need more proof to believe her, though. Something he could see for himself. Too bad she had no clue where to find it.

Unless . . .

Was that what the clue in the compass was for? To have her clear the Black Swan's name?

Was that why they were still hiding?

Let the past be your guide.

But whose past would guide her?

Grady's?

"You're doing it again," Dex said, nudging her with his elbow. "That thing where you stare into space, totally oblivious to everything around you. Usually means you're planning some secret thing that'll end in an emergency Elwin call."

"I'm not planning anything."

Planning would mean she'd at least have *some* idea what to do.

"Yeah, well, whatever you're *'not planning'*—just . . . if you need me, I'm here, okay?"

"I know, Dex." But she'd put him through enough already. More than she'd realized.

She picked up the broken piece of gadget he'd been playing with. "So what is this thing?"

"Right now it's a pile of junk, but I'm hoping I can turn it into a gadget that'll transmit my thoughts as telepathic signals."

Sophie smiled. "There are much cooler things you could do with your talent."

Dex shrugged and snatched the piece away from her. He twisted the broken wires together, reconnecting them to other pieces of the metal.

"You know, if you took technopathy training, you'd—"

"Not gonna happen. Just a little more than a week and I start ability detecting again, and I'm going to work as hard as I can to make sure they trigger something."

"School starts in a little more than a week?"

She'd known it was coming up, but that suddenly felt very, very soon.

"Yep. The Opening Ceremonies are next Friday and school starts the following Monday. Didn't you get your Foxfire uniforms yesterday?"

"Not that I know of."

She told herself to stay calm—that everything had been settled at her final Tribunal. But the Council couldn't have changed their minds about letting her return to Foxfire, could they?

"I should go home and look for them," she said, getting up and pulling out her home crystal.

"Yeah, you'll want to make sure your costume fits."

She was so distracted by her worries that she didn't catch what Dex said until the warm light was already pulling her away.

Costume?

"Please tell me this is a joke," Sophie begged as she trudged down the stairs into Havenfield's living room in a tight bodysuit covered in a shaggy brown fur.

It had sewn-in feet.

Feet!

Apparently her Foxfire uniforms, along with the monstrosity they called an "Opening Ceremonies costume," had arrived the day before. But Sandor—who had given her a twenty-minute lecture on how dangerous it was for her to leave Slurps and Burps without telling him—had insisted on inspecting the package before delivering it to her.

What was next? Was he going to start searching her laundry before the gnomes delivered it to her room? Worried the kidnappers might attack her with deadly socks?

"You forgot your headpiece," Edaline said, picking up a folded piece of brown fabric from the pile on the couch. She slipped the band of fur around Sophie's forehead, adjusting the narrow strip of cloth attached so that it hung down the center of Sophie's face and ended just below her waist. "There. Now you're a mastodon."

There were many, *many* questions racing through Sophie's mind as she scratched her neck where the furry collar was tickling it. But the most important one was probably, "Why am I dressed like a shaggy elephant?"

"Mastodons are the Level Three mascot."

Right, but . . .

Edaline fanned out the elbow-length crescents of fabric that draped off the sides of the headband like droopy ears. "It's part of the Opening Ceremonies."

"You're going to love them," Grady added as he came in from the front pastures. Neon feathers stuck out of his hair, which made him look more like himself again. "Everything okay?"

The nervous lines creasing his face told her he wasn't referring to the elephant-costume-of-doom.

"Yeah. Everything's good." She'd find a way to prove to him that he was wrong about the Black Swan. And in the meantime, she was happy to settle on a truce.

If only she could find such an easy solution to her furrybodysuit problem.

"I seriously have to wear this?"

"Don't worry, all the other Level Threes will be too," Edaline promised. "And you'll see how fun it all is when you're at rehearsal on Monday."

Somehow she doubted that.

"Wait—rehearsal? What am I rehearsing?"

Grady smiled. "The choreography."

Excitement and nerves tangled in Sophie's stomach as she and Dex arrived at Foxfire on Monday morning. The grounds buzzed with strange activity, but it was still the same familiar campus, and walking the paths with Dex safely at her side felt healing, somehow. Like she'd taken another piece of her life back—even if she was currently being trailed by a seven-foot goblin and everyone was staring at her because of it.

At least they weren't whispering about "the girl who was taken."

Plus, it was nice to have a morning off from bathing the verminion—especially since she was also dealing with a restless alicorn and a jealous imp. Silveny hated to be alone, but she still wouldn't let anyone except Sophie near her. And Iggy had started hiding sludgers—the giant slimy worms he ate— in Sophie's shoes and pillows to punish her for spending so much time outside. Grady and Edaline thought it was hilarious, but Sophie kept worrying about Silveny's slow progress. If she didn't find a way to make the stubborn alicorn start trusting people, Bronte would have Silveny shipped off to the Hekses for sure.

Dex knew a shortcut through the fields of purple grass, but they had to weave around gnomes poking the ground with thin metal rods. More gnomes were balanced on the roof of the U-shaped main building, draping the crystal walls with garlands of dark green leaves. Each of the six colored towers now bore a banner with a jeweled mosaic of the mascot for that grade level: an onyx gremlin for the Level Ones, a sapphire halcyon for the Level Twos, an amber mastodon for the Level Threes, an emerald dragon for the Level Fours, a ruby saber-toothed tiger for the Level Fives, and a diamond yeti for the Level Sixes.

Sophie couldn't decide which costume would be more embarrassing.

Then again, mastodons were the only ones with a trunk.

"What are they doing?" Sophie asked, pointing to another group of gnomes struggling to brush the outside of the five-story glass pyramid in the center of campus with teetering copper poles.

"Decorating for the Ceremonies."

As they got closer Sophie could see that the gnomes were actually painting a snotlike slime over the pyramid's walls. She gagged when she caught the musty smell.

Hadn't the elves heard of streamers and balloons?

The Opening Ceremonies would be in Foxfire's main auditorium, and rehearsal was held there as well. The huge stadium had a gleaming golden dome and thousands of empty seats inside. Mentors in bright orange capes separated the prodigies by grade level, and Sophie felt a little smug as she passed the Level Twos to join the Level Threes.

Sir Harding—a broad-shouldered elf with warm brown skin and shoulder-length black hair woven into a simple braid—introduced himself as their physical education Mentor and called for everyone to gather around him so he could demonstrate their choreography. Sophie ordered Sandor to try to hide as she lined up with her classmates.

When Sir Harding finally had their attention, he tossed his cape to the side, held out his hands, and launched into the most complicated dance Sophie had ever seen, stomping and spinning and jumping. He ran through the full routine three times—none of which made any sense to Sophie—and then told everyone to split into small practice teams so they could get a feel for how the choreography worked as a group.

"I still don't see what this has to do with school," Sophie grumbled as she followed Dex and Biana to a patch of empty floor space. Jensi rushed up beside Biana, and for a second Sophie didn't recognize him. His usually messy brown hair had been slicked with too much gel, making his round face look even rounder.

"Not everything at Foxfire is about learning," Biana informed them. "The Opening Ceremonies are about celebrating promise. This is our chance to show the older generations what we can do."

"By dancing like elephants?"

Dex laughed. "It's weird, but it's fun."

"Yeah, and we get showered with candy at the end—this really cool kind that falls from the ceiling like snow—and it lasts for months and months and months if you take some home," Jensi said in his usual *I had too much sugar this morning* way.

"That's *not* the point of the Ceremonies," Biana corrected, making Jensi blush before she perfectly recreated the stomp-stomp-spin-step-twirl move Sir Harding had shown them.

"The mascot dance represents the qualities we'll be developing this year. Mastodons are fast learners that rely on each other as a team. The choreography is designed to showcase that."

"Uh-huh," Sophie mumbled as Biana dipped the final curtsy with a natural grace that made Sophie kind of wish she'd slip and fall. Especially since her own feet refused to cooperate. It didn't help that someone kept testing different colored spotlights and dimming parts of the room, making it hard to see.

"You're forgetting the middle part," Jensi told her. He bent until his hands touched the floor and spun in a series of tight circles. "See?"

Sophie tried to copy him but the turns made her dizzy, and as she glanced up to clear her head, one of the spotlights flashed in her eyes.

A headache flared, blinding her from the pain. She started to topple, but a pair of arms caught her before she hit the ground.

"Whoa—you okay?" Dex asked from what sounded like very far away.

Her ears were ringing and the world was a blur of too-bright colors. But as Sophie sucked in slow, steady breaths, the room faded back into focus and she realized Dex was holding her, expecting her to answer his question.

"Yeah," she said, hating how shaky her voice sounded. "Sorry. Guess I spun a little too fast."

Dex helped her straighten up, and she wobbled as the blood rushed to her head.

"Are you sure that's all it is?" he asked. "Maybe we should see if Elwin's here."

"Can't you do *anything* without needing a physician?"

Sophie sighed as she turned around, almost crashing into Stina's beanpole body. "Why do you care?"

"I don't. But clearly my dad's right about the Council. Choosing *you* over us? Guess that's the perk of having the Vackers protect you all the time."

Biana rolled her eyes. "My family isn't protecting her, you sasquatch."

"Still pretending to be Sophie's BFF, are we?" Stina asked her.

"I'm not pretending—"

Sophie grabbed Biana's arm. "Don't let her get to you," she whispered.

Biana may have originally become friends with her because her dad told her to, but they'd been through enough that Sophie knew their friendship was real now.

"Aw, aren't you guys cute?" Stina sneered. "Better watch out, Biana. It's only a matter of time before she drags your whole family down to her level."

"That's still way higher than your family," Sophie snapped back.

Stina grabbed Sophie's tunic. "Whatever you *think* you know about my family—"

"*Unhand her!*" Sandor growled—though coming from him, it sounded more like a squeak—as he bolted out of the shadows and yanked Stina away.

Sophie laughed as Stina squealed. Maybe having a bodyguard wouldn't be so bad after all.

"Are you okay, Miss Foster?" Sandor asked.

"I'm fine, thank you."

"Good." He turned back to Stina, patting the weapon at his side. "I have my eye on you."

"You look scared," Dex told Stina as she watched Sandor melt back into the shadows. "Did you pee your pants?"

"I don't talk to trash."

Stina stalked away, but Dex called after her. "Better be nice to me. I'd hate you to have exploding farts at the Opening Ceremonies."

"If you even *think* about slipping me one of your stupid elixirs, I will have you booted to Exillium so fast you won't know what hit you."

"Kinda like what happened to your dad?" Marella asked, joining their group just in time to block Stina's path. She tossed her blond hair and stood on her tiptoes to get in Stina's face. "That's right. I know *all* of the Heks family secrets."

"You wish, Redek," Stina grumbled. But she looked nervous as she shoved the tiny girl aside and made her way back to her two giggly minions.

Marella grinned. "I'm a few minutes late and I miss all the fun."

"Don't worry, I'm sure Stina will pick plenty more fights with me before the year is over," Sophie told her.

"Looking forward to it."

Sophie had no doubt she was. The only thing Marella liked more than causing trouble was gossip—which was why she seemed to know everything.

Biana and Jensi showed Marella the choreography, which Marella perfected on her first try. Sophie tried not to sulk as she asked, "So what did you mean about Stina's dad?"

Marella glanced over her shoulder and motioned for everyone to come closer. "Stina's dad never manifested a special ability, but he tries to hide it. He even tried to fake one when he was younger so he could still take the elite levels and join the nobility. But of *course* he got caught, because, dude—you can't fake a special ability. They expelled him and he had to finish his education at Exillium."

The name always made Sophie ill. She didn't know much about it, just that it was where they sent prodigies who were ruled "hopeless cases."

"I also heard that the only reason Stina's parents weren't ruled a bad match was because her dad's sister is married to someone who works at the Matchmaking Office and they rigged the results," Marella added quietly. "Of course there's no way to prove that, but come on. How else would someone without a special ability end up matched to an Empath?"

Dex's hands curled into fists. "If that's true—"

"Of course it's true," Marella interrupted. "Why do you think her dad took her mom's name? And he keeps using the Hekses' gift with unicorns to elevate his own status. My mom thinks it's only a matter of time before the Council makes him an Emissary. He'd be the first Talentless to do it."

That explained why Timkin had been so insistent on taking Silveny, and there was no way Sophie was letting him anywhere near her again.

"What's up with him?" Marella asked as Dex wandered away from their group.

Dex's parents had been ruled a bad match when they got married, because his dad never manifested an ability either. Dex had been teased his whole life because of it.

Sophie moved to his side. "Hey," she said, nudging him until he looked at her. "Think you can help me master these dance moves before the Ceremonies next week?"

A small grin spread across his lips. "I don't know. I can't exactly work miracles."

"Hey, I'm not *that* bad."

He grabbed her hands as she tried to shove him, and his face turned serious. "You're not bad at all. You're awesome."

He blushed after he said it, and Sophie dropped her eyes to the ground.

Sir Harding saved them from the crushing awkwardness when he clapped his hands and announced, "That should be enough rehearsing for everyone. I'll see you all at the

Ceremonies. And don't forget to collect your schedules from your lockers before you leave."

The rest of the prodigies cheered, but Sophie had to force herself to smile.

She'd been dreading her schedule since the Council approved her for another year at Foxfire. Her admission came with a condition. . . .

She trudged a few steps behind her friends as they made their way to the main campus building. Biana showed them how she'd gotten her nexus off early, and they were all so busy telling her how cool that was—especially Jensi, who seemed glued to Biana's side—that they didn't even notice. Not that Sophie minded. Biana deserved a few moments of fame after so many years in Fitz's shadow.

It did make Sophie wish she knew when she'd be allowed to remove her own stupid nexus, though.

The halls changed from black to blue and then to the weird, amber brown color of the Level Three wing. They went straight to the atrium, the huge central quad filled with crystal trees and an enormous mastodon statue that was sleek and smooth, like it'd been carved from a gigantic piece of amber. A Mentor whom Sophie didn't recognize handed her a tiny square of paper with her name and a rune, and she made her way to the walls lined with narrow doors, searching for the one labeled with the matching rune. She found it in the darkest corner—or maybe it just felt that way as she licked the thin silver strip, which thankfully tasted citrusy, and pulled open the locker door.

Inside she found a neat stack of textbooks, a few rakes and shovels, and a small scroll on the top shelf.

She needed several deep breaths before she reached for the scroll and unrolled it.

Elvin history, PE, elementalism, and multispeciesial studies—nothing to worry about there. She'd had the same subjects as a Level Two, and even though she had new Mentors, she knew she could handle them. Linguistics and agriculture didn't sound too bad either—and explained why they'd given her gardening supplies.

The second-to-last session was the one that made her palms sweat.

Inflicting.

With *Councillor Bronte.*

Who'd already sworn to fail her.

Alden had told her not to worry, but that was a very worrisome thing.

Though seeing the session officially listed wasn't what made her heart pick up speed. An unexpected note underneath her telepathy session triggered that.

Fitz Vacker will also attend this session.

SEVENTEEN

S O WHAT'D YOU GET?" DEX ASKED, snatching Sophie's schedule.

He frowned as he read the list, and she knew he had to be thinking the same thing she was.

Why was Fitz in her telepathy session?

Except for PE—where they needed teams—all Foxfire sessions were taught one-on-one between Mentor and prodigy, so the curriculum could be customized.

"Aw, are you guys sad that your lockers aren't next to each other?" Marella asked, nudging her way between them. "Because I might be willing to trade mine for a few rare Prattles' pins." She pointed to a locker a few doors down from Sophie's.

"Maybe later," Dex mumbled, still glaring at Sophie's schedule.

Marella read over shoulder. "Whoa—you have a session with Fitz Vacker?"

"I guess."

"Fitz *Vacker*," Marella repeated. "You get to spend four hours a week alone with Fitz. Vacker?"

"Not *alone*," Sophie whispered, wishing Marella would keep her voice down. Several heads had turned their way, and Dex was turning redder by the second. "Sir Tiergan will be there too."

"Still." Marella's eyes turned dreamy. "You're the luckiest girl alive."

"Oh, please," Dex muttered.

"Man—why can't *I* be a Telepath?" Marella said, ignoring him. "I'd better manifest a special ability this year—and it better be something good, like Vanishing. Though I'll probably be a Guster like my dad. Controlling the wind—whoop-de-freaking-do." She let out a dramatic sigh. "Meanwhile Sophie gets *three* ability training sessions."

"Only two," Sophie corrected.

"Uh-uh. Linguistics is an elite subject, so the only reason you're in it is because you're a Polyglot."

"Wait—an elite subject? Like, the elite levels?" Sophie asked.

Marella nodded. "Level Eight, I think. No point in learning to speak Ogre if you aren't going to be nobility, ya know?"

She'd be learning to speak Ogre?

"Whoa, it says your session is in the Silver Tower," Dex said, holding out her schedule to show her.

"Wait—you get to go inside the Silver Tower?" Jensi asked as he and Biana joined the group. "Do you realize how insanely cool that is—no one's allowed in the elite towers except elite prodigies—you have to tell us what it's like!"

"I'll try," Sophie said, struggling to wrap her head around this *huge* new information.

How did she go back to being the super-young-prodigy-with-all-the-older-kids? She'd done that already as the twelve-year-old high school senior—and it hadn't exactly gone well. Not to mention she'd be totally lost in the new building, and it wasn't like she knew anyone there who could help show her around.

Well . . . she did know one person, or know *of* him anyway—but that was actually worse.

She'd always been relieved that she didn't have to worry about running into Prentice's son, Wylie. He had his part of the school, and she had hers, and they never had to meet.

What if they did now?

What would she say?

What would *he* say?

"You're still coming over today, right?" Biana asked, interrupting her mounting panic.

Sophie shook her head to clear it. "Sorry. Yep. I just need to run home to change first and then I'll head over." Alden was back from wherever the Council had sent him and she was planning to finally show him the clue.

"Oh, good, you're spending *more* time with Wonderboy," Dex muttered under his breath, earning himself a glare from Sophie.

Marella laughed.

"What?" Dex snapped.

"Oh, nothing." She tossed her hair and grinned at Sophie. "I just have a feeling this is going to be a *very* interesting year."

As much as Sophie hated to admit it, she had a feeling Marella was right.

The towering fence around Everglen glowed so brightly Sophie had to shield her eyes as the gates parted to let her inside. The gleaming metal absorbed incoming light, blocking anyone from being able to leap directly inside the grounds without permission—a rare security measure Alden had installed, though Sophie sometimes wondered why he'd felt the need, since crime was supposedly so unheard of.

Sandor had insisted on accompanying her to the gate, but he didn't follow her inside. Everglen was one of the few places Sophie was allowed to go without him.

Biana pushed the button to lock them safely inside the grounds. "I thought you were going to change."

"I did." Sophie smoothed the embroidered hem on her loose gold tunic, which was—admittedly—very similar to the loose gold tunic she'd been wearing during rehearsal. But this one had longer sleeves and a black sash instead of brown.

Biana, on the other hand, looked like she was ready to have her picture taken. Her fitted teal tunic—the exact same shade as her eyes—had intricate pink embroidery that matched her perfectly glossed lips. She'd also swept her dark wavy hair back with jeweled combs, which sparkled with every step as she led Sophie along the winding path lined with rainbow-colored trees toward the main house.

The expansive grounds of Everglen made the pastures of Havenfield seem like a shoebox—and the estate itself was more like a castle than a house, complete with crystal towers and golden accents and humongous glittering rooms. All elves were given a birth fund with more money than they could ever spend in their lifetime. But somehow the Vackers seemed to have *more*. Maybe it came from having so many generations of their family in the nobility.

"'Bout *time* you got here," Keefe called as they crested a hill and entered a grassy meadow peppered with tiny blue flowers. "I was getting tired of stomping Fitz to a pulp in bramble."

"Only because you cheat!" Fitz shouted, tossing a red tri-pointed ball at Keefe.

Keefe caught it and whipped it back so fast Fitz had to dive to avoid being smacked in the face. Then the strange ball curved back like a boomerang and Keefe caught it one-handed. "Only losers play fair. Which is why I call Foster for *my* team today."

"Hey—why do you get her?" Fitz asked, dusting grass off his dark pants as he picked himself up off the ground. "I think the Telepaths should be together."

"Yeah, because *that's* fair," Biana argued. "Sophie's with me and we're playing boys against girls."

"Wait—what are we playing?" Sophie asked.

"Base quest. And you're with me. Together we shall be *unstoppable!*" Keefe pumped his fist at the sky.

Now she knew why they all wanted her on their team. Base quest was a strategy game, a bit like capture the flag meets hide-and-seek. And thanks to her ability to track thoughts telepathically, Sophie was undefeated.

"How about we play without special abilities?" she suggested. "That'll make it fair for everyone."

Fitz shrugged. "I'm up for the challenge if you are."

"Lame. I vote for The Unstoppable Team Keefe! Or Team Foster-Keefe if you're one of those egomaniacs who needs your name in there. I can share *some* credit."

"Whatever you guys want," Biana said through a sigh. She may have gotten her nexus off early, but she hadn't manifested a special ability. And she was several months older than Fitz had been when he became a Telepath.

Sophie suspected Biana's frustration had more to do with the fact that Keefe didn't want to be on her team, though. "Looks like 'no abilities' wins. So why don't you team up with Biana, Keefe?" she tried.

"No way," Keefe said. "If abilities aren't allowed then I'm with Fitz. He'll let me cheat."

"He better not. And you guys have to quest first." Biana pointed to a nearby tree with lavender leaves that swirled up the trunk like stripes on a candy cane. "That's our base. You have five minutes to hide and then we're coming for you."

"Sounds good," Fitz agreed.

And you're going to regret the no special abilities rule, he transmitted to Sophie.

She jumped this time, surprised that his mental voice felt louder than usual. His words were still echoing when she transmitted back, *Hey, I had to give you guys a fighting chance for once.*

He grinned.

Keefe looked back and forth between them and rolled his eyes. Then he grabbed Fitz's arm and pulled him into the woods.

When the five minutes were up, Biana took off after them. Sophie went the opposite way, in case they'd split up or doubled back. Usually she stood guard at the base and transmitted Fitz and Keefe's location to Biana. But if she couldn't track the guys' thoughts, they both needed to go hunting.

She ran up the nearest hill, hoping to catch a glimpse of the boys from above. But there was no sign of them anywhere. She stopped to catch her breath, trying to decide which way to run next when a bird startled out of a bush at the bottom of the hill.

Fitz and Keefe burst from the leaves and took off running.

Sophie raced after them, channeling all of her core energy to her legs to speed her downhill sprint. Somehow the guys managed to stay ahead of her, though, and as they drew dangerously close to the base, she focused on the warm hum in her mind, trying another brain push. The rare skill wasn't *technically* cheating, since she was just channeling a different energy that most people couldn't feel. But as her mental energy mixed with her burning muscles, she felt a strange sort of pull.

Her vision narrowed to a singular point—a speck of light in the distance—and as she rushed toward it she felt her feet leave the ground without realizing she'd decided to jump.

Wind whipped against her cheeks as she soared so high and fast she felt like she was flying. Then she started to drop and her vision cleared and she realized the purple branches of her base tree were far, *far* too close.

This was going to hurt.

EIGHTEEN

SOPHIE FLAILED AND TWISTED AND barely managed to grab on to a branch that stuck out a little farther than the others. Pain shot through her arms as she fought to hold on, but she gritted her teeth and . . .

Found herself stuck twenty feet above the ground with sharp bark slicing into her palms and her strength quickly fading.

But she was alive!

"What the . . . ?" Keefe shouted as Fitz transmitted, *Are you okay?*

I'm fine, she told him, searching for a way to get down. She really didn't want to have to admit she was stuck like a treed cat. *I just overestimated my strength, I guess.*

I'll say.

She kicked her legs, hoping that if she could swing to a more steady position, she'd be able to climb down.

Craaaaaaaaaack!

Before she could even scream, Fitz shouted, "I got her!" and two arms wrapped around her waist. The momentum from his jump pushed them sideways and somehow he managed to flip them before they crashed, sending them tumbling across the soft grass.

"Are you guys okay?" Keefe asked, rushing to where they'd landed.

"I think so." Sophie wasn't sure which was hurt more, her bruised body or her pride.

She wiped a giant splotch of mud off her cheek, trying not to think about how soggy and dirty her shirt felt as she pulled bits of leaves from her hair. At least her pants looked pretty normal. The black fabric hid the grass stains.

"Dude—Fitz—you should've seen how high you jumped to catch her—and the way you guys curved through the air and flipped across the ground? *Awesome.*"

Fitz laughed and rubbed his shoulder as he sat up.

"Are you really okay?" Sophie asked him.

"Yep. I'm just glad I caught you."

He smiled as he said it and Sophie thought her heart might explode from the flutters. "Me too."

"And *you,*" Keefe said, shoving between them. "What was

up with the whole Amazing Flying Foster routine?"

She bit her lip, wondering if she should confess to the brain push. The only time they'd seen her do one was during a splotching match against Fitz, and they'd all been pretty weirded out by it. "I guess I'm still learning how to channel."

"Uh—it was a little more than that. When did you learn how to blink?"

"Blink?"

"When you let the light pass through you and disappear. It's like what Vanishers do, but it only lasts for a second," Fitz explained. "Remember, I did it the day I found you—when you wouldn't believe you were an elf?"

"That's right, I'd forgotten about that. You almost gave me a heart attack."

Fitz laughed. "I felt the same way when I realized you were one of us."

"Okay, you guys are seriously bumming me out with all this sappy reminiscing. Not to mention, uh, hello—Foster just *flew*. And blinked in and out while she was doing it. You aren't developing another special ability are you? 'Cause seriously— save some for the rest of us."

"Actually, I think she just wanted to distract you boys so we could win," Biana said, tagging Fitz and Keefe from behind.

Keefe groaned. "If that really was your plan, you guys are evil geniuses,"

"It wasn't our plan," Sophie admitted.

"But the win still counts," Biana added.

"No way—I'm calling shenanigans. You shouldn't be able to—"

"You're bleeding," Fitz interrupted, lifting Sophie's hand and examining her palm. Thin streams of red dripped down her skin. "These look bad, Sophie. You should get them treated."

"I'm fine," she said, trying not to think about the blood, or the fact that Fitz was technically holding her hand, since both things made her head spin way too fast. "Really. It's not a big deal. We don't need to call Elwin."

Fitz grinned. "Actually, I was thinking we could just ask my mom. She always keeps some basic first aid in the house just to be safe."

"Oh," she mumbled, feeling her face flame.

Keefe snorted. "Only Foster has a physician on standby."

"This might tingle a bit," Della told Sophie as she smeared a bright orange salve along both of her palms.

Sophie tried not to flinch as the cream sank into her skin, zinging like tiny jolts of electricity. Fitz, Keefe, and Biana were watching her, and she didn't want them seeing how squeamish she still was about medical things. Especially since elvin medicine didn't use things like needles or machines like humans did.

"That should do it." Della wiped the sticky orange goo away, revealing soft, scrape-free skin. "And I have something that will help with the bruising, too."

She tossed her chocolate brown hair and stood, her aquamarine gown shimmering with the movement. No matter how many times Sophie had seen her, she couldn't help staring at Della. There was something unreal about the beauty of her wide, cobalt blue eyes and heart-shaped lips. Though it might've also had something to do with the way Della disappeared and reappeared with every step she took. She didn't realize she did it—Vanishers rarely did—but even after almost a year it still made Sophie wonder if her eyes were playing tricks on her.

Was that what she'd looked like as she was blinking?

The crystal walls of Everglen were cut like prisms, shooting streaks of color in every direction as Della crossed the room. She removed two round green vials from the drawer of a small apothecary cabinet and handed one to Sophie and one to Fitz when she returned. "This will ease any aches from the fall."

The label said ACHEY BREAK and it had the Slurps and Burps logo.

Sophie swallowed the bitter serum, and it rushed through her like warm bubbles floating into all the places she'd felt sore.

"Drink this, too," Della said, handing her a clear fluted bottle labeled YOUTH. The water had a special enzyme that helped keep everyone healthy. "And why don't you change into something of Biana's? I can ask the gnomes to clean your tunic before we send you home. That way Grady and Edaline won't know about your little 'accident.'"

"Eh, I'm sure they're used to Foster's catastrophes by now," Keefe said, clapping her on the back. "She has one every other week."

Sophie sighed as everyone laughed, hating that he was right.

"Are you staying for dinner?" Della asked.

"You have to," Biana told her. "We're having an aurenflare to celebrate school starting."

"Um, great." She still needed to talk to Alden anyway.

Keefe smirked. "You have no idea what that is, do you?"

"It's . . ."

It's a special kind of bonfire, Fitz transmitted.

It was hard not to smile—and Sophie was careful not to look at Fitz as she folded her arms and told Keefe, "It's a bonfire."

Keefe glanced at Fitz, then back to her. "Telepaths," he grumbled.

Fitz grinned at her, and this time everything inside Sophie turned fluttery. *Thanks.*

Anytime.

Biana gave her a red tunic with a white silk sash and tiny white roses embroidered along the V-neck collar. It was too bright and too fancy and too fitted—but Biana had insisted and told her to clean up and meet her downstairs.

Biana's bathroom was like a shrine to all things *girl*, complete with hair-curling elixirs and rosy-cheek powder. For about half a second Sophie thought about trying some. Then she washed her face, brushed as much of the mud out of her hair as she could, pulled the parts that were still crunchy back with one of Biana's jeweled barrettes, gathered up her dirty tunic, and headed back downstairs to rejoin the others.

"Well, if it isn't Sophie Foster."

Sophie backed up to find Alden sitting at his huge black desk in his round office. Half the wall was a curved window overlooking the lake behind the mansion. The other half was a floor-to-ceiling aquarium, filled with all kinds of strange floating creatures.

He motioned for her to come inside. "I almost didn't recognize you. I take it Della and Biana have been playing dress up?"

"Well, they sort of had to." She held out her muddy tunic and explained what happened. She even admitted she'd used a brain push.

"How far did you fly?" he asked, standing to look out the window.

She moved to his side and pointed to the hill she'd climbed, explaining that she'd jumped from about midway down and flown to the tree with the lavender leaves.

"That's an incredible distance," Alden said after a second. "An *impossible* distance. And you blinked as you were doing it?"

"I guess. I wasn't trying to."

"Fascinating," Alden whispered.

"So . . . how weird is that, compared to, like, normal people?"

"You *are* normal, Sophie. That doesn't mean you can't also be exceptional."

"You realize those two things are opposites, right?"

"Actually, someday you'll find that when you stop equating normal with acceptance, the two are far more similar than you think."

"I have no idea what that means."

Alden laughed. "Give it time."

Sophie glared out the window. She hated when adults said things like that.

Glints of silver caught her attention, and she focused on two graceful birds floating on the lake. Their necks were hooked like swans and their heads were crested with wispy feathers. Long silver tails like peacocks trailed behind them as they glided along the reeds.

"Are those . . ."

"Moonlarks." Alden finished. "I borrowed them from the Sanctuary. Thought it might be good to study their behavior—see if it gave me any insights."

The Black Swan had dubbed Sophie's creation Project Moonlark because moonlarks lay their eggs in the ocean and let the tide carry them away, forcing the babies to survive on their own. In Sophie's case they'd hidden her in a sea of humans, though they'd at least left her help—even if Mr. Forkle had been grumpy and smelled weird and used to drive her crazy.

Mr. Forkle cared.

"Did you learn anything interesting?" she asked quietly.

"Yes. They're fascinating creatures. Which reminds me. I seem to remember you needing to tell me something when I was last at Havenfield. I'm sorry I haven't followed up. I've been a bit . . . overwhelmed."

He sank back into his thronelike chair, and Sophie noticed how tired he looked. Faint shadows made his bright eyes look sunken, and there was a tight crease between his brows.

"Anything I need to know about?" she asked, expecting him to say his standard, *No reason to worry.*

Instead he frowned and murmured, "Our world is changing, Sophie."

He stared into space for so long she thought he must be done. But then he added, "What happened to you and Dex frightened people. Shattered their sense of safety and confidence in the Council—not that anyone blames you, of course."

Some of the people in Mysterium seemed to. . . .

"But we'll have it under control soon," he promised. "Silveny is a wonderful symbol of hope, and the Council is planning a huge celebration for when we move her to the Sanctuary. The sooner you have her ready, the better."

Great, like she needed more pressure.

And wouldn't catching her kidnappers be a much better way to restore people's sense of safety?

"So what was it you needed to tell me?"

She bent and reached into her ankle pocket. "I found this

on my tree in the Wanderling Woods. Notice anything strange about the locket charm?"

She handed him the bracelet.

"The sign of the swan," he whispered as he opened the compass. "I'm guessing the inscription is in code?"

She was surprised he couldn't read it. "It says 'Let the past be your guide.'"

The crease between his brows deepened. "It specifically says 'guide'?"

"Yeah. Is that important?"

She waited for him to answer, but he just watched the strange creatures floating in his aquarium as the sunset turned the sky orange and pink.

"It certainly gives us a lot to think about," he finally said, handing her back the bracelet.

"That's it? Come on, I'm not stupid. I know there's something you're not telling me."

"I would never think you're stupid, Sophie. I simply need more time to consider this from every angle. Give me a few days to go through my files and see if a compass holds any specific significance to the Black Swan before we discuss anything. And you should search your memories, see if you can trigger anything. But not tonight. Tonight"—he stood, offering her his hand—"we have an aurenflare!"

She really wasn't in the mood for a fancy bonfire thing, but she stuffed the silver bracelet back into her pocket, glad he at least wasn't keeping the charm. Before she took his hand, though, she had one more thing she needed to ask.

The words stuck in her throat and she almost lost her nerve. But if she was ever going to figure this out, she needed to know what he thought.

"Do you think the Black Swan murdered Jolie?"

NINETEEN

ALDEN FROZE, AND THE PANIC IN his eyes made Sophie worry she'd gone too far. But he blinked it away and whispered, "I hope not."

That . . . wasn't the answer she was looking for, but it was better than yes.

"Why do you ask?"

"Because I don't think they did." It felt good to say it out loud. Made it feel real. "And I think the clue might have something to do with that. Something in the past they want me to find that would help clear their name."

"I suppose it's possible," Alden said slowly. "But whose past? Yours?"

Sophie shook her head. She didn't know her past—not her real one anyway. She didn't even know who her real parents were. All Alden had learned from Prentice was her DNA.

She gasped. "What if it's Prentice?"

"Prentice?" Alden repeated, turning pale.

"Yeah. He's the one who led you to me, right? So he probably knows everything about me. Maybe if you brought him to me I could—"

He grabbed her shoulders. "Stop right there, Sophie. I know what you're going to say and you do not realize the danger. A broken mind *cannot* be probed. The Black Swan knows that. Everyone knows that. Prentice is not the answer. Prentice is nothing. Believe me, I can't tell you how much I wish it weren't so."

His voice cracked on the last part and he looked away. When he turned back to her he looked fifty years older.

"Yo, Foster!" Keefe shouted from somewhere down the hall, "What's taking so long? You have another medical emergency?"

"Ignore him, Sophie," Della called. "Beauty should never be rushed!"

Something passed across Alden's face, lightening some of the shadows and erasing the hard lines. He released her shoulders. "We should go. People are waiting for us. People who *need* us."

Sophie nodded. She wasn't ready to drop the Prentice idea yet, but Alden was clearly done with the conversation. Maybe he'd change his mind after he did more research.

Otherwise she had no idea how she'd ever get to Prentice on her own. Exile wasn't a place she could just drop by for a visit—not that she'd ever be crazy enough to go there.

She followed Alden to the back of the mansion, resisting the urge to duck as colored streams of water shot over their heads in graceful arcs all through the hallway. An arched golden door led outside to a wide stone patio overlooking the glassy lake where everyone had gathered.

"Oh, Sophie," Della gasped when she saw her. "You really should wear that color more often. Makes your eyes even more striking. Especially with your hair that way."

"Mom, you're embarrassing her," Biana said, pushing past Della and Alden and dragging Sophie over to an ornate silver bench. "She is right, though," she whispered. "Red is definitely your color."

"Thanks," Sophie mumbled.

She slouched, feeling like she was back in her first day at Foxfire when Dame Alina flashed a giant spotlight right at her.

"What?" she asked, when she caught Fitz and Keefe staring at her.

"Nothing," they both mumbled.

Three gnomes broke the uncomfortable silence as they dragged a bundle of enormous black fan-shaped leaves to the footed silver basin in the center of the benches. They carefully formed the leaves into a tower, and Alden lit the top with a long copper match. Flames in every color of the spectrum raced down the stems, growing into an enormous teardrop-shaped bonfire that filled the air with a sweet, sticky aroma, like melting sugar.

Della passed out skewers with green brattails speared on the ends, and they roasted them in the flames. When the sausage-flavored tubers turned an ashy brown, they wrapped them in a soft yellow bread that tasted like melted cheese. Sophie felt ready to explode after devouring three, but Della insisted she still try a ripplenut and handed her a skewer lined with round yellow nuts. The shells turned orange as they roasted, and Biana showed her how to crack them open and suck out the juice inside. Sophie's eyes watered as the warm goo coated her tongue, but it was worth the heat. It tasted like butter and vanilla and honey melted together with a hint of cinnamon and caramel.

When Keefe finished his, he used his skewer to poke the flames, showering Sophie and Biana with rainbow-colored sparks that felt like cool splashes of water. Biana giggled, but Sophie had to force herself not to flinch as every spark flew, and her skin tingled with the memory of her burns.

I guess a bonfire wasn't the best thing to invite you to, huh? Fitz transmitted as she rubbed her wrists

She winced.

What's wrong?

Sorry, you just transmit really loud sometimes.

I do?

Yep. It's like you're screaming in my head.

His cheeks flushed. Or maybe it was the light of the auren-flare. *Why didn't you tell me? Is this any better?*

Not really.

How about now?

A little.

You're just saying that, aren't you?

It's not bad, really. It just takes a second to get used to.

He frowned. *Do you want me to stop?*

Of course not! It's not a big deal.

Well, maybe Sir Tiergan can help me figure out what I'm doing wrong. You know about that, right?

Just saw it on my schedule today.

I guess it was my dad's idea. He wants to see if Sir Tiergan can figure out why I can do this now. I keep telling him it's because I'm super talented—he grinned—*but my dad wants to make sure.*

Make sure of what?

"Dude—will you guys quit it?" Keefe interrupted. "Normal people talk *out loud.*"

"Yeah, but this is Sophie," Biana reminded him. "She never does anything the normal way."

Everyone laughed—and not in a mean way—and Sophie did her best to smile. But paired with what Fitz had just said, she'd found a new reason to worry.

"Oh, this is the best part," Biana said as the fire made a tiny *pop!* The tower of burning branches collapsed and a stream of rainbow flames erupted into the sky.

The fire split into flecks of light as it hit the atmosphere, spreading like fireworks. But they didn't flash away—they lingered above them, surging brighter each second until they finally exploded with a blast of white light that burned Sophie's eyes and triggered a headache so sharp she could barely breathe.

Are you okay? Fitz asked, and she had to fight not to cringe.

It's just a headache. It'll go away in a minute.

Does that happen a lot?

Sometimes, she admitted.

Have you told Elwin?

Not yet—but I'm sure it's not a big deal.

I think you should tell him. What if something's wrong?

I'm fine, she promised. And she tried to believe it.

But when she crawled into bed that night and closed her eyes, a thin halo glowed in her vision, like the light from the aurenflare had burned into her eyelids. And in the last restless moments between wake and sleep, with her head still pounding and her mind replaying all the strange events of the day, she found herself asking the same question Fitz had.

What if something's wrong?

TWENTY

ABURST OF SHARP, COLD TERROR ripped Sophie from her nightmares, like her brain had just been stabbed with an icicle. She stumbled out of bed and ran to her door as Silveny filled her head with an image that made Sophie's chest so tight she thought she might choke.

Figures in black cloaks, looming outside the enclosure, trying to get in.

This time Sophie didn't argue when Sandor insisted she wait inside while he searched the pastures for any sign of intruders, and Grady and Edaline sat with her as she watched the door, tugging out loose eyelashes and trying not to imagine the kidnappers storming the house.

She jumped when the door slammed open, but it was only Sandor returning. His weapon was sheathed and he looked much more calm than Sophie had expected as he loomed in the doorway.

"Well?" Grady asked him.

"The alicorn is terrified and screeching whenever anything comes near her pen, but I could detect no unfamiliar scents or signs of intruders. The yard is clear. The Cliffside gate is locked. All seems normal."

"But Silveny saw them!" Sophie could hear the hysteria in her voice, but she couldn't stop it. "She sent me an image of black-cloaked figures."

Edaline rubbed Sophie's back. "Maybe Silveny had a nightmare. Weren't the Hekses wearing dark clothes when they came for her?"

"Yes," Sophie admitted.

"Well, then maybe she relived that in a dream tonight and it scared her."

That did sort of make sense, but . . . "It seemed so real."

"Nightmares always do."

"You said you didn't detect any unfamiliar scents," Grady said to Sandor. "Can you still detect the Hekses?"

Sandor turned his head and sniffed the outside air. "Hints of them, yes."

Sophie jumped to her feet. "Do you think they tried to take Silveny again?"

"Why would they do that?" Grady asked.

"Timkin wants to be in the nobility. Wouldn't training Silveny help make that happen?"

"If the Council sanctioned it, yes. But stealing her in the middle of the night would merit a Tribunal—and how else would they explain why they have her? Unless . . ." Grady started to pace, and he'd passed Sophie three times before he added, "I suppose they could've been trying to help Silveny escape so they could rescue her and use that to prove our incompetency."

Sophie could *definitely* see them doing something like that. "Can we do anything to stop them?" she asked.

"I'll talk to the gnomes tomorrow about adding some extra security measures around her pen," Grady decided.

"I should check on Silveny."

"Absolutely not," Sandor said, blocking her. "Not until I've done a more thorough sweep. I'll patrol the grounds tonight. No one can get past me."

Sophie tried to go back to sleep, but Silveny kept filling her mind with waves of panic and pleas for Sophie to let her go free—plus several words Sophie's mind couldn't translate. And no matter how many times she tried to convince Silveny that she was safer in her enclosure, the stubborn horse wouldn't believe her.

She survived the long hours by rumpling Iggy's pink curls,

and when the first rays of dawn finally erased the night, she stumbled out of bed, threw on some work clothes, and made her way downstairs to try and calm Silveny.

Grady was already awake, sipping tea at the kitchen table.

"Good, you're up," he said, offering her his last slice of some sort of brown stringy fruit that reminded Sophie way too much of sludgers. "The gnomes and I tried to get started on Silveny's pasture, but every time we get close to the bars she whinnies and flies around. Think after breakfast you can help keep her calm while we work?"

Sophie nudged the icky fruit away. It smelled even worse than it looked. "Actually, I can go now."

Grady laughed. "You're missing out. Squirmigs are delicious."

Somehow she doubted that.

She wanted to gag as Grady shoved the rest in his mouth and motioned for her to follow him outside.

"Looks like she's still doing that weird diving thing," he said as Silveny's enclosure came into view.

Weird was right.

The glittering horse kept tucking her wings and nose-diving from the highest part of her enclosure. At the last possible second she'd pull up and circle back to the top to repeat the process. Over. And over. And over.

Calm, Sophie transmitted, repeating the command until the alicorn broke her pattern and landed. She stamped her hooves as Sophie approached the bars.

Sophie held out a handful of swizzlespice. *Friend.*

Fly! Silveny replied, sending Sophie another image of her flying free in the starry sky.

It's safer here, Sophie promised. But as she stared into Silveny's sad, pleading eyes she couldn't help wondering if that was really true. Silveny had survived on her own for who knew how long without the elves interfering. Couldn't she take care of herself?

"Are you sure we shouldn't let her go?" Sophie asked as she stepped closer and reached through the bars to call Silveny over. Silveny stayed out of reach.

"Why would we ever do that?"

"She seems so sad in her cage."

"She's had a rough night. Once she calms down she'll be okay."

"But I don't think she wants to be here."

Grady sighed. "None of the animals want to be here at first, Sophie. That's part of their rehabilitation."

"Then why do we do it to them?"

"You of all people should know how dangerous it is for animals in the wild. Predators. Pollution. Not to mention what would happen to a creature like Silveny if she were ever spotted by humans. And there are other threats too. Ogres do not value animal life the way we do. The trolls aren't so great either. The only way we can guarantee a creature's protection is to move them to our Sanctuary—and once they're there, they love it. But we can't bring them until we know they're ready. That's why you've been assigned to help Silveny adjust."

"But how?" It had been almost a week and she'd made no progress at all.

"Patience, for one thing. Lots and lots of treats help too," Grady added as Silveny finally caved and moved close enough to chomp down the swizzlespice Sophie was offering. "But really, it's about figuring out what she needs."

"She's told me that already. She needs to be free."

"No—that's what she *wants*. What she *needs* isn't the same thing. I doubt Silveny even knows it herself."

Sophie sighed. Why couldn't anything ever be easy?

"Think she's calm enough for us to work on her enclosure now? I need to add a padlock to the gate, and the gnomes are going to add some extra poles to make the gaps between bars more narrow."

"That's all you're doing?"

"What more do we need?"

Sophie wasn't sure. But stopping anyone from getting to Silveny was way different than stopping an intruder from setting foot at Havenfield in the first place. Part of her wished their house could be more like Everglen, with its massive gates that absorbed all the light. It probably got annoying that they were never able to leap directly home, but it had to be nice knowing no one could get to them.

She couldn't tell Grady and Edaline that, though.

Alden and Della had offered to let her live with them when Grady and Edaline cancelled her adoption, and if she told them now that she wished their house was like Everglen, they might think she regretted her choice—and she didn't.

But it would be nice to feel safer.

Silveny must've agreed because she twitched or whinnied every time Grady or the gnomes made a sound, and she kept filling Sophie's mind with images of the black-cloaked figures.

Safe, Sophie kept repeating. *I promise you'll be safe here.*

She intended to keep that promise.

Silveny was trapped there because of her—because *she'd* heard Silveny's thoughts and followed them and leaped her to Havenfield and coaxed her into the enclosure. And the only reason she wasn't undoing all of that and letting Silveny fly away was because she believed Grady. It was a dangerous world for a sparkly flying horse.

But if she was going to take away Silveny's freedom, then she was going to make *sure* the alicorn truly was better off. So when Grady and the gnomes were done with Silveny's enclosure, Sophie wandered the grounds, searching for some clue that Sandor might have missed that would tell her if Silveny had been right about the intruders.

After several hours of finding nothing, Sophie was ready to concede that it really had been a nightmare.

But then she found a pair of footprints in the tree line.

TWENTY-ONE

THESE PRINTS HAVE NO SCENT," SANDOR repeated for probably the twentieth time. He was down on his knees, nose to the mud, inhaling every inch. "If they were not shaped like feet, I would think they were made by boulders."

They'd already compared everyone's footprints—including the gnomes'—and found no match. The prints *had* to be from an intruder—though everyone kept using the word "visitor," like that somehow made it less scary.

Grady ran his hands through his hair as he paced back and forth. "Couldn't they be old prints? Wouldn't the scent have faded over time?"

"These prints are too fresh."

"I don't understand," Edaline whispered as her grip tightened on Sophie's hand. She'd latched on the second she saw the two impressions in the mud, and it seemed like she had no intention of letting go. "How could the prints not have a scent?"

Everyone looked at Sandor, who seemed to debate with himself before he answered.

"There . . . is a way to trick our senses."

"*What?*" Grady and Edaline asked at the same time.

"It's knowledge we guard very closely so that it cannot compromise our strength as bodyguards—and it's an extremely complicated feat to achieve. But if someone knew what they were doing, it's possible they could hide from me."

"I thought you said no one could get past you," Sophie snapped. "I trusted you!"

"And you can still trust me," Sandor replied calmly. "Only a select few have this information. But this is why I'm always telling you to *stay by my side*, in case something somehow sneaks up, so I can be ready."

"Who knows about this?" Grady asked after a second, and the strain in his voice suggested he felt just as betrayed as Sophie.

"The Councillors, and a few select members of the nobility. No others."

Grady mumbled to himself, listing off names Sophie didn't recognize, like he was trying to guess who might know.

He stopped pacing. "Vika Heks has many family members in the nobility. Do any of them know?"

"It's possible. I do not know the full specifics."

Grady nodded, and the lines on his forehead seemed to fade. "It has to be them. They're the only ones that make sense."

"Not the only ones," Edaline said, squeezing Sophie's hand so hard it cut off her circulation.

Grady went back to pacing, and he'd worn a small groove in the mud before he said, "I know what you're worrying about, Eda—I'm worrying about it too. But we both need to remember: They weren't here for Sophie. Look where the prints are—nowhere near the house. Silveny's the one they were interested in."

Edaline's death grip slackened. "I suppose."

Sophie wished she could relax as easily. She had a hard time imagining the Hekses being skilled enough to trick Sandor's senses. She doubted Stina was skilled enough to walk and chew gum at the same time.

Maybe it was the Black Swan—but why would they care more about a sparkly winged horse than her?

Though, what would the kidnappers want Silveny for?

Sophie's brain hurt trying to figure it out, and she realized only one thing really mattered: If Silveny was the one they wanted, she needed to work extra hard to get Silveny ready for the Sanctuary so she could finally be somewhere safe.

"That's a lot of bodyguards," Dex said as he stood next to Sophie at Silveny's pasture, watching a goblin who made Sandor look puny give orders to four others before they all raced away in opposite directions to resume their patrol. "Anything I should know about?"

"They're not for me, and I'm not allowed to say more than that."

The Council had ordered extreme silence when it came to what they had dubbed "the suspicious incident." *No* one was allowed to know of the possible threat to Silveny. The last thing they wanted was more paranoia spreading.

Dex sighed.

Sophie felt like doing the same.

She offered Silveny a handful of swizzlespice through the bars, but Silveny simply sniffed the air and stared at Dex.

Scared.

"Scared" was Silveny's new favorite word. She'd been transmitting it constantly for the last few days—when Sophie left her alone, when someone so much as breathed too close to her enclosure, when she wanted anything at all. And despite Sophie's renewed efforts to get Silveny to respond to *someone* besides her, the traumatized horse refused to get anywhere near anyone Sophie brought over.

Silveny even panicked around other animals. Especially Iggy—though it hadn't helped that the mischievous imp decided to launch one of his toxic Iggy-farts into Silveny's face when Sophie introduced them. Silveny had gagged for about ten minutes, and Sophie couldn't blame her.

At least it had been *all quiet on the alicorn front* since the extra goblins arrived. Not so much as a bent blade of grass had been found on the grounds for the last three days.

"Sorry I haven't been around this week," Dex mumbled, fidgeting with the silver band on his wrist. It was the Disneyland watch Sophie had given him at the end of midterms last year. "My parents needed me to help out at the store."

"You don't have to be sorry," Sophie said, feeling bad that she hadn't noticed. Thanks to Silveny and her nightmares Sophie had barely slept, and the exhaustion was starting to get to her. She'd even started to consider asking Elwin for an extremely mild sedative, but she was afraid he might want to examine her. And after her talk with Fitz she was afraid of what he might find.

It was easier not to know—at least for right now when she had so much to deal with. She hadn't had a headache since the aurenflare, so whatever the problem was, it couldn't be that big of a deal. She'd look into it later.

"But I *like* coming here," Dex said, interrupting her thoughts. His ears turned red and he added quickly, "It's nice to get a break from my parents. They've been a lot more annoying, ever since . . ."

He glanced toward the Cliffside gate. Sophie felt a knot form in her throat.

"I knew I'd find you hard at work on your assignment," Alden said as he appeared behind them. "Sorry, I know I come unannounced. I have sort of a last-minute . . ."

His voice trailed off as Silveny flapped her wings and took off to circle her enclosure. "Such an incredible creature," Alden breathed.

Incredibly annoying was more like it.

"Sort of a last-minute . . . ?" Sophie prompted.

"Yes, right. Sorry. A last-minute assignment." He glanced at Dex. "I'm sorry, Dex, I need to discuss something classified with Sophie."

"Oh." He turned to Sophie. "Should I go?"

She nodded and Dex reached for the home crystal hanging from his neck. "Wait—is this about the kidnappers? Because I think I deserve to know what's going on with that too."

Alden smiled—though it was a sad smile. "You definitely do, Dex, and I'm hoping I'll have some new information for both of you soon. But this is a special assignment from the Council that I need Sophie's help with."

There was a strained tone in his voice that made Sophie tug out an eyelash. Dex must've noticed too because he asked, "Is it dangerous?"

"Dangerous isn't the right word."

"What is the right word?" Sophie asked.

Alden didn't look at either of them as he said, "Difficult."

The word felt like ice. But when Dex asked Sophie if she

would be okay, she nodded. Alden would never let anything bad happen to her.

"I guess I'll see you at the Opening Ceremonies tomorrow, then?" Dex asked.

"Of course you will," Alden answered for her. "And thank you, Dex. I trust you'll keep the fact that I was here to yourself?"

"Yeah. Sure." He hesitated as he held up his crystal, but Sophie smiled and mouthed that she'd be okay. He nodded and stepped into the light, leaving her alone with Alden.

"So . . . what's the assignment?"

Alden kicked a pebble, sending it skipping across the grass. Several endless seconds passed before he whispered, "You're still so young, and you've already been through so much. I hate that I have to ask this of you."

She waited for him to continue, but he just stared at the grass like he'd forgotten she was there.

"Ask me what?"

He glanced over his shoulder, where Sandor stood in the shadow of a tree. "I can't say here. No one is allowed to know where we're going."

"Sandor's not going to like that."

"I'll take care of him. Go put on your best walking shoes. We have a long journey ahead."

Wherever they were going, they used a black crystal to leap there.

Clear crystals leaped to the elvin world. Blue crystals leaped to the Forbidden Cities—and were restricted to only certain members of the nobility.

Sophie had never seen a black crystal.

The shiny black stone was long and thin and had only one facet. It was set on a thick silver chain Alden wore around his neck, and when he'd held it to the sun, the beam it cast looked more like a shadow. The light felt cold as they stepped into it, like billions of snowflakes were fluttering under Sophie's skin, until an icy wind blasted them away, sending her scattering in a million directions. She had just started to panic when the chilly blast vanished and the scenery blurred back into focus.

A scorching, empty desert.

Arid dunes stretched in every direction. No plants, no rocks, no signs that anyone had ever set foot where they stood. Waves of heat radiated off the blinding sand, making Sophie squint.

"Where are we?" She had to shout over the dry desert wind.

"According to my instructions, this is the Gateway to Exile."

Sophie shivered despite the searing sun. Exile was the one place she'd promised herself she'd *never* go.

Though maybe this was the chance she'd been waiting for.

Prentice was in Exile.

Alden shaded his eyes as he took her hand and led her through the dunes. "I think this is the right way. Their directions were rather vague."

"You haven't been here?"

"Generally only the Councillors are allowed to come. But they made an exception for us."

"Why?"

"I'll explain in a moment. First we must get somewhere more private."

Sophie looked around at the empty, barren land surrounding them. Where was more private than this?

"I'm sorry, I know I'm being vague. But this assignment is at the absolute highest level of confidentiality. I can't reveal anything further until I'm certain we're somewhere no one can overhear." He glanced over his shoulder, like he expected someone to burst out of the mounds of scorching sand. But the desert stayed as empty as ever.

Alden counted his paces as they walked, mumbling something about "following the rivers of sand." Sophie tried to shield her face from the sun, wishing she'd worn a hooded cape. For once it would've been useful.

"This has to be it," Alden said, pausing at a circle of sand surrounded by low dunes. "I've been told the next part of our journey is going to be rather unpleasant. All I know is that we need to ignore our instincts and trust the trap."

"What does that mean?"

"Just don't fight against the pull—and make sure you hold your breath and keep your eyes closed. You ready?"

"Not really."

He smiled. "I know what you mean."

He sucked in a huge breath and she copied him, filling her lungs with as much air as they would hold.

Her legs shook as he led her into the circle. The ground sank with each step, and within seconds she was up to her knees.

Quicksand.

She tried to break free but that only made her sink faster, the hot sand now up to her waist.

Alden's instructions echoed through her thoughts as his grip tightened on her hand and his eyes met hers. He nodded, like he was telling her it was okay as they sank up to their shoulders.

Her last thought was, *Trust the trap.*

Then the sand swallowed them whole.

TWENTY-TWO

OPHIE'S LUNGS SCREAMED FOR AIR and her brain screamed for help and it took everything in her not to actually scream as the scratchy darkness pulled them downward.

Trust the trap. Trustthetrap. TRUSTTHETRAP!

She clung to Alden's hand, her only connection to any sort of reality, as they sank deeper into the darkness.

Sooner or later she would need to breathe.

They sank farther still, and panic overwhelmed her. But as she thrashed and kicked, the darkness turned thinner and her body turned lighter and the air turned smoother.

Air?

She gasped for breath, wanting to cry when the burning in

her lungs faded. She opened her eyes and found they were free-falling through darkness, dropping so fast she didn't have time to scream before they collided with the ground.

A sand dune cushioned their fall. She knew she should be grateful for the soft landing, but at the moment she never wanted to feel sand again.

She coughed, feeling grains and grit between her teeth. Alden pounded on her back as he wheezed and hacked as well.

"*Most* unpleasant," he rasped.

A pale blue light cut through the darkness. When Sophie's eyes adjusted, she realized they were in a small round cavern. The walls were smooth and the ceiling was sand, and she wondered if this was what it felt like to be trapped in an hourglass. Any second she expected the grains to fall and bury them alive.

The light flickered as Alden dusted sand off his clothes, and she noticed the glow was coming from a small blue crystal strung around his neck. She stood and tried to shake the sand out of her hair, but she had a feeling she'd be finding it in unpleasant places for weeks.

"Some water?" a deep, gravelly voice asked from the shadows.

Sophie ducked behind Alden as he pointed the light toward the far wall. A brown, hairy creature with a pointed snout, bulbous nose, and squinty eyes pulled itself the rest of the way out of the ground and held up a flask that looked to be made from the same black crystal as the stone that had leaped them there.

Alden bowed. "Thank you." He took the flask and handed it

to Sophie as the creature nose-dived back into the ground, its hairy hands tunneling effortlessly into the soft sand.

"What was *that*?" she asked as she took a tentative sip from the flask. The water was ice-cold and even sweeter than the bottles of Youth they drank every day. She had to stop herself from guzzling the whole thing.

"A dwarf."

"As in *Snow White and the Seven . . .*?"

Alden smiled as she handed the flask back to him, and he took a long drink before he answered. "Most likely, no. Dwarves are one of the five intelligent creatures we've made treaties with. They're rarely seen above ground—the light is far too bright for them. But their tunneling skills are unmatchable. We've relied on their help many times throughout the centuries, when we needed to build something secret—or hard to reach. Like this place."

Hard to reach was a bit of an understatement.

"And this is . . . Exile?" Somehow she'd expected it to be bigger. With dungeons and chains and screaming prisoners or something.

"No, this is the Entrance to Exile."

"I thought that's where we were when we were above ground?"

"That was the Gateway to Exile. It's confusing, I know—which is intentional. Exile was designed so that you have to know exactly where to go and what to look for—and be willing to endure some discomfort—if you want to reach it. We're now one of about twenty people who know where it is—besides those exiled of course. Has it triggered any memories?"

"No, none of this feels familiar."

Alden frowned.

"Did you think this was where the Black Swan was telling us to go with the charm?"

"I still believe it is." Alden handed her back the flask and Sophie was surprised to see it was full again.

"It collects moisture in the air," he explained.

"Crystal can do that?"

"Not crystal. Magsidian. An exceedingly rare mineral the dwarves mine from the deepest recesses of the earth. It has an inherent field that draws things to it, and you can change what it draws by how you carve it." He pointed to the irregular shape of the flask's mouthpiece. "These careful cuts make this flask draw water from the air. Whereas *this*"—he dug under his tunic and pulled out the black crystal pendant, holding it up so she could get a better look at it—"was cut to draw certain types of light, which will be important when it's time to leave."

Up close the stone was a much more specific shape than Sophie had realized, with seven sides of seven different lengths, all etched around the edges.

"It's another security measure," Alden explained. "Regular light isn't strong enough to push someone up and out from this deep underground. Which may be why the Black Swan was unable to plant any memories of this place in your mind. Perhaps they've never been. If anyone came here uninvited, they'd be trapped."

The walls felt like they were closing in and Sophie sucked in a breath, reminding herself that *they* weren't trapped. At least, she hoped they weren't.

"Magsidian is also how the dwarves know we're here," Alden added, "and why they knew we weren't a threat when we arrived. They can sense its presence. We only have twelve magsidian stones in our possession, one for each member of the Council. They were gifts from the dwarves when we signed the treaty. If someone were to set foot here without carrying any, the dwarves would assume they're here without the Council's permission and restrain them. For us, they could feel the magsidian from Councillor Terik's pendant, so they sent someone to refresh us for the next leg of our journey. Which we should probably get started on. Are you ready?"

She wasn't. Not even a little bit. But she'd come this far.

Alden approached the wall, tracing his fingers across the smooth surface until he found a narrow slit hidden by shadows. He slipped the magsidian pendant into it and twisted like it was a key. Air hissed and stone scraped and the ground rumbled as the heavy wall spun clockwise, scattering clouds of dust as it slowly revealed a narrow doorway leading into darkness beyond.

Alden handed her a clear crystal on a slender gold chain. "Breathe on it," he told her as she slipped it around her neck. "The warmth reignites the balefire."

She did, and tiny blue sparks flickered to life inside the crystal. "Did Fintan make these?"

His name felt wrong on her tongue.

Fintan. The elf she'd accused of sparking the Everblaze.

The elf who *claimed* he was innocent—though he was clearly hiding something.

Balefire had been his trademark, before pyrokinesis had been forbidden. It was a special flame that required no fuel and could be contained in crystal.

Alden took a closer look at his pendant. "These were probably made by one of his apprentices. But it's still rather ironic, I suppose, that we're using them to light our way, given that we're coming to see him."

"So . . . he's been exiled?" Last she'd heard, the Councillors were giving him a chance to confess before they took such a drastic measure.

"They moved him here earlier in the week. I'll admit, I was surprised. Normally, they wait until after . . ."

"After what?"

He shook his head and gestured toward the doorway, signaling for her to go first. "I'll tell you in a minute."

Her legs felt heavy as she moved forward, especially when she spotted the narrow, winding staircase that descended into the darkness. Even with the blue light of the balefire pendant she couldn't see where it ended.

Words couldn't explain how much she didn't want to go down the scary-stairway-of-doom—but as she hovered in the doorway, she reminded herself that this was the chance she'd been waiting for.

Somewhere at the bottom, behind however many locked doors, was Prentice.

Her *past*.

Maybe the answer to the Black Swan's clue.

Every step forward brought her closer to the truth.

TWENTY-THREE

OWN.

Down.

Down, they climbed.

One step at a time.

One foot in front of the other.

No light, except from the balefire crystals around their necks. No sound except their feet slapping against stone.

Stomp.

Stomp.

Stomp.

For a while Sophie tried to count the stairs, but she gave up once they'd passed a thousand. Her legs burned and her feet ached and the air grew hotter and stuffier the farther they went, until her hair was plastered to her head with sweat.

"Where is this place?" she asked. "The center of the earth?"

"Exactly."

"You're serious?"

"I'm guessing humans taught you the earth's core was either a big pool of magma or a solid ball as hot as the sun."

That *was* what she'd been taught—but she wasn't about to admit it. "But . . . how is this possible?"

"The dwarves can tunnel anywhere, and we can make anything habitable. Combine that with the fact that Exile needed to be impossible to reach, and this was really the only logical option."

"Only elves would call tunneling to the center of the earth 'logical.'"

"And only a girl raised by humans would think otherwise."

She couldn't decide if he meant that as a good or a bad thing.

"So, can you tell me what we're doing here yet? Or are you still worried about eavesdroppers."

"No, I think this is sufficiently secluded."

She'd taken at least ten more steps before he added, "The Council has ordered me to perform the memory break on Fintan."

"Oh."

She tried to say more but the words lodged in her throat, making it hard to breathe.

"He still refuses to reveal what he's hiding, and we're positive he knows something important about the Everblaze." Alden's voice was hushed, but it echoed through the suffocating silence of the dark stairway. "I've been ordered to give him one last opportunity to confess. If he remains silent, I'm to probe his memories—by any means necessary."

"Have you ever done a memory break before?" Sophie whispered. She didn't know much about them—only that they shattered the person's sanity.

"Not personally. They're quite rare. Quinlin performed the last one, since he's a stronger probe than me—"

"You mean the one on Prentice?" Sophie interrupted.

"Unfortunately, yes."

The sadness in his tone made the question she'd been afraid to ask slip out before she could stop it. "Do you think breaking Prentice's mind was . . . ?"

"A mistake?" Alden finished, when she didn't.

She nodded.

If the Black Swan really were the good guys, then Prentice had *technically* been innocent. He did hide something from the Council—but he was hiding *her*. Probably trying to protect her from the *real* bad guys.

"I try very hard not to think about it," Alden said quietly.

Sophie had been trying to do the same thing.

"So why did you bring me here?" she asked after several steps of silence.

Hopefully, he didn't need her to officially accuse Fintan.

She firmly believed that Fintan had been involved with the Everblaze somehow. But she wasn't sure if she could stare into his eyes and condemn him to madness.

Alden cleared his throat. "A memory break should never be performed alone. You must send your consciousness so deeply into the victim's that it's possible you could get lost in the mental chaos and never return. The only way to protect yourself is to have someone there to guide you back."

She stopped so abruptly Alden crashed into her back. "Please tell me you aren't expecting *me* to be your guide."

"I understand your hesitation, Sophie. I've wrestled with the idea myself, ever since you showed me that charm."

She whipped around to face him. "*That's* what you think the clue means?"

"I do. The Black Swan would never use the word 'guide' by coincidence, especially mere days before the Council ordered a memory break—the first one ever ordered on an Ancient mind. So I can only assume that they're telling us to have you guide me, probably to make sure we're able to unearth whatever he's hiding before he shatters. That'll be much more difficult with thousands of years' worth of memories to wade through."

"But . . . that doesn't make sense. If I'm the 'guide,' then what do they mean about 'the past'?"

"I'm guessing that's referring to the fact that Fintan is one of the Ancients, and therefore the very essence of our past. Or perhaps they're hinting that the memory we need is deep in Fintan's past."

"But—"

"I realize it's not a *perfect* match, Sophie—and believe me, I've done everything I could to reject this theory. I've researched 'guide,' and compasses, and spent every waking hour trying to find some other meaning. This is the only idea that makes sense."

"What about Prentice?"

Alden looked away, shaking his head as he ran a hand through his hair. "How many times do I have to tell you, Sophie—Prentice is *useless*."

The emotion in his voice knocked her back a step—but she couldn't tell what it was. Sorrow? Anger?

"I'm sorry," he said after a second, rubbing his temples. "I just . . . I wish I could change . . . But I can't."

He sounded so incredibly weary.

Before Sophie could think of anything to say he took a shaky breath and added, "I'm not going to force this on you, Sophie. I had to bring you down here because I couldn't tell you the plan until we were completely alone—but if you don't want to do this, we will leave right now. No questions. No problems. Certainly no hard feelings. I'll come back with someone else as my guide. The choice is completely yours." He held out the magsidian crystal. "Say the word and I'll take you home."

Her reflection looked fractured in the dark facets. Sophie felt just as torn.

"What if something happens to you?" she whispered, wishing she could block the horrifying thoughts racing through her head.

Alden, staring at her with wild eyes, like Brant. Curled up on the floor of a cold, empty house, rocking back and forth.

"Nothing's going to go wrong," Alden promised.

"How can you know that? You wouldn't need a guide unless there was a really good chance something could go wrong during a break, right? And what if I'm not strong enough to help you?"

Alden stepped closer and squeezed her shoulders. "I have no doubt that you're strong enough, Sophie. Think of all the amazing things your mind can do. You're impenetrable to other thoughts and transmissions—"

"Not Fitz's."

"Okay, *one* person can get past you—"

"Silveny, too."

A smile peeked from the corners of his lips. "Fine. One person and an alicorn—that's still *far* superior to our strongest Keeper, who's had dozens of Telepaths slip through. And when you pair that with your incredible concentration levels and consider the fact that no one can block you, it's almost like the Black Swan made you for this task."

Sophie cringed. She didn't want to be *made* for anything.

"I know how frightening this is. And trust me, this is the *last* thing I would *ever* ask of you—not because I'm worried for me. I know I'll be fine. But I want *you* to be fine. If you don't want to, say the word."

"It's not that I don't *want* to. It's just . . . if something happened and it was my fault—"

"Nothing is going to happen, I promise. But even if it does, it wouldn't be your fault. No—don't shake your head. Listen to me. You are—by far—the strongest Telepath in our world. If you can't guide me back, no one can. *No one.*"

She could tell from his eyes that he meant every word.

And if he believed in her that much . . .

She swallowed, barely able to find enough of her voice to whisper, "Okay."

His smile was sad as he pulled her in for a hug. "Thank you, Sophie. I'm so sorry you have to go through this. I'll try to make it as easy as possible."

She was too stunned by what she'd just agreed to do to think of anything to say to that, so she turned back around and continued their descent.

The rest of the walk was a blur as she tried to remember everything Tiergan had ever taught her in their telepathy sessions. It all seemed so trite and useless now. What did it matter that she could project her thoughts on paper or read the minds of animals or transmit miles and miles away? How would any of that pull Alden back if he started to lose himself?

She was so absorbed in her own worries that she didn't notice they'd reached the bottom until she tripped, her feet expecting another stair and finding sandy floor instead.

The room they'd entered was small, square, and empty. The only distinct feature was a huge metal door with a small black slit in the center.

"They call this place 'the Room Where Chances are Lost,'" Alden whispered.

The sand rustled in front of them, and Sophie barely managed not to squeal as another dwarf twisted out of the ground.

"Permission has been granted for you to enter," the strange creature murmured in a dry, cracked voice as he shook the loose grains from his shaggy fur and squinted at them with his dark, beady eyes. "I am Krikor. I shall be your attendant."

Alden gave a slight bow and Sophie fumbled to copy him.

"Are you ready?" Krikor asked, moving toward the metal door.

Alden reached for Sophie's hand—probably to reassure her, but he was trembling so much it was hard to feel comforted.

"As ready as we'll ever be," Alden whispered. Then he pulled Sophie forward and inserted his magsidian pendant into the keyhole in the center of the door.

Metal latches clicked, but nothing happened until Krikor slipped a rounded disk of magsidian into a thin slot hidden in the shadows at the edge of the door, like putting a coin in a soda machine.

A thunderous *Boom!* reverberated through the chamber and a seal broke along the edges, letting bright orange light seep through the cracks.

"Focus on the floor as you walk," Krikor advised as he pushed open the door. "It will spare you from seeing the madness."

The first thing Sophie noticed was the smell.

It wasn't rot or decay or waste like she would expect from a prison. Nor was it sulphur or magma, like the center of the earth should smell. The only word she could think to describe it was "bleak." If hopelessness had an odor, it would smell like Exile. Sharp and stale and bitter.

Also noticeable was the sound. It wasn't loud or angry. No screaming or raging. Just constant muffled moans. Cries of misery. Or insanity.

"How big is this place?" Sophie asked, her voice echoing off the cavernous walls. The metal hallway was lined with porthole-size windows and seamless doors, and it curved up ahead, disappearing into the gloomy light.

"Not as big as you think," Alden told her as they made their way down the hall. "The structure is a spiral, curling in on itself."

Still—there were a *lot* of doors. "I thought crime was supposed to be rare."

"Exile is the prison for *all* the worlds. That's why we have to keep its location so secret. Not all species are as peaceful as ours."

Almost on cue, some sort of creature screeched and crashed against the walls of its cell. Sophie moved closer to Alden.

Despite her fears she ignored Krikor's warning, scanning the doors and hoping to spot Prentice's name in the glowing labels above them. But then a face appeared in one of the windows—moss green skin and slits for a nose and brown fangs peeking through its flat lips. Sophie looked away, but she could feel it staring at her with its bulging milky eyes as they passed.

After that she focused on the smooth, sterile floor, watching her reflection warp and skew as she tried not to imagine what other monsters hid behind the metal walls. On and on they walked until Sophie felt dizzy from winding round and round and round. And yet it still felt too soon when they stopped, and Krikor announced, "The prisoner you seek is in here."

TWENTY-FOUR

I S IT SAFE?" SOPHIE ASKED AS ALDEN slipped the magsidian key into the plain silver door labeled FINTAN.

It felt wrong to enter a prison cell with only a short, hairy dwarf to protect them—where was Sandor with his bulging muscles and giant weapon when she actually wanted him?

"The prisoner is in controlled confinement, and we have restrained him," Krikor answered.

"But stand behind me just in case," Alden warned.

He started to twist the key, but Krikor blocked him. "Your pendants," he said, holding out his furry hands.

"I can't believe I missed that." Alden removed his balefire crystal and handed it over.

Sophie copied him. Her wrists tingled with the memory of her burns as Alden explained that Fintan would've been able to call sparks back to a flame, and she hoped this would be the last Pyrokinetic she'd ever face.

Krikor stepped out of the way, and Sophie hid behind Alden as he turned the key.

Moist, frigid air blasted them when he pushed the door open, and a raspy voice said, "I guess this means the Council has decided to make good on their threats."

"Unless you'd like to make this easier on everyone," Alden told him. "It's not too late."

"Oh, it's far too late. Far too late."

The resignation in Fintan's voice pricked at Sophie's heart. Even if he'd brought this on himself, what must it be like knowing you were about to turn into one of the mindless drones filling the hallway with their lifeless wails?

"I'll admit, I didn't think they'd send you," Fintan added quietly. "I guess I should see it as a compliment. They sent their star."

Alden sighed and took a few steps forward. "Fintan. I implore you to see reason—"

"Ah, you're not alone. I'd wondered," Fintan interrupted. "You—hiding back there. No need to be afraid. They've gone to great lengths to make sure I'm *perfectly* harmless."

Sophie peeked around Alden's side.

Fintan was thinner than she'd expected. Almost fragile-looking, with sky blue eyes and slender features. Not someone she would ever suspect of being wrapped up in a conspiracy to massacre the human race. He wore bright red clothes and was bound to a plain metal chair in the empty, icy room.

"Amazing," he whispered, staring into her eyes. "You're the girl who bottled the Everblaze, aren't you?"

Sophie nodded, focusing on his ears. The tops curled into more prominent points than Bronte's, sticking out of his messy blond hair.

His dry lips stretched into a grin. "Wasn't it magnificent? The Everblaze," he clarified when she frowned. "It's been ages since I've seen it. But it was a remarkable thing to behold." He stared into space, like he was reliving the memory. "Couldn't you just *feel* the way the fire breathed with power and energy and life?"

Fluorescent yellow flames danced through Sophie's mind, and she could almost feel the searing heat and the choking smoke as the fires closed in around her. "Mostly I just wanted to get out of there alive and stop it from killing any more innocent people."

His smile toppled to a scowl. "I suppose only a Pyrokinetic can truly appreciate the majesty of an unstoppable flame. The fire of the sun on the earth. I would've loved to see it again, before . . ."

He closed his eyes.

"If you'd tell us what you know, there wouldn't be a 'before,'" Alden reminded him.

"We both know I'm never leaving this cold, empty room with no warmth, no kindling—nothing but solid metal and fireproof clothes. A life with no heat—no fire—isn't worth living."

He shivered.

"Besides," he added, shifting as much as his bonds would allow. "Some secrets are worth protecting."

"So you admit, you *are* hiding something," Alden asked him.

Fintan's hands curled around the metal arms of his chair, turning his knuckles white. "Our world is *broken*, Alden—and all the Council does about it is condemn anyone brave enough to acknowledge that we have a problem. Break our minds, lock us deep in the earth, convince themselves that we are the criminals. But who are the ones ruining lives? Destroying families? Forbidding people from using their abilities, relegating them to working class—"

"Pyrokinesis was forbidden because your insatiable craving for power killed five people. You supported the decision when you resigned from the Council."

"That was a regrettable mistake," Fintan whispered. "And I understood the need for change. But then I *lived* the life they'd relegated me to. Treated like the Talentless—with no way to satisfy my craving for flame. It's a daily struggle not to let my sanity slip away."

"I'm not so certain you've succeeded."

Alden's voice was cold, but Sophie couldn't help feeling a

tiny stab of sympathy for Fintan. Having a special ability meant everything in their world. She could imagine how frustrating it would be to have one and have to deny it. And if his body actually craved it . . .

"And that's only a small problem," Fintan added, his voice building steam. "Left to their own devices the Council will let everything we've built crumble to dust. Someone had to stand up and fight for what matters—and while I'm not the one who cast the first sparks, I *am* willing to help keep the flames alive."

"The flames have been extinguished!" Alden shouted.

Fintan snorted a laugh. "That's the funny thing about rebellions. You can't stop them until they've consumed everything that fuels them. And from where I sit I see *plenty* of kindling." His eyes locked with Sophie's. "She's as much a part of it as I am—never forget that."

"She's not a part of anything."

"If that were true, then why is she here?" He stared at Sophie again, the kind of stare that made her want to squirm or hide because it was like he was looking through her instead of at her. "You're choosing the wrong side, Alden. If anyone's mind should be broken, it's hers. *She's* hiding more secrets than anyone."

Alden grabbed his shoulders. "That's enough!"

Sophie forced air into her lungs and tried to shove his horrible words out of her mind, but they'd already rooted themselves to her fears.

"Enough," Alden repeated. He took a deep breath and turned to face Sophie. "Are you ready for this?"

She gave a shaky nod.

"Doing this brings me no joy, Fintan," Alden told him quietly. "But this group—this rebellion you're protecting—*will* be stopped. I'll do whatever it takes to protect what matters."

Fintan's glare screamed a million snide insults. But all he said was, "Well, then I guess you'd better get started, shouldn't you?"

"Yes, I believe I should." Alden stepped back, smoothing his hair and rubbing his temples. "Last chance."

All the color had drained from Fintan's face, but he still gritted his teeth and said, "I'm not the first to sacrifice myself for the cause—and I won't be the last."

"And your sacrifice will be for nothing. I'll find whatever you're hiding in the break."

"You'll never find it in time. I know how to protect my secrets. And if I can, I'll drag you down with me."

"You'll only hurt yourself if you try." Alden turned to Sophie. "I'll need you to keep physical contact with me."

Sophie stumbled over to him, her palm slick with sweat as she curled her fingers around his wrist. "What am I—how do I—I don't know—"

"Relax, Sophie. Your job is incredibly easy. All you have to do is open your mind to mine and stay connected. If you feel my thoughts start to slip away, simply call for me to guide me back. Think you can handle that?"

"But he said he can drag you down."

"He's just trying to scare you. The worst he can do is block me from finding what he's hiding before his mind shatters. Just keep your eyes closed and try not to pay attention to anything you see. I'll work as fast as I can."

"How long will it take?" she whispered.

"No more than a few minutes."

Fintan laughed, cold and sharp. "That's what you think."

Alden ignored him, placing his hands on Fintan's temples. "Go ahead and connect to my thoughts, Sophie. Let me know when you're ready."

She felt too overwhelmed to think. But she closed her eyes and tried to stretch out her mind and . . .

. . . thought she might be sick all over the floor.

She took a deep breath and tried to tell herself that this was no different than trying a new skill in her telepathy session. It didn't help as much as she'd wanted, but when she tried again she was able to spread out her consciousness enough to reach Alden's mind.

Alden's thoughts filled her head, rippling like a soft breeze

There's no reason to worry, Sophie. I trust you.

Telling her not to worry was like telling her not to breathe. But all she said was, *Be careful.*

You too.

She counted each passing breath, wondering how she would know when the memory break started. Would something change? Would it feel suddenly different?

Then Alden's mind dimmed and turned cold—and Fintan started to scream.

TWENTY-FIVE

SOPHIE TIGHTENED HER GRIP ON ALDEN'S wrist, forcing herself to stay connected as a flood of images poured through his mind. She tried not to focus on them, tried to let them all wash through her consciousness and fade away.

But the Everblaze burned too brightly to be ignored.

She watched through Fintan's eyes as he and five other elves in deep orange capes stretched their arms toward the night sky. She felt his head throb as he concentrated on the tiny pricks of heat radiating from the twinkling stars, but he focused through the pain and counted to three. Together as one, the six of them called the warmth down to earth.

For a second the heat ignored them. Then six lines of

neon yellow flame streaked toward the elves, gaining speed with every second. The others gasped and backed away, but Fintan held his ground, opening his palms and ordering the fire to bend to his will. The flames twisted and coiled into an elephant-size fireball that hovered above him.

Tears pricked his eyes as he soaked up the power of a purer, richer, more magnificent fire than had ever graced the earth before. But the blaze refused to stay contained and the fireball erupted, raining bits of scattered flame.

Fintan shielded his face with his cape, but the falling sparks attached to the fireproof fabric and ignited. He tossed the garment to the hungry flames and jumped through the fire line, tumbling across a patch of cool grass that hadn't yet succumbed to the blaze.

Coughs racked his chest, and his skin was red and raw and throbbed with a pain he didn't understand, like being stabbed by hundreds of scalding needles.

His first burns.

But he was alive.

And he was alone.

Flashes of orange thrashed among the yellow flames, and Fintan stumbled to his feet, realizing they were the figures of his friends. He shouted at the heat to subside, but the blaze swelled higher, crackling like it was laughing at him. All he could do was watch their agonized faces as the fire attacked. Then he dropped to his knees and vomited.

Sophie felt like doing the same.

She tried to shove the horror out of her mind, but it was like the memory was seared behind her eyes. She could only watch helplessly as Fintan fumbled for his pathfinder, hating himself for ignoring the bone-chilling cries of his friends as he held it up to the light.

Before he glittered away, the memory shattered.

Sophie yanked her consciousness back as the scene splintered to a million glinting shards that were swallowed by the darkness of Fintan's mind.

Alden groaned.

Are you okay? she asked, squeezing his wrist.

He's destroying the things he doesn't want me to see. I have to work faster. Brace yourself.

The shower of images turned into an icy downpour. Then to a raging flood. But the memories kept warping and twisting, and when Alden tried to focus them they vaporized to a thick fog that clouded everything.

His Ancient mind is too strong, Alden told her. *If I'm going to salvage any memories, I need you to boost me with your concentration.*

How do I do that?

Send some of your energy into his mind. It's like transmitting, but with force instead of words. Can you do that?

I'll try.

Sophie shoved any other thoughts out of her head and

pulled all of the energy stored in her inner core into her mind. It tingled and hummed as she wrapped her consciousness around it, and when she had a firm hold, she shoved it into Fintan's head, filling it with warmth.

The thick fog thinned, but didn't melt away.

I'll have to find another way, Alden told her—but his mental voice sounded weary.

Wait—let me try something.

Mental energy seemed to be more powerful than core energy—maybe a brain push was what they needed.

She focused on the energy buzzing at the edge of her consciousness, letting it surge and swell until her head felt ready to explode from the pressure.

Ready? she transmitted, not wanting to catch Alden off guard.

On three, he replied.

One.

Two.

Three!

She pushed the mental energy out of her head in a rush of heat.

It wasn't until the force collided against the other energy that she remembered her disastrous splotching match against Fitz—the first time she'd performed a brain push. Mental energy and core energy couldn't mix, and with the two trapped inside one mind they twisted and swirled around each other, forming a cyclone of heat that made Fintan scream.

Sophie panicked, trying to draw the energy back—but Alden ordered her to wait. She held her breath as the vortex of energy wound tighter and tighter. Finally, the pressure was too much and it collapsed and imploded, melting away the mental fog and revealing a memory hidden underneath.

An elf in long red robes. The features of his face were a murky blur of shadow and color, but Sophie watched through Fintan's eyes as he helped the elf stretch out his arm and curl his fingers into some sort of very specific fist and point it at the sky. Then Fintan jumped back as the elf flicked his wrist and a small ball of neon yellow flame sprang to life, hovering above his palm.

Everblaze.

Alden tried to force the memory into focus, but before he could, Fintan shouted and a wave of heat shot up Alden's arm, burning Sophie's hand.

The scene shattered.

The entire stream of memories cracked and splintered, crumbling into tiny, unrecognizable shards. Sophie pulled her concentration back before she was sucked into the chaos, but she felt Alden's consciousness slip away, leaving her suddenly cold.

She ripped her eyes open as his wrist slipped from her grasp and his body hit the floor with a thump. Her head throbbed and her hand ached, but she ignored the pain as the room came into focus.

Fintan sat slumped in his chair, muttering incoherently.

Alden lay unconscious, a large gash on his forehead streaking his face with red.

Her stomach heaved at the sight, and she tried not to look at the blood as she dropped to her knees and grabbed him by the shoulders.

"What happened?" Krikor asked, rushing into the room as Sophie shouted Alden's name and tried to shake him awake.

"I don't know—he must've hit his head when he fell."

She shook Alden again but it made no difference. Neither did Krikor's slapping Alden's cheeks.

Krikor wiped the blood away with the fur of his arm and examined the wound. Then he pried Alden's eyelids open, frowning at the blank whites. "I do not think the problem is physical."

Sophie glanced at Fintan, who was rocking back and forth. His cracked lips were turned up at the ends in a twisted smile.

Could he have dragged Alden down with him?

Tears turned everything to a blur, but Sophie blinked them back. Now was not the time for crying. Now was the time to be a guide.

She placed her shaky fingers against Alden's temples, transmitting his name over and over as she pushed her consciousness into his mind. His head felt cold and dark and was hauntingly quiet. No whisper of thoughts. No trace of memories. It was like Alden was *gone* and she was wading through an empty shell.

You promised nothing would go wrong, her mind screamed as she fanned out her thoughts, trying to feel in every direction at once. The cold pounded against her brain, and a tiny trickle felt like it was seeping in. But as she waded through the darkness she found something *warmer.* Clearer, somehow. She followed the feeling until she reached what felt like a small space. A warm nook.

But it was empty too.

Come back, she ordered him. *We need you.*

She filled the space with memories of Fitz and Della and Biana, the people who loved Alden and needed him and would never be the same if he left them.

You have to come back for them.

A tiny speck of light flashed through the darkness. Sophie wrapped her consciousness around it, like cupping her hands around a fledgling flame, shielding it so the shadows couldn't snuff it out. She fed it more images of Alden's family and friends and pulled it into the nook. A safe place to let it grow.

Brightness and warmth seeped around her, flooding the space with memories—happy scenes of family and friends. She stared at her own face, surprised to find herself in the mix.

Then Alden's mind whispered, *I'm here.*

TWENTY-SIX

SOPHIE WASN'T SURE IF SHE WANTED to collapse or cry as she threw her arms around Alden and squeezed as hard as she could. His heartbeat rang in her ears and his chest rose and fell with slow, steady breaths, promising that he was alive.

"I'm so sorry," he whispered, his voice weak and shaky.

She leaned back to take a better look at him. His beautiful teal eyes looked dull and tired, and his hair was matted against his forehead from the blood still streaming down his face.

She gagged.

Alden wiped his cheek, frowning when he saw the red on his hand. "It's just a cut," he told her as he pressed his palm against the wound. "No reason to worry."

"Here," Krikor said, handing him a magsidian flask shaped like a star. Inside was a thick gray sludge and Alden smeared some onto his forehead. It hardened like cement, stopping the bleeding.

"Thank you, my friend," he said as he gave the flask back.

Krikor nodded.

"Are you really okay?" Sophie asked.

"I'm perfect. Well, other than this burn."

He showed her his blistered hand.

Sophie's palm looked about the same, and Krikor offered no remedy. She pressed the tender skin against the metal floor, letting the chill soothe the burn as she asked, "What happened?"

"Fintan drew the warmth from my body and used it to burn me—us," he corrected, pointing to her hand. "Are *you* okay?"

"I've had worse."

"Yes, I suppose you have." He turned to where Fintan sat slumped against his chair, babbling and staring at nothing. "You *fool*! Was this really worth it?"

Fintan didn't answer.

"Did you learn anything from him?" Sophie asked quietly.

"Unfortunately, no. He did a very good job burying anything he didn't want us to see. The extra energy you sent was able to sweep away his defenses, but the burn broke my concentration before I could focus the images, and when I fought my way back in, his mind shattered and dragged me under. Now he's too far gone for us to risk any further searching."

Alden punched the ground with his good hand, uttering a word Sophie had never heard before. She assumed it wasn't a good one.

"Do you think we should try probing his mind again?" she asked quietly. "Maybe there's something—"

"It's far too dangerous, Sophie. A broken mind is like quicksand. It pulls your consciousness down, trapping you inside." His eyes dropped to his hands as he gently bent his singed fingers. "If you hadn't pulled me back, I would've been lost there forever. How did you find me?"

"I have no idea. I just tried everything I could think of. I wasn't going to lose you."

Alden pulled her in for another hug and Sophie sank into it, letting his steady heartbeat reassure her that he was okay.

He asked her for specifics, and she told him about wading through the icy darkness and following the trail of warmth to the small nook in his mind.

"A nook?"

"Yeah. It felt like it was a safe spot, somehow. It was easier to concentrate in there, so I tried calling you to me. You didn't respond at first, but then I filled the nook with images of your family, and after a few minutes, you found me."

"I remember that. Sort of." He let her go and wiped his eyes.

"What else do you remember?" she whispered, hoping it was okay to ask.

"Not much. I had no idea who I was anymore—but I did feel like there was something missing. Something I needed to know that was just out of my reach. I kept fighting my way toward it, but I wasn't getting anywhere until I felt a trickle of warmth and followed it. There were suddenly images all around me, people who felt familiar even though I couldn't remember who they were. Not until I saw your face in the mix and heard your voice—then everything snapped into place, and I realized I had to fight for the people I care about. That gave me the strength to pull myself free."

Fresh tears streamed down his cheeks. Sophie had to wipe away a few of her own.

"I am so incredibly sorry for what you've had to endure today, Sophie. But I'll confess . . . I'm glad you were here. I never would've made it through this if you hadn't been my guide."

"But I lost you—"

"No—I lost myself. And trust me, no one could've saved me like you did. In all my years, I've never heard of anything like this 'nook' you found. I suspect the uniqueness of your mind makes you the only one who can reach it."

She straightened. "Do you think that means I could save Fint—"

"Fintan is *broken*, Sophie, not lost. Those are two very different things." He turned to Fintan, who now had a thin string of drool running down his chin. "There's nothing more that can be done here. We should get home."

Alden stood, wobbling so much Krikor had to steady him. "I'm fine," he promised when he noticed Sophie's frown. "Just weak from the headache." He pointed to his wound, which had swelled to a giant red mound around the crusty cement.

"Will Elwin be able to fix it?" she asked as she followed him out of the cell.

"I have yet to encounter an ailment that Elwin can't heal—though you've seemed determined to stump him these last few months."

Sophie forced a smile. She could've done without the reminder about her latest medical problem. She was still hoping it would go away on its own.

Krikor closed the door, muffling Fintan's moans. He handed them their balefire pendants and pointed to the left. "I trust you can find your way to the exit? I need to tend to the prisoner."

"Of course." Alden gave him back the magsidian water flask and bowed his head, wincing slightly. "We cannot thank you enough for your assistance."

Krikor nodded, shoved the flask somewhere in his shaggy fur, and returned to Fintan's room. Fintan's faint, broken laughter filled the hall before the door closed, and Sophie had a horrible feeling the sound would haunt her nightmares for months to come.

She kept her head down as she turned to follow Alden through the curved hallway, but a nagging thought kept repeating with every step.

They were leaving with *nothing*.

They'd gone all that way. Risked Alden's sanity. Broken Fintan's mind.

For what?

Nothing. Nothing. Nothing.

The tiny pieces they'd learned couldn't have been what the Black Swan wanted. Their clues always led somewhere, gave her something new to go on.

Alden had to have been wrong. The clue had to mean—

Sophie's head snapped up, her eyes searching the glowing red letters over the doors, hoping she hadn't already passed the most important one. She read name after name—most so long and foreign she couldn't begin to pronounce them—and just when she was starting to give up, she spotted the one she needed.

Prentice Endal.

She knew Prentice's mind was supposed to be useless—but Prentice had been a Keeper. He knew how to tuck secrets away in unreachable places. Maybe the Black Swan had even trained him to do that, and that's why they sent her the clue.

"What's wrong?" Alden asked as she stopped walking. "Are you . . ."

His voice trailed off as his eyes found the name over the door.

Sophie braced for another lecture. But Alden just stared at the glowing letters, turning paler by the second.

They stepped toward the porthole without a word, almost like it was drawing them to it. Sophie had to work up the courage to peer through.

The room was small and dim, with padded walls. A hunched figure in some sort of tangled-looking straitjacket sat on a narrow bed, swaying lightly from side to side. His dark skin was slicked with sweat and his glazed eyes twitched as he muttered to himself.

"He didn't deserve this," Alden whispered after a minute. "I shouldn't have let . . ."

His voice cracked.

Sophie thought he was going to cry, but instead he shouted, "Why didn't you tell me the truth? I would've understood!"

Prentice didn't respond. He didn't even blink. Just kept swaying and muttering and twitching, like he really was as useless as Alden claimed.

But he had to be the answer.

Had. To. Be.

Nothing else fit the clue—and when would she have another chance to probe the mind of someone from the Black Swan?

Her brain was so tired from everything she'd put it through, but Sophie rallied any extra energy she could, pressed her palms against the glass, and imagined that she was touching the skin around Prentice's temples.

"What are you doing?" Alden asked as she closed her eyes.

Sophie didn't answer.

The last thing she heard was Alden shouting, "Don't!" Then the rest of the world faded away and she pushed her thoughts into Prentice's mind.

TWENTY-SEVEN

A T FIRST ALL SOPHIE FELT WAS thick, scratchy black, poking and prodding and pressing against her mental barriers. She tried to fight back, but the shadows were relentless, and the coldest ones found a way to seep through.

Images followed—as sharp and clear as normal memories. But they were *wrong*. Every color felt off. Every sound felt distorted. It felt like reality had been stripped and smashed and reassembled into something else. Something terrifying.

Trees rained from gray-green clouds, their dark branches reaching for her like clawed hands as they fell. Beasts sprang from a ground lit with stars, bared their fangs, and chased her across the sky-covered hills. Glowing eyes peeked through bushes covered in blue ears, and butterflies with bright red lips whispered sounds like mush. Sophie searched for some clue, some key to translate what she was seeing, but there seemed to be no rhyme or reason for anything.

Just the twisted thoughts of a twisted mind.

The images tangled, coiling around her, pulling her deeper. She whipped through more darkness and fell into the streets of a ruined city. The clouded and cracked crystal buildings were a hodgepodge of structures Sophie had seen throughout the Lost Cities: the swirling castles from Eternalia sandwiched among the silver-tipped spires from Atlantis mixed with gleaming mansions that wrapped around the pyramid of Foxfire. There was a fountain in the center of it all, two golden figures standing in a round pool, holding hands as colored streams of water showered them from every direction. A shadow of a girl appeared between them and took off through the buildings, shattering everything she touched before she dove into a sea of shards.

Sophie plunged after her.

Down down down she sank, feeling Prentice's mind turn colder—thicker—as she landed in a blank space, void of any sound or color. A bubble of nothing. She pressed against the sides, but a force slammed her back. Then a face appeared in front of her, pale and featureless except for two teal jewels for eyes. The more she stared into them, the more her head spun until she couldn't tell which way was up or down or where she'd come from or how to get back.

"No reason to worry," the face whispered as laughter erupted around her. The sound was young and childish at first. Then deep and dark as the face shattered to a million tiny flecks that surrounded her, stinging like needles. Some part of her mind knew she wasn't actually being touched—but that didn't make the pain any less real. She wanted to scream or cry or call for help—but she had no mouth. No voice. She was just a blip of consciousness.

A bodiless mind.

The needles of light turned electric, zapping with tiny shocks over and over and over until the only reality she knew was their pricks and pain. She was trapped. Stuck in this nightmare world where shadows tricked and light attacked and she was nothing. No one.

No.

She was someone.

But who was she?

It was a question she used to know, but the answer felt like it had been erased by the panic and pain, shoved out of her reach—beyond the burning lights.

She had to find it. Even if it was hard. Even if it hurt.

She pushed through the shards of light, letting them scrape and singe and strip more of her consciousness away. And then she was falling again. Down down down, with no end in sight. Dropping so far she knew she'd never pull herself up.

But without the tormenting stings, she found the answer to her question.

I am Sophie Foster.

She transmitted the words to make them more real and a thin strand of white light cut through the black. She wrapped her mind around it, clinging to the lifeline and hovering in the dark with no idea where to go or what to do. The cord of light flickered. Then a whisper of warmth trickled around her, building to a hum as the shadows bent and twisted into a shape. A dark bird.

A black swan.

It spread its wings and dove. Sophie watched it fall, wondering if she could trust it.

Let the past be your guide.

She released her hold on the strand of light, falling falling falling so fast, so hard, she caught up with the swan. She grabbed its wings and held on tight as it swooped and swept and swerved, finally crashing into a world of sunlight and blue sky and green grassy hills. But the world was too bright, too shimmering. Almost blinding.

The swan—now a real bird—tumbled with Sophie across soft ground until they collided with the legs of a woman, knocking her down. Her musical laugh rang through the air as she fell into their tangled heap. Then she pulled herself free, cradling the flapping swan in her arms and whispering for it to be calm.

She looked about twenty, with long blond hair that hung in soft waves and a violet gown. Sophie had never seen her before, but something felt familiar about her, especially when she smiled. The smile made her turquoise blue eyes sparkle the exact way Edaline's eyes did in the rare moments when she broke free from her grief.

Jolie.

Can you see me? Sophie transmitted, knowing it was crazy.

Jolie didn't respond. Instead she looked back to the swan waddling at her feet and reached to stroke its black feathers.

I don't understand, Sophie transmitted, wishing she could scream when silence was the only response. *What does this mean?*

Jolie laughed. "It'll be okay."

Her voice was so similar to Edaline's, Sophie felt chills. Jolie turned toward her then, and the clarity in her stare felt different than the other visions—like it wasn't a dream or a memory this time.

"We have to trust," she told Sophie, her smile fading.

Trust what? Trust who?

Jolie didn't say. She just glanced at the sky and said, "You have to go."

How? And what are you doing here? What does this mean?

Jolie swept up the swan with long, graceful arms and tossed it to the bright white clouds. "Follow the pretty bird across the sky."

The swan spread her wide black wings and flapped as the scene splintered to dust. But the shadows that rushed in pushed Sophie up instead of down. Shards of memories tried to grab her as she rose but she was moving too fast, blurring through the darkness until it turned gray and then white, and then she was back in her body, gasping and heaving and thrashing inside two strong arms that held her in a viselike grip.

"Don't you *ever* do that again!" Alden shouted.

TWENTY-EIGHT

SOPHIE WAS NO STRANGER TO HEADaches, but she'd never experienced *anything* like the thunderbolt that crashed into her brain when she opened her eyes—pounding and tearing and smashing and searing.

"Just breathe," Alden whispered, squeezing her hand. "It will pass."

She did as he said, trying to count her breaths to distract from the pain. But she couldn't concentrate and had to keep starting over. The third or fourth time she passed one hundred, the headache retreated, crawling back to whatever dark place it had come from.

She opened her eyes slowly, giving her brain time to adjust.

The faint blue glow from Alden's balefire pendant provided the only light, and the room they were in had a sandy floor and a massive metal door. Alden must've carried her to the Room Where Chances Are Lost at some point—though she had no idea when. Had she blacked out?

Alden helped her sit up, leaning her against his shoulder.

"Thanks," she croaked, wincing when she heard her broken voice. "So, I guess that was a pretty bad idea, huh?"

Alden didn't respond.

"I know you're angry—"

"You think I'm *angry*?" His shout echoed off the walls—which sure made it seem like he was angry. "I thought I'd lost you, Sophie."

"But I'm here. I'm fine." She forced herself to sit up on her own and tried not to sway too much as the blood rushed to her head, turning everything fuzzy. "I just . . . I thought Prentice might've hidden something important for me to find."

"His mind is *ruined*!" Alden wiped his eyes, taking several deep breaths before speaking again. "All he has left are shattered memories that have smashed together—a maze of madness so convoluted it sucks you in and never lets you escape."

"I know. But I thought that since he was a Keeper, there might be a memory he'd tucked away, waiting for me to find."

Alden sighed. The epic kind of sigh that sounded weary and frustrated and hopeless all at the same time. "Was there?"

"I don't know," she admitted.

She closed her eyes, picturing the swans she'd seen among the chaos. The shadow swan had only formed after she'd transmitted her name, almost like it had been sent for her. And it led her straight to that warm, safe place with Jolie and the real swan, which didn't feel like a memory so much as . . .

"Do you think Prentice could've communicated with me?" she asked quietly.

"Why?" Alden leaned forward, his eyes stretched almost too wide as he took her by the shoulders. "Did you see something?"

"I saw a black swan with . . . a woman."

She thought about telling him who. But if she told Alden she'd seen Jolie communicating with a black swan, she knew he'd think the same thing she was. The same thing it felt like Prentice had been *trying* to tell her.

Could Jolie have been part of the Black Swan?

What would Grady think if he knew?

"Did you see the woman's face?" Alden asked.

"I'd never seen her before." It wasn't totally a lie. She'd never seen Jolie in person—and she'd never seen pictures of her that age. "But she was talking to the swan. And then . . . it felt like she talked to me. She told me to 'follow the pretty bird across the sky.' Does that mean anything?"

"I . . ." Alden let her go and buried his face in his hands.

"Are you okay?"

"My head . . . I'm just"—he pressed his palms against his forehead like he was trying to squeeze the headache out—"I'm sorry. It's been a long day. And I know you think this is what the Black Swan meant for you to find, but Prentice isn't capable of having rational, coherent thoughts anymore."

"Couldn't part of him still be there somewhere? Locked deep away?"

"Let's hope not, Sophie. Let's hope for Prentice's sake that he's not even aware he's still alive. To be trapped forever in constant madness would be a far worse fate. Far, far worse." He shuddered.

She knew Alden was right. But she couldn't shake the feeling that some tiny piece of Prentice had tried to tell her something. Something so important he'd clung to that last bit of his sanity all this time.

Alden rubbed his temples, wincing with each press of his fingers. "Did you see anything else?"

"Nothing that made sense. It was all such a jumble of images. The only other thing I really recognized was you."

"Me?"

"Well, I'm pretty sure it was you. I saw a face with teal jewels for eyes. It leaned in to stare at me, and then it whispered, 'no reason to worry.'"

Even in the dim light of the balefire Sophie could see Alden turn pale. "Th—that was the last thing I said to him. Before the break. He begged me to make sure his family stayed safe and I promised he'd have no . . ." His voice faded and his whole body shook. "He *remembers*. I can't believe—I never thought he—I—"

He clutched his head in his hands and moaned.

"What's wrong?" Sophie asked as he toppled forward.

"My head," he managed to groan. Then his body went limp.

She rolled him to face her, calling his name and shaking his shoulders. The gray cement over his wound had cracked, releasing fresh streams of blood. "Alden, please, you're scaring me."

He didn't respond.

Sophie looked around for Krikor, wishing he'd pop out of the sand. But it was just her and Alden in an empty room in the center of the earth. And she had no idea what to do.

She fumbled for the magsidian pendant, holding it to the blue balefire—but the light was too dim to cast a beam. There had to be a trick she didn't know—and there was no way she could carry him up all those stairs.

"Please, Alden—wake up," she begged as she dug out her Imparter and shouted Elwin's name.

The silver square stayed blank—and it wouldn't respond to Grady's or Edaline's name either.

She shook Alden harder. "How do I get us home?"

Still no answer.

Fitz, she transmitted, forcing herself to concentrate through her panic. She pictured Everglen in her mind, trying to remember what she'd done when she'd been hostage and called for Fitz from halfway across the world. *Fitz, please, tell me you can hear me.*

Silence.

Tears pricked her eyes, and she struggled to think of anything else she could try.

Fitz, please. I don't know what to do.

Sophie? Can you hear me?

Fitz! Now she was crying. *Fitz—you have to help me, he's hurt and he won't respond and I can't leap us out of here—*

Whoa, whoa—slow down. Who's hurt? Where are you?

I . . . I'm not allowed to tell you. . . .

Sophie, come on—if you need help, you have to tell me where you are.

She glanced at Alden. His wound had opened wider, soaking the sand with red.

I'm in Exile.

EXILE???

Yes—with your dad—and he hurt his head. He's bleeding. A lot.

Leap him here. I'll have Elwin meet you at the gate.

I can't. We have to use this magsidian pendant thing and I don't know how to make it work. Do you know anything about it?

I've never heard of magsidian. Can't you ask someone?

There's no one else here—and I can't get your dad to wake up.

But . . . maybe she didn't need to.

The information was in Alden's memory somewhere. If she probed his mind, she would surely find the answer.

She took a deep breath, rallying her concentration.

Sophie, are you there? Fitz transmitted. *What's happening? What should I do?*

Hang on—I'm trying something.

Before Fitz could argue, she blocked his transmissions and pushed her consciousness into Alden's mind.

It felt different than she expected. Cramped and dim.

And *sharp.*

His thoughts had edges—rough bits that scraped and scuffed as she waded through, transmitting Alden's name over and over. At least his mind wasn't empty. There were memories to cling to, but they were tangled and twisted into an icy jumble and she didn't know how to make sense of them.

Streams of cold trickled into her consciousness, but she ignored the chills and focused on the thin threads of warmth she could feel scattered around Alden's mind. She gathered them together as she begged him to come back, telling him how scared she and Fitz were, how much she needed his help.

For several terrifying seconds nothing happened. Then Alden gasped and opened his eyes.

His chest heaved and he cradled his head as he hacked and wheezed. "What happened?" he asked between coughs.

"I don't know—you just collapsed and you wouldn't wake up." A small sob slipped out as she said it and Alden looked at her, his eyes suddenly clearer.

He's awake, she transmitted, hoping Fitz could hear her. *We'll be there soon.*

"Oh, Sophie, I'm so sorry. I thought . . . I don't even know." His shaky hands fumbled for the magsidian and he held it next to his balefire pendant. "Let me get us out of here."

He spun the balefire crystal until he found the facet he wanted and touched the point of the magsidian to the edge. The black stone turned iridescent, flashing an almost blinding beam of light toward the ground.

Alden couldn't stand as he grabbed Sophie's arm and told her to concentrate. But he rolled them into the icy light, blasting them out of Exile.

The sudden sunlight nearly blinded Sophie as she tumbled across the sand—but the scorching heat was a relief after the arctic chill of the leap. She felt like she'd been swallowed by an avalanche and launched through a blizzard.

A dusty breeze swept across the desert, closing off her throat. Alden sputtered and coughed as he slowly sat up beside her.

"I'm sorry," he mumbled when his breathing calmed. "I'm so sorry for collapsing down there. This head injury must be worse than I thought."

Sophie tried not to look at the wound. "We need to get you to Elwin. Are you up for another leap?"

"I think so." He squinted at the sand where tiny spots of red speckled the bright white. "My eyes are a bit blurry, though, so I might need your help with the pathfinder."

He fumbled to pull the slender wand from the pocket in his sleeve and gave her instructions for how to twist the crystal to the right facet. Sophie locked it into place and reached for his hand.

"I know this day has been quite the adventure—but there's no reason to worry now, Sophie. Everything's going to be okay."

She wrapped most of her concentration around him anyway. Her head ached from the extra strain, but she wasn't taking any chances during the leap.

She was bringing Alden home *safe*.

"It's about time!" Fitz shouted as the glowing gates of Everglen came into focus. He sprinted to their side with Elwin right behind him.

"I'm sorry." Sophie tried to stand, but was hit by a wave of dizziness. "I got us here as fast as I could."

She noticed Alden's confusion and explained about transmitting to Fitz for help.

Elwin picked at the cement on Alden's wound. "What is this stuff?"

"A dwarven remedy." Alden took Fitz's hand and Fitz pulled him to his feet—but he couldn't stand on his own. Fitz threw Alden's arm around his shoulders and steadied most of his dad's weight.

Elwin whistled. "Well, you're a mess all right—but we'll get you fixed up *properly* in no time. And what about you?" He squatted down to examine Sophie, snapping his fingers and forming a blue orb around her.

The light flashed in Sophie's eyes, triggering another headache.

"You're a mess too," Elwin told her as she winced. "I'm start-ing to think your accident-prone ways are contagious."

Alden gave a weary laugh. "This one was my doing, Elwin. And I was very lucky to have Sophie along." He squeezed his son tighter. "Very, very lucky."

"Why were you in Exile?" Fitz demanded.

"It's classified, Fitz. You weren't even supposed to know we were there."

"Sorry," Sophie mumbled.

"You have nothing to apologize for, Sophie. You were in an impossible situation. The fault is mine. As it is for so many things . . ."

He tightened his grip on Fitz again, but this time it looked like he was clinging to him.

"Well, come on," Elwin said, lifting Sophie over his shoulder.

"I can walk on my own!"

"Maybe, but I'm not taking any chances."

"Alden's the one who collapsed—not me."

"True enough. But you're the one who's faded."

TWENTY-NINE

I DON'T UNDERSTAND," SOPHIE SAID AS ELWIN set her down her on a giant canopied bed in one of Everglen's enormous upstairs guest rooms. It was the same bed she'd woken up in when she'd nearly faded away. "How can I be faded? I'm wearing a nexus."

"That's what I'm trying to figure out." He grabbed her wrist, squinting at the meter on the underside. "Did you do anything differently during the leap?"

"I wrapped some of my concentration around Alden to make sure I brought him home safe. But my nexus is supposed to keep me together no matter how much I concentrate, right?"

"That's what it's designed for."

She looked away as Elwin flashed orange around her

wrist, not wanting to trigger another headache.

"The nexus *is* working," Elwin said after a second.

"Then there has to be some mistake."

"Oh, there's no mistake. See for yourself." He handed her a silver mirror from the dressing table.

Sophie's eyes widened.

All her color had been washed away, leaving her lips and cheeks the same pale white as her skin. Even her eyes looked more gray than brown.

"Don't worry—it looks worse than it is. When it's serious your skin starts to turn translucent. And when it's deadly you're practically clear. There were parts of you I could barely see when Fitz found you last time."

Sophie shuddered. "You can fix it, right?"

"Yeah, I just have to make up some of that limbium-free Fade Fuel that Kesler came up with. And in the meantime, I want you to drink this"—he handed her a bottle of Youth—"and try to rest."

He smeared purple balm on her burn and wrapped her hand in a damp silk cloth. "I have to go take care of Alden. Will you be all right?"

Sophie nodded. "Is he going to be okay?

"Of course. He's a little beat up, but it's nothing I can't handle. Just try to relax. I'll be back in a few."

She downed the bottle of Youth, trying not to stare at her pale hand as she set the bottle on the bedside table.

She was going to be *fine*.

She didn't even feel different. Just tired and sore.

She closed her eyes and leaned back against the pillow, hoping to get some much needed sleep. But the nightmares refused to let her rest.

Fire and chaos from Fintan's memories. Madness and mayhem from Prentice. All the horrors she'd seen during her probes, mixed with her own fears and sandwiched together into the ultimate horror show in her mind.

But the worst was a memory she didn't remember seeing.

Prentice, strapped to a chair in a round room with projections on the walls. Sophie had been there once, when Alden brought her to Quinlin's office in Atlantis. But this time all the screens projected the same image.

The sign of the swan.

Prentice stared quietly at his lap as Quinlin circled him, shouting questions. Finally Quinlin wrung his hands and reached for Prentice's temples. Prentice didn't struggle—didn't resist—didn't do anything except stare at the person whose eyes Sophie was seeing the memory through.

Alden.

Sophie could feel Alden's anger and sadness as Prentice thrashed and screamed, and she jolted awake, hoping to bury the devastating memory so deeply in her mind that it would never resurface. But she had a feeling it would haunt her the same way it must be haunting Alden.

Sorry, didn't mean to startle you," Fitz said, making her jump.

No, it wasn't you," Sophie said when she could breathe normally again. "I just had a bad dream."

He sat next to her on the bed. "Sorry."

Sophie shrugged. "How's your dad?"

"Sedated. Elwin needed to do some deep tissue repair to his head wound, so he put him under."

"But he's going to be okay?"

"According to Elwin. And Bullhorn's not freaking out either, so I guess he's right."

Banshees only screamed when someone was in mortal danger—though it was worse when they lay down next to someone. That meant death was far too close.

"What happened down there?" Fitz asked quietly.

"Pretty much one disaster after another."

"I'll say." He held up a small blue vial with an atomizer. "Elwin made this for you. Breathe in."

He spritzed near her nose and Sophie inhaled the medicine, coughing as the tingly moisture hit her sinuses.

"Just like old times," Fitz said sadly. "I used to sit right here, giving you a dose every hour, watching the bits of color slowly return to your face and hoping you'd wake up."

"You did?"

He nodded.

If she could've blushed, she would have.

"Then of course you woke up during one of the few times

my mom forced me to get some rest." He grinned, but there was still sadness in his eyes.

"I'm so sorry, Fitz."

"It's not your fault—though you really know how to give me a heart attack. When your transmissions cut away today I almost leaped to Eternalia and banged on the Councillors' doors until they took me to you guys."

"I'm glad you didn't do that."

"Me too. I guess. Though it looks like you could've used some help."

Sophie stared at her hands, relieved to see a hint of pink returning to her fingertips. "Elwin said it's not a big deal this time."

"Yeah, that's what he told me, too. But he also said I have to make you wear this." Before she could react he grabbed her left arm and clamped something teal and sparkly around her wrist. "It's Biana's old nexus. Elwin wants to be extra careful."

Sophie scowled as he twisted the jeweled cuff until it clicked, leaving her wrist covered in pink and purple flowers.

Great, now she had *two* nexuses.

"How long will I have to wear it for?"

"Until he can figure out why you faded."

"It had to be the stress."

"Maybe."

He fidgeted with the bottle of medicine. *You really can't tell me what happened? Or what you were doing in Exile?*

His transmission felt like a hot poker stabbing her brain.

Still too loud? he asked when she winced.

Sophie nodded.

"Sorry. Hopefully Sir Tiergan can figure out what's wrong."

"Yeah," Sophie told him, hoping the same thing.

She was hoping even harder that the problem wasn't with *her*.

"I never should have let you go with Alden," Grady practically growled as he and Edaline helped Sophie up the stairs at Havenfield. Sandor trailed behind, grumbling about how nothing would've happened if he'd been allowed to do his job.

Edaline squeezed Sophie's hand. "Elwin said she's going to be fine. And he'll check her again in the morning to be safe. Maybe we should just have him move in."

Sophie felt her jaw drop slightly as Edaline smiled at her joke.

Since when was Edaline the calm one?

The good news had been that Elwin didn't find anything wrong with her—and he'd tested her every imaginable way. The bad news was he had no idea why she'd faded, or why she kept getting headaches or any of the other weird things that she'd finally told him about. All he could do was insist on weekly checkups until he either figured it out or the problems went away.

"Besides, I don't think we *really* had a choice," Edaline added quietly. "Alden was on assignment from the Council."

"Yes, and I suspect there were other forces involved too." Grady gave Sophie a look and she became very interested in her feet.

She didn't have the energy for another debate about the Black Swan. Especially since there was a chance now that Jolie had been involved with them. Could her death have had something to do with the Black Swan after all? Even if it wasn't murder?

Sophie would have to find out, though she had no idea where to start.

They left her alone to shower and change, and Sophie hoped the subject was dropped. But when Grady and Edaline came back to tuck her in, Grady kissed her good night and whispered, "Please be careful, Sophie. I just don't think you realize who you're dealing with."

"I—"

"I'm not going to say anything else. Just rest."

He left without another word.

Edaline handed her Ella and brushed a few strands of hair off of her forehead. "You really do need to sleep, Sophie. Are you sure I can't make you some slumberberry tea?"

The last thing Sophie wanted was to close her eyes and relive any more nightmares—but fading again had renewed her resolve. "No sedatives."

Edaline frowned, but didn't argue as she kissed Sophie's cheek.

Iggy settled on Sophie's pillow, and Edaline turned off the lights and left them alone. But when the sound of Edaline's footsteps had disappeared, Sophie crept out of bed and recorded all of the crazy things she'd seen in Fintan's and Prentice's minds into her memory log. The images were even more terrifying on paper, and she shoved the book out of sight, grabbing her Spyball before burying herself under her covers.

"Show me Mr. Forkle," she whispered, not surprised when it flashed UNKNOWN. She wasn't really in the mood to see him anyway. She needed something that didn't involve broken minds or the Black Swan or exiled prisoners or fire and doom.

"Show me Connor, Kate, and Natalie Freeman," she whispered.

The silver orb flashed, revealing her dad, mom, and sister snuggled together on the couch eating popcorn and store-bought cookies. Movie night was a Foster family tradition, and Sophie soaked up the normal scene, hoping it would fill her dreams. Then something caught her eye. A floppy-eared beagle puppy curled in her sister's lap.

One of the few requests Sophie had made when Alden left to relocate her family was to get them a house with a yard big enough for them to finally get the dog they'd always wanted.

She was happy to see they finally had it.

But it hurt, too—so much more than she ever thought it would.

Tears burned her eyes and she grabbed Iggy and nuzzled

his fuzzy nose, trying not to feel so alone and afraid, and wishing she could go back to a time when she didn't have to worry about things like fading and kidnappers and memory breaks.

It helped a little, but what finally helped her regain control was Silveny's quiet voice filling her mind.

Calm.

Friend.

Silveny repeated the words, transmitting a strangely soft warmth, and Sophie sank into the feeling, letting it wrap around her consciousness like a blanket.

For the first time in a long time, she drifted off into a dreamless sleep.

THIRTY

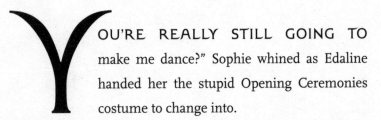

YOU'RE REALLY STILL GOING TO make me dance?" Sophie whined as Edaline handed her the stupid Opening Ceremonies costume to change into.

Why, *why* did she let Elwin tell everyone she was one hundred percent recovered when he checked her that morning? She should have asked him for a Get Out of Dressing Like an Elephant Free card.

"Being part of the mascot dance at the Foxfire Opening Ceremonies is a tremendous honor, Sophie," Edaline told her. "Tonight will be a night you'll remember for the rest of your life."

Oh, she had no doubt about that. She just had a feeling it

would go down in history as The Night Sophie Foster Tripped on Her Trunk and Fell on Her Face In Front of the Entire Elvin World.

But Edaline looked so proud and excited—and it would be nice to do something *fun* with her family for a change. Plus, she'd get to see Alden again. Elwin had assured her that he was completely healed, and Fitz had told her the same thing when she'd tried reaching him with her Imparter that morning. But she needed to see him for herself, with no more gash on his forehead or burn on his skin. Then she'd *really* know he was okay.

So she didn't argue—too much—as Edaline left her to get ready.

She tried pulling back part of her hair and even put on one of the lip glosses Biana had given her, but Iggy still made a snickering sound when she put on her costume. Sophie was glad her mirror wasn't a spectral mirror. Vertina would've had *quite* a lot to say if she could've seen her in all her floppy-eared glory.

Her furry feet made it even harder to walk as she climbed the stairs to the Leapmaster, and she slipped on the smooth floor, landing on her butt with a thud. At least the costume had some extra padding to cushion the fall.

"You're going to love this," Grady told her as he rushed to help her up.

Somehow she doubted "love" was ever going to be a word to

describe this process. But it was nice to see a smile on Grady's face again. He looked almost regal with his amber-brown cape clasped at the base of his neck with the Ruewen crest. Edaline stood beside him, looking like a Disney princess in her long amber-encrusted gown and silky cape.

It really wasn't fair that they got to look stylish and elegant and she had to look like a shaggy elephant. Even Sandor had changed into amber brown pants.

"Does he really have to come?" Sophie whined. "Thousands of people are going to be there—there's no way the kidnappers are going to try anything."

"One can never be sure of such things," Sandor corrected. "It is just as possible that they could decide the chaos of a crowd is the perfect opportunity to make their move—and I'm not going to allow that risk. You're not leaving my side again. Except for your performance, of course."

"Are you sure that's safe? Maybe I should sit with you on the sidelines. . . ."

Grady laughed. "Nice try, kiddo. You're dancing."

Sophie glowered at the ground.

Sandor handed her a flat golden disk, about the size of a human penny. "I assume you have a pocket hidden somewhere in that fur? Keep that inside it."

There were dozens of pockets running down each of her legs—which Sophie thought was strange—but she hesitated before slipping the disk into one. "What is it?"

"A tracking device. I've had them sewn into all of your permanent clothes, but not your costume, since you'll be returning it."

He'd put trackers in her clothes?

How many different ways was she being watched?

She was tempted to fling the tracker back at him—and insist they be removed from the rest of her things—but it wasn't worth the fight.

At least not *that* night.

"Whoa," Sophie whispered as the Foxfire buildings glittered into focus.

A vibrant orange *F* glowed across the glass pyramid, casting a fiery haze over the entire campus. Thin blue strands of light hung like luminous icicles in all the trees and dangled from the garlands that were draped across the main building. But the most striking effect was the glowing green mushrooms blanketing every inch of the grassy fields.

Sophie smiled, remembering how much she'd teased Fitz about attending a school named after glowing fungus. Now they were decorating with it.

The mushrooms were as big as her feet and Sophie crouched to get a closer look. "I thought bioluminescent plants only grew in caves?"

"They usually do," Grady said as he crouched beside her. "But these are a special type of mushroom the gnomes cultivate just for this event."

Sophie stood, squinting at the *F* on the pyramid, which seemed to shift between orange and yellow. "Is that fungus too?"

"It's actually a kind of mold. And the blue lights are a rare type of glowworm."

"*What?*"

"Don't worry, they're far too busy eating the mandible leaves they're dangling from," Edaline promised. "And they're harmless anyway."

"But . . . why are they here?"

The glowing fungus she understood—sort of. But *worms?*

Grady laughed. "Bioluminescent light is the only natural light in the deepest, darkest places on this earth. And Foxfire Academy is all about training our future generations to shine just as boldly. What better way to mark the start of a new school year than by lighting our path with their special kind of glow?"

Sophie was tempted to point out that worms and fungus didn't seem all that special. But then she took another look. The campus really was breathtaking. Even if it did make her skin crawl.

She kept toward the center of the path as they wound their way past the outbuildings to the main auditorium, and Sandor placed his meaty hand on her shoulder as they walked. For once she didn't mind. The black capes the Level One parents were wearing made it all too easy to imagine the kidnappers wandering among them.

The crowd gathered along the edge of the round courtyard

in front of the auditorium's entrance. All the bushes that lined the circle had been twisted and trimmed into the six Levels' mascots and lit with more glowworms. The mastodon was by far the largest, and Sophie couldn't help feeling a bit proud to be a Level Three. Especially when she saw how ridiculous all the other costumes were too. The gremlins had black noses and furry gloves, and the halcyons had blue feathered arms and red beaks, and the dragons had leathery green bodysuits with spikes running down their backs, and the saber-toothed tigers had long red-orange striped tails and pointed white fangs hanging from their hoods, right next to their eyes. But the worst was the yetis in their head-to-toe bushy white fur.

Sophie tried to find her friends, but with the shadows and the costumes it was impossible to tell who was who. Maybe that was the point. No one was popular or unpopular, important or unimportant. They were all just Foxfire prodigies, waiting to start the next year.

The chimes rang with the same fanfare Sophie remembered hearing in Eternalia, and as everyone fell silent, the twelve Councillors appeared in all their finery in the center of the courtyard. The crowd erupted with applause—though Sophie noticed that several of the adults around her didn't clap. And each Councillor was flanked by two bodyguards.

"Welcome to the beginning of another year at Foxfire!" Councillor Emery announced, raising his arms. "We fully expect this year will be the greatest year the Academy has ever seen—

and we look forward to watching all of the greatness unfold."

"Maybe they should spend less time watching and more time actually *doing* something for a change," someone near Sophie whispered, and someone else snorted in agreement. "Maybe then we wouldn't have to worry about our children being taken."

"We understand things have been a bit . . . uncertain in recent weeks," Councillor Emery continued, almost like he'd heard the murmurings. "And we want to assure you that we are working tirelessly to restore the peace and order we've enjoyed for millennia. Our world has changed—but change is not always a bad thing. When we resolve this situation—and it *will be* resolved—our world will be stronger, smarter, more prepared for whatever else time may throw our way. Make no mistake that we *will* endure this unrest, and bring an end to these rebellions."

There was a smattering of applause, but Sophie suspected it wasn't the resounding celebration the Council was hoping for. She could see Bronte's scowl deepen, even in the dim light.

"We also have some other news, which we suspect you will find most encouraging," Councillor Emery added, his voice booming even louder. "Some of you may have already heard the rumors about the timeline being reset, and we are happy to confirm tonight that the rumors are indeed true. A second alicorn has been discovered—a healthy, magnificent female!"

The collective gasps made Sophie smile. If they only knew how stinky and annoying Silveny could be.

Though she was extremely grateful for the peaceful night of sleep Silveny had given her.

"The remarkable creature is currently in the process of being rehabilitated, but we are confident she will be moved to the Sanctuary soon," Councillor Emery continued. "And we will prepare her to bring forth not just a new life for her species, but a new hope for our world. A promise of restoration. A promise of survival."

This time the cheering and applause was so loud it hurt Sophie's ears. Maybe she was imagining it, but the Councillors' smiles looked relieved as Councillor Emery promised an update soon and welcomed them once again to the Opening Ceremonies. "And now," he added, stepping back in line with the other Councillors, "let us celebrate our future."

The Councillors flashed away amid more applause. Then another chime sounded and the intricate golden doors to the main auditorium slowly parted, bathing the crowd in the yellow glow from inside.

Dame Alina stepped onto the landing and smiled at the crowd as she smoothed the silky fabric of her elaborate orange cape and gown. She tossed her dark wavy hair and raised her hands to quiet everyone.

"Lords and Ladies. Sirs and Madams. Parents and prodigies. As Foxfire's principal it is my great honor to welcome all of you to tonight's festivities. Let the Foxfire Opening Ceremonies begin!"

THIRTY-ONE

A MENTOR AT THE DOOR DIRECTED Grady and Edaline to their seats in the stadium and sent Sophie down to the floor level with the other performers. Sandor tried to follow, but the Mentor insisted the rehearsal area was for prodigies and faculty only.

"I'll keep an eye on her," a familiar voice volunteered.

Sophie grinned as she spun to face a tall Mentor with olive skin and light blond hair. "Sir Tiergan!"

"Just Tiergan," he corrected—true to form. "You seem surprised to see me. Have you been hoping they'd find you a Mentor who could actually match your incredible abilities?"

"Actually, I already have that."

"You're very kind. But we both know I can never match you."

Sandor protested as Tiergan led Sophie away, but Tiergan reminded him that only Mentors and prodigies were allowed where Sophie was going, and that he'd be much more useful to her by keeping an eye on the audience, where any real threat would be hiding. Sandor didn't look happy about it, but he stalked off to catch up with Grady and Edaline.

"I take it you've seen the change with your telepathy session this year," Tiergan said as he brought Sophie down the stairs to the cold silver room that served as the preparation area. Costumed prodigies shouted over each other and groups of Mentors struggled to line them up by grade level. "I hope you don't mind having Fitz in there with you."

"No, I like Fitz—I mean, I don't *like* him—we're friends, not anything . . . It's fine," she finished, feeling her face burn.

"Well, it wasn't my first choice," Tiergan mumbled, fidgeting with the topaz-encrusted *F* pinning his bright orange cloak. "But if he can get past your blocking, I suppose it'll be worth investigating. Even if he is a . . ."

He didn't finish the sentence, but Sophie had a feeling she knew what he meant. Tiergan might've been the only elf—besides Dex—who didn't admire the Vackers. Especially Alden. Tiergan had been close friends with Prentice and had pleaded for mercy on his friend's behalf after he'd been arrested. But Alden had gone forward with the Tribunal and the memory break anyway, and Tiergan had never forgiven him.

It had to be even harder for him now that the Council was working to join forces with the Black Swan. Especially since Tiergan had adopted Prentice's son and personally lived with the devastation of Alden and the Council's decision. But now that she thought about it, she couldn't help wondering what had made him so sure of Prentice's innocence.

Did he know something about the Black Swan?

The question was on the tip of her tongue when Tiergan told her, "I need to take my place for the Ceremonies. Will you be okay if I leave you here?" He pointed to the line of Level Threes.

"Of course."

"See you Tuesday, then." He'd vanished into the crowd before Sophie realized she'd forgotten to tell him about Silveny's transmitting. She'd have to wait for their first session.

She tried to imagine how it would be having her, Fitz, and Tiergan alone in a small, plain telepathy room, working so closely together. Just the thought made her heart feel fluttery. She scanned the crowd to distract herself, shouting for Dex when she *finally* spotted him among the chaos. He shoved his way toward her, dragging three Level Ones with him. Two boys and a girl, all with wild strawberry blond hair sticking out around their gremlin ears.

"Hey," Dex said, tugging on Sophie's mastodon trunk and making a trumpeting sound. "Been looking everywhere for you."

"I know—it's crazy here. I thought I'd never find you. Are these the triplets?"

"Yep. Rex, Bex, and Lex. My dad thinks he's hilarious," he added when Sophie laughed at the rhyme.

"Ooh, you're Sophie?" the girl—who Sophie assumed was Bex—asked. "My brother talks about you all the time."

"No I don't—and get back here, Lex!" Dex grabbed one of the boys by his furry collar and jerked him back to his side.

"Yes he does," the other boy—who had to be Rex—corrected, flashing a huge grin with a big black space where one of his front teeth was missing. "He *liiiiiiiiiiiiiikes* you."

"I do not!"

"Yes you do!"

Sophie stared at her furry feet as all three kids made kissing noises and Dex threatened to destroy everything they owned and dragged them away.

"Sorry," he said when he returned, gremlin free. "My parents made me watch them."

"I didn't realize they were going to be Level Ones this year."

Dex never talked about his siblings—they were kind of a sore subject. Multiple births were incredibly rare in the elvin world, and quite a few people thought the triplets existed because Dex's parents had been a bad match.

"Yeah. I'm not happy about it." He fidgeted with his left mastodon ear, unraveling a thread at the end. "I'm sorry they said that, by the way."

"Huh?"

"When they said that thing, about me—"

"It's fine! They're just giving you a hard time."

Her sister had been a master tormenter when she was growing up—though she actually missed it now, crazy as that sounded.

"Yeah," he mumbled, and they both stared at their feet until Marella and Jensi joined them in line. Marella's "ears" hung crooked on her head—and she'd managed to get her furry bodysuit wrinkled.

"Where's Biana?" Jensi asked, scratching at the collar of his costume, which hung loose on his skinny frame.

Marella snorted. "Ten lusters says she's hiding in the bathroom, not wanting anyone to see her in her trunk."

Sure enough, Biana joined them at the last *possible* second—though she still looked ten times better than everyone else. She got in line behind Sophie right as the Mentors called for silence. They gave instructions that didn't make *any* sense—probably because as a Level Three, Sophie was supposed to know that stuff by now. She was glad she had Dex in front of her and could follow his lead.

Dame Alina introduced each grade level as they marched into the stadium, and when all six levels were in position, the spotlights focused on the Level Ones. Dame Alina gave a quick speech about the qualities the prodigies would be learning that year, and then the music started—a raspy tune that sounded like it was made of muffled growls—and the Level Ones skulked and somersaulted, moving uncannily like the gremlins Sophie had seen at Havenfield. The audience cheered when they made their final bow, and then it was the Level Twos' turn. Sophie tried to pay attention as the halcyons flapped and fluttered to a melody of high-pitched chirps, but she couldn't stop thinking, *We're next.*

"Just follow me," Dex whispered as the halcyons filed away and Dame Alina started her speech about teamwork and cleverness. Then their pounding, trumpeting song started and all Sophie could think was *don't trip don't trip* and *why why why do we have to do this?* as she filed out to the center of the stage. Blinding spotlights flashed in her eyes and Sophie braced for a migraine. But all she felt was a dull buzzing as Dex squeezed her arm to cue her.

Maybe Elwin had fixed the problem!

She couldn't tell for sure, but her head felt clear as she squinted at Dex to copy his movements. Her feet kept stumbling and her leg muscles burned, but she was surprised to realize she was smiling behind her stupid elephant trunk. She made the final series of twirls, nearly losing her footing but managing to stay upright, then dipped an ungraceful curtsy.

She did it!

She didn't do it *well.* But she made it through a major school event without falling on her face, needing medical attention, or almost burning down the building. And even though she couldn't see them in the crowd, she knew Grady and Edaline were cheering for her like crazy.

The rest of the dances passed in a blur, and then Dame Alina stepped up for the closing remarks. Sophie leaned on Dex, not really listening to the speech, but something Dame Alina said caught her attention.

"Foxfire is about more than just a top-notch education. It's about helping our youth find their place in this world. Discovering where they belong. And it is our goal that by the time they complete their studies, they're not only ready to handle whatever life throws at them—but to truly know who they are."

Sophie gulped down the words like they were cold water in the scorching desert.

She had the exact same goal.

And for the first time in a few weeks, the future was feeling bright.

THIRTY-TWO

"GET READY," DEX SAID WHEN DAME Alina thanked the audience.

A bell chimed as she dipped an exaggerated curtsy, and everyone leaned back and opened their mouths to catch the white confetti that started raining over the auditorium. Sophie copied them, surprised that the confetti felt warm on her tongue and tasted like coconut and strawberries and other sweet fruits she couldn't name.

"Grab as much as you can!" Dex shouted, stuffing handfuls of the candy anywhere he could store it. Now Sophie understood why the costumes had so many pockets.

She filled everything but the pocket with the tracker, and by the time she was done, the confetti shower had stopped and the Mentors were herding the prodigies outside to the lawn with the mascot-shaped bushes. Dex left to round up the triplets, and Sophie wondered how she was ever going to track down Grady and Edaline in the chaos. But then she spotted Sandor's flat-nosed face towering over the crowd at the far end of the courtyard.

She tried to make her way through the mass of parents and prodigies, but kept getting bumped and rerouted away. She was about to turn back and try a different path when she heard a familiar voice behind her.

"So I wagged my tail when I was supposed to flick it—what's the big deal?"

Keefe.

And the voice that responded was a voice Sophie had been hoping to avoid hearing again.

"The 'big deal' is that this was your chance to impress the faculty—and instead you've shown them you're just as ridiculous as ever. When are you going to start taking your education seriously?"

Lord Cassius—Keefe's arrogant and overbearing father.

"Hey, I'm a year ahead—what more do you want from me?" Keefe asked him.

"I want you to live up to even a *fraction* of your potential."

"No, you want me to be like you."

"And what would be wrong with that?"

Sophie knew she shouldn't listen, but she'd been curious

about the relationship between Keefe and his dad ever since she'd run into them after midterms and seen the way Keefe seemed to wilt in his father's presence. Not that she could blame him. She'd probably done the same thing the moment she'd looked into Lord Cassius's far-too-intense eyes.

"This is why I didn't want to leave you," Sandor squeaked, shoving his way to her side. "How can I protect you in all this commotion?"

Before Sophie could answer she heard someone near her whisper, "That's the girl who was taken." Several others mumbled something about "unsafe" and suddenly the crowd around them had scooted away, leaving a wide bubble of space.

Sophie's face flamed.

"You sure know how to clear a path, Foster," Keefe said behind her, making her cheeks feel even hotter. He smirked when she turned to face him. "Nice trunk."

"Nice fangs." It was hard to recognize him with the hood covering his messy hair and the white fabric pieces dangling on each side of his face.

"We seem to have a habit of running into each other, don't we, Miss Foster?" Keefe's dad asked, forcing her to finally look at him. He smoothed his immaculate blond hair and treated her to one of his tight smiles, which never quite reached his eyes.

"Only twice now, Lord Cassius." And she would do everything she could to make sure there wasn't a third. She hated the way he stared at her. Like any second he expected her to sprout an extra brain and use it to take over the world.

"How goes your progress with the alicorn?" he asked. "I hear you've had some *trouble*."

The way he emphasized the last word made her wonder if he'd heard about their suspicious intruder. But she wasn't supposed to talk about that, so she just shrugged and said, "Silveny's really stubborn, which makes things a little harder."

"Well, *that* I can definitely understand." He glared at his son.

Sophie waited for Keefe to snap back with a joke, but he just stared at his feet like he hadn't heard.

She kind of hoped he hadn't.

"Well, I should get back to Grady and Edaline," she said, slipping away before Lord Cassius could stop her. "I'll see you on Monday, Keefe."

"Let the Foster Adventures begin," Keefe called after her.

Sophie could hear them return to arguing as Sandor led her to where Grady and Edaline were. But she stopped paying attention when she spotted Alden and Della.

Alden laughed as Sophie ran to his side and strangled him with a hug. "It's good to see you, too, Sophie."

She dried her tears on his orange cape. It felt so good to hear him sound like *Alden* again. She knew Elwin and Fitz had promised her that Alden was fine, but she still pulled back from the hug to examine him herself. He looked *much* better, but there was a line on his forehead where the gash had been.

Alden touched the scar. "It'll be gone in a couple of days. Some wounds need a little more time. But there's no reason to worry. How about you? You look a little different since the last time I saw you."

He tugged on her floppy ears.

Sophie smiled. "Can I take this stupid thing off yet?"

"I wish," Biana grumbled as she and Fitz—who somehow managed to look good as a saber-toothed tiger—joined them. "We still have to do the elite dedication."

"That's my favorite part," Della said, reaching for Alden's hand.

Sophie followed their gaze to the two twisted towers that stood on their own in the distance, one made of pure silver, the other of gold.

"I still can't believe you have a session in the Silver Tower," Biana said as the spotlights around the towers dimmed.

"Seriously?" Fitz asked. His eyes widened when Sophie nodded. "Well . . . wow. That's crazy."

He smiled as he said it, but Sophie could hear a hint of envy in his voice. If he only knew how much she was dreading it. Now that she'd seen Prentice, it would be even harder to face Wylie if she ran into him.

"How many prodigies live in the towers?" she asked, hoping it was a *lot*.

A loud chime drowned out Fitz's answer and the crowd fell silent as the arched doors on each building parted. Two streams of prodigies in silver and gold cloaks filed out and lined up around their towers, facing the crowd. Sophie tried to guess which one could be Wylie, but it was hard to tell in the dim light. Before she could spot him, they turned away and raised their hands toward the stars.

A flash of purple gleamed from the roofs, bathing everything in an unearthly glow.

"The splendors just bloomed," Fitz explained as everyone applauded. "They're a rare plant that only flowers once a year, and every elite prodigy has to cultivate one to have it bloom at the Opening Ceremonies. It's their gift for future generations."

"Why does it smell like feet?" she asked, gagging.

Biana plugged her nose. "It is pretty gross. But it draws the flickerwings."

She pointed to the sky, where thousands of twinkling sparks were sweeping in from every direction. At first Sophie thought they were fireflies, but when they got closer she realized they were some sort of glowing moth or butterfly. They landed on the towers, coating the gleaming buildings in iridescent flecks as a slow, lilting melody began to play, and the elite prodigies started to dip and twirl and spin.

The dance was supposed to be calm and peaceful, but Sophie felt the opposite when she spotted a dark-skinned elf who looked uncannily like his father.

"That's Wylie, isn't it?" Sophie whispered to Alden.

Alden tensed at the name, and his voice cracked as he looked where she'd pointed and said, "Yes, I believe it is."

She watched Wylie leap and sway to the music and wondered if he was wishing the same thing she was.

That his dad could be there to see him.

"Do you think he blames me for what happened to his father?" Sophie asked, barely able to find her voice.

Several seconds passed and she wondered if Alden had heard her. But then he murmured, "No, Sophie. He blames me."

The sorrow in his tone made her wish she could tell him that wasn't true. But if Tiergan blamed Alden, it was pretty safe to assume Wylie did too.

It probably didn't matter. No one could change anything that had happened. If Wylie did blame her, all she could do was avoid him and hope he didn't cause a scene if they somehow ran into each other.

The music faded to silence, and the audience erupted into applause as the boys bowed and the girls curtsied and the tower chime sounded again, sending the flitterwings scattering. By the time the last flitterwing had fluttered away, the elite prodigies had formed two perfect lines and were filing back into their gleaming towers as the purple glow faded. Dame Alina's voice cut through the darkness, thanking everyone for coming to support the future generations. Then the chimes in all the towers began chiming an intricate melody as the crowd applauded and turned to disperse.

"What's wrong?" Della asked, sounding suddenly worried.

Sophie glanced at Alden, surprised to see how pale he looked. And he was shaking.

He reached up, pressing his forehead, where the wound had been. "My head . . ."

His words trailed into a moan.

"What's wrong, Dad?" Fitz asked, shoving past Sophie to steady Alden as he started to sway.

"I—I can't—" Alden tried, but a groan swallowed the thought and he collapsed into Fitz's arms.

For a moment everyone just stood there as Alden trembled.

Then Grady took charge. "We need to get him home. I'll hail Elwin and tell him to meet us there."

He held up a pathfinder and helped shoulder Alden's weight as he and Fitz leaped away. Edaline took Della and Biana with her, ordering Sandor to take Sophie back to Havenfield. They vanished into the light before Sophie could protest.

She stared at the empty space where they'd all been.

No one around her seemed to notice the Vackers' sudden departure, too busy laughing and eating candy and gathering their children to head to their own homes.

"I should've gone with them," Sophie said, ripping her stupid headpiece off and flinging it on the grass.

"Lady Ruewen instructed me to take you to Havenfield," Sandor said as he retrieved the stupid piece of costume. "I'm sure they'll be joining us as soon as Elwin arrives to tend to Lord Vacker."

"But I should be there!"

Why didn't they take her with them?

Sandor placed a hand on her shoulder. "You should be where your family instructed."

She stalked away, looking for someone—anyone—who could take her to Everglen. But everyone was avoiding "the girl who was taken," like they'd rather pretend she didn't exist.

"Whoa—what's going on, Foster?" Keefe asked as he rushed over from shadows. "I can feel your panic from, like, halfway across the courtyard."

"I . . . I don't know." She tried not to cry as she explained, but a few tears still leaked down her cheeks.

"Hey—it's okay," Keefe said, raising his arms like he might hug her and then dropping them back to his sides. He pushed back his hood, rumpling his messy hair before he said, "Alden's going to be fine. Remember—Elwin's a genius. Look at how many times he's brought you back from the dead."

He meant it as a joke, but Sophie couldn't get past the word "dead."

"If you'd seen how pale Alden looked . . . ," she whispered.

"Yeah, I'm sure it was pretty scary. But trust me, Sophie— *nothing* was scarier than the way you looked when you were fading away. I really didn't think . . ." He cleared his throat. "Anyway, my point is, Elwin got you back to normal. If he could do *that*, he can do anything."

Sophie tried to nod, but her mind was too distracted by memories of the vivid streaks of blood that had streamed down Alden's face in Exile.

Could Alden have *permanent* brain damage?

No—Keefe was right. Elwin *always* had a cure. He must've missed something the first time.

But how could he miss something?

"Hey," Keefe said, stepping closer. "Don't worry, okay? Am I ever wrong?"

"Yes."

"That hurts, Foster. And I'm right about this. Elwin will fix everything, I promise."

"Come on, Miss Foster," Sandor said quietly. "I need to get you back to Havenfield. Your parents might already be waiting for you."

"He's right," Keefe told her. "Go home. And plan on me giving you a great big 'I told you so' tomorrow."

She wanted to resist—but what choice did she have?

She pulled out her home crystal and held it up to the light.

Keefe reached for her hand like he was going to grab it, but at the last second he pulled back and gave her a small salute instead, promising that he'd check on the Vackers the next day.

Sophie wished she could feel as confident as he did. But as the rushing warmth pulled her away, she had a horrible feeling everything was about to fall apart.

THIRTY-THREE

BIANA DIDN'T SMILE AS SHE OPENED
the gleaming gates to let Sophie into Everglen
the next morning. Her pale green tunic was
wrinkled and tied with a sloppy knot, and her
hair was pulled back in a boring ponytail. With hair bumps.

"Is it that bad?" Sophie asked, feeling her already knotted
insides twist even tighter.

When Grady and Edaline had come home the night before,
all they could tell her was that Elwin was working on Alden
and they were sure he'd be fine. And when Sophie had tried
hailing Alden with her Imparter first thing in the morning,
Della had simply told her to come right over.

"My mom keeps saying he'll be okay," Biana said, her

gloss-free lips trembling slightly. "But, I don't know . . ."

They rushed down the winding path, and Biana explained how Elwin had been there all night trying different balms and medicines, but so far the only thing that helped were sedatives—and even those didn't work the right way. By the time they reached the mansion, Sophie felt like she couldn't breathe.

Alden *had* to be okay.

"Oh, Sophie," Della said, appearing out of thin air in the hallway. "Thank you for coming."

Della wore a pale pink strapless gown with a full skirt of wispy tulle that swished as she moved, and her lips were painted with sparkly pink gloss. It seemed strange that she would be so dressy, but Sophie wondered if Della was trying to prove that nothing was wrong. Her human mom used to do that sometimes when she didn't want her or her sister to worry.

It only made her worry more.

"Can I see him?" Sophie whispered as Della wrapped her in a hug, squeezing a bit too tight.

"Of course." Her hands shook as she let Sophie go, and she took a deep breath and smoothed the feathery layers of her skirt before she turned and motioned for Sophie to follow.

A few steps in, Sophie realized Biana wasn't with her. She turned back and Biana shook her head, sinking into the nearest chair and wrapping her arms around herself.

"She's having a hard time," Della whispered. "Best to just give her some space."

"Is Alden—"

"He's going to be fine."

Della led her up the twisting silver stairway to the third floor, and every step they took seemed to thunder off the crystal walls. Della blinked in and out of sight in the prismlike hallway, finally stopping at two arched doors that led to one of the mansion's many crystal towers. A jeweled mosaic had been carefully assembled across the gleaming metal—yellow birds with scarlet beaks soaring through a cloudless sky. Della knocked quietly, waiting for Elwin to call "Come in" before pulling open the door.

Sophie's mouth went dry as she entered the wide round room. Thin columns of white silk cascaded from the peaked crystal roof and draped around a silver-posted bed. A vine with bell-shaped flowers trailed down each swath, anchoring the fragile fabric to the ground—which was blanketed in white petals. The room should've been bright and breathtaking, but a strange sort of gloom hung over everything. Even the yetis on Elwin's tunic seemed dull and sedate.

Glittering hallways branched off the sides of the room, leading to other private spaces, but Sophie forced herself to finally look at the pale figure in the bed with his eyes closed.

"How is he?" she asked, relieved when she noticed his chest moving. Breathing was a good sign.

Elwin flashed a purple orb around Alden's head and adjusted his iridescent spectacles. "I have no idea. His wound healed perfectly. His cells are clean, no signs of any toxins.

I've checked his nerves, his veins, his muscles, not to mention I searched him head to toe for some other injury I missed. There's nothing *wrong* with him—and Bullhorn agrees." He pointed to the slinky gray creature curled up in the corner, watching them with his beady purple eyes.

"But clearly I'm missing something," Elwin said, pointing to Alden's unconscious form.

"He's sleeping, though—that's good, right?"

"That's just the sedative. And they're wearing off unnaturally fast. He'll need more in a few minutes."

Della turned toward the curved windows that were draped in silky white curtains, and her figure slowly faded until she was completely invisible. Sophie had seen her vanish many times, but this time it looked more like the sunlight swallowed her—like Della was too weak to fight against it—and she could hear whispers of sobs coming from where Della hid.

"Here we go again," Elwin said as Alden's eyes ripped open and he screamed and clutched his head.

Della rushed to Alden's side as his whole body started shaking.

"Same thing happens every time the sedatives wear off," Elwin mumbled, rummaging through the brown satchel strung across his chest and pulling out vials in every shape and color.

"What are you giving him?" Sophie asked.

"Not sure yet. We're at the trial-and-error stage here."

Alden wheezed and Della wiped the beads of sweat off his brow. Watching them made the lump in Sophie's throat so thick she thought it might choke her. Elwin finally settled on a small vial filled with a thick silver sludge, and Della pulled Alden's lips open so Elwin could pour the elixir down Alden's throat.

"Until I find the problem, all I can do is guess and keep him sedated so he's not in pain. But I *will* figure this out," Elwin promised, squeezing Della's hand.

Alden's thrashing calmed to a weak tremble as the drug settled into his system. Della stroked his cheek and buried her face in his neck, whispering something only he could hear— though Sophie wasn't sure if he was listening.

"Why don't you give us a few minutes?" Elwin suggested when he saw the tears streaming down Sophie's cheeks. "We'll come get you when he's calm again."

Sophie stumbled out of the room, sinking to the floor as soon as the doors were closed. She leaned her forehead against her knees.

"It's hard to watch, isn't it?"

Sophie jumped. She hadn't noticed Fitz standing across from her—and she almost didn't recognize him with his messy hair and red puffy eyes.

He sat beside her, so close their arms touched. Her heart pounded so loud she almost didn't hear him as he whispered, "It seems much worse this time."

"I know."

"What happened on that assignment, Sophie? And don't tell me it's classified."

"But it *is* classified."

"Who cares? My dad is *sick*."

"Fitz is right."

Sophie sucked in a breath as Alvar stepped out of thin air. He blinked in and out of sight as he approached, crouching in front of them and smoothing his slicked, dark hair. "We need to know what happened in Exile."

Fitz glared at his older brother. "Mom said you weren't coming."

"No, Mom told me I didn't *need* to come, because she's trying to pretend this isn't a big deal. But we all know it is. So if there's something you know that might help," he added, turning back to Sophie, "please. Tell us what it is."

Sophie chewed her lip.

"Just tell us what you know!" Fitz shouted. "Don't you want to help him?"

"Of course I do! How can you even . . ."

She took a deep breath to calm down. She knew Fitz was just scared and angry—she felt the same way, and Alden wasn't her father.

And maybe what she knew *would* help.

What do you want to know? she transmitted, making Fitz flinch as her voice filled his mind.

Everything. Anything. His transmissions were louder than ever. *What were you guys doing down there?*

Sophie sighed, hoping she wasn't breaking a major law. *We went there to perform the memory break on Fintan.*

WHAT? He ran his hands down his face as he processed that. *Please tell me you weren't his guide.*

I tried to talk him out of it. But Alden said it had to be me.

Fitz shook his head. *It always has to be you.*

What does that mean?

Nothing.

She considered telling him about the charm and the clue— but had a feeling that would only make things worse.

Something happened during the break, didn't it? he asked.

She rubbed her hand, remembering the blisters.

Fintan burned us when we got near the memory he was protecting. It broke our concentration and I was barely able to pull free. But Alden got lost—

"He *what?*" Fitz shouted, jumping to his feet.

"Oh good, so you *are* going to include me in your secret conversation," Alvar said as Sophie stood too. "Care to catch me up?"

"Sophie lost Dad's consciousness during a memory break," Fitz said, his voice as cold as his glare. "How could you not tell us that?"

"Because I brought him back!"

"You can't bring someone back if you lost them!"

"Then why was he fine yesterday?"

"I don't know, but he's not fine anymore!"

"That's not my fault!"

She said the words with as much conviction as she could. But part of her was secretly wondering if they were true.

"Okay—whoa, slow down," Alvar said, stepping between them. "I'm not a Telepath so I don't know as much about this stuff as you guys do. But I thought lost meant *lost*."

"It does," Fitz snapped.

"Then how could Dad have come home afterward? I talked to him yesterday and he was totally normal."

"I don't know," Fitz admitted, pinching the bridge of his nose. "But you can't tell me you don't think it has something to do with why Dad is unconscious in there right now."

"No, I can't." Alvar glanced at Sophie. "We should tell Elwin, see if it changes his treatment."

"Way ahead of you," Fitz said as he rushed into the bedroom without knocking.

Sophie and Alvar were right behind him, and all three of them froze when they saw Alden thrashing on the bed in a seizure.

"Clearly the last elixir I gave him wasn't the right one," Elwin explained, pinning Alden's shoulders and holding him steady as Della held his legs down.

Alden started to moan and Sophie covered her ears—but it couldn't stop the sound from crawling under her skin.

He sounded just like the prisoners in . . .

She smothered the thought as Fitz pushed past Elwin, reaching for Alden's face.

"What are you doing?" Della and Elwin asked at the same time.

"Searching his mind."

"What for?" Elwin asked.

"Something went wrong during the memory break Sophie did with him a couple of days ago, so I'm checking to see if the problem's in his head."

"I think Sophie should do it," Alvar said as Fitz placed his hands over Alden's temples.

"She's done enough."

The fury in Fitz's voice knocked Sophie back a step, but Alvar pulled her forward with him.

"Seriously." Alvar grabbed Fitz's shoulder and yanked him back. "I know you want to help—but Sophie's mind is stronger than yours."

Fitz shoved him away. "Please, she's just a kid."

Sophie stared at the ground, hoping no one could see the tears that had slipped out before she could fight them back.

"Fitz," Elwin said after a second of painful silence. "I know you're upset about your father—"

"Then let me help him!"

"Maybe I should go," Sophie whispered.

Alvar blocked her as she turned to leave. "We may need you."

"No, we won't!" Fitz snapped back.

"I don't think this is a good idea," Elwin started to say, but Fitz was already pressing two fingers against Alden's temples and closing his eyes.

Alden's head twitched and a tiny moan rattled from his chest.

Then Fitz started to scream.

Elwin yanked him away and Fitz collapsed to the floor in an unconscious heap.

Alden didn't move.

"Idiot," Alvar muttered as Elwin dropped to Fitz's side, shaking his shoulders and smacking his face.

No response.

"I think we're going to need that help now, Sophie," Alvar said, dragging her out of her stupor and nudging her forward.

Sophie tried to force away her panic as she sank to her knees. She placed her shaky hands on Fitz's forehead, transmitting his name over and over. When he didn't respond, she pushed into his mind.

His head felt cold.

And *empty*.

She refused to think about what that meant as she transmitted Fitz's name, screaming for him to come back. Icy cold trickled into her consciousness as she searched, but she ignored the shivers, shoving deeper into his mind until she finally found a thread of warmth. She followed it to the nook, calling for Fitz over and over and filling the space with images of his friends and family until the warmth surged all around her, and Fitz's mental voice whispered, *Sophie.*

She pulled her mind free and Fitz's eyes popped open, wild and wide and darting all over the room. He shook so hard his teeth chattered.

Elwin fumbled through his vials of medicine as Della dropped to the floor next to Fitz, her huge skirt fanning out with a swoosh of air. She cradled him in her arms and brushed his sweaty hair back from his forehead with gentle fingers. "What happened?" she asked Sophie. "I don't understand."

Sophie didn't answer as she stumbled away, needing space to breathe.

She could only think of one possible explanation—but it couldn't be that.

Please, don't let it be that.

Fitz wrapped his arms around his mom, still shivering. "Dad's mind was cold and dark and everything felt . . . wrong. I couldn't get back out."

"No," Sophie whispered, grabbing the nearest thing to steady herself. It turned out to be Alvar's arm.

"What does that mean?" Alvar asked as she leaned her full weight on him.

Sophie closed her eyes, unable to look at anyone as she forced the words out of her mouth—the words that would change everything.

"I think it means Alden's mind is broken."

THIRTY-FOUR

O!" DELLA SHOUTED AS SHE RAN
to Alden's side and shook him. "He's still
here. He's not some mindless, broken . . ."

Alden started twitching and groaning,
silencing her argument.

"Maybe I should try prob—"

"No," Elwin snapped, blocking Sophie as she tried to get to
Alden.

"But what if I can help him? I helped Fitz."

"You didn't help me," Fitz said, trying to sit up and only
managing to flail.

"You'd be lost if it weren't for her, Fitz," Alvar said quietly. "But
lost is different than *broken,* Sophie. You're sure my dad is . . ."

"That's the only reason why Fitz would get pulled under. And why everything in Alden's mind would look *wrong*. But maybe I should check."

"No! No one is going to try *anything* else," Elwin yelled. He shook his head as he gave Alden another dose of sedative. "I don't need any more bodies piling up."

"Bodies?" Della whispered. She glanced from her moaning husband to her trembling son and . . .

Collapsed.

Elwin sighed as he bent to check her, flashing an orange orb around her face. "I think it's time for Della to rest."

He looked to Alvar, who blinked, like he was coming out of a daze. "Yes, whatever you think is best."

Elwin turned Della's chin toward him and poured a sedative down her throat.

"We should move her," he said as he lifted her limp body and passed her to Alvar.

Alvar stared at his unconscious mother, his eyes turning glassy. "I—I guess I'll put her in one of the guest rooms tonight, so she won't wake up and see . . ."

"Good idea," Elwin told him, squeezing his arm.

Alvar stood there for a few more seconds, like he hadn't quite figured out how to make his legs work. Then he made his way to the door, and for once he didn't blink in and out of sight as he carried Della away.

Elwin handed Fitz a vial of sedative. "Your turn."

"I'm fine." Fitz tried to sit up again, but was still too weak. "I need to talk to Biana."

Sophie stepped forward. "I can talk to—"

"You've done enough!" Fitz yelled.

Sophie was too stunned to move—to think. She barely remembered to breathe as she watched tears stream down Fitz's face.

"This is *not* Sophie's fault," Elwin said, glancing at Sophie as he crouched next to Fitz. "It *isn't*."

Fitz snorted.

Elwin sighed. "Look—I understand you're angry and in shock, Fitz, but you don't want to say things you're going to regret later."

"I won't regret them."

"How about this, then?" Elwin grabbed Fitz's arms. "If you don't take that sedative right now, I'm going to pour it down your throat."

Fitz glared at him, but he must've realized Elwin was serious, because he uncorked the vial and swallowed the contents, his shaky hands spilling part of it as he did.

Sophie looked away as his head lolled back, reminding herself that Fitz would wake up again.

He'd probably still hate her—but he'd be awake.

Unlike Alden . . .

She glanced at the bed, relieved that Alden had calmed. If she didn't know better, she would think he was just asleep.

"We can't give up," she decided, digging her Imparter from

her pocket with shaky hands. She could think of one person who might know how to bring Alden back.

People had thought she was dead when she was still alive.

Maybe there was still a chance.

Alvar decided he should be the one to tell Biana—and Elwin needed to stay nearby in case she needed to be sedated. Which left Sophie to go open the gates of Everglen. Alone.

The midday sun warmed her shoulders as she walked the familiar path, but it couldn't erase the chill that had settled into her heart. The grounds felt darker, emptier without the promise of Alden's smile and deep, accented voice to greet her when she got back. She couldn't imagine a lifetime without him. There had to be something someone could do.

Had to.

It took her a minute to find the small button hidden on a sundial next to a blue-leafed tree, but when she pressed it, the gates swung open, revealing a figure in a black tunic and pants, nervously shuffling his feet.

"Tiergan!" She ran to his side and threw her arms around him. He tensed in her embrace, but she needed something to hold on to. "Thank you for coming."

"Of course." Tiergan patted her back awkwardly. "What's going on? You said Alden's sick?"

She nodded against his chest and then forced herself to let go, wiping her eyes and clearing her throat so she could explain the situation, in all its devastating detail.

"That's . . . impossible," Tiergan said, squinting at the sky. "I—I have to see him."

He hurried down the path. Sophie had to run to keep up with him, and they didn't stop until they'd reached Alden's room. Sophie was sure Tiergan could hear her heart pounding as he pulled open the heavy doors.

He sucked in a breath. Sophie did the same.

More color had drained away from Alden's skin, turning him pale.

Lifeless.

Tiergan made his way to Alden's side, lifting Alden's arm and letting it fall limply. "Is he sedated?" he asked Elwin.

"For the moment. When he's awake he gets tremors and babbles to himself. But the sedatives don't last." Elwin wiped his eyes, and his voice was thick as he asked, "Is there anything you can do?"

"It depends."

Tiergan's fingers grazed Alden's forehead, settling on his temples. He took a deep breath, closed his eyes, and . . .

Jumped back, furiously shaking his head and gripping one of the silver bedposts.

"I can't," he whispered, swallowing several times as he rubbed his forehead. "I'm sorry. His mind is too much chaos."

Every tiny hope Sophie had been clinging to slowly unraveled. "So he's really broken?"

Tiergan met her eyes as he nodded.

Only once, but it was enough.

The room turned to a blur as Sophie's knees collapsed—but something stopped her from crashing onto the floor. Someone's arms maybe? She couldn't think through the panic and grief swelling inside, clawing up her throat, choking her. Someone shouted something she couldn't understand, and then something cold pressed against her lips.

"No!" she screamed, twisting away.

"It's not a sedative," Elwin promised, pressing the vial against her lips again. "It's just to help clear your head. Please, Sophie, trust me."

She stopped struggling and let him pour the cool, salty medicine down her throat. She gagged, but the liquid stayed down, and as it rushed through her body, the spinning slowed and the blurry blobs morphed back into faces she could recognize. But the room didn't just become clearer—it became brighter. Lighter. Things weren't so bad, really. How could they be when there was this cool rush racing through her, filling her with life and energy and lifting her higher . . .

"Whoa—what did you give me?" she asked, fighting back a giggle that wanted to burst from her lips as she pulled away, ready to stand on her own again.

"Something to help your mood."

This was more than *help*. This was weird, unnatural giddiness.

Her heart was still broken but her head was floating and flying, making it impossible to be sad.

"It's strong," she said, covering her mouth with her hand to hide the smile that had forced its way across her lips.

Elwin ran his hands down his face as he leaned against the bed, staring sadly at Alden. "At least one thing's working right. He's really beyond any repair?"

"I can't believe it either." Tiergan twisted his fingers so tightly it looked painful. "His mind was one of the strongest I've ever seen."

Was.

Not *is.*

"And you're sure you can't . . . ?" Sophie meant to whisper, but her voice came out loud and clear.

"Positive."

"Maybe we should call Quinlin. See if he can—"

"There's nothing that can be done for a broken mind, Sophie," Tiergan interrupted. "Trust me. I've spent the last thirteen years trying."

He turned away, walking to the windows and staring out at the sky. Sophie knew he must be thinking about Prentice.

Broken, *ruined* Prentice.

Was that Alden's future? A straitjacket and a cell in Exile?

"So that's it?" she asked, hating her cheery tone. "We just *give up?*"

Tiergan nodded sadly. "There's nothing else to do, except help the family."

A sob bubbled up Sophie's chest as she tried to imagine the Vackers without Alden, but by the time it slipped from her lips it came out like a squeaky hiccup. She kicked the carpet, scattering flower petals everywhere. Part of her wanted to kick something harder, louder, something that would break into pieces. The other part wanted to giggle and roll in the silky flowers.

Stupid confusing elixir.

"It just . . . It just doesn't make sense," she decided. "He was *fine* before he got the headache. How does someone go from fine to broken in five minutes?"

She could still hear him laughing as she'd tackled him with a hug.

"Something must have happened to set it off," Tiergan said quietly.

"But nothing did. He was just standing there, watching the elite prodigies present their stinky flowers and dance and . . ."

Her voice trailed off as a memory flashed back.

Wylie, spinning gracefully in a silver robe.

She'd been so worried about seeing him at school that she'd leaned over and asked Alden if he thought . . .

And he said . . .

"No," she whispered as her hands darted to her mouth. "No. No. No. No. No. No."

"'No' what, Sophie? What's wrong?"

She shook her head, feeling her eyes burn. Either Elwin's happy-elixir was wearing off, or the truth was so real and painful it cut through the fake haze.

"Fitz is right," she whispered. "It is my fault."

THIRTY-FIVE

I T'S NOT YOUR FAULT," ELWIN AND TIERGAN both said in unison.

"It is."

Sophie looked at Alden.

Kind, wonderful, *broken* Alden. "It was guilt."

"Guilt," Tiergan repeated.

"But, what could Alden possibly be guilty of?" Elwin asked.

Tiergan knew, even before Sophie said the name.

"Prentice."

"That's crazy," Elwin argued. "The Council ordered that break—not him."

"Alden was the accuser, though," Tiergan said as he slowly crossed the room to where Alden lay. "And he was wrong."

He wiped a tear from his cheek and grabbed Alden by the shoulders. "Why didn't you just listen to me when I told you he was innocent? Was this worth it?"

Sophie choked back a sob. She'd seen the sadness in Alden's eyes as he'd watched Prentice in Exile, and the hurt in his features when she told him Prentice remembered him, and his sorrow and regret as he watched Wylie dance—but she'd been so caught up in her own plans and worries she never thought . . .

"If I'd paid closer attention, I could've gotten him help or—I don't know. Maybe he wouldn't be—" The room dimmed and her legs turned to rubber.

"Don't you dare!" Tiergan shouted, grabbing her arms and holding her up. "This was *not* your fault. It was *his* guilt that did this and it would've caught up with him eventually. You can't run from the truth."

"But maybe he—"

"Don't. Do not let any guilt cloud your mind—I mean it, Sophie. Not unless you want to end up like him."

The fear in his eyes was enough to clear her head.

"Good girl," he said, releasing her. "If *any* thoughts like that start to rear up, you must shove them away—immediately, do you hear me? Guilt is a treacherous thing. It creeps in slowly, breaking you down bit by bit. I'd wager Alden's been on the verge of a break since he learned the Black Swan were on our side."

"That was my fault too," she whispered.

Technically the whole thing was her fault. Prentice had been hiding *her*.

"If we're playing the blame game, it's just as much my fault," Elwin mumbled. "I should've noticed what was happening and stopped this."

Tiergan shook his head. "Mental breaks aren't physical things. There's nothing you could've done. And I need both of you to listen to me. The *only* one who could've stopped this was Alden. He let it fester. Which is why both of you *must* shove any guilt away—do you understand me?"

They both nodded, but Sophie was only half listening, too busy replaying her memories from when she was in the Room Where Chances Are Lost.

The headache Alden had when they were down there—had that been a break too?

They'd been talking about Prentice at the time it happened, just like how they'd been talking about Wylie at the Ceremonies. And yet he'd pulled through that and came back to normal.

Why did seeing Prentice's son affect him so much more?

Or did it?

Did he make it through because she somehow helped him?

And if she had, could she do it again?

She pulled away from Tiergan and went to Alden's side, trying to seem like she was just saying goodbye as she focused her concentration. She knew what Tiergan would say, but she had to know, had to risk it, had to try. She owed it to Alden, after everything he'd done for her.

When her mind was as clear as it could be, she pressed her fingers against Alden's temples and pushed into his mind.

The fractured memories were even sharper this time. Daggers and needles and icicles swirling in a dark vortex—tiny splinters of faces and places that were already smashing together into a nightmare world like Prentice's mind. She tried to shove her way through, but the further she pressed the more she could feel the blackness latching around her like cold hands, squeezing and straining and dragging her under.

She fought back, transmitting Alden's name over and over as she searched the mayhem for something—anything. A thread of warmth. A fleck of light. Something she could hold on to and draw Alden back. But there was nothing but freezing shards, and as she started to sink deeper, she realized that if she didn't break free, she'd be swallowed into the madness like she had with Prentice, and who knew if she'd ever be able to escape.

She rallied her strength and yanked her mind free, collapsing backward into someone's arms.

"That was hands down the most foolish thing you've *ever* done!" Tiergan shouted, and Sophie was surprised to realize he was the one hugging her. "What were you thinking?"

"I'm sorry." Her words were muffled by the fabric of his

tunic. "I had to make sure I couldn't help him. If there was any chance I could . . ."

Tiergan sighed and let her go—and she was immediately grabbed by Elwin. He spun her around and flashed a blue orb around her face.

Sophie cringed as the light hit her eyes, feeling a headache flare.

"You look okay," Elwin said, flashing orbs in other colors. "But evidently I can't see mental damage or distress, so who knows?"

"Only Sophie," Tiergan said quietly. "How do you feel?"

Devastated, exhausted, angry, scared. Pick an emotion—she was feeling it.

But all she said was, "Fine."

"Then you're a very lucky girl. I barely managed to pull myself free and I was only in his mind for a second."

"How long was I in there for?"

"At least a minute. I really wasn't sure you'd come back."

"Well . . . I did."

"And you will *not* try that again, understood? I need your word on that, Sophie."

"It didn't work anyway."

"I still need your word."

"I really thought it would work."

"*Sophie!*"

"Fine! You have my word. I just—I don't understand. Why

can I bring back someone lost but not someone broken?"

"Because *lost* and *broken* are two very different—"

"Yeah, I *know*." If she had to hear that one more time, she was going to lose it. "I guess . . . I just thought it might be possible. I can do so many other impossible things. Why not this?"

The only one that mattered.

Tears pricked her eyes and she fought back her guilt, remembering Tiergan's warning.

Which made her wonder . . .

"Can guilt be reversed? Like, if we could make Alden not feel guilty for what happened to Prentice—convince him it wasn't his fault or something—would it heal him?"

Tiergan sighed. "He's not capable of coherent reasoning anymore."

"But what if we could get through somehow?"

"You saw for yourself how ruined his mind is."

But it wasn't empty. There was still *something* there. And she'd seen even more in Prentice's mind. He could still think and communicate.

If Prentice could still function—after all that time—then maybe Alden could . . .

A new spark of hope caught inside her, kindling in her heart and pumping through her veins.

Maybe Alden could still heal himself.

If she could find a way to show him that he had nothing to

feel guilty for, maybe whatever small part was left would find the strength to fight his way back.

She didn't know if it was possible, but she had to try.

And she could think of one thing that could definitely erase Alden's guilt.

If Grady was right about the Black Swan.

THIRTY-SIX

OPHIE NEVER THOUGHT SHE'D *WANT*
to be the creation of a band of murderers—but
now she wished for it more than anything else
she'd ever wished for.

So what if Mr. Forkle had cared?

That didn't mean the rest of the Black Swan did. Grady was
convinced they were evil, and she needed him to be right.
She'd worry about what that meant for *her* life later.

All that mattered was bringing Alden back.

For that she'd need proof. Something she could show Alden
to call him out of the darkness, seal the cracks in his mind,
make him *him* again.

"Someone will need to alert the Council," Alvar announced, appearing from nowhere.

Sophie clutched her chest, wondering how long he'd been standing there.

"I can go," he offered, noticeably not looking at his father. "I believe the Councillors are in their offices right now."

Tiergan held up his hand. "I think we should wait. We need to prepare a place in the house where Alden can comfortably stay. Otherwise they'll want to move him to Exile."

Sophie tried to block the image of Alden locked up in one of those cold, tiny rooms from her mind, but it wormed its way in anyway.

"But if they find out we kept this from them—" Alvar argued.

"They won't. And even if they do, we can explain that we were giving it time to make sure nothing changed. I'm sure they'll be especially accommodating in your father's case. He was one of their best Emissaries."

"But—"

"We're going to wait a day!" Tiergan insisted. "I'll take full responsibility if they're unhappy."

Alvar stepped into Tiergan's personal space. "Since when have you had even the slightest concern for anyone in my family? In fact, shouldn't you be celebrating right now?"

"I may have disagreed with your father on certain things—but I have *never* wished ill on him, or anyone else in your family. I am simply trying my best to help, and as the most senior official in this room, what I say will be what goes."

Alvar's eyes narrowed, but he didn't argue. "I guess I'll go check on my sister, then," he said as he stalked out of the room.

Tiergan rubbed his temples. "I'm probably not the best person to be assisting with this situation."

"They're going to need all the help they can get," Elwin said sadly. Alden started to thrash again and Elwin forced more sedative down his throat. "It's wearing off quicker and quicker."

"Soon it won't work at all. You can't alter consciousness when there's no consciousness to alter."

"So there's still some consciousness left?" Sophie asked, unable to hide the hope in her voice.

"Not the way you're thinking, Sophie. When your sanity breaks, it continues to break, splintering into smaller and smaller pieces. In the beginning the shards are big enough to still react to certain things. But as they shatter further they'll become completely unresponsive."

"How long will that take?"

"It's different with every person. With Prentice it was slow, because his mind was so strong."

Alden's mind was strong too—supposedly one of the strongest in their world. Hopefully that meant she had more time.

"You really think they should keep him here?" Elwin asked as he wiped the sweat off Alden's forehead. "Won't it be too hard?"

"It's better than locking him away in Exile. I've been there, it's . . ." Tiergan looked away.

"He's right," Sophie agreed—though she had another reason for not wanting Alden moved. Once she'd figured out how to fix him, the last thing she wanted was another trip to that horrible place.

Elwin sighed. "I guess I'd better talk to the gnomes. We'll need to set him up somewhere he can't hurt himself if he thrashes."

"And somewhere they won't be able to hear his wails." Tiergan's voice shook as he said it.

"I should probably go home," Sophie mumbled. She was dreading telling Grady and Edaline the sad news, but she needed to start looking for the proof to save him.

"I'll go with you," Tiergan offered. "I should talk to Grady anyway."

He didn't say about what, and Sophie decided not to ask. She had enough to worry about.

She refused to look at Alden's pale, unconscious form as she dug out her home crystal and reached for Tiergan's hand.

This was only temporary. The next time she saw Alden she'd be bringing him the news to pull him back from the darkness.

Friend? Silveny called as she spotted Sophie across the pastures. *Friend! Come! Fly! Trust! Fly! Fly! Fly!*

Silveny, not now—please, Sophie transmitted, rubbing her temples.

"What's wrong? You're not getting a headache, are you?" Tiergan asked.

"No. Silveny's just calling for me, and it's hard to concentrate because I can't block her."

His eyes widened and she realized she'd never told him about her unusual connection to the alicorn. "What do you think that means?" she asked when she was done explaining.

"I can't even begin to guess. I'd long suspected the alicorn we had in the Sanctuary had a mind far superior to any creature we'd ever encountered before. But I never thought—"

"Tiergan? Is that you?" Grady called from the back door. "And, Sophie, you're back from Everglen already? How's Alden doing? I haven't been able to get ahold of Della."

Sophie tried to figure out how to respond, but she couldn't find the right words.

"Why don't you wait out here while I answer their questions?" Tiergan said quietly.

Sophie couldn't begin to express how much she wanted to take him up on that offer. But she knew Grady and Edaline would need her. "No, it's okay. I'll tell them."

Tiergan smiled sadly and offered her his hand. They'd walked several steps before Sophie realized how natural the gesture felt. Tiergan's usual awkwardness around her seemed almost forgotten. Like he'd stepped into Alden's role without even realizing it.

She was grateful for it. But it made her sad, too.

"What's going on?" Grady asked as he got a closer look at their expressions. "Is Alden's injury serious?"

"We have much to discuss," Tiergan told him. "But I think we should be sitting down."

Grady wasn't sad. He was *furious*—shouting hateful things about the Council, the Black Swan, memory breaks, even Alden. Edaline wasn't sad either. She was *worried*—trying to force a dozen elixirs down Sophie's throat, no matter how many times Sophie assured her she was fine. Tiergan ordered them both to drink a mild sedative and they finally calmed, sinking into their chairs.

"I'll have to talk to Grady about the other matters tomorrow," Tiergan said as they stared blankly into space. "Hopefully he'll have accepted the news by then."

Sophie hoped so.

"Maybe I should stay. I'd hate to have you here alone."

"I'll be okay. I have Sandor here with me."

Tiergan nodded. "I must say, you're handling this very bravely. Alden would be proud."

Would he?

Or would he think she cared less than the others who kept falling apart?

"I suspect your upbringing helps you process grief better than the rest of us," he added, like he knew what she'd been thinking. "Death and loss are so much more common for humans."

"Then how come you're not more affected?"

Tiergan fiddled with the edges of his sleeves. "I've known more loss than anyone. Anyway, if you'll really be okay, then I should go. There is much to do before I go to the Council tomorrow. I'll be back here in the morning."

Sophie nodded.

Tiergan made her promise to hail him if she needed anything. Then he vanished into the light, leaving behind a silence so thick Sophie wondered if it would smother her.

Sandor helped her lead Grady and Edaline upstairs, and by the time they were settled into their enormous canopied bed, Sophie could barely stand. She turned to head to her room, but her body felt ready to collapse. Or maybe she did collapse, because the next thing she knew, Sandor was setting her gently down on her bed.

"I'm worried today's events will give you nightmares, Miss Foster. Perhaps you should try some of that tea Elwin has suggested. Slumberberry?"

"No sedatives."

Sandor sighed—a wheezy, squeaky sound that would've made her giggle any other time—but didn't push her. Instead he untangled Ella from the blankets and handed her the familiar bright blue elephant.

"Thanks," she mumbled, burying her face between Ella's ears.

"If you need me, I'm right outside." He clapped his hands, closing the drapes along her walls and leaving her in darkness.

Sophie closed her eyes, waiting for the exhaustion to pull her weary mind into unconsciousness. But sleep wouldn't come.

Iggy's wood chipper snore echoed through the silent room, which felt cold and empty. Sophie was tempted to ask Sandor to station himself inside for the night, but she pulled the blankets over her head, squeezed her eyes shut, and curled up as tight as she could.

The coldness was inside her, though. Shards of ice slicing her apart.

The shivers turned to heaving sobs that shook her so hard she wondered if she'd be bruised the next day, and cold tears soaked her pillow, mixed with snot and drool.

Friend?

Silveny's soft call echoed through her mind, but Sophie was too lost in the grief to respond.

Friend! Silveny called again—more urgent this time.

When she still didn't reply, a warm buzz filled Sophie's mind, soft and sweet, like the crunch of fresh grass between her teeth or the rush of the wind on her feathered wings or the gentle touch of a slender blond girl, brushing her fingers through her mane.

Sophie's eyes popped open.

Silveny must have opened some sort of channel between them and was filling her head with feelings and memories that weren't hers. Panic and instinct told Sophie to shove the foreign thoughts away—but there was something so calming about the pure simplicity of the sensations. No grief. No worry. Just the easy pleasure of running at top speed through a dew-covered meadow, or soaring through a cloudless sky with the crisp breeze blowing in her face. But stronger than anything else were the images of *her*. Silveny shared memories of smiles and laughs that Sophie had felt rather than seen, and she could feel the downy fur of her nose being tickled by soft fingers. The gentle strokes sent tingles rippling all the way to the tips of her hooves—filling her heart with a warm burst of joy. Lightening a darkness and emptiness so deep inside that Sophie had never noticed she felt it—but she realized that was because it wasn't hers.

It was Silveny's.

Hundreds of years of running, flying, hiding anytime anyone came close. Until one day a soft voice entered her mind as she fled, and convinced her to stay.

Friend? Sophie transmitted, feeling the word circle and buzz in Silveny's mind, sweeping away even more of the loneliness.

Friend, Silveny repeated. *Calm.*

The word carried authority, like Silveny was ordering her to relax, and Sophie couldn't help smiling at the thought of being mothered by a glittery winged horse.

But Silveny took her job seriously. She filled Sophie's mind with memories of vivid desert sunsets and moonlit beaches with silver-tipped waves and rich green meadows with flowers in every color of the rainbow. Cities and forests and islands and icy tundra. Empty, isolated places that felt like the world had forgotten them, and crowded, cluttered places where voices smiled and laughed as Silveny hid in the shadows, listening.

It was two or three lifetimes' worth of memories, and Sophie's last thought was to wonder how a single alicorn could possibly have been and seen and known so many places. Then her mind finally drifted off to sleep.

THIRTY-SEVEN

SORRY, DIDN'T MEAN TO WAKE YOU," Grady said when her bedroom door creaked, jolting Sophie from her strange, alicorny dreams. "I just wanted to check on you."

Sophie sat up, rubbing the sleep from her eyes as Grady crossed the room and sat on the edge of her bed. "I also wanted you to know how sorry Edaline and I are that we got so upset yesterday. *We* should've been comforting *you*—not the other way around."

"It's okay. It was hard news."

He cleared the thickness from his throat. "I still can't believe it. But I went to Everglen this morning and saw for myself how . . ."

He didn't finish, and Sophie was grateful.

"Wait—what time is it?" She clapped her hands to open her drapes. The sun blazed high in the sky, like it was almost midday. "How long did I sleep?"

"We didn't want to wake you. Dex stopped by, but we told him we were letting you rest and you'd see him tomorrow. You've been through so much."

She had. But still—how many hours had she lost?

"Edaline's over at Everglen, trying to help Della figure everything out. Will you be okay if I leave you alone here?"

"Of course. Where are you going?"

His hand moved to the Ruewen crest clasping his jewel lined cape, and Sophie realized he was dressed in an embroidered tunic and fine linen pants, with his hair immaculately combed. He looked almost regal as he sighed and said, "I'm going with Tiergan to speak to the Council. Someone will need to take over Alden's duties."

Sophie frowned. "You're agreeing to be an Emissary?" She was glad he'd finally come around, but . . . why was he willing to do it for Alden and not her?

"Alden did so much for us," he said, reaching out and stroking Sophie's cheek. "It's the least I can do."

His eyes brimmed with the tears, and Sophie felt her own well up too. She blinked back the sadness. She wasn't going to cry for Alden—she was going to fix him. And if Grady and Edaline weren't going to be home, she knew exactly where to start.

She hugged Grady goodbye and waited for the house to fall silent. Then she threw her covers off and ran for her bedroom door and . . .

Slammed into a wall of rock-hard goblin muscle.

"Ow, Sandor!" She rubbed her forehead. "What are you doing?"

"I could ask you the same question."

She tried to move past him, but he blocked her with his beefy arms.

"Will you relax?" she asked. "I'm not going anywhere."

"If you're not going anywhere, then why won't you tell me what you're doing?"

"Aren't I allowed to have any secrets?"

"Secrets hinder my ability to protect you."

"I don't need your protection for this."

"You always need my protection."

His stubbornness made her want to tear out her hair. She settled for tugging out an eyelash.

"Fine," she said after several deep breaths. "I need to look around a room that Grady and Edaline don't like me to go into, and since your job is to report everything I do—"

"That's not my job," Sandor interrupted. "If it were, I would've told them how you sneak out of bed to read by the light of the moon jars you keep in your desk."

Her jaw fell slightly.

His thin lips twisted into what she assumed was a smile.

"You didn't really think I couldn't hear you, did you? My senses detect everything."

Everything except the mysterious "visitor" who tried to take Silveny.

"My job is to protect you, Miss Foster," he continued. "If you're awake, so am I. But I'm not here to chaperone you. If something you do isn't dangerous, there's no reason for me to report on your behavior. So it would be easier for both of us if you would stop trying to hide things from me."

Sophie studied his face, trying to decide if she could trust him—though she didn't really have a choice, thanks to his super-goblin-hearing.

"Fine—if you must know, I need to look around Jolie's room."

"You're trying to find out if she was murdered." It wasn't a question, so Sophie didn't answer, and it proved once again how closely Sandor was paying attention.

"So will you let me by, or not?" she asked.

"On one condition. If this quest you're on takes you beyond these walls, I *will* be coming with you—and you will not try to stop me."

Sophie sighed. Having an enormous weapon-toting bodyguard on her tail was going to make the whole "stealth" part of investigating pretty impossible. But she doubted she'd really be able to sneak away. "As long as you don't tell anyone what we're doing until I'm ready."

His eyes narrowed as he considered that. Then he extended his hand and they shook, cementing the deal.

He stepped aside to let her pass, but shadowed her down the stairs and through the quiet second floor hallway, stationing himself outside Jolie's door.

"I'll keep lookout, in case your family comes home," he explained.

"I . . . Thanks."

Maybe having Sandor on her side wouldn't be such a bad thing. Especially since she had a feeling she was going to need all the help she could get.

Sophie tried not to think as she rummaged through Jolie's things. Then she didn't have to feel bad about disturbing the careful peace of a dead girl's bedroom. She was just a mindless force with a single purpose: find something.

Something to tell her . . . well . . . *something*.

It wasn't much to go on, but it was all she had.

She checked all the obvious places first: under the bed, between the mattresses, in the desk. Nothing seemed out of the ordinary—though it was strange how much Grady and Edaline had kept everything the same. Books were still marked to the page Jolie had been reading, tiny pots of lip color—long since dried up—were still carefully arranged on her dressing table, even a half-finished bottle of Youth still waited on the small table next to the bed.

Sophie moved on to the closet, which was filled with fancy gowns covered in frills and lace. Most of them were in shades of purple—another detail about the vision Prentice had shown her that seemed far too accurate to be coincidence. But it still didn't give her any clue what the scene meant.

On the highest shelf Sophie spotted two small silver chests that were stacked on top of each other. She pulled them down, coughing as a shower of dust rained around her. The bigger chest was filled with small trinkets, most of which Sophie couldn't identify—tokens that must've meant something for Jolie to keep them, but told Sophie nothing. But the second chest was filled with folded slips of pink-toned paper, bound with a red satin ribbon. Sophie stepped out of the closet, peeling back the lace curtains on the nearest window so she'd have enough light to see the words written in faded black ink.

The pages were all signed, *Yours always, Brant.*

"What do you think you're doing?" a high-pitched voice shouted, startling Sophie so much she dropped the stack of letters.

Papers fluttered everywhere, and Sophie glared at Vertina's face in the mirror. "Don't worry about it."

Vertina's eyes narrowed. "Listen, girlie, I've lived here a lot longer than you—so if you think I'm going to just sit here and let you raid Jolie's things you're—"

"Lady Ruewen just leaped back on the property," Sandor called from the hallway.

"—seriously delusional." Vertina finished. "You can't just—"

Sophie scrambled to the floor, ignoring Vertina's ongoing tirade as she tried to gather all of the scattered letters.

She knew she wouldn't have enough time to put the letters back in the closet—and she hadn't had a chance to look through them anyway—but she wasn't sure how to sneak them out. She wished the Black Swan had made her a Conjurer as she stuffed them behind her back in the waistband of her pants, hoping she'd be able to slip up to her room without Edaline noticing the rectangular bulge under her tunic.

She ran for the door and ducked into the hallway *right* as Edaline came up the stairs.

"Sophie?" she asked, frowning as she glanced from her to Sandor, to Jolie's room. "What are you doing?"

"Sorry," Sophie mumbled, trying to think of an explanation that wouldn't seem suspicious. "I know I'm not supposed to go in there. I just . . . I was worried about Vertina. She seemed so lonely the last time I was here, I thought maybe I should come visit her occasionally."

She held her breath and tried not to move when she felt Sandor reach behind her and grab the letters from their horrible hiding place. If he ratted her out, she was going to strangle him—but he slipped them behind his back as Edaline sighed and shook her head.

"You have no reason to apologize, Sophie. This house is your home. I'm sorry if you felt like there were places you weren't supposed to go."

"You don't have to say that. I know this room is special."

Edaline smiled. But it wasn't a happy smile. "No, this room *was* special. Now it's just a room. And I think . . ." She hesitated for a second, then stepped forward and threw open Jolie's door, letting her eyes wander over the space before she said, "I think it's time to let go."

"I—wow—really?"

"I don't know . . . I watched Della today, clinging to every tiny thing Alden had ever touched like it could somehow bring him back, and I could see how much worse it made everything. This *stuff* isn't going to change anything. So maybe . . ." Her voice faded away.

Sophie struggled to think of something to say.

"We can't live in the past," Edaline added, her voice louder. Resolved. "We have to let the hard things go—what happened to Alden proves it. I'm going to ask the gnomes to pack all of this up, and we can make this room into whatever you want."

"Maybe you should—um—check with Grady first." Sophie knew Edaline was right about moving on, but she needed more time to search Jolie's things before they packed them all away.

"I guess," Edaline agreed, letting Sophie lead her toward the door. "But you're right about Vertina. We shouldn't leave her alone in this dim room anymore. Would you like me to ask the gnomes to move her up to your room?"

It was hard not to groan.

Then again, the obnoxious girl did know Jolie. Maybe she knew something that would help. "Sure . . . but make sure they put her in a corner."

Edaline smiled. "I don't blame you for that. And then I think we should do something fun today. You start your first full year at Foxfire tomorrow—we should celebrate. Start some new traditions. No more living in the past."

Sophie tried to smile back—but it felt wrong to celebrate and start a new year at Foxfire when Alden hadn't been healed yet.

But Edaline was right, too. Life did have to go on. So she went upstairs, stashed Brant's letters in the bottom of her desk drawer, changed out of her dusty pajamas, and spent the rest of the afternoon with Edaline, feasting on freshly made mallowmelt and custard bursts and playing with Iggy, who soaked up the attention. Grady came home in time for dinner, and even though he looked weary, he jumped right on board with the *starting new traditions* plan. He even promised they'd bring her to Atlantis whenever she wanted, so she could pick a new charm for her bracelet. It was one of the best nights she'd had in a long time.

After they'd tucked her in, though, Sophie snuck out of bed and retrieved Brant's letters and her memory log. She started to grab a moon jar, but then she realized there was no point sneaking around. She snapped her fingers, flooding her room with light as she crawled back under the covers. Iggy curled up next to her, and she rumpled his still-pink fur as she unfolded the first letter.

My Dearest Jolie, the message started, followed by what might have been the sappiest love letter ever written. Sophie mostly skimmed—it felt strange reading something so personal—and moved on to the next, which might have been even sappier. Same with the one after that. Brant seemed to *really* miss his girlfriend while she was sequestered away in the elite towers—which was strange that he wasn't there with her. Was he older than Jolie?

The next letter was some sort of gooey love poem, and Sophie was about to give up on the whole pile. But the next letter felt heavier than the others, and as she unfolded it, a small photo slipped into her lap.

She sucked in a breath as she stared at the happy couple before the fire destroyed them. Jolie looked exactly like she had in the vision Prentice showed her—which meant he must have known her in real life. And without the scar, Brant looked like a rock star, right down to the tousled hair and crooked smile.

Jolie had a silver cape with a unicorn pin clasping it across her shoulders, so the photo had to have been taken when she was a Level Eight, the last year of the elite levels. Unicorns were the final mascot.

Which meant it was only a few months before she died. Maybe even weeks.

Brant wore a green tunic with a black stripe across the chest and a crest over his heart: a red triangle crisscrossed by two gray lines set against a background of blue. Something felt familiar about the symbol—but Sophie couldn't place what it was.

She closed her eyes, focusing on the blurry image forming in her mind. A blue sleeve with a similar symbol—though the colors were different. She couldn't remember anything else, and it was only a quick flash. Like the rest of the memory had been lost.

Or *taken.*

She dropped the photo and scrambled for her memory log, projecting the blurry image before it slipped away. As she stared at it, another foggy image resurfaced in her mind.

Curled, squiggly lines stretched along the edge of a hot pink page.

She recognized the paper from an old journal she'd used to write in when she was younger—until she got bored with it. She only remembered using it to complain about the annoying things her sister did. But had she written something else?

She poked at the memory, tried to force it into focus before she projected it onto a fresh page. The image was dim and fuzzy, but she could see the sparkly edge of the pink book and the faintly curved squiggles written in the margin. She didn't remember writing them, and they were too blurry to read what they said. But she could tell one crucial detail.

They were elvin runes.

THIRTY-EIGHT

HER MEMORY LOG CRASHED TO THE floor as Sophie raced for her bookshelf, whispering, "Please please please." She scanned the rows but found no sign of any sparkly pink journal.

She ran to her desk, tearing through the drawers.

"What's going on?" Sandor asked as he burst into her room—but she was too busy sprinting to her closet to answer.

She flung aside her shoes and unearthed a small pile of wrinkled jeans and T-shirts she'd long since forgotten. But what she needed was the purple canvas backpack underneath. It felt empty when she picked it up, but she still checked each zippered section. All she found were a few crumpled candy wrappers and a broken pencil.

She sank to the floor, rubbing her temples as she tried to think. She remembered rushing up the stairs in her parents' cramped house, stumbling down the hall and shutting herself in her room to pack. She'd only taken a single backpack, feeling like most of her things didn't belong to the new life she was starting.

"Please," Sophie whispered again as she ran through a mental checklist of the items she'd thrown in the bag. Shirts, pants, socks, and underwear to last a few days. A scrapbook she'd made with her mom, full of old family pictures. Her iPod. And . . .

That was it.

Fitz had gone back and grabbed Ella for her a few minutes later. But she left the long forgotten journal in the same place she'd shoved it years ago—the bottom of her old desk drawer, buried under a pile of schoolbooks.

"Miss Foster," Sandor said, pulling her out of her spinning thoughts. "Are you okay?"

"Yeah," she mumbled, trying to keep the frustration out of her voice. "I'm fine."

But she wasn't. Not even close.

She'd left behind what was probably the most important clue to the Black Swan—the most important clue to who she was.

She had to find a way to get it back.

"That color actually looks good on you," Vertina told her as Sophie adjusted the mastodon pin on the stupid half-cape of her Foxfire uniform.

She frowned at her reflection. "Really? You don't think I look like a rotten orange?"

"No, you do. But at least it almost matches your freaky eyes."

Sophie stepped out of Vertina's range, wishing she could throw a blanket over the obnoxious mirror. Too bad she was *trying* to be nice and get Vertina to trust her. So far Vertina had answered all of her questions about Jolie by shaking her tiny head and telling her it was "none of her business," and Sophie had no idea how to bribe a mirror into talking.

She grabbed her Foxfire satchel, ignoring Silveny's demands that she come play as she climbed the stairs to the Leapmaster. The muffin she'd eaten for breakfast churned in her stomach, but it wasn't the usual first-day-of-school jitters. Worrying, *Who will I sit with at lunch?* or *What if my Mentors don't like me?* or even *Will people make fun of my monstrous goblin bodyguard?* seemed pointless in the wake of Alden's loss.

Grady and Edaline were waiting for her under the crystals.

"You look so grown-up," Edaline whispered, wiping her eyes.

Grady looked choked up too, but Sophie was more affected by his dark blue cape. It looked just like the one Alden usually wore.

"Try not to be nervous about today," Grady said as he wrapped Sophie in a hug. "One thing that should make it easier is that the Council has decided to keep what's happened to Alden quiet until they figure out how best to proceed. The news will come as quite a blow to many, and they want to make sure they figure out how best to deliver it."

"Can they really keep it secret?"

"They can for a few days."

It seemed strange to hide something like that from everyone, but . . . if Sophie was honest, a tiny part of her was relieved, too. One less thing to worry about—for a few days at least.

Though it didn't solve the biggest problems on her mind.

What would she say to Fitz and Biana?

Or worse.

What if they still blamed her for what happened?

"There you are!" Dex said, rushing to the corner Sophie was hiding in on the bottom floor of the glass pyramid. "I've been looking all over for you."

"Sorry, I didn't want Sandor to freak anyone out."

She'd made him stand against the wall and squat down to be more discreet—though really, she'd been hiding from Fitz and Biana. So far she'd seen no sign of them, and she was hoping to keep it that way as long as possible.

Plus, it felt weird being surrounded by so much excitement and laughter. All the prodigies around her were talking, sharing schedules, trading Prattles' pins, like there was nothing wrong in the world. She wondered how Fitz and Biana were handling it. It had to be hard pretending like everything was normal when their dad was . . .

Sophie refused to finish the thought. As far as she was concerned, Alden was just sleeping. She'd find a way to wake him up soon enough.

"Were you listening to anything I just said?" Dex asked, dragging her back to reality.

"Um . . ."

"Ugh. Never mind. The drama getting the triplets ready for school this morning wasn't that interesting anyway."

"I'm sorry. It's just been a hectic few days."

"Yeah. How was that assignment thing that I'm not supposed to know about?"

"I'm . . . not allowed to say."

Dex heaved a sigh as Marella joined them and asked, "Not allowed to say what?"

Sophie was saved from an interrogation by Dame Alina's projection flashing across the far wall. She gave her most dazzling smile, welcomed them to a new year at Foxfire, and launched into a string of announcements that Sophie couldn't make herself pay attention to because she was too busy imagining how Dame Alina would take the news about Alden. It was a well-known fact that she'd pined for Alden for years—even tried to steal him away from Della on his wedding day.

"She's tuning us out again," Dex said, and it took Sophie a second to realize he meant her.

"Sorry."

Marella shrugged, but Sophie could tell Dex was annoyed, so she did her best to pay attention as they walked to the atrium and Dex and Marella argued over what would be a fair trade for Marella's locker, finally settling on two of Dex's rarest Prattles' pins. She also forced herself to listen when Jensi walked her to her first session, even though he was mostly wondering why he hadn't seen Biana, and every time he said her name it gave Sophie a nervous stomachache. She even tried to listen to Sir Beckett—her new elvin history Mentor—when he launched into a mind-numbing lecture on the establishment of the dwarven treaty. But his dry, toneless voice was almost hypnotic, and the only thing that stopped her from dozing off was the high-pitched wheeze of Sandor's snoring.

Sophie would never forget the way his eyes bulged when Sir Beckett shook him awake, and she was tempted to ask for recordings of his lectures. Finally, she'd found Sandor's weakness.

Her smile faded as she made her way to the cafeteria for lunch. Fitz and Biana usually sat at her table, and she had no idea what she'd say to them if they did.

She had no idea what she'd say if they *didn't* sit with her either.

But in the end it didn't matter.

The Vackers weren't there.

Marella and Jensi were speculating about where they could be when Sophie sat down, but she was able to distract them by pointing out that Keefe wasn't sitting with them either. Jensi told them he'd heard that Keefe had already gotten detention, and Marella had all kinds of wild theories about what he could have done. Sophie spent the hour playing with her brown mushroom sludge, glad she wasn't actually hungry.

Apparently, another Foxfire tradition was to make the mushrooms grown for the Ceremonies into some sort of stew that was supposed to make everyone smarter. Mostly it tasted like dirty dishwater, and Sophie was too afraid that the glowworms might also be part of the recipe to eat more than a bite. She hoped the food would be back to normal the next day.

"Are you nervous about your next session?" Dex asked, and it took Sophie a second to remember what her next session even was.

"That's right—you're going to the Silver Tower!" Jensi said, scooting closer. "You have to tell us all about it—you'll be allowed to, right?"

"I think so." Sophie honestly didn't know. She was still try ing to figure out why she had to take linguistics in the place. Didn't being a Polyglot make that unnecessary?

She pretended to be excited as the bells rang and sh friends to head to the elite towers. But as she mad lonely walk across the purple fields to the twiste ver towers, she was tempted to flee back to Da and request a different session. Or at least

The only thing that kept her moving the Councillors were the ones who'd d doubted even Dame Alina had the p

SH

The gleaming elite towers were so tall they blocked out the sun, and as Sophie climbed the shadowed steps to the Silver Tower's door, she couldn't help feeling like an Oompa Loompa in her ugly orange-and-white uniform.

The arched door wouldn't open, so she knocked, and the thick metal seemed to swallow the sound. Seconds later a tall elf with far too much shiny gel in his jet black hair opened the door just far enough to lean out and tell her, "You kids don't seem to realize that interrupting elite study time merits a week's detention."

"I'm sorry. The door was locked, and I've been assigned a ~ssion in here."

~nticism was obvious as she handed over her schedule,

~d into a smile when he read the tiny scroll.

~dence was forced to return for?"

~th a clank

~ç.

to

~hirst

~e left her

~e the long,

~d gold and sil-

~ne Alina's office

~n explanation.

~orward was knowing

~nosen her schedule. She

~ower to make any changes.

THIRTY-NINE

I'M IN CHARGE OF ENFORCING THE RULES," Master Leto explained, pointing to an official-looking badge pinned to his silver cape. "I'm happy to let you in today, but in the future you should access the tower by submitting your DNA here." He pointed to a silver strip set into the door about a foot over her head. "Oh, you're too short to lick it. Hmm. I suppose that means I'll have to open the door for you twice a week."

Great—because *that* wasn't going to be embarrassing.

Then again, the idea of a shared DNA access strip made Sophie want to gag. She still got grossed out licking the one on her locker, and she was the only one who used it.

"Wait—twice a week?" she asked, checking her schedule

again. Sure enough, her inflicting session with Bronte was also in the Silver Tower.

Awesome.

Master Leto motioned for her to come in, but blocked them as Sandor started to follow. "Only approved prodigies may enter."

"I've been charged by the Council to protect Miss Foster wherever she goes."

"And *I've* been charged by Dame Alina to only admit *approved prodigies.*"

Sandor reached for his weapon, but Sophie grabbed his arm. The last thing she needed was to be the Girl Whose Bodyguard Threatened the Beacon. Even if she had no idea what a Beacon was—and thought it was stupid that she had to call him "Master."

"Is this the only way in or out of the towers?" she asked Master Leto.

"It is."

"Then if you station yourself out here," she told Sandor, "you'll still be protecting me from everything. Right?"

Sandor looked like he wanted to argue, but Sophie pleaded with her eyes until he nodded and stepped back. Master Leto moved aside to let her pass.

"A goblin escort," he mumbled as they entered a cramped, low-ceilinged room. Blue balefire sconces provided dim lighting, and the only decoration was a statue of the Level Eight mascot, a silver unicorn staring at them with glittering black eyes. Master Leto placed his palm against the wall next to the door, which made a loud click, like the door had just latched. "Is that the popular new accessory these days?"

He laughed like his joke was the funniest thing he'd ever heard, and it pretty much cemented for Sophie that she wasn't going to like Master Leto.

"Actually he's there to make sure no one tries to kill me again."

"Yes, I realize. And it's a good thing you left your problems at the door. The elite towers are a place for study and private contemplation. Everything else must be set aside. It's why we're sequestered away from all distractions and worries. To clear the mind for true enlightenment." He crossed to the far wall and placed his badge against a small black sensor, opening a compartment filled with silver cloaks. He handed one to Sophie. "No one may progress farther without wearing the noble color."

Sophie tied the cape over her shoulders, scowling when at least a foot of it dragged along the ground.

"I suppose we aren't properly prepared to have a . . ." He made a strange series of crackly sounds, and it took Sophie a second to realize he'd called her a "wonder child."

She blushed.

"So you can understand my dwarven," he muttered, mostly to himself. "Then clearly the problem's not there."

"Problem?"

"Yes. We've all been trying to guess why Lady Cadence would need to be forced back to Mentor you. Most were assuming there's some problem with your education that needs to be fixed. You *were* raised by humans, weren't you?"

He walked away before she could answer—not that she had anything she wanted to say to that.

The room had no doors except the one they'd entered through. But when Master Leto pressed his palm against the left wall, a panel hissed open, creating a doorway.

He motioned for her to go first. "Your session is this way."

She forced her shaky legs to work, entering a round stadium-size sitting room. Silver chandeliers dangled from the ceiling, and chrome bookshelves packed with books thicker than Sophie's head covered the curved walls. The massive space was broken up with plush silver armchairs grouped around crystal tables filled with balefire, which reflected off the silver floor and painted the room with soft blue light. Everything looked sleek and modern and immaculate. A place where the best of the best went to mingle among other greatness. But at the moment it was empty, save for a few silver-cloaked prodigies who rushed past without so much as glancing at Sophie.

"Tardiness is a serious offense," Master Leto said, leading her to a spiral staircase that wound its way up from the center of the room. He explained that everything in the tower went vertical, not horizontal, and as they passed floor after floor after floor, Sophie wished the tower had an elevator. Especially since the staircase bent sideways and slantways and upside down—leave it to the elves to defy gravity—as the tower itself twisted around the Gold Tower.

They had just passed floor number seven when Master Leto paused. He turned around and gestured for her to do the same.

"This is the Hall of Illumination," he announced as he led her into a round room lined with mirrors. At least twenty Sophies stared back at her—but each reflection was slightly different, kind of like funhouse mirrors, though instead of making her look stretched or warped, the changes were much more subtle. Some had different shadows, or parts of her were blurred, or places were blasted out by light.

"Each reflection is designed to teach us something about ourselves," Master Leto explained, "and one of the requirements for commencement is to learn what all of them mean." He pointed to a mirror directly across from them. "That's the one everyone always solves first. Any guesses?"

Sophie stepped closer, hating to admit she didn't see anything different about it. But maybe that was the lesson. "To be true to yourself?"

He frowned and moved to her side. "This is a *human* mirror. Their mirrors invert and reverse everything as they reflect it back. Look at the *F* on my badge."

She wanted to roll her eyes and tell him she was familiar

with how human mirrors worked. But . . . how had she not noticed that elvin mirrors were different?

"So what's the real lesson?" she asked.

"That's for you to figure out. Master them all, and you've achieved true wisdom. In the meantime, we'd better move along."

She turned to follow him back to the stairs, but light reflecting off one of the mirrors flashed straight into her eyes. She braced for a headache, but instead she felt a strange pull, and a hum of energy started to build under her skin—a warm simmer that grew hotter by the second, until she felt like her insides were on fire.

"Are you all right?"

Sophie blinked, and it took tremendous effort to step back. Once she had, her head cleared. But the hum of the warmth lingered, buzzing in her mind like a swarm of bees—not that she wanted Master Leto knowing that.

She plastered on her best smile and said, "Of course."

Master Leto opened his mouth to say something, but a tinkling chime, like the clinking of hundreds of water glasses, reverberated through the tower.

"That's the warning bell. It means you have two minutes to get to session or you'll be late. Lady Cadence will be most unpleased."

"What's she like?" Sophie asked as she followed him up the stairs.

"Tremendously talented."

Not exactly the information she'd been hoping for, but it was all he said as they climbed past several more floors. Between the humming in her head and the topsy-turvy staircases, Sophie was incredibly dizzy when they finally stopped at a narrow platform that sloped at a strange angle. Two silver unicorns stared at her with deep black eyes from the center of a room lined with doors.

Master Leto pointed to one marked with a rune she couldn't read. "That one's you."

When she didn't move, he nudged her forward, and she tripped on her too-long cape and slammed against the door, which swung open and sent her toppling into the room.

She could hear Master Leto snickering as a Mentor with raven black hair and midnight blue eyes leaned over her and said, "This is going to be far worse than I imagined."

"How was your first day?" Grady asked after Sophie leaped into the Havenfield pastures. He was up to his armpits in dinosaur fluff, giving Verdi her weekly bath.

"I lived."

Grady smiled. "That bad, huh?"

Sophie shrugged. Her topple-through-the-door had turned out to be the *high* point of her linguistics session, which basically consisted of Lady Cadence pummeling her with phrases in other languages and muttering "so pointless" when Sophie translated them correctly. It was the first time she'd gotten in trouble for being *good* at something.

It hadn't helped that the strange humming in her head had lingered the entire session. She'd almost considered having Elwin check her—but she knew Keefe would tease her mercilessly if she went to the Healing Center on her first day. Plus, the sound was fading. Only a hint of it remained now that she was home, and she was sure the rest would be gone by morning.

Verdi thrashed, spraying them both with soggy feathers that smelled like dirty lizard. But Sophie didn't mind. She actually liked seeing Grady back to his regular job. It felt like things were still normal.

"The Councillors are easing me into my new position," Grady said, like he knew what she'd been thinking.

"Is it as bad as you thought it would be?"

"It's *different*. But right now everyone is still so shocked by what happened that we're all scrambling a bit." He glanced over his shoulder, to where Silveny was trotting back and forth along her fence. "Which is actually something I need to talk to you about. The Council is hoping to be able to move up the celebration they've been planning for Silveny's introduction into the Sanctuary. *Significantly*."

"How soon?"

"Soon. I realize it's going to be challenging for you, but I agree with their reasoning. Our world is going to desperately need something happy once the news of Alden's tragedy breaks."

"Have they decided when they're planning to tell people?"

"This Saturday."

If hearts could sink, Sophie's would have.

"There'll be an announcement sent to all residences in the morning," Grady said quietly. "And the afternoon will have a planting in the Wanderling Woods."

"But Alden's not dead!"

Grady swiped the feathers off his tunic and wrapped an arm around her. "I know it's hard to let him go, but we have to. That's why the Council decided to treat it like he's passed away. We all need to grieve, and then move on."

The others could move on if they liked. She wasn't giving up on him.

"But that's why they want to move Silveny to the Sanctuary on the coming total eclipse."

"The eclipse in three weeks?" She couldn't imagine how she would get Silveny ready so soon. "Can't they give me at least a month?"

"No, it has to be that night. Every time there's a total eclipse, Orem Vacker—one of the Ancient members of the Vacker family—uses his incredible talent as a Flasher to put on a spectacular light show called the Celestial Festival. It's one of our world's grandest traditions, but Alden's loss will surely put a damper on the occasion—and that's the last thing the Council needs. They need everyone to feel calm and happy, assured that our world is safe and stable—"

"But it isn't," Sophie interrupted. "It won't be until they catch the kidnappers." And she doubted they expected to catch the kidnappers in the next three weeks.

"The Council realizes that, Sophie. And they *are* working on it. But in the meantime they have to try something else to calm the unrest. Unrest leads to rebellion, and rebellion leads to tragedy." He kicked the ground, and she knew he was thinking of the Black Swan—but all he added was, "We need to make people feel comfortable again. And what better way to do that than by celebrating the creature that will reset the timeline—and the girl who discovered her? The girl everyone has wondered about."

Sophie snorted. What Grady should've said was, *the girl everyone is afraid of.*

"Our world needs this, Sophie. More than you realize. I'll do everything I can to help, but we need to make this happen. If you don't think you can handle it, the Council would be willing to reassign Silveny to the Hek—"

"No," Sophie interrupted again. No way was she letting that happen. "What do I need to do?"

"Better go inside and change. You and Silveny need to practice flying."

FORTY

OPHIE HAD HOPED THAT—THANKS TO her enhanced concentration—*maybe* this would be the year she finally wouldn't be a disaster in PE. But after hours of flying with Silveny and using muscles she hadn't known existed, even walking felt like a tremendous effort.

At least she'd figured out how to steer Silveny by teaching her simple commands like *left* and *right* and *if you dump me into another pile of sparkly manure, I will clobber you.* But the Council expected her to whisk into the Sanctuary on Silveny's back, circle the crowd a few times, and then land in the center of the Councillors. And Silveny still bucked and thrashed whenever anyone besides Sophie got too close to her.

Between the bruises from getting thrown from the back of a terrified alicorn and an entire morning of stumbling and falling because her tired muscles couldn't keep up with the other prodigies, Sophie finally swallowed her pride. She skipped the cafeteria and used her lunch break to visit the Healing Center.

"What is *that*?" she asked, pointing at the picture of her hanging above the bed she was currently sitting on. Or, more accurately, the picture of her in her humiliating mastodon costume in the middle of an awkward dance step at the Opening Ceremonies.

Elwin snort-laughed. "Figured this year I should pay you proper tribute. Just be glad I didn't take Keefe's suggestion and rename this place the Foster Center."

Sandor laughed from his spot in the corner and Sophie glared at both of them. But it was hard to stay mad after Elwin handed her a vial of Achey-Break, and the cooling serum rushed through her muscles and made the pain go away.

She'd just have to steal that photo later.

"You seem like you're sleeping better," Elwin said, studying her face. "Glad to see that. I was afraid you might be worse, what with . . ."

Sophie stared at her hands.

She *shouldn't* be sleeping so soundly—she should be working round the clock trying to find another clue to get to the truth about the Black Swan. But she couldn't block Silveny's transmissions, and the alicorn's emotions were so irresistibly soothing. No matter how hard she fought to stay awake, sleep always pulled her under. And it was such a relief to have sweet, happy dreams after so many weeks of nightmares.

But she was letting Alden down.

Every second she wasted was a second she left him trapped in the darkness.

"Hey," Elwin said, jostling her shoulder. "You're not giving in to any guilt, right?"

She shook her head, trying not to shiver at the reminder.

"Good. Keep it that way. But still." He snapped his fingers, flashing a bright yellow orb around her face.

The bright light hit her eyes and pain exploded in her mind.

"What's wrong?" Elwin asked, but all she could do was curl up in a ball and focus on breathing. Something wet touched her lips and she readily swallowed the sweet serum—not even caring if it was a sedative. She just wanted the pain to stop.

Fortunately it did.

She took several more breaths before she chanced opening her eyes.

"Thank goodness," Elwin said as he wiped the sweat off her brow. "Do you have *any* idea what you just put me through?"

"Sorry. That migraine came out of nowhere."

"It was more than a migraine," Tiergan said, and Sophie turned her head, surprised to see him there. "Elwin sent Sandor to get me when you wouldn't wake up. Do you remember anything about the last hour?"

"Hour?" She had no idea the pain lasted that long.

"Do you really not remember me calling your name or shaking your shoulders or trying to get you to swallow different elixirs?"

"I guess I blacked out." But she didn't remember blacking out. She thought she'd been awake.

Elwin ran his hands through his already mussed hair. "Do you see any problems, Tiergan? Because I can't find anything physically wrong."

Tiergan squinted at Sophie and shook his head. "I can't get past her blocking—but I assume that's a good sign."

"A good sign for what?" Sophie asked, not sure if she wanted to know the answer.

"If your mind were"—Tiergan shook his head like he couldn't say it—"I'd think I'd be able to slip through the cracks. But your thoughts are as silent as ever."

Sophie pulled herself up, moving her head different ways, checking for any remnant of the pain. "I feel fine now. I think it's just all the stress—it's been a rough few days."

No one could argue with that, and she was relieved, even though her stomach was churning and her heart was racing and her brain kept remembering all the times the light had affected her weirdly. She'd gotten better for a few days, but it seemed worse than ever now.

But if Elwin and Tiergan didn't see anything wrong, she had to believe that she was fine. She couldn't worry about one more thing.

"I think you should go home and rest," Sandor suggested.

"If I go home early, Grady and Edaline will worry—and they're dealing with enough right now. I'm fine, really." Sophie stood up to prove it. "How hard is it to sit through an hour of study hall?"

Sandor's glare didn't falter, but Elwin nodded. "I guess you can rest here until the end of the session—but you're going to *rest*. And I'm going to check a few more things as you do."

"Deal."

"I don't like this," Sandor grumbled. Everyone ignored him.

Tiergan excused himself, promising to see Sophie on Thursday and ordering her to hail him if she needed anything. She nodded as she lay back down on the cot and closed her eyes, ignoring the sound of Elwin's fingers snapping. She used the time to try and think of a plan for helping Alden. Her only possible lead was her old journal—but she had no idea what happened to it. The elves wouldn't have left any trace of her existence for humans to find. Would they have destroyed the things she left? Or brought them back to the Lost Cities?

She *really* hoped it was the latter, but she wasn't sure how to find out. Usually she went to Alden with those kind of questions. Who else would know?

The Councillors would—but she couldn't exactly hail them on her Imparter and ask for a favor, could she?

She still hadn't come up with an answer when the bells chimed the end of session. Sandor tried one last time to convince her to go home, but Sophie thanked Elwin—promised she would call him if she felt even the slightest headache—and headed to study hall in the glass pyramid. Dex waved her over to the table he'd saved.

Sophie grinned as she took the chair across from him and got a better look at his hair. It looked like he'd stuck his head out a car window going ninety miles an hour down the freeway. "How was ability detecting?"

"So annoying. They were testing to see if we were Gusters, so we basically spent two hours in a wind tunnel."

That explained the hair. She glanced over her shoulder, then leaned in and whispered, "You *could* be taking technopathy instead."

"Yeah, and be studying the stupidest ability ever," he whispered back.

"It's not stupid—it's awesome. Have you at least told your parents?"

"No. My dad would tell *everyone*, trying to prove that his son's not Talentless like he is."

"Or maybe because he'd be proud of you. It's an amazing ability."

"Yeah, right. I can play with gadgets—who cares?"

"I do. That iPod trick you set up for me was so cool. I never thanked you for that, by the way."

Dex's cheeks turned bright pink.

"Ooh, are we making Dex blush?" Marella asked as she grabbed the seat next to Dex. "That's one of my favorite games."

"Mine too," Keefe said, snatching the seat on the other side of Sophie. "Though it's also fun making Foster blush."

Sophie felt her face get hot and he smirked at her.

"See?"

"Mr. Sencen!" Sir Rosings—the Mentor monitoring study hall—called, slamming his skinny arm on his desk. "Would you like me to extend your detention?"

"Tempting. But I think I'll pass."

The room erupted with giggles as Sir Rosings glared at Keefe—or Sophie assumed he was glaring. It was hard to tell. He had the kind of face that looked like he'd just licked a lemon.

"Shouldn't you be sitting with the Level Fives?" Dex hissed as Jensi dragged over a chair.

"Nah, *somebody* had to keep Foster company." Keefe scooted his chair closer to Sophie's—earning himself an eyeroll from Dex—and pulled out one of his textbooks, flipping through the pages so quickly Sophie doubted he was reading them. He may have had a photographic memory, but even *she* couldn't learn that fast.

"Hey," Keefe whispered, nudging Sophie with his arm but keeping his eyes glued to his book. "Do you know what's going on with Alden?"

"I . . . um . . . have you talked to Fitz?"

"He isn't answering his Imparter."

"Oh. Yeah. He's . . . got a lot going on."

"Aw, come on, Foster, don't hold out on me. Every time anything weird happens, you're always involved."

Sophie knew he was joking, but there was a touch of truth to his words. Keefe must've felt her mood shift because he turned toward her. "Everything's okay, right?"

Sophie bit her lip. "I think Fitz should be the one to tell you."

"That's another day of detention, Mr. Sencen," Sir Rosings shouted. "And one for you, Miss Foster!"

"Ooh, we can be detention buddies again!" Keefe said as Sophie shot him a death glare and went back to her homework.

But she couldn't stop thinking about Fitz.

He was home mourning his father. And she hadn't even checked on him—or Biana.

She felt queasy just thinking about it—but she was their friend, and she couldn't keep avoiding them just because she was afraid of what they might say.

They needed her now more than ever.

FORTY-ONE

SOPHIE SHIELDED HER EYES AS SHE approached the glowing gates, afraid of what might happen if she focused too intently on the light. Her light leap home from school had made her head fuzzy, and leaping to Everglen had made it even worse.

Or maybe it was the nerves.

All the hairs on her arms were sticking straight up, and her knees knocked together as the gates swung open. Edaline—who'd been spending most days there—gave her a sad smile as she held out her hand. Sophie took it, leaning on her as they made the long trek to the house.

"Sophie Foster returns," Alvar said, appearing out of thin air from his spot on the steps outside the mansion. "Welcome to the most miserable place on earth."

She couldn't argue with that. Especially with the raspy, eerie song ringing in the background. "What's that sound?"

"My mom. Today she's singing."

"Singing?"

Alvar sighed. "My mom studied music with the dwarves. She thinks it'll bring my dad back. Just like making his favorite foods should've done yesterday and showing him every picture we've ever taken the day before."

"It's hard to let go," Edaline whispered, wiping a tear. "I'd better go check on her. Will you be okay?" she asked Sophie, and Sophie nodded, even though she felt anything but okay.

"You came to see Fitz and Biana?" Alvar asked, motioning for her to take the seat next to him.

"Yeah—if they'll see me."

He shrugged. "Everyone handles this stuff differently. My mom's trying to 'fix' it. Biana's hiding and not talking to anyone. And Fitz is trying to figure out who's to blame."

"Me," she whispered, feeling tears burn her eyes when Alvar nodded.

"And Prentice. And the Council. He's basically mad at the world."

Sophie watched Alvar shoo away a fly that was buzzing around his face. She felt about as small and unwanted.

"Should I not go in, then?"

"No, you're here. You should see them. Maybe it'll help. *Something* has to."

That left her no choice but to get up and head inside. But before she opened the door, she turned back to Alvar. "How are *you* doing?"

He smoothed his hair and gave her a weak smile. "It's one day at a time."

Sophie had hoped Fitz and Biana would be separate, so she could talk to them each alone. But she could hear them both in Everglen's gigantic kitchen and had no choice but to head there and face the firing squad.

Biana froze when she saw her, turning into a Biana statue that didn't move, didn't blink, and barely breathed. That was way better than Fitz, though. He slammed his bottle of lushberry juice on the table as he stood and snapped, "What are you doing here?"

"I . . . just wanted to check on you guys and see if there's anything I can do."

"No—you've done enough, thanks."

The words stung, but she'd heard them before. And she'd been expecting them. She'd thought about telling them she might have found a way to fix Alden, but it wasn't right to get their hopes up until she knew for sure. So she went with the answer she'd practiced, reminding herself that she was there to help them. "If you want to blame me, go ahead—"

"Wow, I didn't realize I needed your permission," Fitz interrupted.

Sophie ignored him, sticking to the script she'd rehearsed the whole walk there. "I just want you to know that I know you're going through a lot and . . . if blaming me makes that easier for you—do it. You don't have to feel bad later or apologize. I understand."

"Oh, you understand?" He laughed and glanced at Biana, but she was still in stunned statue mode. "So you *really* get why I'm mad, then?"

She didn't, but her best guess was, "Because I went to Exile with him instead of you, and you think that would've changed something."

"No. Because you went with him even though you were hiding the fact that your brain has problems!"

"*What?*"

He stalked closer. "You told me that day—when you did that weird thing with the blinking. You told me you were getting headaches. And you told me you were going to talk to Elwin. But I *asked* Elwin. He had no idea. Not until you came back faded. And I'm guessing my dad didn't know either—did he?"

"No," Sophie mumbled, trying to sort through the questions and memories and horrifying possibilities that were crashing around her head.

Was he right? Did that make it worse?

"That's what I thought," Fitz growled. "So you let him bring you, let him trust you with his life, and you never warned him something might be wrong."

"I told him I didn't want to do it but he said it had to be me!"

"Yeah, well, maybe he wouldn't have said that if he'd known you were damaged!"

The word felt like a slap in the face.

Damaged.

Was that what she was?

"I think that's enough, little brother," Alvar said, appearing in the room. Sophie's head was spinning too much for her to wonder how long he'd been there. It didn't matter. Nothing mattered if she was damaged.

Fitz rolled his eyes and mumbled something about his brother being clueless as he grabbed Biana's hand and dragged her out of the room.

"You okay?" Alvar asked as Sophie fought back her tears. She tried to nod, but she was afraid if she moved, she might crumple to the floor in a heap.

Alvar moved closer and grabbed her shoulders. "Hey. Don't let what he said get to you. Even if he's right—which I doubt he is—it was *guilt* that broke my dad. Guilt for something that happened a long, long time ago—before you were even born."

But she was the reason behind *that* too.

Alvar sighed. "Look, I don't know how to make you believe me but just . . . remember, if you fall apart, then all of this was a waste. Breaking Prentice led us to you—and my dad always believed you were the key to everything. It's why he worked so hard to find you. So if you let the guilt break you, then everything he did was for nothing. Do you want that?"

"No," Sophie whispered, repeating his words until they cleared the fog from her head. "You're right—I won't let this break me."

"Good," he whispered back.

He seemed to realize he was still holding her shoulders and let her go, dropping his arms to his sides. "You should probably head home. Before my idiot brother starts any more drama."

She nodded, but not because she was afraid of seeing Fitz. She needed to get home and come up with a *plan*—a real one this time.

Alden gave up everything to save her. It was time she did the same for him.

FORTY-TWO

A M I INTERRUPTING SOMETHING?" Grady asked, peeking through her doorway. Sophie scrambled to close her notebook as he made his way into her room. "Nope. Just . . . doing homework."

She'd actually been listing the pros and cons of all the Councillors, trying to figure out who was the best one to ask for help finding her journal. Something the Black Swan didn't want her to know was in there. Maybe it would tell her what they were really about.

Grady sat on the edge of her bed. "Edaline said things got a bit tense at Everglen today—or that was what Alvar told her."

Sophie looked away. "It's fine. I was expecting it."

She figured he was going to give her some long lecture on patience and forgiveness, but all he said was, "I'm sorry."

"Me too."

He tugged at the collar of his cape. "I really hate wearing these ridiculous clothes."

He unfastened the pin securing the two ends around his neck and let it slide off his shoulders to the floor. Then he undid the laces on his jerkin, and the top button of the collared shirt underneath. "We all have to do things that are unpleasant sometimes. Which is what I wanted to talk to you about." His eyes dropped to his hands. "Bronte's planning something very difficult for your session tomorrow. Something the Councillors and I . . . well . . . He says it's necessary. And there's a chance it won't even work, but I want you to take this with you tomorrow in case you need it." He handed her a small vial filled with a milky white liquid.

"Dex and Kesler made it just for you. They said this one was especially hard to do without the limbium, but they found a way. It won't be quite as effective, but it should help you clear away any darkness."

"Darkness?" Sophie could hear the tremble in her voice.

He didn't clarify. Just squeezed her shoulder and told her that Elwin was there for her if she needed him. Which only made her more nervous. What was Bronte going to do to her?

"Get some sleep," he told her as he grabbed his cape and left her alone in her room.

She stared at the tiny white bottle in her hands.

Yeah—like she was *ever* going to be able to sleep now.

Her inflicting session was at the very top floor of the Silver Tower—so high that Sophie lost count as she followed Master Leto. The room was bare except for a gleaming silver throne, which Bronte didn't even bother getting up from as she entered.

"Isn't it customary to curtsy when approaching a Councillor?" he asked as Sophie tried to figure out where to stand.

"Sorry, Sir—*Councillor* Bronte." Sophie dipped an awkward curtsy as Bronte shook his pointy-eared head.

Bronte turned to Master Leto. "No matter what you hear, you would be wise not to investigate unless I call for you. Otherwise I will not be responsible for your pain."

"Understood." Master Leto gave a quick bow before he turned to leave, and Sophie tried to convince herself she'd imagined the look of pity in his eyes.

She dropped her satchel in the corner and leaned against the cold metal wall opposite Bronte, crossing her arms and giving him her best, *you don't scare me* look. She had a feeling it wasn't very convincing. Especially when he smiled.

He folded his hands in his lap and leaned back in his throne. "Let's be honest, Miss Foster. You're here because your *creators*—in their infinite absurdity—decided to give an insolent, uneducated girl the ability to inflict pain. And *I'm* here to make sure you don't abuse your power."

A dozen angry retorts pressed against her lips, but Sophie bit them back. She knew Bronte was pushing her, trying to get her to slip up so he'd have a reason to expel her.

He scowled, probably annoyed she hadn't fallen for his trick. "I hear you're not a fan of this ability. Is that true?"

"Yes," she admitted.

"And why is that?"

Because it's scary. And cruel. But all she said was, "Because I don't like hurting people."

"And I suppose you'd rather make everyone feel happy and loved."

"Is that possible?"

"Once again your ignorance astounds me. Only *negative* emotions can be inflicted, Sophie. Fear and pain and hopelessness work best. Though anger works too." He crossed his arms. "Well, go ahead, then."

"Go ahead, what?"

"What do you think?"

"You want me to inflict on . . . you?"

"Do you see anyone else here?"

"No."

His eyes narrowed. "I won't ask you again, Sophie."

Not sure what else to do, she closed her eyes and tried to muster up the right amount of rage. It was hard with no impetus.

Bronte's sigh was so loud she was surprised it didn't shake the walls. "That's what I figured."

"I don't know—"

"Oh, no need for explanation. I'd expected nothing less. You have no knowledge or appreciation for your talent, because it doesn't occur *naturally*. They just twisted your genes, giving you any powers they wanted with no rhyme or reason. And now the Council wants you to harness a power that your mind doesn't understand. Which is why I've had to come up with a way to help you learn how to interpret it."

Maybe she was imagining it, but she swore there was glee in his eyes as he lunged for her, pinning her against the wall.

"What are you doing?" she asked, trying—and failing—to squirm away.

"Something several of the Councillors think I won't be able to do."

He closed his eyes and his hands started to shake.

"You're going to inflict on me?"

He didn't reply—but the icy darkness that seeped into her head told her she was right. She shivered as the cold gnashed at her mind with sharp teeth, pressing and scraping and thrashing. But the pain wasn't unbearable. It didn't leave her doubled over on the floor, flailing and writhing, like the other people she'd inflicted on.

Bronte gasped for breath and the force changed, turning bright and hot. It melted the darkness, consuming everything it touched like fire. The harder Sophie tried to fight the heat, the hotter it burned. And just when she thought it couldn't get any worse, a trickle of the fire pushed deeper.

Sophie screamed and felt her body collapse as the searing heat raged through her mind like an inferno. She thought about resisting, but she'd lost the will. What could she do? She was just a worthless, broken girl with no actual power. She should curl into a ball and give up.

"I *knew* you weren't as strong as everyone thought!"

She gritted her teeth. She wasn't going to let him win.

With the last of her strength she dragged her shaking body to her satchel, forcing her eyes to focus as she fumbled for the vial Grady had given her. She spilled a few drops as she tore out the cork, but she managed to choke down the rest of the creamy liquid.

Ice rushed through her veins and white clouds filled her head, lifting her up and away from everything. She couldn't feel, couldn't think, just lay there and soaked up the freedom of being so light, so calm, so completely unburdened.

She had no way to know how much time passed before the clouds melted like fog in the sunlight, but eventually her head cleared and she rolled to her side, noticing for the first time a figure leaning over her. His bright white teeth were all she could focus on as Bronte bent down and said, "I was right about you. And now everyone will know."

"Told ya you should've named this place the Foster Center," Keefe announced as Elwin handed Sophie a bottle of Youth to drink.

Master Leto had insisted on helping Sophie down the tower stairs—even though she'd told him she felt fine after she'd taken the elixir. He kept mumbling that she was far worse than she realized, and when he brought her to Sandor, he demanded that Sandor rush her to the Healing Center. Not that Sandor needed an order to freak out and become overprotective about her safety.

At least it got her out of lunch detention—though she'd have to make it up the next day.

And it gave her something else to think about besides Bronte's words, which were still swimming around in her head, making her queasy every time she tried to process them.

What was he going to tell the Council?

"I think I should start a pool to see who can guess how many times you'll end up here this year," Keefe said, leaning back in his bed. "I could make a fortune."

"Hey, you're a patient too," Sophie reminded him, pointing to his cloth-wrapped hand.

Keefe shrugged. "It was easier than ditching."

Elwin handed Sophie a small vial filled with a teal elixir. "The serum you took seems like it did its job, but I want to be extra cautious, given what happened yesterday. Inflicting takes a pretty heavy toll."

He didn't have to tell her. She'd never forget the pain—though the all-encompassing hopelessness that had swallowed her was worse.

"So what'd you do?" she asked Keefe, to stop herself from thinking about it.

Keefe smirked. "You're not the only one who can be mysterious."

"He shattered the bottle he was using to catch a tornado and cut his hand on the glass," Elwin answered for him.

"Whoa—way to kill all the fun," Keefe complained as he unwrapped his hand and flexed his fingers. "And it was more like a scratch."

"A scratch that needed three coats of Wound Wipe to seal it."

"And you get on me for being bad at elementalism," Sophie teased.

"Hey, Miss I've-Almost-Exploded-the-School—I am *awesome* at elementalism, I just . . . couldn't concentrate today."

Elwin turned to look at him. "Everything okay?"

Keefe glanced at Sophie. "You tell me. I tried to stop by Everglen after dinner yesterday and the gnomes wouldn't let me in. Said the family 'wasn't accepting visitors.' And Fitz still won't answer my hails."

Sophie became very interested in the edges of her cape.

"Come on, Fitz is my best friend." When she still didn't say anything, he added a quiet, "Please."

She studied him, noticing a tiny dent between his brows. It was the closest Keefe came to actually looking stressed.

Elwin must've noticed it too, because he said, "Maybe we should tell him. The news will be public in a few days anyway."

"Are we really allowed to tell people?" Sophie half hoped they weren't. She didn't feel like reliving all the sadness *again*. Plus, what if Keefe blamed her just as much as Fitz did?

"Come on, Foster—how would you feel if your best friend had something major going on and no one would tell you what it was?"

"I know," she mumbled. He was right. He deserved to know, no matter what. "But . . . it's not good news."

"That's why I want to know."

She sighed. Then she opened her mouth and tried to force the words out. But her voice had left her.

"Alden's mind is broken," Elwin said when she couldn't.

Keefe blinked. "You mean like . . . he has a wound from when he cracked his skull, right?" He turned back to Sophie. "That's what he means, right?"

Sophie shook her head, fighting back tears as Elwin explained what little he could about the Council's mission and Alden's guilt about Prentice. Every new word made Keefe turn paler.

"Are you okay?" Elwin asked, grabbing Keefe's shoulder as he started to sway. He helped him lean down and put his head between his knees.

After a series of deep breaths Keefe sat back up, wiping sweat off his brow. "I just—I can't—I mean, it's *Alden*. He's always been like . . ."

He didn't finish, but Sophie knew what he meant.

Alden felt like a father to her, too.

Keefe sniffed and smudged away a tear. "Sorry," he mumbled. "I just . . . I never thought"—his voice cracked and he cleared his throat—"And there's nothing anyone can do?"

Elwin sat next to him on the edge of the bed. "Apparently not. All of the Telepaths who've checked him have said it can't be undone."

"Is that true?" Keefe asked Sophie.

It took her a second to remember to nod.

She might be clinging to a weak hope with both fists locked tight, but that was *her* secret.

Keefe's eyes narrowed, but he didn't say anything else as Elwin checked his hand and gave him a blue serum to drink. When the chimes announced the end of lunch, Sophie slipped away before he could ask her any more difficult questions. Or decide that it was her fault.

She tried to pay attention in multispeciesial studies—Lady Evera was even lecturing on goblins, and she wouldn't have minded learning a few more Sandor facts. But her mind kept flashing back to Keefe, pale and doubled over as he tried to process the news.

If he'd taken it that hard, how much worse would it be when the whole school knew?

"Hey, earth to Foster," Keefe said, grabbing her arm as she made her way to study hall. "Whoa, calm down, Gigantor," he added as Sandor moved to shove him away. "I just need to talk to her for a second."

"I'll be watching *closely*," Sandor warned him.

Sophie tried to stay calm as Keefe pulled her to the side, but she had a feeling he was about to freak out on her just as much as Fitz had. "What's up?"

"I was going to ask you the same question. I know you too well, Foster—you obviously know something about Alden that you're not telling me, something that's helping you stay so calm about this."

"I'm not—"

"I won't tell anyone, if that's what you're worried about. But whatever you're planning, I want in. I want to fix Alden just as much as you do, and if we work together, it'll happen twice as fast. Actually, three times, since clearly I count for double."

"Keefe, there's nothing anyone can do to fix a broken mind."

"I'm not talking about *anyone*. I'm talking about *you*. And I know you're up to something. I can feel it." He grabbed her hand, sucking in a slow breath as the crease between his brows relaxed. "I can feel your hope. It's not much—but it's there. And there has to be a reason for it. Besides—you're going to need my help. Who knows the Vackers better than me?"

He did make a valid point. But . . . trusting *Keefe*?

"Please, Sophie," he whispered. "I need to do *something* or I'm going to go crazy."

Sophie sighed, looking at all the prodigies around them, many of whom were clearly eavesdropping. "We can't talk about it here."

"Look at you, wanting to ditch study hall. Some people might say I'm rubbing off on you—which is an awesome compliment, by the way."

"I didn't mean *now*. But . . . come to Havenfield after school."

She walked away before she could change her mind.

"It's a date, Foster!" Keefe shouted, turning every head in the corridor and making her grit her teeth so hard her jaw hurt. "Looking forward to it."

That made one of them.

FORTY-THREE

S O, THIS IS WHERE THE GREAT SOPHIE Foster lives," Keefe said as he plopped down on her bed and grabbed Ella from among the pillows. "Wow—you really sleep with this thing? I thought Fitz was kidding when he gave it to you when you were recovering."

Sophie snatched Ella away and placed her on the desk chair, wondering why she'd thought it was a good idea to bring Keefe up to her room. The first time she'd had Dex up there had been embarrassing enough.

At least Iggy was happy. He curled up in Keefe's lap, squeak-purring like crazy as Keefe tickled his belly.

"Only you would have a pet imp—and dye it hot pink."

"Actually, the pink is Dex's fault."

"Ah yes, I forgot about Dex. He comes over a lot, doesn't he?"

"We *are* best friends. And I've been thinking—"

"Oh good, at least one of us should."

"I'm *serious*, Keefe. Before I tell you anything, I need you to agree to three conditions."

"And those conditions would be?"

"Okay, number one: Anything I tell you can *never* be repeated, to anyone—ever. Not even Fitz."

"Ooh, I get to solve all the Foster mysteries—awesome!"

She sighed. "Two, *I'm* the one who makes the decisions—and you don't get to argue with them."

"I don't see how that's fair."

"I didn't say it was fair. You either agree or you're out."

He grinned. "Fine, Foster's the queen of the universe—agreed. What's the last one?"

She stared at her hands, trying not to think about the fury she'd seen in Fitz's eyes the day before. "That no matter what you learn . . . you won't hate me."

"Why would I hate you?"

"Just promise, okay?"

"Uh, that one's a no-brainer. Still not so sure on the whole letting-you-boss-me-around thing. But the last one's easy."

She nodded, still not looking at him.

"So . . . that's it, right? We have a deal?"

"Actually there's one more thing," Sandor announced, marching into the room. "Whatever you guys are planning, I'm in too."

"That might not always—"

"I go where you go," Sandor insisted, cutting Sophie off. "Or I head downstairs and tell Edaline everything I just heard—and more."

Sophie glared at him, but she had no doubt he would make good on his threat.

"Okay, so Gigantor's on the team," Keefe decided.

"And let's get one thing straight, Mr. Sencen," Sandor said, leaning down in Keefe's face. "I am here to keep Miss Foster safe, so you will do what I say or I will leave you behind. Is that clear?"

"Is he always this cuddly?"

Sophie couldn't help smiling.

"All right, so I think everything's settled," Keefe announced. "Team Foster-Keefe—and our goblin mascot—is official. Where do we get started?"

That was a very good question.

"This isn't *nearly* as exciting as I thought it would be," Keefe complained as Sophie finished explaining her theory about removing Alden's guilt and how she was trying to track down her own journal. "When do we get to, like, fly into the line of fire or sneak away to the Forbidden Cities?"

"Hopefully we won't have to do any of that." She scanned her notes on the Councillors. She'd narrowed it down to

Emery or Kenric—either of whom she'd probably be okay with approaching. But the problem was figuring out how to ask them. She doubted she could just leap to Eternalia and knock on their doors. And she'd tried her Imparter and been told those names were "restricted."

"Ugh, this is so boooooooooooooring," Keefe whined as he got up to wander. He'd circled her room several times before he said, "You know, you have *way* less girlie stuff than other girls. Actually, you just have less *stuff*. I see maybe ten things in this whole room that say 'Sophie lives here.' What's up with that?"

"I don't know," she said, surprised to realize he was right. "I guess I haven't bought that much since I moved here. I've been a little busy with school and friends and—"

"Almost dying three times? Or is it four? I can't keep count anymore."

"Yeah. And that."

"But still, I was expecting all kinds of cool human stuff."

"I didn't take much when I left."

Maybe if she had, she'd have her journal—though she doubted it. She'd forgotten all about it.

"Do you ever think about them?" Keefe asked quietly.

"Who?"

"Your old family. It's gotta be kinda weird knowing they're still out there. . . ."

"It is," she admitted. "But it's better this way."

"Of course it is. You belong with us. And you got some pretty cool guardians to live with. Be glad the Council didn't stick you with my family—I'm sure my dad would've volunteered. He finds you *'fascinating.'*"

Sophie tried not to cringe. "Your dad seems . . . intense."

"That's putting it mildly. Do you know we have an entire room at our house dedicated to the Wonder That Is Him? He's covered the walls in portraits and awards and has a life-size statue of himself in the center—carved out of Lumenite, so it glows. I used to have nightmares about it coming to life and trying to eat me. And when I started Foxfire he cleared out the room next to it, saying we'd fill it with all my honors. So far, all it has is a pile of detention slips."

He laughed as he said it, but it sounded slightly bitter.

Sophie tried to imagine living with that kind of expectation. Even with her human family, she'd never been pressured to succeed. If anything, they were always trying to slow her down, let her enjoy being a kid. It used to drive her crazy, but maybe she didn't realize how lucky she'd been.

"What about your mom?" she asked, realizing that in all the months she'd known Keefe, she'd never once heard him mention her.

"She's a perfect match for my dad."

"I'm sorry."

"Eh, it's fine. Disappointing them is actually pretty fun. And they gave me my stunning good looks, so that makes up for it."

He ran his hands through his hair, disheveling it even more—which somehow made him look even better.

Sophie looked away before Keefe could realize she'd noticed.

Grady knocked as he peeked his head through the doorway. His brows shot up when he noticed Keefe. "Oh. I thought you were up here with Dex."

"Nope. Keefe's helping me with . . . something."

"I'm teaching Sophie some tricks for using her photographic memory," Keefe jumped in. "Figured it can't be too early to help her get ready for midterms, given what happened last year."

"Hey—I passed all of my midterms!"

"Barely."

Grady smiled, but he didn't look convinced by Keefe's story. "Well, either way, I need you to come downstairs."

"Is something wrong?"

"Not necessarily." He sighed. "Bronte was a bit *concerned* after what happened during your session today, and he's demanded a demonstration to see how Silveny's progress is coming along. I tried to stall them until the weekend, but I was overruled. The entire Council is waiting for you outside."

Grady looked nervous, but Keefe cracked up. "Only Foster gets the Councillors to make house calls."

FORTY-FOUR

RADY PULLED SOPHIE ASIDE AS
she and Keefe followed him and Sandor
downstairs.

"You're okay, right? The session—Bronte
didn't . . . ?"

"I'm fine," she promised, wishing there hadn't been a
tremble in her voice as she said it. "The elixir fixed everything, and Sandor brought me to Elwin just in case."

Grady's hands curled into fists. "I'm so sorry you had to go
through that."

Sophie stared at the floor. "Why is the Council concerned
about what happened? Why does it matter if Bronte can inflict
on me?"

"They're just a little concerned that your mind . . . isn't as strong as they thought it was."

She swallowed as she processed that. "Why would that affect Silveny?"

Grady sighed. "If Bronte's theory is right, it would affect everything—but it's *not* right. And that's what you're going to show them right now."

"What's Bronte's theory?"

"It's not important."

"Kinda sounds like it is," Keefe jumped in, grinning as Grady spun to face him. "Forgot I was standing here, didn't you?"

"No—I—what *are* you doing here, Keefe?"

"Foster invited me." He reached out and brushed Grady's arm. "Whoa—that is some serious tension radiating off of you. Is it that bad?"

"Is it?" Sophie asked as her pulse picked up speed.

"*Empaths*," Grady grumbled as he turned back to Sophie. "There's *very* little chance that Bronte's right, Sophie."

Very little chance.

That was way different than *no* chance.

"I need to know," she whispered. "What is he saying about me?"

"It's not worth repeating, Sophie—it's just going to upset you."

"Please. I have to know."

When she didn't back down, he shook his head. "Fine, if you *really* want me to tell you, I will—but I completely disagree with him." He ran a hand down his face, closing his eyes as he said, "Bronte thinks that you're . . . malfunctioning."

Malfunctioning.

"He thinks that the new abilities the Black Swan triggered aren't working right—and that it's affecting your other abilities. Why Fitz can transmit to you now and why you can't block Silveny's transmissions and why he was able to inflict on you today."

"Because I'm . . . *malfunctioning.*" Sophie wasn't sure if she should be angry or embarrassed or really really scared.

Fitz said she was damaged—but malfunctioning felt worse, somehow. More fundamental.

"He's wrong, Sophie. Bronte's been wrong about many things—and this is another clear example."

"Of course he's wrong," Keefe agreed. "If anyone's *malfunctioning*, it's him—I heard him try to laugh one time and he sounded like a freaked-out banshee."

"Exactly. It doesn't mean anything," Grady promised.

Sophie knew they wouldn't stop trying to console her until she agreed, so she gave them her best *there's nothing to worry about* smile and said, "I guess I need to prove him wrong," as she headed for the door.

She tried to stay calm as they walked toward Silveny's enclosure. But the word "malfunctioning" had taken root in her head, branching out through her brain, weaving together connections she'd never considered before.

She'd already known she was an anomaly. The way the Black Swan had tweaked her genes was something no one had ever seen or done before.

What if the Black Swan had miscalculated something?

That would explain why she had brown eyes—and an allergy.

"Hey, ease up with the walking panic attack, Foster," Keefe whispered. "Remember, Bronte's just trying to get in your head. If you let him, he wins."

He was right—Bronte had been trying to rattle her from the moment he'd met her. But if Keefe knew all the things she knew . . .

She glanced at the sun, feeling the now all-too-familiar ache in her skull as the light seeped in. Was that another symptom?

Friend! Silveny transmitted when she spotted Sophie approaching. *Friend! Friend! Friend!*

Silveny's eager transmissions only made her panic worse. Were they more proof that her abilities were slowly unraveling?

"Ah, Miss Foster, thank you for agreeing to this demonstration," Councillor Emery said as she dipped an especially shaky curtsy. "We're very excited to see what you can do."

The twelve regal elves stood a safe distance from Silveny's pasture, giving the jittery alicorn her space. Sophie couldn't help trying to guess which ones were siding with Bronte. She hoped it was the Councillors who'd never spoken to her.

"What do you want her to do?" Grady asked, squeezing Sophie's shoulder.

"How about a flying demonstration?" Emery suggested.

"One that doesn't involve feces," Bronte added.

"Especially *glittery* feces," Kenric joked, flashing Sophie a wide smile.

"Whoa—what's this about sparkly poop?" Keefe asked.

"What is the Sencen boy doing here?" Bronte snapped.

"I'm Foster's personal bodyguard now. Gigantor wasn't cutting it."

"Keefe was helping Sophie get an early start preparing for midterms," Grady jumped in. "She has some difficult sessions this year"—he glared at Bronte—"but back to the reason we're here. Sophie, do you think you can control Silveny enough to fly her outside her pasture?"

The plea in his eyes made it pretty clear what her answer should be.

Things must be *really* desperate for him to want her to take such a risk.

"Just give me a minute to explain to her what we're about to do."

"Of course," Councillor Emery agreed.

Sophie made her way to the purple bars of Silveny's enclosure, stroking the horse's iridescent snout. *Fly?*

Fly! Fly! Fly! Silveny repeated, whinnying and nuzzling Sophie's arm.

It's going to be different this time. We're going to fly free. She could feel that Silveny didn't understand the difference, so she sent her an image of Silveny streaking through a bright, cloudy sky. *Fly free!*

The winged horse's enthusiasm quadrupled and she stamped her hooves. *Fly free! Fly free! Fly free!*

"I think she's ready," Sophie told them as she made her way to the gate, hoping she'd be able to explain to Silveny that they had to come *back.*

Stay, she transmitted as Grady undid the lock and let Sophie inside. She could see Silveny twitching like she wanted to take off running, but she stayed put, bowing her head to let Sophie climb on.

"Don't fly too far," Grady ordered as Silveny slowly trotted to the gate. "And remember, you're the one in charge."

Ready? Sophie asked Silveny.

Fly free!

Sophie barely had time to tighten her grip before Silveny spread her wings and launched them into the sky. The crisp ocean breeze made her shiver, and Sophie gasped when she glanced down and saw how high they'd already flown.

Easy, she transmitted. *We have to stay close.*

The giddy horse ignored her, swooping past the cliffs and taking them over the shimmering ocean. Sophie refused to think about how very far down the water was.

Silveny curved farther away from Havenfield.

Not too far.

FREE! Silveny responded.

I know. But we have to stay safe.

She tried transmitting images to help Silveny understand, but Silveny just kept saying *Free!* and flying even farther away.

Sophie glanced behind her and could see Grady—or the tiny speck she assumed was Grady—waving his arms like he was trying to call her back.

Left, she told Silveny, repeating the command over and over until the stubborn alicorn reluctantly obeyed, making a wide loop through the puffy white clouds and heading back toward the house. But she filled Sophie's mind with scenes of forests and meadows and wide-open spaces.

Free, Silveny transmitted again. *Come, friend!*

Sophie hated to admit how tempting the invitation was. Maybe it was Silveny's emotions surging through her veins, or the horrifying fear swimming around her mind, but part of her wanted to let the glittering horse pick a direction and keep flying until they were far away from anyone and everyone who knew what she was.

Havenfield grew closer, and as Sophie stared at the caped figures silhouetted by the sunlight, her insides twisted so tight she wasn't sure if she wanted to groan from the pain or throw up.

Calm, Silveny transmitted, sending a rush of warmth. But Sophie couldn't calm down.

She couldn't face the Council—couldn't face their questioning, condemning stares. Couldn't face what they thought she was. Or the possibility that it was true.

She didn't want to go back.

Not yet at least. She wasn't ready to face that reality.

Free? Silveny transmitted.

Yes.

Sophie didn't transmit the thought, but Silveny seemed to hear it anyway. Her glimmering body surged with a new rush of energy as she tucked her wings and dove.

FREE!

Down down down they went, flying faster faster faster as the ground rushed toward them.

Fly! Sophie transmitted, but she wasn't sure the alicorn could hear her. Silveny's mind hummed with a strange new energy, one that seemed to swell and spread through both of them as the seconds passed, until Sophie's head was filled with so many tingles she thought she might burst.

Trust, Silveny told her as the energy exploded with a thunderous clap and a crack opened in space.

Sophie's scream echoed in her ears as they rocketed into the oblivion beyond.

FORTY-FIVE

THE FORCE OF THE VOID WAS SO strong Sophie felt like her body was being pulled and stretched and twisted. It didn't hurt. She honestly couldn't feel anything except a tugging and twirling as she whipped through the cold emptiness.

Silveny filled her mind with a crisp image: a lush meadow surrounded by snow-capped mountains. Then white light flashed and thunder cracked and everything squished back together, leaving her in the middle of a valley, staring at the same mountains she'd seen in Silveny's thoughts.

"Whoa," she breathed as Silveny touched down on the grassy floor, right next to the misty river. If she hadn't been able to feel tiny drips of the cold water splashing her skin, Sophie might've thought she was hallucinating.

She clung to Silveny's neck with all the strength she could muster, afraid that if she let go, Silveny would fly away and leave her there—wherever *there* was. "What was that?" she screamed, hearing her voice echo off the valley walls. "Did we just..."

She didn't even have a word for what just happened. One second they'd been at Havenfield, and then the sky tore open and now they were somewhere else—and it definitely hadn't been a light leap.

Free! Silveny told her, leaning down to take a drink. Sophie tumbled forward, and only her death grip on the alicorn's neck saved her from toppling headfirst into the rushing river. But she still drenched her legs as she landed on her feet in the shallows.

What did you do? she transmitted as she waded back to dry land. Her soggy shoes squished with every step.

A sound echoed through her head, and it took a second for her brain to translate the word.

"We *teleported?*"

Silveny whinnied.

Sophie didn't even know that was possible—though she supposed it explained how Silveny had visited so many places. And why alicorns were so elusive. It was hard to catch something that could rip an opening in the sky and vanish into it.

A wave of panic hit her as she considered what that must've

looked like to the Council—or what they must be thinking now that she'd disappeared.

You have to take me back!

Silveny munched on the long stalks of grass. *Free.*

Sophie looked around for some clue to tell her where they were, but all she could see was that they were in the middle of nowhere—and that it was breathtakingly beautiful. She could understand why Silveny didn't want to go back to Havenfield and be caged again. Something about the pen must keep her trapped—maybe there wasn't enough space for her to get up to speed to teleport. That would explain why she'd seen Silveny dipping and diving sometimes. Trying to get away.

But they *had* to go home.

Grady was probably having a heart attack.

How could she convince the stubborn horse to take her home? She couldn't exactly teleport them back on her own.

Or maybe she didn't need to. There was more than one way to leap around the world.

She grabbed her home crystal and held it up to the sunlight, imagining her consciousness wrapping around Silveny's glimmering body. Before Silveny figured out what she was doing, she pressed her palm against the horse's neck and stepped into the light, letting the rushing warmth whisk them both away.

To say Sophie arrived back at Havenfield to pandemonium would have been understating things. *Greatly.*

Bronte was screaming at Grady, Grady was screaming at Sandor, the Councillors were screaming at each other—the only one not freaking out was Keefe, who was also the first one to spot her. He gave her a thumbs-up and she tried to smile, but everything was spinning and blurring and her ears were ringing and her head was throbbing and her body felt too heavy for her weary legs.

Silveny whinnied and the screaming quadrupled as everyone noticed them and shouted something like *"Wherehaveyoubeenareyoucrazywhathappened?"*

But Sophie couldn't answer. She didn't remember falling but she did feel the pain as she hit the muddy ground.

"Somebody call Elwin," Grady ordered, and she was surprised to realize he was cradling her in his arms. "I'm taking her up to her room."

"I'm fine," she promised—but she didn't feel fine. And she knew what Grady was going to say even before he said it. She could tell from the worried look everyone was giving her. Especially Keefe.

"You're not *fine*, Sophie. You've faded again."

"Looks like you get a new accessory," Elwin told her as he handed her the blue vial of the special limbium-free Fade Fuel strung to a cord. He squeezed the atomizer on the end and she inhaled the medicine before he tied it around her neck. "How you can fade with *two* nexuses is beyond me. But at least you got your color back quickly this time. I want you to inhale a dose of this every time you leap, just to be safe."

"I'm sure the fading only happened because of the teleporting," she said, trying to convince Elwin as much as herself.

"Maybe," Elwin agreed. "Though I have to say, *teleporting*? Will you ever stop being full of surprises?"

"That was Silveny, not me." She climbed out of her bed and checked her reflection in the mirror.

"Whoa, what happened to you?" Vertina asked, and Sophie jumped back to get out of range. Clearly her color wasn't all the way back.

Grady opened the door a crack and peeked through. "You're up."

"Can't keep that girl down," Elwin said as Grady ran across the room and strangled Sophie with a hug.

"You can't disappear on me like that," he told her. "Never again."

"I won't," she promised.

He cleared his throat and let her go, wiping his eyes on his cape. "Are you up to facing the Council? They obviously have some questions."

She nodded, though she had no idea what she was going to say. "Did this make it worse?" she whispered.

"It definitely didn't help. But once you talk to them, hopefully . . ."

He left the thought unfinished, and Sophie had no choice

but to follow him down the stairs and back outside where twelve very serious-looking Councillors—and a smirking Keefe—were waiting for her.

"Are you all right, Miss Foster?" Councillor Emery asked, and the crease between his brows made Sophie wonder if he'd switched to the Sophie-must-be-malfunctioning camp.

"Yes," she said, glad her voice sounded strong. "Teleporting just takes a lot out of you."

The word unleashed an explosion of questions, most of which she didn't know the answer to. She gave them what little information she could and they switched to arguing among themselves again.

Friend? Silveny transmitted, and Sophie tensed, realizing she'd forgotten all about the finicky alicorn. She spun around, relieved to see Silveny safely cantering around her enclosure.

"How did you . . ."

"Keefe calmed her down and lured her to her pen," Grady answered. "Clearly she responds well to Empaths."

"Or maybe Silveny just has good taste," Keefe said, stepping close enough to lean in and whisper, "Just so you know, you're pretty much my hero now. It takes serious talent to freak out the entire Council. I may need you to give me some pointers!"

Sophie rolled her eyes.

"Though I gotta say, you look much better with color, Foster. The faded look, it just"—his smile vanished—"well, don't do it again, is all I'm saying."

Sophie squeezed the vial hanging from her neck. "I won't."

"It's quite remarkable, isn't it?" Councillor Terik interrupted, making everyone turn to face him. "All these centuries we've had an alicorn in our custody and we never knew its secrets. But now, thanks to an uncannily talented thirteen-year-old girl, we've discovered the first animal with a special ability—a special ability none of us have ever developed. Our world will never be the same."

Everyone murmured their agreement.

"What did teleporting feel like?" Kenric asked, before Sophie could figure out how to respond to that. "Did it hurt?"

"Not really. It was kind of like I was a rubber band being stretched as thin as I could go before I snapped back into form once we got there—and if you're going to ask, I don't know where we went. Some valley in the middle of nowhere."

They pummeled her with more questions until Grady finally stepped in and reminded them that she'd had a very exhausting day and they could continue this conversation later.

Sophie knew she should be relieved—but the glare Bronte gave her as he leaped away told her she had *not* satisfied his doubts in her abilities. And she couldn't even blame him. She was starting to doubt them herself.

The rest of the Councillors slowly glittered away, and Keefe elbowed Sophie. "I guess that's my cue to leave too." He dipped an exaggerated bow and held his crystal up to the light, saying, "I'll see you tomorrow, Foster," as he leaped home.

Grady rubbed his temples. "So . . . Keefe Sencen?"

"What about him?"

"What about Dex?"

"What *about* Dex?"

Grady held out his hands. "Never mind. We should head back inside. Elwin said he wanted to check you again before he leaves."

Someone cleared their throat behind them, making Sophie and Grady turn.

"Councillor Terik?" Grady sounded as surprised as Sophie felt. "I thought you'd left."

"I had. But I realized I'd forgotten to say one thing to Sophie."

When he didn't continue, Grady said, "I guess I'll wait in the house."

Sophie watched him walk away, trying to guess what Councillor Terik could possibly want. She hoped not another descrying session.

"Can I see your Imparter?" he asked, when Grady had closed the door.

Sophie dug it out of her pocket and handed the silver square to him.

He flipped it over to the dull side and pressed his finger in the center of the square, holding it there until the Imparter flashed with a deep green light. "Permission granted," he said, and the light turned blue. "There—now you'll be able to reach me. Just say my name and if I'm within range, it'll hail me."

"Um . . . thank you."

"I know that you used to rely on Alden when you needed advice, so I want you to know that you are welcome to come to me any time. Don't let that the fact that I'm a Councillor make you feel like you shouldn't bother me. I am *always* here for you, Sophie."

She nodded, feeling dazed as he pulled out his pathfinder and leaped away.

"What did he want?" Grady asked as soon as she set foot in the living room.

"I'm not sure. I think he just wanted to help me."

"Help you?"

"He said he wanted me go to him with the kind of things I used to go to Alden with. He even adjusted my Imparter so I can call him whenever I need."

"You can come to me, too, you know," Grady said quietly. "I know you and Alden had a different kind of relationship than you and I do. But . . . I'm here if you need me. For *anything*."

"Even if it's about the Black Swan?"

She bit her lip as his eyes narrowed, wondering if she'd pushed too far. But when he answered he said, "Yes, Sophie. I still don't trust them—but that doesn't mean you can't come to me. I promise I will try to be objective. Okay?"

"Okay."

She was halfway up the stairs before he added, "I would be

careful, Sophie. I'm sure Councillor Terik means well, but that won't change the fact that as a Councillor he is bound by our laws at all times. If you ever asked him about something that turned out to be illegal, you could end up in a mess of trouble."

A lump formed in her throat as she imagined another Tribunal . . .

"I'll be careful," she promised—and she would.

But as she made her way to her room, she realized that she *finally* had a way to track her old journal down. So as soon as Elwin left, she pulled out her Imparter, needing a second for courage before she gave the command.

"Show me Councillor Terik."

FORTY-SIX

COUNCILLOR TERIK HAD SEEMED surprised to hear from her so soon—and even more surprised by her request. Apparently the elves *had* packed up all of her old human things after she'd left them behind and brought them to Eternalia to be inspected. But they'd found nothing significant, and he had no idea if they'd since been discarded.

"Can I ask what you're looking for?"

"I'd rather not say." Sophie held her breath, hoping she hadn't just committed some sort of treason or perjury or other Exile-able crime.

Councillor Terik laughed. "I've always admired your

gumption, Miss Foster. I'll do my best to find out what I can, and I'll be in touch tomorrow."

His image clicked away.

Sophie stared at the blank screen of her Imparter.

She was used to seeing Alden's face there—his bright teal eyes crinkling around the corners as he smiled.

What if she never saw him do that again?

She blinked back the tears and forced the fear to the same corner of her mind where she'd shoved all the other worries she couldn't let herself think about. She only had energy for the things she could control. Finding her journal. Figuring out what memory had been stolen. Learning the truth about the Black Swan. Terik promised her answers *tomorrow.* In the meantime, she just had to wait.

"What's going on with you and Keefe?"

Sophie nearly dropped her satchel as she turned to face a scowling Dex. The glass pyramid felt especially crowded that morning during orientation—though maybe that had something to do with the heavy glare Dex was directing at her.

"Nothing. Why?"

"I heard he went over to your house after school yesterday."

"I heard that too," Marella said as she squeezed in beside them. "Dedra told me after she heard it from Maruca."

"Yeah, and I heard that from Huxley who heard it from Audric," Dex added.

"Okay—who *are* those people? I've never heard of most of them."

"So he didn't come over, then?" Marella asked.

"Well . . . okay, he did—but it wasn't a big deal. He was just helping me with something." She couldn't believe they were even talking about this—especially when there were so many bigger, more important problems to deal with.

Dex was clearly sulking about it, though, so she made sure to be his partner during channeling practice in PE, and that helped him get over it. Or it did until Keefe hooked his arm through hers on the way to lunch.

"Better get moving, Foster. You and I have a date with detention—remember?"

Sophie groaned. She'd forgotten all about that.

She mouthed *Sorry* to Dex as Keefe led her toward the glass pyramid, up to the cramped floor just below the apex. Sophie hadn't been sent there since the time she stole the midterm information from Lady Galvin—a mistake she'd paid for with almost a week of torture—and she'd hoped to never return. Especially since the punishment changed every day, depending on the Mentor in charge.

She really hoped there'd be no screeching sirens or humiliating dancing this time.

"Who's monitoring us today?" Sophie asked Keefe when she noticed the Mentor's desk was empty.

"No idea, but let's hope it's not Sir Donwell. On Monday he

made us listen to him read classic dwarven poetry. I'm pretty sure I'll be traumatized by anything that rhymes from now on."

The door opened and Sophie made a silent wish for it to be anyone but Bronte. But it was almost worse.

"Oh good, the queen of the alicorns is here," Stina grumbled as she stalked across the room. "I'm surprised you're not covered in glittery poop, Sophie. I hear that's your favorite perfume these days."

"She still smells better than you," Keefe called back, before leaning in and whispering, "Dude—you *have* to give me some of this magical substance. I can think of *several* uses. I bet Dame Alina—"

The door opened again and Keefe fell silent as the monitoring Mentor strode into the room.

"Wow—I thought I knew all the Mentors," Keefe mumbled as he stared at the dark-haired woman in the gleaming silver cape.

Sophie slouched, hoping to hide from her horrible linguistics Mentor. But Lady Cadence noticed her right away.

"Miss Foster. How unencouraging it is to see my alleged *star* prodigy in detention the first week of school." Her words felt like they'd been sharpened into knives. "Though I suppose I shouldn't be surprised given what I've read about you in your file."

Stina snickered, but Keefe held up his hand like he wanted her to give him a high five. Sophie ignored them both, staring at the grains of wood in her desk, wishing she could crawl underneath it.

"Anyway, I'm incredibly behind on my research, thanks to my being moved to teach here, so I've volunteered to cover as many available detentions as possible. Those of you who are repeat offenders will get to spend lots of time with me—though you may decide after today that whatever mischief you like to cause is simply not worth the price."

She snapped her fingers, and piles of round brown vegetables appeared in the center of everyone's desks. They looked a bit like potatoes, but they most definitely were *not* potatoes. If millions of skunks sprayed a mountain of poop, Sophie would've chosen to roll around in *that*. Even living around Silveny breath and Iggy-farts, Sophie had never smelled anything as vile.

"These are curdleroots," Lady Cadence explained. "The ogres use them to make an incredibly toxic poison that I'm trying to make an antidote for. I need them all peeled and juiced before lunch is over, so I suggest you get to work. And in case you're wondering, yes, the smell will wear off. In a few days."

She smiled as they all whined.

Sophie reached for a curdleroot, trying not to gag when she discovered it was squishy like a rotten tomato.

And moist.

The thick peel reminded her of an orange, and she tore it with her fingers, removing it in long, slimy strips.

"So that's your Mentor, huh?" Keefe asked, coughing as he peeled his own curdleroot. "Congratulations, I think you found someone worse than Lady Galvin."

"You should try inflicting with Councillor Bronte."

"Yeah, Dame Alina was clearly out to get you when she gave you that schedule."

More like the Council.

"So, did you make any progress on our little project after I left?"

"Actually, I did." Sophie glanced over her shoulder to where Stina was glaring at them. "I'll tell you later."

"I never said you were allowed to talk, Miss Foster," Lady Cadence snapped from her desk, where she had surrounded herself with tiny candles, probably to block the smell.

"You never said we weren't allowed to either," Keefe reminded her.

"That's just the kind of sass to earn yourself another detention," Lady Cadence retorted. "Another for you, too, Sophie. And if you think today's punishment is unpleasant, just *wait* until tomorrow's."

"Wow, that is *quite* an aroma," Tiergan said, coughing as Sophie sank into the chair across from him.

The extra chair that had been added for Fitz was noticeably empty, and Sophie tried not to look at it as she said, "Yeah, Lady Cadence is evil."

"I don't know if 'evil' is the right word."

"Have you met her?"

"A few times—but it was a while ago. She's been living with the ogres for decades. In fact, I was quite surprised when the Council brought her back to Mentor you."

"So was she," Sophie grumbled. "Do you know why?"

"I have a few suspicions. But I wanted to talk to you about something else." He sighed, fidgeting with the ends of his cape. "I know you've heard Bronte's *theory*."

She slouched in her chair, wishing she could shrink away from this conversation. "You mean the one about me being defective?"

"I believe 'malfunctioning' was the word he used but . . . yes. Are you okay?"

She kicked the back of her shoe. "I don't know, do *you* think I'm malfunctioning?"

He was quiet for a long time, twisting the edge of his cape so tightly she was surprised it didn't rip. "I . . . I think sometimes we forget that you—like all of us—have limitations. Just because the Black Swan tweaked your genes to refine your abilities doesn't mean you're *perfect*."

"But what if I was supposed to be?"

"Then the Black Swan had impossible expectations."

"Maybe," she mumbled. "How much do you know about them?"

"Not as much as I'd like."

"Do you realize that you never *actually* answer any of my questions?"

A hint of a smile peeked from the corners of his mouth. "I'm sorry. I wish I could tell you what you want to hear. The only thing I know for sure is that *they* control what they want you to know. I have no doubt that someday the Black Swan will give you the answers you seek. But it will be when *they* decide the time is right. Not a second sooner."

Sophie scowled. She was really getting tired of sitting back and waiting on *them*. Especially since they'd done nothing since they gave her that charm. No notes. No clues.

Unless Prentice had tried to give her one.

"Does, 'Follow the pretty bird across the sky' mean anything to you?"

His brow creased as he nodded. "I believe it's part of an old dwarven poem. It's been ages since I've heard it, but I think it goes:

> "*Sing swan, Spring swan,*
> *Then let's fly.*
> *Follow the pretty bird across the sky.*
> *Call Swan, Fall Swan,*
> *Then let's rest.*
> *Tucked in the branches of your quiet nest.*"

"It's about *swans*?"

"Yes," he said carefully, like he knew where her mind was

already headed, "but it's an *old* dwarven poem. Centuries and centuries. Long before the Black Swan was even a whiff of an idea. Not to mention very few of us pay any attention to dwarven poems. My mother happened to have an affinity for them, which is the only reason I know it."

That explained why Alden hadn't heard of it. "But maybe they've decided to use it for something. Some sort of code word or password or . . . I don't know."

"I suppose anything is possible, Sophie. But it's like holding a key but no lock. If you don't know where to use it, the key is meaningless."

She sighed, hating that he was right.

But she was right too—she could feel it. It *couldn't* be a coincidence that the poem was about swans. Which meant Prentice told her that line for a reason. And if she could figure out what it was, maybe it would lead her to the Black Swan—or at least to another clue.

Most of the prodigies kept a wide berth from Sophie—and the other stinky detention survivors—during study hall. But Dex still sat in the chair next to her.

"I deal with funky-smelling stuff all the time at the store."

"Gee, thanks."

He grinned. But his smile faded when Keefe plopped into a chair across the table and whispered, "So, Foster, what time am I coming over—and I'm *hoping* it'll be after you shower."

She fanned his stink away. "Uh, I hope you're planning on showering too."

"He's coming over *again*?" Dex whined, turning several heads.

"We're working on something," Sophie whispered.

"Can I help?"

"Miss Foster, Mr. Dizznee, and Mr. Sencen—one more peep and I'm giving all three of you detention," Sir Rosings called.

Keefe rolled his eyes. "Someone is *begging* for a desk full of sparkly poop."

"That's it—one day of detention each."

Sophie glared at Keefe as she took out her notebook. She started to review her history notes, but Dex pulled the thin book away and wrote something in the margin. Then he scratched it out and wrote something else. Scratched that out and wrote something else, staring at it for several seconds before he finally nudged it back, not looking at her as he did.

I never see you anymore.

Sophie felt her lips stretch into a smile.

I miss you too, she wrote, and slid the notebook back to him, just as her Imparter beeped in her pocket. She pulled it out, surprised to find a brief message in glowing orange letters.

> Found what you were looking for. Meet
> me at my office. —CT

Sophie's heart sputtered into overdrive.

"I take it that's good news," Keefe whispered, raising one eyebrow.

"I'll tell you later—I have to do an errand after school."

"Can I come?"

"Me too!" Dex added, but Sophie shook her head at both of them.

This was something she wanted to do alone.

Keefe teased her about being mysterious as Dex grumbled something about "worse than Wonderboy," but Sophie was too excited to care.

The pieces were *finally* coming together.

FORTY-SEVEN

SOPHIE SQUINTED AS THE SHIMMER-
ing city of Eternalia glittered into view. In the distance the jeweled buildings glinted in the sunshine, and members of the nobility trolled the streets in all their finery. But Sophie inhaled a blast of Fade Fuel and turned the other way, crossing the glassy river lined with Pures—special trees with fan-shaped leaves that filtered the air—and heading toward the row of twelve identical crystal castles with twisted, swirling spires.

The offices of the Councillors.

The low heels she'd worn cut into the sides of her toes, but Sophie was so relieved to be in clothes that didn't smell like curdleroots that she didn't mind dressing noble. She'd had to shower three times to get the stench out of her hair.

"You haven't explained what we're doing here," Sandor said, his hand poised over his weapon as he scanned the path ahead.

"Technically, you never said I had to tell you everything. Just that I would let you come."

Sandor scowled, but didn't argue.

She made her way to the farthest castle on the end, and the front door swung open before they reached the top step.

Councillor Terik stepped onto the shimmering landing, his face stretched with a wide smile as he said, "Always a pleasure to see you, Miss Foster. And I forgot about the bodyguard."

"Is that going to be a problem?"

"Not at all. Though I must admit, it's been a long time since I've done an assignment with so little information upfront."

"Oh—I, um—"

"It's okay, Sophie. I understand that you don't know me well enough to open up to me like you did Alden—yet. I'm happy to earn that trust, for now." He held his pathfinder up to the sunlight and offered Sophie his hand. "You ready?"

She willed her palms not to be clammy as Sandor took her other hand and she asked, "Where are we going?"

Councillor Terik smiled. "You'll see."

"Mysterium?" Sophie asked as they reappeared on the familiar narrow streets lined with identical buildings.

"What better place to keep our storage?"

Councillor Terik's tone implied no insult, but the snobby words still made Sophie cringe.

At least she wasn't the *only* one getting stares and whispers as they made their way down the street—though the reaction seemed to be verging on panic this time.

Why is a Councillor here?

Is there something they haven't told us?

Is it safe?

Councillor Terik frowned as the majority of the crowd ducked out of their way and rushed inside. Only a few stragglers remained, watching them with wary eyes.

"I hadn't realized the fear had spread this far," he mumbled. "I rarely walk among the masses like Bronte and Kenric do. This must be why they're pushing so hard for the alicorn's relocation."

Sophie watched a mother drag her two children into the nearest building. "Do you really think a sparkly flying horse is going to help?"

"You'd be surprised at how powerful *hope* can be, Sophie."

Actually, she knew that firsthand.

"Please let it be there," she whispered as they turned down a narrow alley and stopped at a building no different from any of the others, with a rune on the plain gray door that Sophie couldn't read.

Councillor Terik placed his palm against a small black panel next to the rune and the door clicked open. "I haven't inspected any of this myself. But I've been assured that everything brought out of the Forbidden Cities was moved here."

Sophie nodded, her mouth suddenly dry as she stepped into the dimly lit room.

It felt like stepping backward in time.

She walked a few steps forward, past her old couch and coffee table, and the old TV that didn't get very many channels but that her dad refused to get rid of as long as it was working. Ahead was the hallway that led to the kitchen and to the right were the stairs that led to the bedrooms. It was like the elves had carved out the inside to her old house and moved it there, right down to the carpet and paint. But they couldn't do that—could they?

"I didn't realize they took *everything*," she whispered.

"Of course they did. We had no way of knowing if anything was important. Though, as far as we could tell, there's nothing significant in here."

Sophie hoped that wasn't the case as she climbed the stairs and made her way down the hall to her old bedroom. She half expected to see Marty—her parents' fluffy gray cat—curled up outside her door. But the place was empty and dusty, and had clearly not been visited in a very long time—which made her sadder than she wanted to admit.

She reached for the handle of her door, hesitating before turning the knob.

"Everything okay?" Councillor Terik asked.

"Yeah . . . it's just . . . Can I have a few minutes alone?"

As the words left her mouth, she realized she'd basically just asked a member of the Council to go away.

"Sorry, I didn't mean—"

"It's okay," Councillor Terik told her with a smile. "Take all the time you need."

Sandor looked like he wanted to stay, but Councillor Terik placed a hand on his shoulder and Sandor sighed, saying, "I'll be right downstairs."

"Thanks," she whispered as they walked away.

Their heavy footsteps echoed through the quiet space, and Sophie couldn't help smiling when she heard the couch springs creak, trying to imagine a goblin and elvin royalty lounging in her old living room. Then she squared her shoulders, turned the doorknob, and stumbled inside, not daring to look until the door was safely closed behind her.

Her jaw dropped slightly.

Every tiny detail of her room had been precisely recreated, right down to the way she used to arrange her stuffed animals by height—though there was a gap where Ella should've been. She sank onto the bed, running her hands over the tattered blue-and-yellow quilt her mom had made for her. The fabric felt coarser than the elvin fabrics she was used to now, and she could see the stain from the time she'd spilled orange juice as a kid, but she still wanted to curl up in a ball and bury her face in it.

She hadn't realized how much she'd left behind.

Textbooks and notebooks and trophies and ribbons from her

days in human schools. Tacky knickknacks and figurines her parents had given her over the years. Silly crafts she'd made with her mom and sister. Books she'd read so many times the bindings were creased and frayed—though they looked a bit ridiculous now with their wizards and dragons and demigods on the covers.

In fact, *everything* looked ridiculous. Dull and dusty and completely useless—at least in her new world of power and light.

It was hard not to feel just as useless.

She clutched her registry pendant—proof that despite her differences, this world was where she belonged. Then she stood, smoothing the wrinkles she'd left on the bed and focusing on the reason she was there.

She pulled open the bottom drawer of her desk, coughing as bits of dust and cat hair erupted in a plume. It was stuffed with notebooks and old school projects and cell phone chargers, and she was starting to worry it wasn't there when her fingers brushed against the scratchy edge of something covered in glitter.

She couldn't help smiling when she saw the hot pink cover with sparkly unicorns staring at her. Their purple eyes and rainbow manes and tails were almost as absurd as the rainbow walkways they were posed on or the floating hearts in the sky. She wanted to pore over it page by page, but she wasn't sure how long she could keep Councillor Terik waiting.

As she turned to leave, a small part of her wanted to take more, keep a few more memories and things that were *her*.

But was this *her*?

Or was this just her past?

She glanced around again. Then left everything behind.

"Is that what you were looking for?" Councillor Terik asked as she came down the stairs. He pointed to the journal she'd been hugging to her chest, and she nodded.

"Can I see it?"

Sophie froze.

"It's okay," he promised. "I just want to satisfy my own curiosity, nothing more. In fact"—he reached up and removed his circlet, and held it out to her—"let's trade. For the next few minutes, consider me a citizen."

Her grip tightened on the journal and her head screamed for her to keep it secret. But he'd trusted her enough to bring her there without question. Couldn't she do the same? Besides, any runes she'd written would be the Black Swan's cipher. She doubted he'd be able to translate.

Still, her hands shook as she took his circlet and gave him the journal. She stared at her warped reflection in the enormous emeralds as he flipped through the pages.

And then flipped through them again.

And again.

He finally laughed. "Well, as far as I can tell, other than being a rather humorous glimpse of how much your younger sister drove you crazy, there's nothing significant in here. Though there are a few pages missing toward the end."

He held out the journal, pointing to scraps of torn paper running along the inner spine. She had no memory of tearing those out.

Tears burned her eyes—but not sad tears.

Angry tears.

"I'm guessing you don't want to tell me what you were hoping to find," Councillor Terik asked quietly. "Remember—the crown's still off."

"It doesn't matter. It's not there."

She tried not to imagine Mr. Forkle's chubby, wrinkled body skulking around her house when she wasn't home, tearing out the pages.

Or maybe she had been home.

An image of him looming over her while she slept filled her mind. When else would he erase her memories?

"Are you okay, Miss Foster?" Sandor asked as she started to sway.

Mr. Forkle may have cared that day in Paris, but he'd also messed with her life in so many creepy, unimaginable ways.

She had to get out of there.

"Thank you for bringing me here," she said as she handed Councillor Terik his circlet and fumbled for her home crystal.

"Anytime, Sophie. And don't forget this." He held out her old journal.

Sophie couldn't make herself take it.

Sandor grabbed it for her, and Sophie tried to act normal as she held her crystal to the light. But inside she was panicking.

The Black Swan had stolen more than her memories when they tore out those pages.

They'd stolen her only lead to save Alden.

FORTY-EIGHT

THERE YOU ARE!" KEEFE CALLED FROM outside the pterodactyl enclosure.

Grady was brushing the teeth of a bright orange male and Keefe was leaning against the bars watching. His gray tunic was streaked with mud, and tufts of purple fur were stuck in his especially messy hair.

"Grady's been keeping me busy while you were gone," Keefe explained.

"I can see that. Sorry. I told you I'd be home later."

"Yeah, well, my dad started into one of his lectures on the importance of me living up to my potential. Anything's better than that. Plus, it gave me a chance to play with Glitter Butt."

"Glitter Butt?"

"Way better name than Silveny, right?"

"Wait—you've been *playing* with Silveny?"

"It's bizarre," Grady answered for him. "I had him help me feed her, since she responded to him last time. Next thing I knew she was nuzzling his neck, just like she does with you."

"What can I say? Glitter Butt loves me."

"Her name is not Glitter Butt."

"It should be. She likes it better."

"She does not."

"Wanna bet?"

"I wouldn't do it, Sophie," Grady warned her. "She *really* likes Keefe. Which is great for us. She's finally accepting another person."

But . . . did it have to be *Keefe*?

Sophie rushed to Silveny's enclosure, and as soon as the gleaming horse spotted her, the transmissions began. *Friend! Fly! Trust! Fly!*

But there was a new word in the mix.

Keefe!

"See? I told you she likes me."

"You don't know that."

"Actually, I do. I can feel her emotions without touching her—just like I can with yours. I didn't notice it the last time I was around her because I assumed what I was feeling came from *you*. But now I can tell the difference."

Keefe!

"Hey, Glitter Butt—did you miss me?"

Keefe! Keefe! Keefe!

Do you realize he's calling you Glitter Butt? Sophie transmitted. She sent a picture of a large, sparkly horse hind to illustrate.

Glitter Butt, Silveny repeated. *Keefe!*

Sophie rolled her eyes.

"If you're jealous because you don't have a cool nickname, we can start calling you Sparkle Fanny," Keefe offered.

"Thanks, I'll pass."

"Suit yourself. Personally, I insist that you call me Shimmer Booty from now on."

Keefe! Silveny added. *Keefe! Fly! Keefe! Glitter Butt!*

Sophie rubbed her temples. Just when she thought the transmissions couldn't get any more annoying.

"So where were you anyway?" Keefe asked.

"Yeah, I've been wondering the same thing," Grady said behind them.

When Sophie didn't answer, everyone looked at Sandor.

"She was perfectly safe," he assured them.

"I went to see Councillor Terik," Sophie said, before Grady could grill Sandor further. "I'd asked him to help me find my old human things so I could pick up something."

"Is that a *diary?*" Keefe asked as Sandor handed her the sparkly journal.

He tried to snatch it, but Sophie yanked it away just in time.

"I wrote it when I was five. All the entries are like three sentences long and they were just me plotting to annoy my sister."

"Um, who *doesn't* want to know more ways to annoy people?"

"Trust me, you already know them all."

She caught Grady frowning at her. "It was fine," she promised. "There's nothing in the journal that could get me exiled—and Councillor Terik's not like that anyway. He even took off his crown before he checked through the journal."

"His circlet is merely a representation of his power. With or without it—"

"I know. I'll be careful."

"Don't worry, I'll keep an eye on her for the rest of the day," Keefe said, offering a cheesy salute as he hooked an arm through Sophie's.

Somehow Grady didn't look comforted as Keefe led her away.

"Don't you dare," Sophie said, blocking Keefe as he tried to flop on her bed. "You smell like a wet rat. You can sit on the floor."

He laughed and scooped up Iggy, scratching his fuzzy head. "Bet she treats you this way too, huh? Like it's your fault your breath smells like something died inside you."

Iggy squeaked and nuzzled Keefe's hand. Sophie had to give him credit—he had a way with animals.

"So now that we're alone, are you going to tell me what's *really* in the rainbow-unicorn-diary thing? And by the way—

that's the kind of awesome human stuff I'd been hoping for. Please, feel free to go get more so I can make fun of it."

Sophie sank to her bed with a sigh. "I'd *hoped* it had a clue in it. I can remember writing something in the margin—but of course the pages I needed have been torn out." She flipped to the section with the jagged scraps of paper.

"Torn out by who? And aren't you supposed to have a photographic memory?"

Sophie explained about Mr. Forkle and the strange gaps in her memory. "Clearly, there's something they don't want me to find."

"Okay, that's just . . . whoa. I mean, how do you deal with that and, like, go to school and hang with your friends and act so calm? I'd be running to Elwin screaming *'someone stole my memories—get them back!'*"

"Elwin can't help," she said, dropping the useless journal on the floor and kicking it away. "No one can."

"Actually, that's where you're wrong. I *knew* you were going to need me. You got a pencil around here?"

She pointed to her school satchel, and he rifled through and pulled out her silver pencils. Then he snatched the journal and started to plop down next to her.

"Nope—stinky boys sit on the floor."

"Sheesh, ungrateful much?" he asked as he sank to the flowery carpet.

He tilted the book a number of angles, then grabbed a

pencil and started to shade the margin with the side of the point. "If you pressed hard enough as you wrote, we'll still see the impression in the next page. Trust me, this trick has come in handy *many* times."

Sophie had no doubt of that as she squinted at the faint white curves and squiggles Keefe had traced. Her heart stuttered as the marks twisted into words.

"I'm guessing this is a good sign," Keefe said as she scrambled for a notebook to write the message down.

A boy who disappeared.

"Should've figured it would have something to do with a boy."

"I was five, Keefe."

"What, and cute boys didn't exist when you were five? Well, it's true you hadn't met me yet, but . . ."

Sophie tuned him out as an image resurfaced in her mind. The same vague symbol she'd seen before, similar to the one on Brant's shirt—but she could see more of the scene now. It was like her mind had zoomed out and she could tell that it was a crest on the shoulder of someone leaning against a tree.

She ran to her desk, grabbed her memory log, and projected the blurry scene before it slipped away.

"Is that a bramble jersey?" Keefe asked, peeking over her shoulder.

"A what? Wait, is that the game you and Fitz were playing?"

"Sorta. We were playing the one-on-one version. There's a team version too, and every three years we have a championship match. They print special jerseys, and everyone who's into the game buys like ten of them and wears them all the time. That one was from—"

"Eight years ago?" Sophie guessed.

"Yeah, I think it was. But wait—is this *your* memory?"

"I think so." She sank to the floor as the room started spinning.

"But eight years ago you were still living with humans."

"I know."

She was living with humans and had no idea elves existed. Her telepathy hadn't even manifested.

And yet, if her blurry memories were right, she'd somehow seen a boy in a blue bramble jersey.

A boy who disappeared.

FORTY-NINE

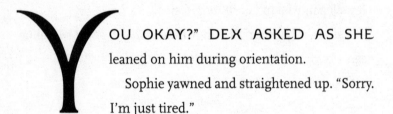

YOU OKAY?" DEX ASKED AS SHE
leaned on him during orientation.

Sophie yawned and straightened up. "Sorry.
I'm just tired."

She'd stayed up late trying to force more of the memory
back, and when she finally gave up and went to sleep, she had
weird dreams about mysterious boys jumping out from behind
trees. It didn't help that Silveny had added Keefe to her night-
time projections. He kept weaving through the nightmares
calling her Glitter Butt, and it made her want to whinny and
run in circles.

If it happened again, Sophie was definitely revising her
policy on sedatives.

She tried to focus during elementalism, but managed to crack three bottles trying to catch a small storm cloud. Lady Veda, a wispy woman with waist-length braided black hair, did *not* look impressed.

Her afternoon session was even worse. Agriculture was held with all the Level Threes in a garden tucked behind the main building, filled with trees, vines, and bushes that grew up and down and sideways and diagonally. A group of gnomes explained that they would be learning how to cultivate the food served in the cafeteria during lunch so they could properly appreciate the work and energy that went into it. But Sophie discovered that it would be another subject where her human upbringing interfered. By the end of the session she'd been corrected for digging, planting, and raking in ways that apparently destroyed the soil/plants/seeds/entire universe, or might as well have, given the way Barth—the ultra-short, green-haired gnome who'd been assigned to work with her—had panicked.

Add to that another stinky lunch detention with Lady Cadence, and Sophie thought the day couldn't get any worse. Then Dame Alina's projection appeared on the walls of study hall.

"Attention, prodigies. I've just gotten word from the Council that a special announcement will be made tomorrow morning. Your parents are being contacted as we speak, but make sure they know to look for an official scroll to be delivered to your homes tomorrow morning with specific instructions for when to read."

She blinked away without any additional explanation, leaving the prodigies to whisper and speculate about what might be happening.

Sophie already knew.

She tried not to cry, tried to remind herself that it didn't change anything.

But all she could think was, *Tomorrow it will be real.*

The letter from the Council was delivered the next morning by a courier in a bright green cape, and came with the instruction to open it at precisely 10:00 a.m. The hour-and-seventeen-minute wait was agony—and even though Sophie knew what the message would say, she still burst into tears when she read the precise black script.

It is with our deepest regrets that we inform you that Alden Vacker has been lost to us all. A seed will be planted in the Wanderling Woods at midday for any who would like to pay their respects.

"You don't have to go," Grady told Sophie as she wiped her eyes.

She shook her head. She didn't want to go—and she was *not* going to say goodbye. But of course she was going to be there.

Grady and Edaline didn't argue, and Sophie excused herself to go to her room. She tried to figure out what she was feeling as she rifled through her clothes—clothes Della had personally picked for her after Fitz brought her to the Lost Cities—but it was a mix of too many emotions.

Calm! Silveny told her, filling her mind with a rush of warmth. Sophie used it to fuel her as she showered and changed into the emerald green gown she'd chosen. Tiny diamonds dotted the bodice, and the full skirt had so many layers of tulle she was guaranteed to trip at least a dozen times. She felt completely ridiculous as she fastened a jeweled velvet cape across her shoulders, tied part of her hair back with a green satin ribbon, and brushed gloss on her lips. But she knew Della would want everyone to dress their best.

"You look . . . wow," Vertina said as Sophie checked her reflection in the full-length mirror. "What's the occasion?"

"You don't want to know."

Something in her tone must've convinced Vertina, because she didn't press further. A quiet knock interrupted the awkward silence that followed.

Grady cleared his throat as he entered, looking more regal than she'd ever seen. "Feels like we keep doing this, doesn't it?" He smiled sadly, and reached into his pocket. "I'm sorry to keep giving you these on such somber occasions, but I thought you might want to wear this."

He handed her a Ruewen crest pin, identical to the one Brant stole.

"Where did you—?"

"I've been in Atlantis a lot lately, so I had the jeweler make it for you."

"Thank you," she whispered as he helped her pin it through her cape.

He looked like he wanted to say something else, but instead he took her hand and they walked to the Leapmaster where Edaline and Sandor were waiting. Edaline's gown was covered in lace and jewels, and even Sandor had changed into silky green pants. No one said anything as they gathered under the crystals, and Grady gave the command for the Wanderling Woods. But Sophie could've sworn she heard Edaline whisper, "Here we go again," as the light swept them away.

FIFTY

OPHIE WAS FAIRLY CERTAIN THE ENTIRE elvin world had packed themselves into the Wanderling Woods—but even the massive crowd couldn't break the unnatural silence of the solemn trees. There wasn't a dry eye in the group, and the grief was so thick it felt almost tangible, like if Sophie breathed too deeply it might choke her.

Grady and Edaline were needed up front with the Vackers, but Sophie hung back with Sandor, hiding on the fringes and hoping no one would notice her. The last thing she needed was for people to start whispering about "the girl who was taken." Especially since goblins weren't supposed to be in the Wanderling Woods. But Sandor had *insisted*.

There was no fanfare as the Councillors appeared on the crest of one of the taller hills, and Sophie was surprised to see they'd brought their bodyguards too. She listened for grumblings about the Council letting goblins near the Wanderlings, but all she saw were stunned stares, and no one said a word as Councillor Emery called for Della to step forward.

Sophie was too far back to see what happened next—but that was better. She didn't want to watch the seed planted, and she reminded herself once again that it didn't mean Alden was *gone*. Her own "grave" was proof enough of that.

A chime sounded and the silent crowd somehow managed to get quieter. Sophie closed her eyes and tried to think of something happy, but she could still hear the ping of shattering glass that rang through the air, and it felt like everything inside her split open.

That was when the sniffling started. Followed by quiet sobs.

Sophie opened her eyes, feeling them burn with tears when she saw the red, weeping faces all around her. She'd never been surrounded by so much sadness, and it made her chest so tight she couldn't breathe. She backed away, shoving through the crowd until she found a pocket of space near a Wanderling. She sank to the ground, resting her head on her knees and sucking in deep breaths.

"I should take you home, Miss Foster," Sandor said, his high-pitched voice sounding way too perky with all the mournful moans.

"No." She couldn't leave without paying her respects to the family. "I'll be fine in a minute."

"Sophie?"

Sophie looked up and found Tiergan frowning at her.

"Are you okay?"

"Yeah. It's just . . . sad," she said as she forced herself back to her feet.

"These always are." He turned to stare at the forest. "Hard to believe only a few short weeks ago I was here for yours."

Had it really only been a few weeks?

"Wait—you were at my funeral?"

"Of course I was. Did you think I wouldn't be?"

"I don't know. I try not to think about it, honestly. It's kind of weird."

"Yes, I suppose it is." He fell silent for a second. "You would've been pleased by how many people came. Almost as many as today."

She couldn't help turning back toward the enormous crowd, which was slowly forming into a receiving line. "Wow, really?"

"Of course, Sophie. Your loss was deeply felt. By *all* of us."

"I . . . guess it's a good thing I'm still alive, then."

He smiled. But when he spoke again his voice was a bit thick. "Yes. It definitely is."

And that's how it will be for Alden, she told herself. This was a mistake. She was going to bring him back.

"I should probably go," Tiergan said, grabbing his pathfinder from his pocket.

"You're leaving? You haven't—"

"The Vackers don't want to see me, Sophie—and this day is hard enough for them. I don't want to do anything to make it any harder."

Sophie stared at her hands. The Vackers didn't want to see her, either. Would she be making it harder for them by staying?

Tiergan tilted her chin up. "*You* should stay, Sophie. Trust me on that, okay?"

She nodded.

He told her he'd see her in session on Tuesday, then stepped into the light.

Sophie stood there, staring at the space where he'd been.

"Grady and Edaline are nearing the front of the line," Sandor said, forcing her to snap out of it.

She turned to make her way back toward her family, but as she wove through the crowd she found herself smack in the center of the Hekses. Sophie locked eyes with Stina and braced for some sort of insult or drama. But Stina just wiped her tearstained cheek and stepped aside to let Sophie pass. Sophie could still hear her crying as she joined Grady and Edaline.

"Excuse me, did someone give you permission to cut?" Keefe asked. He tried to sell the joke with a weak smile, but his eyes were too red and swollen.

"I'm sorry," an elegant woman with blond hair woven into

an intricate braid said. "Just ignore my son if he's bothering you."

"He's not bothering me." Sophie glared at Keefe's mother and leaned closer to ask Keefe, "You okay?"

He cleared his throat and looked away. "I've been better."

Grady wrapped his arm around Sophie. "What about you? How you holding up?"

"Okay, I guess. How about you?"

"It's strange this time. I've only been to two of these ceremonies before—and both times I was the one standing at the front of the receiving line, accepting everyone's condolences."

Grady's voice trailed off and Sophie hugged him tighter, trying to squeeze away his sadness. "I'm still here," she whispered.

"I know," he whispered back. "Let's keep it that way."

Sophie nodded as the line advanced, bringing them close enough to finally see the small sapling that she didn't want to look at but couldn't look away from either. The teal flowers dotting every branch were unmistakable, but the tree seemed frail and thin and not at all like the real Alden. Sophie wanted to rip it from the ground and hurl it away.

They moved forward again and Sophie got her first glimpse of the family. Alvar was his usual immaculate self in an embroidered green jerkin and cape—though his eyes were bloodshot and he seemed especially pale as he held his mom's hand. Della was stunning as ever, but her green gown hung off her suddenly bony shoulders, and Biana's gown looked equally loose. And Fitz . . .

Sophie couldn't look at Fitz.

The Councillors were lined up behind them—all twelve in plain green capes and simple silver-and-emerald circlets. Their faces were blank, and they seemed to stare at nothing as elf after elf greeted the family.

"We are going to fix him, right?" Keefe leaned forward and whispered in her ear. "I *really* need to believe that today."

"I know," she whispered back. "I hope we can."

"Hope isn't good enough, Sophie. Give me a job at least. Something. *Anything.*"

"I'm still trying to figure out what to do."

"Why don't you let me look through the journal? Maybe I'll find something else."

"We'll talk about this later," she told him, hating the way Keefe's dad was so obviously listening to them. Plus, they were moving forward again.

Her chest tightened when she realized she was next to see the Vackers, and she could barely breathe as she took the final steps.

Biana and Fitz were mid "thank you for coming" when they realized who they were speaking to. Biana's voice trailed away, and Fitz's jaw clenched so tight it looked like he might crack a tooth.

"I'm so sorry," Sophie whispered, forcing herself to meet Fitz's gaze.

He didn't nod. Didn't say anything. Just stared at her.

Sophie hung her head. She thought about walking away, but

she couldn't. Not without saying the one thing that needed to be said.

I miss him.

"Don't!" Fitz snapped. "You don't get to—"

"Whoa, chill, man," Keefe said, stepping between them. "This is Sophie."

"Keefe, it's fine." Sophie looked at Della, who'd come out of her daze to notice what was happening beside her. "I guess I shouldn't have come."

"No, you shouldn't have," Fitz agreed.

Biana just glared at her.

There were dozens of things Sophie wanted to say, but she knew none of them would help. So she gave Della the tightest hug she could, curtsied to the Councillors, and hurried away, with Sandor right behind.

"Hey, wait up," Keefe called, running after her.

"I don't want to talk, Keefe."

"I know—I can definitely feel that. But I thought you should know that I could tell what Fitz is feeling, and he's not angry at you."

She gave him a look.

"Okay, he's a *little* mad at you. But mostly his dad. And the world. He's freaking out—which I get, but . . . he has no right to take it out on you."

"Yes, he does."

"No, he doesn't."

Sophie rubbed her temples. She knew Keefe meant well—and in some ways what he was saying did help. But not enough.

"I'm sorry, I just want to be alone," she told him, jogging away.

"I guess I'll see you on Monday, then," he called behind her.

She didn't look back until she'd crested the first hill. Keefe was on his way to the Vackers.

"Are you ready to go home, now?" Sandor asked.

"Not yet."

The last time she'd been to the Wanderling Woods the Black Swan had left her a message at her grave. And as she wound through the forest, searching for her tree, she couldn't help hoping that they might do it again. She was starting to think she was heading the wrong way, but then she rounded a bend and two narrow saplings appeared on a hill ahead.

A lone figure stood between them.

"Dex?" Sophie asked when she got closer.

He sniffled and scrubbed at his eyes. "Sorry," he mumbled, hiding his flushed face. "It's stupid to get upset, right? I mean, it's just a tree."

"I cried when I saw them too."

"Really?"

"Yeah." Her tree still didn't have any fruits or color, and it looked like it hadn't grown at all. Dex's was twice as tall and covered with tiny periwinkle flowers. She tried not to read anything into that, but she couldn't help worrying her *malfunctioning* DNA might have something to do with it.

She saved the worry for later, scanning her scrawny sapling and looking for any sign of a clue. It was nothing more than a tree.

Dex reached out, plucking a flower from his tree and sniffing it. "Wow, this really *is* me. It smells just like I do when I don't shower for a few days."

Only Dex would have a tree with stinky flowers.

"I hate that they're still out there," he whispered.

"Who?"

"The ones who tried to . . ."

"Oh. *Them.*"

"Sometimes I'll think I see them or hear them," he added quietly, glancing over his shoulder.

"We're safe, Dex."

"No—*you're* safe. You have the Council and the whole world trying to protect you."

"The world doesn't want to protect me, Dex. They see me with Sandor and freak out, like being near me will get them taken too. Just like what happened to you."

She didn't mean to say the last part, but it slipped out anyway.

"Yeah, well, they're dumb. The only time I feel safe is around you." His cheeks flamed and he quickly added, "You have the bodyguard, after all."

"Yeah," Sophie mumbled, staring at Sandor. She never realized Dex was wishing for a goblin of his own.

Dex dropped his eyes to his feet. "I guess I know what you

mean, though. My parents worry now. A lot. I have to fight them to go places—even to see you. Not that I've had to do that much lately." He kicked the ground, but then his head snapped up. "Oh! This is what you've been busy with, huh?"

Sophie nodded.

"You could've told me."

"I wasn't supposed to talk about it."

"But you told Keefe?"

"Fitz is his best friend, and the Vackers are like his family. He needed to know."

"So now that the news is out, though—you guys won't be hanging out so much, right?"

"We might be. We're still working on something."

She thought about telling him what, but Dex had always chosen to stay away from the Vackers. He'd never wanted to know them—any of them.

Dex sighed and dropped the flower he'd picked, crushing it with his shoe. "I thought things would be different after we got back home," he mumbled.

"Different how?"

"I don't know. I mean, we went through this *huge* thing. And then I came back and everyone just expected me to go back to normal and act like it never happened. *But it happened.*" He pointed to his tree. "I was there too. I almost died too. It's like no one cares except my family."

"Lots of people care, Dex." She hesitated a second and then

took his hand, waiting for him to look at her. "I care."

"Really? Then how come ever since school started, it's like I don't exist? Before that, actually—ever since that day when Alden . . ."

When he spoke again, it was almost a whisper. "Is that when it happened? To Alden?"

She could barely manage to nod. "It got really bad the next day."

He tightened his grip on her hand. "It wasn't your fault, if that's what you're thinking."

"You can't say that. You don't even know what happened." She tried to pull away, but he held tight.

"I know you. And I know you would never let anything bad happen to anyone if you could help it."

Tears burned her eyes. "Thanks, Dex. I hope you're right."

"I am. And see—when you tell me stuff, I can help. I bet if you told me what you and Keefe are working on, I could help with that, too."

"Maybe."

"Maybe I'm right or maybe you'll tell me?"

"Maybe I don't know." She turned back to their trees, their small, weak little trees that were growing stronger by the day. "Come on, we should probably get back to our families."

Dex kept hold of one of her hands as they walked, and Sophie couldn't decide how she felt about that. But she didn't try to pull away, even when they made it back to Alden's grave.

Most of the crowd had left—as had the Councillors—but the Vackers remained. Grady and Edaline seemed to be trying to get them to go home, but Della didn't want to leave the tree.

Dex went to join his parents and Grady caught Sophie's eye.

I'll be waiting at the entrance, she transmitted, hurrying away as fast as she could without actually breaking into a run. She couldn't face Fitz and Biana again, and they wouldn't want her to. At least they knew she came to the ceremony. That would have to be enough.

The entrance to the Woods was as empty as it had been that first day Sophie had been there, and she leaned against the pillar of the arched entrance, trying to clear her head. But she caught a slight movement in her peripheral vision.

Up the path, a dark-skinned figure paced in the shade of a nearby tree. A bright red tree with tiny purple flowers—the same tree Grady and Edaline had shown her.

He wiped his eyes as he bent to run his hands over the stone marking the grave.

His mother's grave.

"Wylie."

Sophie didn't realize she'd said it out loud until he turned toward the sound. He squinted at her. Then his eyes widened and he backed a step away, like he knew exactly who she was.

"Sophie?" Dex asked, running to catch up with her. "You okay?"

"Yeah, I . . ." Sophie took a step toward Wylie. Just one—just to see how he'd react.

He didn't move.

"I need a second," she told Dex. He looked like he wanted to say something, but he held it back. Sandor didn't follow either.

Wylie's skin was lighter than his dad's, and his features were more pinched. But his eyes.

His eyes were Prentice's eyes—only full of life and a million conflicting emotions. He looked about twenty—which she should've figured, but it'd been easier to imagine him closer to her age and growing up never knowing his real dad. If he was twenty, he would've known him and loved him for seven or eight years before he died. He would've felt every heartbreaking second of his loss.

Because of her.

"It was you, wasn't it?" Wylie asked when she got closer. "You're the one."

Sophie forced herself to nod.

Wylie nodded too.

She waited for him to yell, scream, fling random things, something—anything. Instead he stared at her long enough to make her squirm and then whispered, "What are you waiting for?"

"What do you mean?"

"You're supposed to make it right. He said you would make it right."

"Who did? Your dad?"

"Who else would it be?"

"I don't know. I don't know what you're talking about!"

Wylie's hands clenched into fists and Sandor was instantly at Sophie's side.

Wylie backed away. "He told me before it happened—*if* it ever happened—that I wouldn't have to worry. That you would make it right. So what are you waiting for?"

"I . . . don't understand."

Did he think she could fix his father? She wasn't even sure if she could fix Alden—and the only reason she still had hope was because his mind was shattered by guilt, not a memory break.

She'd seen Prentice's mind. A tiny part of him was still there—maybe. But the rest of him had clearly slipped into madness. How was she supposed to fix that?

Unless that's what he'd been trying to tell her. The clue from the poem—could he have been telling her how to fix him?

But how could following a bird fix a broken mind?

"You were supposed to make it right," Wylie repeated.

She didn't know if that was true, but she supposed it didn't matter because there was one truth that overpowered it. "I'm sorry. I don't know how."

Wylie sighed. A thick sort of sigh that was part snort and part sneer and heavy on the disgust. Then he turned and stalked away without another word.

Sandor placed a meaty hand on Sophie's shoulder. "Do not let what the troubled boy says affect you."

She wanted to agree, but . . .

What if *that* was why the Black Swan sent her to Exile? Not for Fintan, like Alden thought. For *Prentice*.

But not to probe his mind.

To fix him.

It would explain why Prentice submitted to the break. Why he was willing to sacrifice himself and leave his family and give up everything.

What if he thought he would get it all back—that she would "make it right"—and he'd been waiting all this time for her to come and fix what happened?

Which led to the bigger, scarier question.

If that had been the Black Swan's plan, why didn't it work when she probed Prentice's mind?

"What if I really am malfunctioning?" Sophie whispered.

She'd hoped saying it out loud would make it seem wrong and impossible and shake the possibility away.

Instead it felt . . . *right*.

"Miss Foster?" Sandor asked as a tear streaked down her cheek. "Do you need me to find Elwin?"

She shook her head. This was something Elwin couldn't help with.

If Wylie was right, the problem went deeper than her skin or her cells.

It was in her genes.

FIFTY-ONE

OU'VE BEEN STARING AT YOUR reflection so long I've counted all of your eyelashes," Vertina announced, making Sophie blink. "Did you know you have one hundred and twenty-seven on your left eye, and only one hundred and nineteen on your right?"

"No," Sophie mumbled, tugging out a loose one from the left side.

"I didn't say you had to even it out!"

Sophie flicked the eyelash away and went back to searching for some sign that Wylie was wrong—some proof that she was perfectly healthy and normal and all of her talents were working the exact way they should be.

But all she could see were her eyes.

Freaky, brown eyes—eyes that made her stand out from everyone else. The Black Swan couldn't have given her those intentionally, could they? Why would they do that? And what about her allergy? Surely they wouldn't have *chosen* for her to have that. And if those things weren't planned, what other fun surprises did her genetic manipulation have?

She stared at the vial of Fade Fuel hanging around her neck as she replayed Wylie's words for what felt like the tenzillionth time. They still made her queasy and shaky—but they held a tiny hint of hope, too. If he was right—and if she *was* malfunctioning—then it meant there definitely *was* a way to fix Alden. And Prentice. And who knew who else.

She just had to figure out how to fix herself first.

But how? It was too late to change her genetic code. And she didn't even know where the problem began, or how deep it went.

Or maybe she did . . .

She moved toward her wall of windows and stared directly at the sun.

The light swelled in her mind, making her brain throb and the room tilt sideways and somehow she was on the floor, even though she didn't remember falling.

She blinked and rubbed her temples, taking deep breaths until the pain faded and she could sit up again.

Maybe Bronte and Wylie were right.

Maybe the light wasn't bothering her because she almost faded away.

Maybe she'd almost faded away because her newly "enhanced" concentration didn't work right. That would explain why she kept fading—even with two nexuses.

What if her brain was doing something fundamentally *wrong*?

She had no idea if that was something Elwin could fix, but he'd need to know *what* her brain was doing in order to try. And clearly it wasn't something he could see with his special glasses.

Which meant she'd have to find a safe way to test herself for symptoms. Something that didn't involve leaping or fading or anything that could land her in the Healing Center for way longer than she could afford to be—or worse.

She ran through all of her recent "incidents," trying to find a pattern, and the more she thought about it, the more one stood out. The mirror in the Hall of Illumination, and the strange heat that had bloomed inside her mind. All the other incidents had involved headaches. But that one had felt like a fire in her brain.

Maybe if she figured out what that mirror did, she would be able to figure out what was wrong with her.

"Did you hear the news?" Dex mumbled as Sophie licked open her locker, which tasted like lushberries.

"Which news?" She'd tuned out most of Dame Alina's heartbroken Ode to Alden speech during orientation—though she'd caught the part where Dame Alina announced that the Council had moved the Celestial Festival to outside the Sanctuary, and that there would be a special finale involving the prized alicorn. Like she needed *more* pressure.

"Fitz and Biana are back at school today."

The two bites she'd taken of her breakfast turned into a rock in her stomach. "Oh."

"Isn't that a good thing?"

"It is. It's just also going to be weird, I guess, because I . . . don't think we're friends anymore."

She'd expected him to whoop and celebrate that he was finally free of the Vackers. Instead Dex sighed and said, "I'm sure they'll come around. I mean . . . I'm still not in the Wonderboy fan club. But—I bet he's a mess right now. The triplets said my family was pretty much chaos after you and I were taken."

Sophie bit her lip. "I'm so sorry they had to—"

"Stop apologizing. It wasn't your fault. None of this is."

She wished she could believe him, but if Wylie was right . . .

She'd know in a few hours. She had one boring session to get through first.

She reached for her history book, but as she pulled it off the shelf a small roll of paper dropped to her feet.

Her heart pounded in her ears as she bent to retrieve the scroll, skipping several beats when she saw the black seal.

The sign of the swan.

"Is that what I think it is?" Dex whispered as she unrolled it with shaky hands.

The message was only two words written in bold black ink.

Patience
Trust

But when she flipped it over, she found a tiny scrap of hot pink paper attached next to another message.

Stop searching for things you are not ready to understand
Wait for us to give your next command

She read the note again—and then again—getting angrier each time.

Were they *warning* her?

The scrap of pink paper had a tiny unicorn on it, and she recognized the design from her old journal. Which meant the Black Swan still had the pages they'd taken—and instead of giving them back, they'd sent her a warning telling her to back off and wait for them.

Who did they think she was?

Their little puppet.

She crumpled the note, wishing she could fling it across the room but too afraid there might be some crucial clue she was missing.

"Is it bad?" Dex asked quietly.

Oh, it was bad—but not the way he was thinking.

The Black Swan thought they could control her, and maybe that's what she'd let them do before.

Not anymore.

If they didn't want her getting that memory back, then she'd work even harder to make sure she did. She was done with their games and their riddles and their clues. She was going to figure out the truth about them on her own, and there was nothing they could do to stop her.

"You're here early," Master Leto said as he opened the door to admit her to the Silver Tower.

"Yeah." Sophie could tell he was waiting for an explanation, so she squeezed under his arm before he could close her out.

He muttered something under his breath as he crossed to the wall with the cloak panel and handed her a silver cape. Sophie clasped it over her uniform, glad to see it had been tailored to her height.

Master Leto opened the doorway to the tower, and Sophie felt her mouth go dry when she saw how full the great room was. Prodigies in gleaming silver cloaks were clustered around every table, though their conversations were hushed whispers, and no one seemed close to smiling. Sophie wasn't sure if that's how it always was or if that was because of Alden, but she didn't stick around to find out. She tried to keep her head down as she slipped through the crowd, but she still caught a quick glimpse of Wylie as she started up the stairs. He sat alone in the corner, and when their eyes met, he grabbed his things and stalked away.

Part of her wanted to run after him and ask more questions—see if his dad had told him anything else that might help her figure out what was wrong. The other part didn't have time for another emotional scene. And there were far too many curious prodigies in the room, so she made her way silently up, not realizing Master Leto was following her until she made the first curve in the staircase.

"Oh, I know where I'm going," she told him.

"I have no doubt you do." He said nothing else, but continued to shadow her.

Sophie did her best to ignore him as she counted the floors, turning off at number seven.

"The Hall of Illumination?" Master Leto asked. "You realize the mirror assignment doesn't apply to you."

"I'm just curious." She turned her back on him, hoping he'd take the hint.

He didn't.

Which left her no choice but to stare at the first mirror in front of her, waiting for him to get bored and leave her alone. The reflection was sharp everywhere except her face, where it turned slightly fuzzy.

"Any guesses?" Master Leto asked.

He sounded genuinely curious, so she decided to answer. "The face is blurred, so maybe, 'what you look like doesn't matter'?"

He stepped closer to the mirror. "Your face is blurred?"

"Yeah." She squinted to double-check. "Isn't that how it's supposed to be?"

He didn't answer. Just stared so intently at her reflection it made her want to squirm.

She turned away, realizing she was wasting valuable time. Only one mirror mattered. She wasn't exactly sure which one it was, but she knew the general area, and as she stepped closer the blinding light reflected in her eyes.

The pull was so much stronger this time—like the mirror had sprouted hundreds of tiny hands, tugging and dragging and drawing her closer. She tried to back away, but the hands grew claws, digging deep into her skin with tiny stabs of heat that sank deep beneath the surface. The pain swelled with each spark until she couldn't think beyond it—couldn't move, couldn't do anything except stand there and let the inferno consume her.

She heard a deep voice say something, but she couldn't concentrate enough to make out the words. It was just white noise, mixed with searing heat. And the light—

"*Sophie!*" the deep voice shouted as two strong hands yanked her backward. She gasped when the tiny needles ripped away, letting cold and darkness rush into the empty places left behind.

Her knees gave way and her eyes focused, and she stared into the face of Master Leto, who strained to keep her upright. "What's happening?" he asked, shaking her as she felt her head start to cloud over. "What are you feeling?"

Her voice didn't want to work, but somehow she managed to croak, "The light." Then everything went dark.

The blackness turned green. Then blue. Then purple. Then red.

Sophie's eyes snapped open and she jerked upright, bursting the spheres of color that Elwin had formed around her. She waved her arms, trying to fan away the last wisps of glow as Elwin struggled to restrain her. "No more light."

"Easy, Sophie. It's okay. You're okay."

Sophie shook her head, feeling her tears mix with the sticky sweat on her face as his words settled in. She couldn't believe them anymore.

She leaned back, curling her knees into her chest and let the huge, ugly, choking sobs that she'd been fighting so long finally break free. She kept waiting for Elwin to try and pour a sedative down her throat, but he just sat beside her, rubbing her back, and with each stroke of his hand, she felt her breathing slow until the fit had passed and the sobs had turned to hiccups.

"You should drink one of these," Elwin said, handing her a bottle of Youth. He helped her sit up enough to swallow a few sips of the sweet water, but her stomach was too knotted to fit anything more.

He raised his arm, his fingers poised to snap, but she grabbed his wrist. "No more light."

"What do you mean by light?" a different voice asked, and it took a second for Sophie to recognize that it was Master Leto. She followed the sound to where he stood in the shadowy corner, watching her through narrowed eyes.

"He carried you here after you blacked out," Elwin explained.

"I was *perfectly* capable of carrying her myself," Sandor snapped from somewhere behind her.

"When a prodigy collapses in *my* tower, I take it upon myself to find out what's going on. You said something about light, Sophie?"

Sophie nodded—though the shudder that rocked her body probably made it hard to tell. "I keep trying to tell myself it's my body needing more time to heal from when I faded. But it's bigger than that."

She glanced at Master Leto, wishing he would leave but knowing that he wouldn't. She supposed it didn't matter. If she was right, then she'd probably be removed from her elite sessions. Maybe she'd even be sent to Exillium. Foxfire was no place for a "malfunctioning experiment."

She closed her eyes and forced the rest of the confession out before she changed her mind: all the incidents. Bronte's and Wylie's theories. How the mirror seemed to amplify everything.

Elwin turned to Master Leto. "Which mirror?"

"The Lodestar."

The skin on Elwin's forehead creased.

"What's the Lodestar?" Sophie asked.

"A mirror that reflects pure light." Master Leto stepped closer, squinting at her.

"But I've checked her—many times," Elwin argued. "I would've seen if there was something wrong."

"Only if the problem is physical," Master Leto corrected, like he was suddenly the expert on everything. "If it's mental—"

"It's not that either," Sophie interrupted. "There's something in my genes or my programming or whatever. Something the Black Swan messed up."

Elwin shook his head. "I don't think you realize how carefully I've checked you. When you were fading, I personally inspected every single cell to make sure I didn't miss something. I'm happy to check again if it would make you feel better." He snapped his fingers and a purple orb spread around her torso.

She waited for the pain, but nothing happened.

Elwin slipped on his glasses. "See?"

"Try flashing the light right into her eyes," Master Leto suggested.

"Why are you still here?" Sophie shouted. "Don't you need to get back to the tower and do—whatever it is Beacons do."

His lips twitched—almost like he wanted to smile. "It's just a suggestion. That's how the mirror works."

She glared at him as Elwin held his fist in front of her face—but then he snapped his fingers and she couldn't think anymore because the light was pulling and twisting and wriggling inside her head. She swatted the glowing orb away, but even when it was gone the ringing in her ears wouldn't fade.

"What did you feel?" Master Leto asked.

"It felt like it was boring into my brain."

"I don't understand," Elwin whispered.

"It really is the light," Master Leto said, staring at Sophie so intently it felt like his eyes were peering inside her head.

She looked away as Elwin turned to pace, muttering under his breath things Sophie mostly couldn't hear, though she picked up tiny snippets like "physiologically impossible" and "getting worse" and "Lodestar." Each word made the question she was too afraid to ask swell on her tongue until it'd grown so big she couldn't keep it in anymore.

"Can you fix it?" she whispered.

Elwin ran his hands through his hair, mussing it more than usual. "I don't know."

FIFTY-TWO

S O . . . I'VE GOT GOOD NEWS AND BAD news," Keefe said as Silveny nuzzled his shoulder through the bars. Keefe hadn't come over the day before, and the high-maintenance alicorn had clearly missed him. "Which do you want first?"

Sophie rubbed her temples. "Might as well start with the bad and get it over with."

She doubted it could be worse than what she was already dealing with. Elwin had spent hours making her drink different elixirs and then flashing light in her eyes to see if they helped. When she'd felt like the headaches were going to break her brain, he'd finally had to admit defeat. And even though he'd promised he *would* figure it out, she wasn't holding her breath.

The only relief was that he'd agreed to let her wait to tell Grady and Edaline until he had more information. No reason to tell anyone. Yet.

"Well?" she prompted, when Keefe still hadn't said anything.

"I . . . *sorta* had to tell my dad what we're doing—"

"*What?*"

"—but before you freak out, don't worry, I didn't tell him anything important."

"Why did you have to tell him *anything*? I thought you were the king of lying to adults."

"I am. But there's only so much you can hide when you're dealing with an Empath—trust me, I would know—so I had to give him enough truth to hide the lies. Apparently he heard us talking while we were in line to see the Vackers, and he cornered me about it, wanting to know what we were up to."

Sophie was too tired and frustrated to do anything other than sigh.

"Sheesh, will you relax? All I told him is that I was helping you with Silveny because you were having a hard time and needed an Empath's skills. Then I loaded it up with all kinds of stuff about how much Glitter Butt loves me, and how much you love having me around, and all that truth sold him."

"Truth," she grumbled, rolling her eyes. "So if it's not a big deal, why are you telling me?"

"Well, you're cute when you're panicking for one thing—but also, he was *super* excited about this. I mean, I'm sure it's because Silveny is such a big deal and he's imagining me getting special mention from the Council once Silveny is ready to be moved or something. But later that night he gave me this."

He pointed to the pin clasping his cape around his shoulders—a circle with two hands holding a candle with an emerald flame. She'd seen the crest before on his Foxfire uniform.

"Wow," she said, hoping he couldn't feel her surprise.

"What?"

"Nothing."

Keefe laughed. "Clearly you have no idea how to lie to an Empath. What?"

Sophie bit her lip. "It's nothing. I guess I just didn't realize you didn't have a Sencen crest pin."

"Uh, you've met my father—you've seen what he's like. He's always told me I have to earn my place in the family. And I guess now I have."

Sophie smiled. She'd been wondering why he was wearing a cape instead of his usual tunic and pants, and she couldn't blame him. She knew how much it had meant when Grady had given her the Ruewen crest—and she hadn't had to spend a lifetime earning it. "So was that the good news?"

"Part of it. But the *real* good news is he told me I can spend as much time here as I want—so we can see even *more* of each other!"

"Oh. Great."

"Wow, try not to be *too* enthusiastic there, Foster." He

rumpled Silveny's mane. "At least you're excited, aren't you, Glitter Butt?"

Keefe!

"It's just . . . I don't even know where we're supposed to go from here. The only leads we have are a line in an old dwarven song about swans and a tiny piece of an erased memory that the Black Swan has specifically warned me not to investigate."

"Whoa—back the T. rex up. The Black Swan contacted you again and you didn't tell me?"

"Sorry. I guess I forgot." She explained about the warning note and the piece of her old journal attached to it.

"Okay, first—I definitely want to know their trick for breaking into lockers. And second, uh, that's not a warning. That's a dare. Now we know they still have the pages. So we just have to figure out a way to steal them back."

"It's not that easy, Keefe."

"Sure it is. We just have to think one step ahead of them."

"More like five steps. Or ten. Think about it, Keefe—how do they even know I have the journal? They have to be watching me. They're probably watching us right now, making notes on any plan we come up with so they can thwart it."

Keefe glanced over his shoulder. "You really think they're watching us?"

"How else would they know?"

"I guess. But aren't there a ton of goblins trolling these grounds? I swear I've seen two or three skulking in the shadows."

"Goblin senses can be fooled."

"*They can?*" Keefe asked as Sandor shot her a death look.

"Yeah, but it's a secret." Not a very well-kept one, in Sophie's opinion. "Anyway, my point is, how are we supposed to sneak up on someone who knows everything we're thinking about doing?"

"Please—you're talking to a master mischief maker. I'll find a way."

"You do that. In the meantime, I need to practice flying with Silveny."

She was only allowed to fly inside the pasture now, and the Council was redesigning their plans for Silveny's appearance at the festival to make sure there were no more teleporting debacles. Silveny was *not* happy about it, and gave the most pathetic sad eyes ever as Sophie made her way to the gate and reached for the cube-shaped padlock to press her thumb against the sensor.

The sides of the cube parted to release the lock and a tiny velvet sack fluttered to her feet.

A *black* velvet sack, marked with a now all-too-familiar symbol.

"What's that?" Keefe asked as she bent to pick it up.

"Proof that we're not alone."

Sandor drew his weapon and scanned their surroundings as Sophie untied the beaded threads knotting the bag and dumped two items into her palm. A tiny silver alicorn pin with orange topaz eyes and outstretched wings, and a note. The

Black Swan had given her pins as clues before, and this one, like the others, looked like it was a Prattles' pin. When she flipped it over, she found a tiny digital readout that said: #1 OF 2.

So not only had they snuck into Havenfield, tricked the goblin's senses to avoid getting caught, opened the lock that needed her DNA to open, but they'd also managed to get their hands on the rarest Prattles' pin of them all. All so they could lead her around like the perfect little puppet.

Well, they could forget it. She was done being controlled. Especially when she saw the message on the note:

Face your fears.

She started to crumple the paper, but Keefe grabbed her wrist and pried it out of her fingers before she could destroy it.

He grinned as he read the note. "Bring it on."

"No way, Keefe. I'm not playing their game anymore."

She was tired of being asked to blindly trust a group who had been manipulating her life for *years*. A group who probably messed something up in her DNA and made her defective. A group who may have *murdered* Jolie.

"You hear that?" she shouted, looking around for some clue as to where they were hiding. She had no doubt that they were there. "I'm done with the secrets! You want to order me around, you can come out and do it face-to-face."

She held her breath, waiting to see if they would respond.

All she heard was the crunching sound of Silveny gobbling down swizzlespice, and the chirping of a few crickets.

Her hands clenched into fists and her body started to shake as the anger swelled inside her, dimming her vision.

"Whoa—easy now," Keefe said, jerking her shoulder.

Calm! Silveny added, sending a rush of warmth that melted away the fog.

"Sorry," she mumbled, staring at her feet. She really needed to get better control of her anger.

"Keep an eye on her," Sandor told Keefe, "I'm going to order the others to do a full sweep of the property."

He ran for the trees, and Sophie wanted to tell him not to bother—the Black Swan were way too smart to ever let themselves get caught. And hey, maybe this was good news. It probably meant their mysterious "visitor" had been from the Black Swan and not the kidnappers.

"Hey, Captain Mood Swing," Keefe said, gently grabbing her arm. He sighed when she didn't smile. "Look, I get what you're feeling. Shoot, I can *feel* what you're feeling—and I don't blame you. At all. But remember what we're trying to do here. We want to fix Alden, right?"

The last of her anger cooled as she nodded. Shame swelled in its place.

"Hey—no feeling guilty either. You have a right to be seriously ticked. And as soon as this is done, you and I are going to put our heads together and figure out how to send the Black

Swan a few secret messages of our own—preferably covered in glittery poop. But in the meantime I think we need to do what they say."

"Yeah," she mumbled, unclenching her fists and staring at the red dent where the alicorn pin she'd been squeezing had cut into her palm.

"So . . . you're the pro at figuring out their clues. Any theories?" Keefe asked.

"I'm assuming this has something to do with Silveny," she said, holding up the pin. "Especially since they left the clue at her enclosure."

"And the note?"

She sighed. "No idea."

They had to mean *her* fear, since the message said, "Face *your* fears." But what did they think she was afraid of—besides a lifetime of being a useless, malfunctioning creation? She was already facing that.

She didn't like doctors—but she faced that fear all the time too.

What else was she afraid of?

Her stomach turned sour as an idea hit her.

"You figured it out, didn't you?"

She nodded miserably and dug out her Imparter.

"Who are you calling?"

"We're going to need extra help for this part," she said, hating that she had to ask this favor. But she had no other choice, so she squared her shoulders and commanded, "Show me Dex."

FIFTY-THREE

OES HE REALLY NEED TO BE here?" Dex asked, glaring at Keefe.

Keefe smirked. "I was just thinking the same thing about you."

Sophie rubbed her temples. She had bigger problems than two stubborn boys. One big, gray, muscly one in particular.

"We can handle this, Sandor," she told him for the tenth time.

"You're trying to break into a place your parents have not only forbidden you to go, but have built a special locked gate specifically to keep you away from. Be glad I haven't barricaded you in your room."

"Whoa, Gigantor's hardcore. And why are Grady and Edaline

so . . ." Keefe's voice trailed off and his smile faded. "This is where it happened, isn't it? Where you guys were . . ."

Sophie cleared her throat. "Yeah."

The Cliffside gate was in plain sight of the clue the Black Swan had planted—and they'd hidden it inside a lock. That had to mean they wanted her to pick the lock on the gate and go back to the one place she'd vowed never to go again. The cave where it all went wrong.

Face your fears.

"Is that why you needed Dex here?" Keefe asked quietly.

Actually, having Dex there made it worse. He was just as terrified as she was—and she hated putting him through it again. "He's the only one who can open the lock. He's—"

She glanced at Dex.

Dex sighed. "Might as well tell him—he seems to know everything else."

"Oh, more secrets. I love secrets!" Keefe added.

"Dex is a Technopath."

Dex cringed at the word, but Keefe's eyes widened. "Seriously? That is *awesome*! Why is that a secret?"

Dex stared at the lock—a small silver orb that dangled from a chain between the two gates—as he shrugged, his cheeks tinged with pink.

"So you can just, like, make a gadget do whatever you want?"

"Sorta." Dex traced his finger over the metal, making it flash with a rush of runes. "It's more like I understand them. I ask them how to do what I want and they tell me."

"That is the coolest thing I've ever heard—and, dude, we need to team up. Think of all the chaos we could cause!"

Dex's face was tomato red by that point—but he was also grinning from ear to ear. It made Sophie want to hug them both, but then the silver lock flashed green in Dex's hands and clicked open, letting the chain slip free.

"Step aside," Sandor ordered, pushing past them as he drew his curved black sword. "Everyone stay behind me."

He threw open the gate and started down the narrow zigzagging stairway that cut a path down the steep cliff to the sandy cove below. It was a path Sophie had walked dozens and dozens of times—but her legs still didn't want to cooperate.

Dex's didn't seem to be working either.

"Come on, guys," Keefe said, nudging his way between them and hooking his arms through theirs. "Gigantor's got us covered."

Sophie tried to believe him as they made the long, slow descent, but her insides had still tangled into knots on top of knots, and by the time they reached the white sandy beach, she was pretty sure she was going to throw up. Especially when she turned to face the largest cave.

The wide gap in the weathered rocks held good memories and bad memories and the worst memory of them all, the moment where everything got flipped inside out and upside down and ripped apart. When three dark-cloaked figures jumped out of the shadows and took her and Dex away.

Sandor thoroughly inspected each of the caves before giving them the all clear.

"So, we going in?" Keefe asked when everyone hesitated.

Dex dropped Keefe's arm and backed up. "I'm sorry—I can't. I . . ."

"Hey," Sophie said, waiting for him to look at her. "It's okay. You don't have to. Just wait here."

She knew exactly how he felt. But *she* had to face her fears.

"This is for Alden," she whispered as she took a step forward. Then another. Sandor and Keefe started to follow but she held out her arms. "I'd rather do this one alone, if that's okay? I'll call if I need you."

She didn't know what was waiting for her in there, but she wanted to face it on her own. She was tired of being afraid.

Her heart pounded so loudly it drowned out the roar of the ocean as she took the last few steps and entered the dimly lit cave. Shadows danced along the walls and across the packed sand floor, and her eyes were drawn to the spot where she'd collapsed to cry. Right before the arms had reached out and—

She counted her breaths and forced the memory out of her mind. She had one job to do, and she wasn't going to let anything get in the way.

A tiny pile on the floor in the back of the cave caught her

attention, and as she made her way over, her breath caught in her throat.

Freshly churned sand.

She spun around, checking for any sign that she wasn't alone. But whoever had stirred up the ground was gone. They'd left something, though. A small clump of twigs and branches on a nook in the rocks.

A nest.

Tucked in the center was a small, mirrored trinket box with a familiar black curve worked into the latch. She closed her eyes and made a silent wish that this would be the answer she needed, then plucked the tiny cube from the twigs.

Inside she found another scrap of paper and a tiny black swan. Not a pin this time—a charm. Carved much more crudely, with jagged cuts and very little detail, which seemed strange. But she was sure there was a reason. She hoped the clue would make it clearer.

There were two lines of text on the note when she unfolded it, but her eyes only saw the first. A small sob slipped through her lips as she read the four words that changed everything.

We can fix you.

FIFTY-FOUR

Y OU OKAY IN THERE?" KEEFE CALLED, startling Sophie so much she almost dropped the note.

"Yeah. I'm fine. I'll be out in a second."

She sank to the nearest rock, taking deep breaths to stop the shaking.

They could fix her.

They didn't say how—this was the Black Swan, after all. But she was willing to forgive them for the lies and the secrets and the ways they'd messed with her life. Even if they were the bad guys—she would trust them if it could make her right again.

All she needed was to figure out the clue.

The note had another sentence. One that was just as vague and unhelpful as the other times she'd heard it:

Follow the pretty bird across the sky.

She studied the crude black swan charm again. It hardly qualified as a "pretty bird."

Although . . .

She glanced back at the nest, where the sand was freshly dredged. There were no other footprints, almost like someone had popped out of the ground and then tunneled back in.

Dwarves.

Maybe *that*'s how the Black Swan were keeping tabs on her. And if they had dwarves on their side, maybe—

"One more minute or I'm coming in there," Sandor called.

"I'll be right out." Sophie tucked the charm back in its pouch, along with the note, and shoved both in her shoe. Yes, she'd promised Keefe and Sandor she'd keep them in the loop, but this was about *her*. She hadn't even told Keefe she needed to be fixed—and she intended to keep it that way.

But they'd never believe she didn't find *anything*, so she grabbed some of the twigs from the nest and snapped off the ends until they fit inside the box. She checked her pockets, wishing she were more like Dex, always carrying interesting things. Then she remembered the trackers.

She felt along the edge of her cape, relieved when her fingers touched the outline of a penny-size disk near the front corner. She didn't have scissors—or time—so she tore the fabric with her teeth, grabbing the copper circle and slipping it in the box just as two silhouetted figures appeared in the cave's entrance.

"I said I'd be right out," she yelled as she ran to meet them, tripping a few times on the rocks.

Keefe smirked. "Don't even try to pretend you didn't find anything."

"I wasn't going to." She handed him the mirrored box, and he dumped the contents into his palm.

"Twigs and a piece of scrap metal? Can't they just say, 'go here, do this, and have a nice life'? Seems like it would save a lot of time."

"It's not scrap metal," Sandor corrected. "It's a tracker." He glanced at Sophie and she looked away.

"A tracker? Like, to lead us to them?" Keefe asked.

"I think it would only tell them where *we* are," Sophie mumbled, heading out of the cave.

Keefe caught up with her. "So what's the plan, then—and don't lie to me, Foster, I can feel you hiding something."

"It's just a theory right now—I need to think it through."

"You mean *we*," Keefe said, hooking his arm through hers. "*We* need to think it through. Team Foster-Keefe!"

"Uh, now it's team Foster-Dex-and-Keefe," Dex said, marching over and taking her other arm.

Keefe shook his head. "That doesn't have the same ring.

Though it could be handy having a Technopath around."

"Look, guys, I really appreciate the help, but . . . I'm kind of tired, and there's a lot of stuff floating around in my brain. Can we talk about this tomorrow?"

"Depends," Keefe said, narrowing his eyes. "Are you trying to get rid of us so you can go on secret adventures by yourself?"

Sophie willed herself to feel calm as she said, "I just want some time to think."

"Uh-huh. Fine, you can have the night to think—but we *will* be revisiting this tomorrow. Come on, Dex, let's go mess with some gadgets before dinner. I know the perfect place!"

Sophie tuned them out as Keefe plotted and schemed the whole way up the stairs. Dex secured the lock on the gate and asked her if she'd really be okay. She promised him she would, and the boys leaped away to cause who knew what kind of trouble.

Sandor stayed silent as she greeted Silveny, promised her she'd spend time with her later, and made her way inside. But as Sophie closed the door to her bedroom, he held out his hand. "I'll need to ask the gnomes to resew that tracker into your cape before you go to school tomorrow."

"Oh. You caught that, huh?" Why did he have to be so obnoxiously good at his job?

"What was really in the box?"

She stared at her feet. "Another charm. And a note."

"I thought you weren't going to hide things from me."

"I had to this time—you're not going to let me go and I *have* to. They say they can fix me, Sandor—and if anyone can, it's them."

"I thought you didn't trust them?"

"I don't know what to think about them. I just know I have to try. It might be the only way."

His frown sank so deep it looked like his face was cracking. "I'm coming with you."

"You can't—"

"We made a deal. I'm coming with you or I go to your parents."

"You can't come with me, Sandor. Not if I'm right about the clue." She stalked to her desk, digging out the other pieces they'd given her.

One pin, two charms, and two vague notes. Not a lot to go on, but if she put it all together . . .

"See this?" she said, holding up the newest note. "It says the same thing Prentice told me. 'Follow the pretty bird across the sky.' And I think it means this."

She held up the black swan charm.

If a dwarf had delivered the charm, then maybe it was made of magsidian—and maybe the rough, crude cuts affected the pull of the stone, just like the flask that drew water and the pendant that drew light.

She held her breath as she picked up the charm bracelet and hooked the tiny swan next to the compass. Then she opened the locket and held the compass flat in her palm, watching the needle spin and come to a stop on . . .

Somewhere between north and west.

"I knew it! The magsidian is changing where the compass points. So if I follow this direction, it should lead me straight to where the Black Swan needs me to go."

"That can't be right. It could be an impossibly long journey."

"On foot, maybe. But the note says, 'across *the sky*'—and they gave me an alicorn pin."

Sandor's eyes widened. "Absolutely not. You know that unstable creature won't let me near her and I cannot allow you to fly off alone—especially without even knowing where you're going."

"But I *have* to. If they can fix *me*, then maybe I can fix Alden and—and maybe even Prentice."

"That's not worth risking your life for. You could be flying into a trap."

"I'm risking my life anyway. You've seen what the light keeps doing to me. If I don't take this chance, who knows . . ."

"I can't Sophie. Maybe if your parents agree—"

"I can't tell them about this."

"Why not?" Grady asked, pushing his way through the door with Edaline right behind him. He glanced at the notes, and his face turned so red it looked almost purple.

"You have a lot of explaining to do, Sophie. Starting right now."

Sophie had no choice but to come clean about everything: the clues, her plan to fix Alden, her journal, the way the light was affecting her, Wylie's theory. Elwin not knowing how to help . . .

"How could you not tell us about this?" Edaline asked as she reread the notes from the Black Swan.

"I don't know," Sophie mumbled.

Grady ran his hands through his hair, making it stick out. "Sophie, if your health is in danger, you *have* to tell us. We could get you help and treatment and—"

"Elwin already tried everything. If it's really in my genes, then the only ones who can fix me are the ones who made me."

Edaline sighed. "I can't believe you told Elwin before us."

"I didn't. I blacked out at school. And Elwin agreed that we should wait to tell you guys until we knew more. You have enough to worry about already."

"We do have a lot to worry about," Grady said, gazing out the windows as the sunset streaked the sky with red. "But we still always want to know what's going on with you. Honestly, Sophie, I know you've had to keep a lot of secrets in your life, but you have to stop hiding things. We're here to help."

"I know." Sophie sat on the edge of her bed and twisted the ripped end of her cape. "I guess I was just . . . embarrassed."

Edaline sat beside her, taking her hand. "You have nothing to be embarrassed about."

"Of course I do—I'm the Town Freak. Have you noticed

how people react when they see me? And how would you feel if you had people tell you that you were *malfunctioning*—especially if it were true?"

Grady took the notes from Edaline, squinting at them as he sat on Sophie's other side. Several seconds passed before he asked, "So this is why you keep fading?"

"It has to be. How else could I fade with *two* nexuses?"

She held out both of her wrists, and her heart ached when she realized both were gifts from the Vackers.

Grady squeezed the Ruewen crest pin on his cape. "And you really believe they can fix you?"

"I believe they're my best chance. My only chance."

Grady got up to pace. He'd worn a small rut in the petal-covered carpet before Edaline stood and said, "I can't believe I'm saying this, but I think we should let Sophie go."

"What?" Sophie, Sandor, and Grady asked at the same time.

"They *made* her. So if there's something wrong—and Elwin doesn't know what it is—I think we have to let them try to fix it. Otherwise what do we do? Let her keep blacking out and fading? How many times can that happen before she doesn't recover?"

"So we send her blindly into a den of murderers?" Grady snapped back.

"We don't know that for sure," Edaline said quietly. "But we do know that clearly the Black Swan can get to Sophie any time they want"—she pointed to the notes in Grady's hand—"so if they wanted to hurt her, they could've easily done it by now. And they haven't. Maybe Sophie's special because they made her. Or maybe it's because we're wrong about them. Either way, I just can't believe that they mean Sophie any harm. And if they can fix her . . ."

Grady shook his head. "I don't trust them."

"I know," Edaline whispered, wrapping her arms around him. "But I think this time we have to *try*. For Sophie's sake."

"This isn't just about me," Sophie reminded them when Grady didn't say anything. "If they fix me, I might be able to fix Alden, too. Don't you want that?"

"Of course." Grady pulled away from Edaline. "I miss my friend terribly. But . . . do you know why I agreed to become an Emissary again, Sophie?"

"You said it was because Alden had done so much for you."

"It was." Grady wiped away a tear. "And what I wanted to pay Alden back for was *you*. Bringing *you* into our lives."

Sophie felt her eyes burn. "I'm glad he brought me into your lives too."

Grady strangled her with a hug. "I would give almost anything to have him back," he whispered. "But I won't give up you."

"You won't have to, " Sophie promised. "They want to fix me, Grady. I *need* to believe that. I don't want to be broken anymore."

Grady sighed as he let her go, and he flipped through the

Black Swan's notes again as he sat next to her on the bed.

He stopped on the one that had made Sophie the angriest.

Patience
Trust

Grady stared at it for so long Sophie started counting the seconds. Eighty-one had passed before he mumbled, "Okay."

It took a moment for the word to sink in. "So . . . you're going to let me get on Silveny and fly wherever the compass leads?"

"Yes."

She glanced at Sandor. He was scowling—and his hands were clenched into fists—but he didn't argue.

"You know I'll have to go alone? Silveny won't let anyone else come."

"Actually, that's where you're wrong," Grady said. "There is one other person Silveny trusts, and even though he's *not* my first choice as an escort for you, he's better than no one."

Sophie couldn't quite hide her groan. "You realize you're putting my life in the hands of Keefe Sencen, right?"

"So, let me get this straight," Keefe said when Sophie was done explaining the new plan. "We don't know where we're going, or how long it's going to take us to get there, and we're flying to meet the Black Swan—who may or may not be evil murderers—and this whole thing could be a trap?"

"Pretty much," Sophie agreed, tugging on her heavy velvet cloak. Edaline had insisted she dress warm, and it looked like Keefe had the same idea. He wore a thick gray cloak pinned with the Sencen crest, and dark boots and gloves. He *almost* looked responsible.

"Awesome! 'Bout time this project got a bit more exciting." He glanced at Sandor. "Don't worry, Gigantor, I'll keep her safe."

Sandor cracked his knuckles. "You'd better."

It had taken a *lot* of convincing to make the overprotective goblin remove the trackers from her clothes. Sophie was afraid the Black Swan would be able to tell they were being monitored and would keep themselves hidden. Plus, she'd reminded Sandor that he wouldn't be able to follow her anyway.

"And your parents didn't have any concerns with you going?" Grady asked Keefe. "You *did* tell them, right?"

"Of course I told them. Sheesh—you act like I'm some sort of troublemaker." He winked. "Seriously though, they were fine with it. Well, once my dad was done asking me ten thousand questions to make sure I wasn't heading off to recreate the Great Gulon Incident or something."

Sophie's stomach tightened. "You told your dad about—"

"Relax. I only told him that you had to fly with Silveny somewhere and your parents didn't want you to go alone. I got your back, Foster."

"Thank you," she whispered.

"So, we ready to do this? What do you think, Glitter Butt?" He walked over to Silveny's enclosure, letting her nuzzle his hands through the bars. "You ready for a Foster-Keefe adventure?"

Silveny nickered. *Keefe! Keefe! Keefe!*

She'd been giddily chanting that since Sophie told her what was going to happen.

"Are you sure you shouldn't wait till morning?" Grady asked. The last wisps of purple twilight were just fading into the starry night.

"The sooner we go, the sooner we're back," Sophie reminded him, checking for the fiftieth time that the charm bracelet was on her wrist with both charms attached.

Grady didn't nod, and she could see the doubt blooming in his eyes.

"This is the only way to make me better," she whispered. "And maybe if they do, I can heal Alden and Prentice and—"

"They're not the ones who matter, Sophie," Grady said, wrapping his arms around her. "I'm doing this for *you*. You have to come back. Stronger and healthier than ever."

"I will," she promised, trying to convince herself as much as him.

"Don't let them do anything except fix you. And if there's anything strange or scary, you run—make Silveny teleport you away if you need to. Just come home safe. If you don't, I . . ."

"I'll be home soon."

She pulled back to look at him, but he strangled her tighter, whispering, "I love you so much," before he finally let her go.

"I love you too." She almost called him "Dad," but it still felt too soon. It was much closer than it had been a few weeks ago, though. Maybe it came down to trust.

Grady was giving her a lot of it right now.

So was Edaline, as she handed Sophie an overstuffed satchel. "Snacks and drinks, in case it's a long flight. And you have your Imparter?"

Sophie nodded.

"You hail us the first second you can."

"Of course."

Edaline's chin quivered as she pulled Sophie in for a hug, kissing her cheek and whispering that she had to be safe. Then she slowly let Sophie go, tucking a strand of Sophie's hair behind her ear as she whispered, "I'll miss you every second you're gone."

"I'll miss you too."

"Whoa, you guys are hardcore with your goodbyes," Keefe said, shattering the moment. "My mom just told me 'See you, son' and my dad only asked if I'd checked how tight the pin on my cloak was so I wouldn't lose a family heirloom."

Grady frowned, and Edaline reached for Keefe's hand, giving it a quick squeeze.

A bit of pink flushed across his cheeks. Then he cleared his throat and offered Sophie his arm. "So, you ready?"

"Probably as much as I'll ever be."

Grady opened the gate and Silveny trotted out, stretching her wings as she knelt to let them climb on her back.

Sophie's palms turned clammy as she wrapped her arms around Silveny's neck. And when Keefe wrapped his arms around her waist, a big part of her was tempted to jump off and forget the whole plan. But she remembered what the vision of Jolie had told her.

We have to trust.

This was for Prentice.

For Alden.

For *her*.

"Better hold on tight," she warned Keefe as she gave Silveny the order to fly. Silveny stood, flapping her shimmering wings as she galloped forward and took off, slicing through the chilly night air as they went up and up and then up some more.

Sophie's eyes burned as she glanced down to see Grady and Edaline waving—but she blinked back the tears. She would see them again—and things would be right this time. Really right. *Fixed.*

She held out the compass, waiting for the needle to spin.

Time to follow the pretty bird across the sky.

FIFTY-FIVE

ARE WE THERE YET?"

Keefe had already shouted that question over the whipping wind at least fourteen times. If he repeated it a fifteenth, Sophie was going to shove him into the dark waves below.

"No—for the millionth time. You'll know when we are because we'll stop flying."

"Okay, that's how *I'll* know when we're there. But how are *you* going to know? Because it's been a whole lot of stars. And ocean. And oh hey—look! There's some stars! And ocean! And I'm kinda starting to wonder if that's all we're ever going to see."

Sophie held the compass to the moonlight and told Silveny to fly a bit more to the left. "I'll know it when I see it."

She *really* hoped that was true.

Keefe fidgeted behind her, nearly knocking them off balance.

"Careful!" Sophie shouted as Silveny tipped up her wing to catch them.

"Sorry. I'm just trying to stay warm." He fidgeted again. "Can we play a game or something? Oh—how about truth or dare? I can think of some *awesome* dares."

"I kind of need to concentrate here."

He sighed so dramatically Sophie could hear it over the wind's roar.

"I'm guessing a tickle war is out of the question," he asked. "Because you're pretty vulnerable right now."

"Try it and see what happens."

"You *do* realize that just makes me want to do it more, right?"

"I'm serious, Keefe."

"I know—that's the problem." He shifted his weight. "How about you, Glitter Butt—you as bored as me?"

Keefe! Keefe! Keefe!

"What's she saying?"

"That you're annoying and she wants to dump you in the ocean."

"Well, I know *that's* not true. Glitter Butt loves me. Don't you, Glitter Butt?"

Silveny whinnied as he patted her side.

Sophie rolled her eyes.

Keefe shifted again. "Gotta say, Glitter Butt, you are not as comfortable as I'd like you to be. We need to fatten you up next time so you're softer."

"Hopefully there won't be a next time."

"Aw, what, you don't want to make this a regular thing?"

Sophie shook her head "It's a little different for me, Keefe. There's kinda a lot riding on this."

"Like your health and your future and Alden's health and stuff?"

"Which I *thought* you cared about—Alden at least."

He was quiet for a few seconds, and Sophie thought he was going to ignore her. But then he leaned closer—close enough that she could feel his breath on her cheek as he said, "I know I crack a lot of jokes, Sophie, but . . . that's just because it's easier, you know? It's how I deal. But that doesn't mean I don't care. I do. A lot."

She was suddenly very aware of how close he was, and the way his arms were around her. She felt her cheeks flame and hoped he couldn't feel the change in her mood.

"Are you scared?" he asked quietly.

She shrugged, not trusting her voice.

"You don't have to be. I meant what I told Sandor. I'm not going to let anything happen to you."

She wanted to tell him he didn't have that kind of power. Instead she cleared her throat and said, "Thank you."

He leaned back, taking his warmth with him. But at least she felt like she could breathe again.

"So tell me about the Black Swan," he said. "What are we up against?"

"I wish I knew. It's not like they tell me anything."

"Yeah, they do seem to like keeping their sense of mystery. Reminds me of someone else I know." He poked her side.

She smiled at the joke, but it also hit a nerve. "Do you think I hide too much?"

Her voice had barely been louder than the wind, but Keefe still asked, "What do you mean?"

"Grady and Edaline think I keep too many secrets."

"You do," he agreed. "But I'm guessing you've sorta had to, right? I mean, look at the kind of things you deal with. I don't really know how you do it."

Sometimes she didn't either.

She checked the compass again, steering Silveny back to the right.

"You can trust Grady and Edaline, though," he added after a second. "You got good parents there."

Parents.

Not *guardians.*

They were slowly starting to feel like that.

"Things have been a little better with your parents too, haven't they?" she asked, hoping she wasn't intruding.

"Yeah. I guess. I don't know. They only like when I do things *they* want me to do. Like this. My dad *loves* that I'm helping you—probably because everything you do seems to, like, change the course of history and whatever. But it'd be nice if they could be proud of something *I* like to do."

"Maybe it would help if the stuff you liked to do didn't involve gulons or glittery poop."

"Probably. But that's way less fun."

"Maybe you could just try . . ."

Her voice trailed off as a dark shape appeared on the horizon, silhouetted by the moonlight. Tall, rocky cliffs jutting out over the ocean. And when she checked the compass, the needle pointed straight to them.

"Is that . . . ?" Keefe asked.

"I think it might be."

She nudged Silveny to fly faster, keeping her eyes trained on the compass as the cliffs drew closer. The silver-white slopes of the rocky ledges came into focus, bright and gleaming in the pale moonlight, and Sophie felt goose bumps prickle her skin as she noticed a dark smudge toward the top of one of them.

A cave.

"That's it," Sophie whispered as a memory prickled her mind.

The dark cavern had a distinct curved shape, and she could see a perfect image of it in her memory. Which meant they'd always meant for her to find them someday.

She instructed Silveny to land on the ledge outside the entrance. Keefe tightened his grip on her waist as they swooped to a stop, and he helped Sophie slide down Silveny's neck to the rocky ground.

"Okay, the legs are *not* happy," Keefe complained as he took a few wobbly steps. "Remind me never to take up horseback riding."

Sophie's legs were throbbing too—but she was too distracted by the pitch-black entrance to the cave.

"So . . . I'm guessing we have to go into the scary black cavern of doom?" Keefe asked, sighing when Sophie nodded. "Yeah, I was afraid of that. I love that neither of us thought to bring a light, either."

"You don't need one," a gravelly voice said from the shadows, making both Keefe and Sophie scream.

"Dude—that was *not* cool," Keefe said as a hairy brown dwarf skulked out into the moonlight.

The dwarf laughed—a clunky sound like a spoon caught in a garbage disposal. "We need to get out of sight. Can you lead your horse inside?"

"I—I think so," Sophie stammered, wishing Silveny could send her some of her calm. But the jittery alicorn was more terrified than she was.

Trust, Sophie told her. *Come.*

She followed the dwarf toward the cave, and after a few steps Keefe and Silveny followed. As soon as they were inside, the dwarf flipped a switch, and blue-flamed torches sprang to life all along the rocky walls that curved around them. The cave was much shallower than she'd expected.

"Won't someone see the light?" Sophie asked.

"The cloaking is back up. I took it down when I felt you draw close, so you could find us."

"You *felt* us?" Keefe whispered.

Sophie pointed to the magsidian swan on her bracelet.

"Whoa—dwarves are freaky."

"I was not told there would be two," the dwarf grumbled. "Only a girl and a horse."

"My parents wouldn't let me come alone."

The dwarf made some sort of sound—a bit like a growl.

"I think he likes me," Keefe whispered, earning himself another growl.

Sophie looked around. As far as she could tell, it was just a normal cave—smaller than the one at Havenfield, even. "Is this . . . it?"

"Until you eat this." The dwarf handed her a plate with what looked like a cookie on it. A black swan. Written in some sort of icing were the words "THEN LET'S REST."

"Tucked in the branches of your quiet nest," Sophie finished, remembering the final line of the poem. "So . . . this is a sedative?"

"You cannot see where I take you."

"Come on, isn't this whole mystery thing a bit overkill?" Keefe asked.

"Don't worry. There's no cookie for you. You can stay with the horse."

"*What?*"

"But he's with—"

The dwarf held up his hand, silencing them both. "Only you."

Keefe glanced at Sophie. "He's like three feet tall and all fur. I think we can take him."

"That would not be wise." The dwarf stomped his foot and a crack split the ground, stopping just before Keefe's toes. Another inch and he would've been swallowed by the gap.

Sophie cleared her throat and took a deep breath for courage. "It'll be fine, Keefe. In fact, maybe it'll be better. I don't think Silveny would do well here all alone. Keep her company."

"But—"

"There's only one cookie," she told him, picking up the tiny swan.

Keefe stared at the crack in the ground, then back at her. "You're sure?"

She wasn't. But she'd come this far.

Her head screamed at her to toss the horrible, revolting sedative away, but she shoved the cookie in her mouth before she could change her mind. As soon as the sweet, fruity flavor hit her tongue, her head clouded and she could barely swallow the bite.

"I'll be right here when you—" Keefe called, but the darkness stole the rest of his words, leaving her alone in the black.

FIFTY-SIX

AKE UP SOPHIE," A DEEP, raspy voice called, and the déjà vu ripped Sophie out of the thick mental fog.

"Relax," the voice ordered as she thrashed on the soft cushion she was lying on—half expecting to feel bonds restraining her. But her limbs moved freely.

"We're on *your* side—remember."

My side, she told herself as she forced her eyes open—though she had no idea what *her side* was. The light from a single crystal hanging over her head burned her corneas, and it took several seconds to adjust.

How long had she been out?

She sat up slowly, letting her head clear before she turned to examine her surroundings. There wasn't much to see. She rested on a small cushioned cot—almost identical to the cots in the Healing Center. The rest of the space was an empty void of darkness.

"Where are you?" she called, surprised as her voice echoed off walls that were much farther away than she would've guessed.

A heavyset figure stepped into the light. "You kids and your screaming."

Sophie felt her jaw fall open. "Mr. Forkle?"

"That's one of my names, yes."

"Want to tell me the real one?"

A tiny smile played across the wrinkles of his bloated face. "When the time is right."

That wasn't good enough. She'd flown who knew how far and been drugged and dragged to who knew where—she didn't go through all of that to not get answers. She closed her eyes and pushed her mind into his and . . .

Hit a wall of silence.

Mr. Forkle laughed—though it sounded more like a wheeze. "You're not the only one with an impenetrable mind. That's why we're alone right now. Can't have you searching for things you're not yet ready to understand."

Sophie glared at him. "I deserve to know what you're hiding from me. And I want my memories back—and my journal pages!"

"It's not a matter of *deserving*, Sophie. Knowledge is a dangerous thing. Trust me when I say that it's better for you not to know."

"All I ever do is trust you!"

"I know, Sophie. And we appreciate it."

"Then trust *me*. Give me some answers!"

He fell silent, and Sophie wondered if she'd gone too far. But then he said, "All right."

"All right, what?"

"I'll give you one answer. *One*."

"I . . . okay . . ."

"Choose your question wisely, Sophie. I won't give you another."

She nodded, trying to make sense of the tornado of questions swirling inside her head. There were so many things she wanted to know. But what did she *need* to know? What single piece of information would change everything?

"Okay," she said, straightening up. "I have my question— and you have to promise to answer honestly."

"You have my word."

She nodded, taking a deep breath before she met his gaze and asked, "Did the Black Swan murder Jolie?"

The question knocked him back a step. "Is that what Grady thinks?"

"Yes. The fire happened right after someone slipped him a note that said, 'You don't know who you're dealing with.'"

"That . . . is not what that message meant," he said quietly.

"So that's a no, then?" she asked after several seconds of silence.

"Yes, Sophie, that is most definitely a no. Though it explains many things."

Relief poured through her in warm waves—though she was tempted to point out that if they were *clearer* with their messages, they wouldn't have these problems. And she couldn't help wondering, "What does it explain?"

His lips formed a word, then switched to a smile. "I said *one* question. And we have wasted enough time as it is. We have a bigger problem to address. *You.*"

The warmth faded as quickly as it came.

Mr. Forkle moved closer, and the smell of dirty feet made Sophie gag. It was the ruckleberries he ate to disguise his identity. They made the skin swell and wrinkle, like an overweight, elderly human. "I'm afraid your mind is broken."

The room tilted sideways—or it might as well have. "Broken like Alden . . . ?"

He shook his head, running a pudgy hand down his face. "No, not like Alden. And if we'd known you were damaged, we never would've sent you down there. It was a miscalculation on our part. I should've expected that something happened when you faded—especially since I did think it was strange that the Vacker boy could transmit to you after that. But I wrongly assumed he'd found the way through."

"Wait." She rubbed the temples of her still foggy head. "There's a way through my blocking?"

How else do you think I gave you your memories? he transmitted.

His mental voice didn't sound screamy like Fitz's, but hearing it in her head made her want to claw the words back out.

"It's a secret way only I'm supposed to know," he said out loud, "but he's a talented boy and I thought maybe he'd figured it out when your mind was weakened by the leap. But that was my mistake. If I'd checked, I would've realized there are two gaps in your barriers now. And the new gap has absolutely no defenses. It's like a chink in your armor. A weak spot where things you should be able to block push through—some easier than others. Like Fitz's transmissions. Or Bronte's inflicting. Or the dark shards of the broken minds you were meant to heal."

She shuddered at the memory. "So, you *did* want me to fix Prentice. That was what your first clue meant?"

"In part. We needed Alden to take you down there in order for you to have access to Prentice, so the message was also meant to convince him that you should be his guide. But yes. We knew when we started Project Moonlark that we could very well endure some casualties—especially with our Keepers—so we gave you the ability to heal broken minds. That way you could recover anyone who was lost."

"But everyone told me that healing minds is impossible."

"As are most of the things I've enabled you to do, Sophie. I've done extensive research, and I discovered a safe place inside the mind. A nook where things can be hidden. We trained our Keepers to hide a part of their consciousness there during a memory break, so that we could rescue them later."

The words triggered such a mix of relief and terror Sophie didn't know what to do with them.

She could fix Prentice—finally set that right!

But what if she couldn't fix Alden?

He hadn't been trained to retreat to the nook—and she hadn't felt his presence the way she'd felt Prentice's when she tried the probe.

What if there was nothing left to rescue?

"How does it work?" she asked, hoping there was still a chance. "How do I rescue them?"

"The rescue is the easy part. The hard part is getting there. That's why we designed you the way we did. We needed a powerful Telepath with an impenetrable mind to probe past the madness without getting lost. Then once you're there, all you have to do is inflict powerful, positive emotions to build their strength back."

"But I can't inflict positive emotions."

He gave her a knowing look.

"I can?"

"Only in theory—though it's looking much more likely now that I've seen the connection between you and Silveny.

I modeled many of your genetic manipulations on alicorn DNA."

"What?" She was on her feet without deciding to stand. "Are you saying I'm part *horse*?"

A horrifying image of her as some sort of mutant-Sophie-centaur flashed through her head, and she wanted to reach inside her brain and tear it out.

"Of *course* not, Sophie. I just needed something to base my research on, and Silla Heks had noted all kinds of interesting observations about the way her alicorn had affected her emotions. I suspected it meant that alicorns have a way of inflicting their feelings on others—both bad *and* good—so I decided to model some of my tweaks on their DNA. But you're still one hundred percent elf."

Sophie sank back down, too overwhelmed to even begin to process that. Especially when he added, "I have often wondered if that's how you ended up with brown eyes, though."

Sophie buried her head in her hands. How was she ever going to look in the mirror and see anything but a horse face now?

"Don't be so dramatic," Mr. Forkle grumbled. "This is not the tragedy you're making it out to be—"

"Really? So you wouldn't care if someone played Dr. Frankenstein with your genes?"

"Are you any different right now than you were five minutes ago, before you knew?"

"I don't know," she mumbled miserably. "It feels like it."

"Well, you're not."

She rolled her eyes. Her stupid, freaky, horse eyes.

Mr. Forkle started to pace, stepping in and out of the shadows as he moved. "We've gotten off track. What's important is that all my careful plans hinged on your mind being impenetrable. And it was, until you nearly faded away. Then your guard cracked, leaving an opening that light—and somehow Fitz—knows how to get through. I'm guessing you bonded with the light as you were fading, let it become a small part of you. And that bond has turned into a weak point where light— or darkness—can push through. That doesn't explain Fitz, but maybe you pulled him through as you dragged yourself back, and his mind learned the way. Regardless, you made a special pathway straight into your brain, and things have been pushing through or slipping away because of it."

That made almost zero sense—but Sophie supposed it didn't matter. All that mattered was, "You can fix it, right?"

"In . . . theory."

"No—that's not what you said." She fumbled in her pocket for the note and shoved it at him. "See—right there. We. Can. Fix. You."

"We *can* fix you, Sophie." He held up a tiny bottle made of glittering green crystal. "Drinking this will reset everything that's been undone. But you need to understand the risk first." He stared at the bottle instead of her as he said, "The only thing that will fix you is limbium."

She scratched at her arms thinking of the hives. "You know I'm allergic."

"I do. And believe me, I've tried to find another way. But alternatives like this"—he reached for the vial of Fade Fuel dangling from her neck—"simply aren't strong enough. They've helped with the symptoms, which tells me I'm right about the cure. But the only true remedy is *real* limbium. A very strong dose."

A slightly hysterical laugh slipped through her lips. "So, the only way to fix me is to give me something that will kill me."

"No. The only way to fix you is to give you something that will *almost* kill you—and then give you the antidote I've carefully crafted and hope it stops the reaction." Mr. Forkle sighed and sat beside her. His bulky body sank into the cushions, making her lean toward him more than she wanted. "The cure will work. Limbium affects the center of our special abilities, and this strong of a dose will serve as a reset, undoing any changes that have occurred since your abilities developed. But . . . there's still a tremendous risk. Your allergy is a complete mystery to us. We've never encountered anything like it—and it's already almost killed you twice."

"So it *was* limbium that caused my first allergy? The one you erased from my memory because you don't want me knowing what happened?"

He shifted his weight, making the cot creak. "Someday you will understand why that memory was taken. But yes, I gave you a small amount of limbium—not realizing it would trigger such a violent reaction. If the human doctors hadn't stepped in, I'm not sure what would've happened. Which is why I've made this."

He reached into his pocket and pulled out the biggest syringe with the biggest needle Sophie had ever seen.

Spots danced across her eyes and she jumped to her feet, backing away from him into the shadows where he couldn't see her. "Uh-uh—no needles."

"It's the only way."

"No, I have this now." She stepped back into the light, holding up the black vial Elwin gave her to wear around her neck.

"That won't be strong enough."

"It worked last time."

"Yes, because the amount of limbium in that mild serum Dex gave you was less than a drop." He held up the green vial again. "This is an ounce of *pure* limbium, and you must swallow every bit. It will take a lot to jolt your mind to reset—and a tiny bottle of Elwin's medicine is not going to counteract that. This is the only way." He stared at the needle and even *his* hands shook. "Though even then, I can't guarantee it will be able to stop the reaction. This is human medicine I collected and then altered and enhanced. It's completely untested. And the limbium will have to stay in your system for several minutes to allow it time to work, so the reaction will be full fledged by the time I treat you. Which is why this has to be your choice."

She snorted. "Right."

"I mean it, Sophie. Despite what you may think, you are not our puppet. We may give you suggestions and guidance, but in the end the final decision is always up to you. You can leave right now and remain just the way you are."

"Oh, you mean broken." She made no effort to hide the bitterness in her voice. "How nice of you to let me stay damaged and malfunctioning."

"You're only a *little* broken. You can still live a perfectly normal life, so long as you take your medicine to help with the fading."

"But I won't be able to fix Prentice, or Alden, right?"

"No. Your mind will never be impenetrable again. Not without this."

"Well, then, it's not really a choice is it?"

"It is, Sophie. You can choose to protect yourself."

She stared at the bottle in his hands, trying not to think about the burning hives or the heaving pain of her last allergy attack. And the needle . . .

She couldn't look at it.

And what about her family? Would Grady and Edaline want her risking her life for this?

But could she live with herself if she left Alden trapped in the nightmare of his insanity and Prentice drooling in his dim cell in Exile?

"Give me the vial."

A sad smile creased Mr. Forkle's bloated lips. "Your courage never ceases to amaze me."

He stood, motioning for her to lie back down on the cot, and she didn't bother arguing. He handed her the vial when she was settled.

"I'll do everything I can to guide you through this. But you're going to have to fight hard."

"I always do."

She stared at the crystal vial, watching the liquid slosh in her shaking hands. It wasn't too late to change her mind.

Or maybe it was.

She pulled back the crystal stopper and poured the salty, metallic liquid down her throat.

FIFTY-SEVEN

THE SECOND THE LIMBIUM HIT HER tongue it started to swell, and Sophie barely managed to choke the liquid down before she started to gag. Breathing became impossible, and the more seconds ticked by, the more her lungs screamed for air.

The room dimmed and the sounds dropped to a hum—but her consciousness didn't fade away. She felt every second as the liquid burned through her like she'd swallowed something hotter than fire. Like she'd swallowed the sun. Her stomach heaved and her limbs flailed and she tried to think through the pain, count the moments passing, search for some sign that relief was on the way. But the agony was too all-consuming.

She wasn't afraid of the needle anymore. She wanted it—needed it. Where was it? She couldn't hold on much longer. Still the fire burned, rushing into her head and searing so hot she was sure her brain would melt in the inferno. Maybe it did. White light burst behind her eyelids, and for a second she felt the pressure ease.

Was that it? Was she fixed?

She couldn't tell—the relief was too fleeting. And the darkness that rushed in to replace it was so much worse. Cold and thick and empty, and she could feel herself sinking into it, following it somewhere much deeper and blacker than unconsciousness, and she knew with every fiber of her being that she'd never come back. She was shutting down. Slipping away.

Then something stabbed her hand and the new pain dragged her free. Her body thrashed and her insides wanted to explode from the pressure as a soft gray mist swelled inside her mind. She latched on to it, using it to float above the shadows as her insides heaved again, and the pressure in her chest grew so unbearable she wanted to scream. But as she opened her mouth, a rush of air filled her body.

Her first breath.

Followed by another.

And another.

She wanted to count them—cling to them—celebrate each one. But the fog in her head was growing thicker, and she couldn't fight the clouds any longer. She set her hopes and trust upon them and felt them carry her away.

"I let you out of my sight for a few minutes and you go and almost die again," Keefe said, his words like a hammer pounding on her brain.

Sophie forced her eyes open—and immediately closed them as the light burned too bright. She tried to speak, but all she could do was cough and hack, which made her realize her body ached in about a million places.

"Hey, easy. I'm not joking about the almost dying thing. Some wrinkly dude brought you here and said he'd almost lost you—twice—but he thinks you're okay now. Well, other than a truckload of pain, which he said he can't help you with because your mind needs to stay 'unaffected' by any medicines for at least twenty-four hours. Any of that sound familiar?"

"Bits and pieces," she managed to rasp between coughs.

"Good. Then maybe you can translate for me, because he kind of lost me at *she almost died*. Pretty sure Grady's going to kill me when I bring you home like this."

"I'm fine."

"Uh . . . you can't see what I see. You've got this whole sweaty, slightly green thing going on—not to mention this wicked bluish-purplish splotch on your hand."

Sophie ripped her eyes open again, and when they'd focused, she stared at the huge bruise from the needle.

Add it to her list of reasons why she never wanted to see a syringe again.

"I'm fine. They had to give me limbium to fix me, and then a shot of some human medicine to stop the allergy."

"Sounds . . . fun."

"Yeah, it's awesome to be me."

She tried not to think about the other things Mr. Forkle had told her about her genetics, but it was hard to do with Silveny transmitting, *Friend! Sophie! Friend!*

"You're really fixed, though? Like, you think you'll be able to help . . . ?"

He didn't say the name, and Sophie didn't want him to. Not until she knew for sure. "I don't think I'll know until I try and see what happens. Did Mr. Forkle give you any other instructions when he brought me here?"

"He gave me a tiny, sealed scroll—said it was for Grady or Elwin. Who was that guy, by the way?"

"The guy who posed as my old next-door neighbor to keep tabs on me around humans. And apparently he's the guy who made me."

"Made you? So, like . . . he's your father?"

"I—I don't think so." She'd never considered that.

Could he be?

He *was* a Telepath. An *impenetrable* Telepath.

And he created her.

And he *cared*.

She shivered so hard her teeth rattled.

She refused to believe it. A father would never play with his daughter's genes the way Mr. Forkle had. And a father would never be able to leave her half-drugged and alone on the streets of Paris—even if he did believe she'd be okay. Nor would he drop her off on the hard ground of a cold cave with nothing more than her friend, a flying horse, and a scroll, after she'd almost died—again.

Unless he was the worst father in the world.

Then again, Grady and Edaline had let her risk everything to find the Black Swan. . . .

"Hey, you okay?" Keefe asked as she curled into a ball.

She didn't want to know any more horrible things about her past or who she was. It just kept getting worse and worse.

One sob slipped through her lips, and once the floodgates were open, there was no stopping it. She waited for Keefe to tease her, but he just scooted closer, lifting her head so it rested on his knee instead of the rocky ground.

"Sorry," she mumbled when the crying fit finally passed.

"For what?"

"I should be braver than this."

"Um, I don't know if you realize this, but you're the bravest person I know—by *far*. Freak out all you want. If anyone deserves to, it's you."

"Thanks." She concentrated on taking slow, deep breaths to calm down, but each one only made her more aware of how sore she was. She could definitely feel that they'd almost killed her this time. Every part of her ached. A deep kind of pain, like a sharp pin in every cell.

"I want to go home," she whispered.

"I know. But do you really think you're up for that? I mean, it's a long flight. And the old dude said we shouldn't light leap. He doesn't think your concentration can handle it."

"I'm hoping Silveny can teleport us back to Havenfield. We know where we're going this time, so we can take a shortcut."

"Ohhhhhhh, teleporting sounds fun. But do you need to rest a little longer?"

She shook her head and slowly sat up. The pain of the simple movement knocked her breath away and she clutched her chest.

"Whoa—that is intense," Keefe said, his voice strained.

"You can feel my *pain*? I'm sorry—I didn't—"

"It's fine." He stopped her from scooting away. "I only feel a tiny glimmer. Nothing on what you're feeling, which must be unbearable. Seriously, how are you dealing with that?"

"I don't have a choice." He helped her to her feet, and she was relieved when her legs held steady, even if it felt like her muscles were tearing. He pulled her arm behind his shoulders and they hobbled to Silveny, who knelt as they drew close.

Keefe lifted her onto Silveny's back, and she grabbed the alicorn's gleaming neck, really *really* hoping she'd be able to order Silveny to teleport. Otherwise she had no idea how she'd survive the flight back. Her weary legs might actually drop off her body.

"Sorry, am I holding too tight?" Keefe asked as he wrapped his arms around her.

"No—it's fine. I'm just sore. How do we get out of here?" She looked around, realizing the opening to the cave had vanished.

"You ask us to remove the cloaking," a dwarf said as he popped out of the ground.

"Dude—it's evil the way they just pop out of nowhere like that."

The dwarf glared at Keefe as he flicked a switch and the cloaking vanished, revealing the opening to the cave and the dark starry sky beyond.

Sophie urged Silveny to step out onto the ledge, and the fresh air felt good on her weary muscles. *Ready to go home, girl?*

Silveny's fur bristled and Sophie nearly choked on the horse's unease.

Relax, Sophie told her. *There's nothing to be afraid of.*

The thought had barely left her mind when a series of loud clangs shattered the silent night and some sort of strange, black net dropped from the cliff above and covered them.

Silveny reared back, but gleaming metal orbs on the edges of the net weighed it down, pinning them to the ground as five black-cloaked figures rapelled from above, surrounding them.

FIFTY-EIGHT

OT AGAIN.

It was Sophie's only thought as the black-cloaked figures grabbed the net, pulling it tighter around them. Keefe shouted something she didn't hear as she closed her eyes, waiting to feel the fear and rage swell inside her head. But all she could muster was a shudder.

She must be too weak to inflict.

A flash of light shot past her, hitting one of the figures and making him collapse in a trembling heap.

"They have a melder!" another figure shouted as Silveny reared in the loosened net.

"Where did you get that?" Sophie yelled as Keefe raised the silver weapon and fired another shot.

"Grady insisted I take it, but he didn't want me to tell you in case it freaked you out." He fired again, but his aim was wrecked by Silveny's thrashing.

The four remaining figures closed off their circle and one of them reached for a melder of his own.

"Don't hit the alicorn!" one of the others shouted at him.

"Isn't this the point where you develop some new, impossible ability and get us out of here?" Keefe yelled as they ducked a melder blast aimed at them.

"I wish." Sophie squeezed her eyes shut and tried to rally her concentration. "Nothing's working right now."

Even her arms and legs were too weak and slow. All she could do was cling to Silveny's neck with what little strength she had and hope Keefe could either take out the attackers or that the Black Swan would send help.

Keefe aimed at the figure who was armed, but before he fired, one of the other figures nailed Keefe in the head with a rock. The melder slipped from his hand.

"Oh, so that's how it is?" Keefe shouted, whipping one of Sandor's weird throwing stars at him. The silver blades clipped the figure's shoulder, tearing his cloak and making him drop his end of the net.

"Don't let the alicorn get away!" the attacker shouted, flailing to regrab the ropes.

Keefe flung another pointed star, but he missed. "These things are hard to aim!"

"How many weapons do you have?" Sophie asked him.

"Hopefully enough." Keefe tossed a third throwing star, missing again.

"Try cutting the ropes!" Sophie shouted.

Before Keefe could try, Silveny bucked again, rearing back so hard she pulled partially free of the net—enough to spread her wings.

A powerful flap had them airborne, but they'd only moved a few feet off the ground before a black lasso swung around Silveny's neck and jerked her down so hard her legs collapsed.

Silveny's right wing bent backward as she toppled to her side. The majestic horse screeched in pain, and Sophie and Keefe tumbled off her back, rolling across the rocky ground until they crashed into the side of the cave.

"What have you done?" one of the figures shouted as the remaining four of them rushed for Silveny.

Sophie struggled to pull free from the tangle of rope, surprised that none of them seemed concerned with capturing her. Before she could decide what that meant, there was a blinding flash of light and the ground shook, cracking around their attackers and sending them sprawling. Through the thick dust Sophie caught a glimpse of Mr. Forkle and a cluster of dwarves running toward them.

"Get out of here," Mr. Forkle screamed as the hooded figures advanced on him and the dwarves. "Leap Sophie home, Keefe!"

But Sophie wasn't leaving Silveny. Keefe must've been thinking the same thing because he pulled himself up and jumped over the fissure to where Silveny lay thrashing on her side.

"Come on, Foster!" he shouted, holding out his arms to catch her. Sophie pulled herself upright, summoning as much strength as she could as she ran for the opening, jumping at the last possible second. Only one foot caught the ground on the other side, but Keefe grabbed her arms and dragged her over. He wiped her cheek, and when he pulled his hand away it was smeared with red.

Sophie wasn't surprised. He had a huge gash over his eyebrow. She was sure she was just as scraped.

Get up, Silveny, she transmitted, and the injured alicorn struggled to her feet.

Keefe lifted Sophie onto Silveny's back and crawled on behind her. As soon as his hands locked around her waist, Sophie transmitted, *Fly!*

Silveny ran toward the edge of the cliff and leaped off. She flapped her shimmering wings, but the right one was crooked and bleeding and when the wind hit the feathers, it bent backward, sending them dropping like a stone toward the ocean below.

Fly! Sophie's mind screamed, but no matter how hard Silveny flapped and flailed, her wing wouldn't work.

"Now what?" Keefe shouted.

Teleport!

Sophie repeated the command over and over, but Silveny's mind was too clouded by fear and pain to respond.

Teleport now or we're going to die!

"Uh . . . Sophie?" Keefe screamed as several precious seconds slipped by.

Silveny, you have to get us out of here!

Help! the terrified horse transmitted.

I don't know how!

But Silveny just kept repeating *Help!* over and over. And as Sophie imagined them splattering over the rocky shore, something inside her clicked.

She wasn't sure if it was instincts or pure desperation, but it felt like her brain switched into autopilot, feeding off her adrenaline to generate warmth and energy and swirling the two forces together until it felt like an explosion rocketed from her mind. The blast tore an opening in space, and a split second later they crashed through it, into the void.

The gray space felt different now that Sophie was the one in control, and she realized they could go anywhere—everywhere—all she had to do was think it and it would be.

There was only one place she wanted to go.

Before she could fully think the word, the grayness split with a flash of light and they dropped through it, landing in a crumpled heap in the soft grass of Havenfield.

FIFTY-NINE

I THINK I'M MAXED OUT ON ADVENTURE for a while," Keefe said as Elwin flashed a red orb around his chest. Thick scratches covered his arms, and his chin had a gash almost as deep as the one over his eyebrow. "Now I know why you need a physician on standby, Foster."

"Are you really okay?" Sophie asked, feeling a bit dizzy every time she looked at the red streaks on his skin. She hoped they didn't hurt as much as the deep cut across her right cheek.

Grady and Edaline had rushed outside the second they'd heard Silveny's agonized screeching. They'd helped Keefe and Sophie pull themselves away from the thrashing, wounded horse, and they'd hailed Elwin and sedated Silveny before she could hurt herself further. But Sophie and Keefe had both insisted on being treated outside, in case Silveny woke up.

Sophie winced as she tried to shift to a more comfortable position on the grassy ground. The instructions Mr. Forkle had sent explicitly forbade elixirs, serums, or sedatives of any kind. All Elwin had been able to do was clean her wounds—which he was *not* happy about. She wasn't a fan either. It would've been nice to at least use a numbing balm, but they couldn't chance it.

"I knew I should've gone with you," Sandor grumbled, slashing his sword at the air like he was slaying imaginary attackers.

Grady nodded as he paced back and forth across the pasture, wearing a groove in the soft ground. Every few seconds he pummeled them with more questions about what happened, most of which Sophie didn't know the answers to. Or didn't want to answer . . .

She didn't know if she'd teleported—or how she'd done it if she had—but she didn't want anyone to know either way. Then she'd have to explain about her crazy alicorn-inspired DNA, and everyone would probably run screaming away from "the girl who was part horse."

Another secret.

But some things she just couldn't share.

"I'm so glad you're okay," Grady said, crouching and wrapping his arms around her. The hug was gentle, but tight, too— like he never wanted to let go.

Sophie didn't want him to. "Thank you for trusting me," she told him.

"Thank you for coming back."

She heard Edaline sniffle and glanced over to where she was busy tending to Silveny. When their eyes met, Edaline whispered, "I love you."

"I love you too," Sophie whispered back.

"I haven't been able to reach your parents," Grady told Keefe. "I tried hailing your father, but he hasn't responded yet."

"Yeah, and it's not like you'd expect him to be waiting up all night for me to come home safe or anything."

Sophie tried to think of something to say, but Grady changed the subject. "I guess this means you were right about the Black Swan, Sophie. I . . . need to let my suspicions go."

"You really do." She tightened her grip around him as she added, "I asked them about Jolie."

His back went rigid. "You what?"

"He let me ask one question, and I asked about Jolie. He said that was not what the message meant, and that they had nothing to do with the fire."

Grady wobbled and leaned back to bury his face in his hands. When he looked up, tears had pooled in his eyes and his arms were shaking. "So it wasn't my fault?" he whispered.

The question made Sophie's heart swell. Now he could let go of his anger *and* his guilt—all the burdens he'd been carrying and battling for so long.

Now he could just be Grady again.

"Did he know anything about the fire?" Grady asked, drying his eyes on his sleeve.

Sophie frowned. "It almost seemed like he'd never considered it a murder, because he said, 'it explains many things.' But when I asked him what that meant, he told me I'd already used up my question."

Grady heaved a heavy sigh, and Sophie couldn't blame him. Then he strangled her with another hug. "Thank you for asking, Sophie. I'm sure there were lots of other things you wanted to know."

"There were," she admitted. "But that was the most important."

And not just for Grady. She may be an anomaly and a freak and created for things she didn't understand, and her real father may or may not be some mysterious elf who kept abandoning her when she needed him most. But she wasn't made by murderers. She wasn't *bad*.

"Explain to me more about these attackers," Sandor interrupted. "I would like to better understand my enemy."

Sophie shivered as the five black-cloaked figures filled her mind. "There were more of them this time, but I didn't recognize any of their voices."

"They had a patch on their sleeve," Keefe added as Elwin flashed more light around his face. "A white circle with an eye in the center, like it was staring at you. Totally creepy."

"Can you project the symbol?" Grady asked Sophie, but she shook her head.

"I didn't see it. I wish I had."

"I'll try to draw it," Keefe offered. "I got a good look as I was aiming those star-blade things. And I sliced one of their shoulders pretty deep. Maybe it'll leave a scar we can recognize."

"Good boy," Sandor told him.

"Yeah, well, who knows what would've happened if the Black Swan hadn't shown up with their dwarves. Things were getting pretty bleak."

"I wonder if they really would've taken us, though," Sophie mumbled, almost to herself. "I think they were after Silveny. She was the only one they shouted at each other about. It was like Keefe and I were just grabbed by default."

Grady turned pale as he processed that. "We'd better warn the guards to be on high alert."

Sandor nodded.

"I don't understand why they'd want her," Sophie admitted.

"Power." Grady went back to wearing a groove in the soil with his pacing. "Silveny is the only one who can reset the timeline. Whoever controls her has the Council at their mercy—to some extent. Which means I'd better alert them immediately."

He pulled out his Imparter and moved far enough away that they couldn't listen to what he said. Which was just as well. Sophie didn't want to hear how Bronte reacted when he found out Silveny had been injured.

"Is she going to be okay?" she asked as Edaline rubbed a thick black balm into the part of Silveny's wing where bits of bone poked through the skin.

"It's hard to tell. She'll definitely live. But . . . she may never fly again. This is a pretty bad break."

Sophie looked away as Edaline set the bone. The crunching sound made her stomach turn—but not as much as the idea of Silveny being grounded for the rest of life. She knew better than anyone how hard that would be for the flight-happy alicorn.

"Speaking of breaks," Elwin interrupted, "congratulations, Keefe, you've cracked four of your ribs. First time I've ever seen that around here."

Keefe gave a weak smile. "I'm sure I'll be proud in a few days—but for now the whole stabbing pain in my chest is killing the triumph."

Elwin handed him four tiny vials in all different colors. "Drink those and you'll be back to causing trouble in a few hours."

"Wow—really?" Keefe poured them all into his mouth at once. "That's almost too easy." He glanced guiltily at Sophie. "You really can't take any?"

"Not yet." She forced a smile, but he didn't look convinced. Neither did Elwin, who stomped over to change her bandages.

"I still can't believe you willingly took limbium. And not just a drop. *An ounce.* Sometimes I think you really do have a death wish, Sophie. And this"—he lifted her hand and pressed gently on the needle's bruise—"is downright barbaric. I don't know what this Mr. Forkle gave you, but he should be ashamed of himself."

Sophie wished she could agree. But the truth was, "He had no choice. It was the only way to fix me."

"*Did* it fix you?" Grady interrupted, rejoining them.

"I . . . don't know. I felt something change during the reaction, but it's hard to say until I try to use my abilities."

"Which you won't be doing for twenty-four hours—and don't even think about arguing," Elwin interrupted again. "If I have to leave you bruised and broken with no pain medicine, then you're not doing *anything* else. And when your time limit is up, I'm treating all your injuries—and doing a thorough exam—before you're allowed to test your abilities. Deal?"

"I'll only agree if you do one thing," Sophie countered. "Flash the light around my face like you did last time, when it went wrong."

Elwin looked leery, so she added, "It's only light. I just . . . need to know."

He sighed and raised his hand. "I'd better not regret doing this," he whispered as he clicked his fingers, and a thin blue orb flashed around her face.

Sophie held her breath, waiting for the pull and the pain. But nothing changed.

Tears burned her eyes as she laughed and waved the light away. "It didn't hurt!"

Even though she knew she shouldn't, she let hope swell and spread until she was filled with an almost giddy warmth that dulled her aches and pains and erased her fears and worries. If that part of the problem was fixed, then maybe everything was fixed. And if everything was fixed, then maybe she could fix a few other things that were broken.

"Can you take me to Everglen tomorrow?" she asked, hardly able to believe that in less than a day she might be able to look into Alden's bright teal eyes and have him actually *see* her. Smile at her. *Talk to her.*

"That depends," a sharp voice barked behind her, and all the warm hope burst with an icy shiver.

Bronte stood at the front of the other Councillors, his arms folded across his chest and a cold glint in his gray eyes. "You all may be exiled."

SIXTY

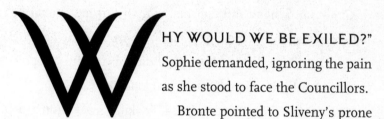

WHY WOULD WE BE EXILED?" Sophie demanded, ignoring the pain as she stood to face the Councillors.

Bronte pointed to Sliveny's prone form. "Look what you've done to the alicorn—do I need to remind you how important she is?"

"The cloaked guys did that—not us!" Keefe shouted.

"Yes, and the only reason they had the chance is because you took the alicorn away from the safety of her pen and the protections we'd put in place, and brought her somewhere incredibly dangerous," Bronte snapped back. "Do you have *any* idea what chaos it will cause if we have to inform the populace that the rebels struck again, this time injuring the only creature who can reset the timeline?"

"So don't tell them," Keefe suggested, earning himself an icy glare from Bronte.

"And how, Mr. Sencen, are we supposed to hide this news when we've announced that the alicorn will be swooping around the Sanctuary in just over a week? She will clearly not be up for flying. We'll be lucky if she's still alive."

His words felt like knives, and Sophie glanced at Silveny. An ugly red stain had seeped through the bandage on Silveny's broken wing, and Sophie sent a silent plea for the glittering horse to be okay.

Grady ran a hand through his hair. "If anyone should be held responsible, it's me. I gave Sophie permission to go."

"So I could get *fixed*! It's not like I did this for fun." Sophie held out her bruised hand. "Does that look like fun?"

"No," Councillor Emery agreed, looking away from the wound. He turned to Silveny's unconscious form. "But you must understand how serious this situation is."

Kenric stepped forward. "I think perhaps we're focusing on the wrong concern. Sophie, do you still have the compass that led you to the Black Swan?"

Sophie started to nod, but as she reached for the charms she realized the bracelet was missing. She checked her pockets, the ground, anywhere—everywhere. "It's gone."

"Of *course* it is," Bronte grumbled.

"Did I have it when they brought me back?" she asked Keefe, who was checking his pockets too.

"I didn't notice. I was kinda distracted by how pale and unconscious you were."

Edaline covered her mouth and looked away.

Grady cleared his throat. "I'm sure the Black Swan didn't want anyone coming back. And I'd bet anything they've abandoned that location anyway, now that the other group has found it. How did they find you, by the way? Do you think they followed you?"

"On what?" Sophie asked. "We flew."

"And there were other ways you could have gotten there," Bronte interrupted. "Safer ways you could've taken instead of endangering the alicorn and likely crippling it!"

Sophie stared at her feet. If she'd known that, she might have gone a different way. But . . . the Black Swan instructed her to take Silveny. That was their idea—not hers.

Maybe they wanted this to happen, a niggling doubt whispered, but Sophie smothered it. No more doubting the Black Swan. They'd fixed her. They didn't kill Jolie. They'd even come to their aid when the rebels attacked. Despite how confusing many of their methods were, they were the good guys.

Councillor Emery rubbed his temples and Sophie could only imagine the headache of arguments that must be raging in his mind as the other Councillors debated with each other.

"I think perhaps it is too early to make any decisions," he

finally announced, holding up his hands. "To decide if punishment is necessary before we know the full extent of the alicorn's injuries would be foolish. My recommendation is that we reconvene tomorrow, after Miss Foster has been treated and Silveny is awake."

The other Councillors murmured their agreement.

Bronte rolled his eyes. "What time can Miss Foster finally take her medicines?"

Elwin stepped forward. "Not until after sundown tomorrow."

"Then we'll be back at sunset." Bronte raised his pathfinder like the matter had been decided.

"Wait!" Sophie called, turning to Councillor Emery. "I need a few more hours than that."

"What for?" Bronte demanded.

"I need to go to Everglen." She couldn't risk that they might haul her away to Exile without giving her a chance to fix Alden. She had no idea if there was any part of him she could rescue, but there was no way she wasn't going to try.

"You really believe you can heal his mind?" Kenric asked quietly.

"According to the Black Swan, I was designed that way."

"Incredible," Councillor Terik breathed.

"More like incredibly complicated," Bronte barked, and Sophie wished she had something to throw at him. Leave it to him to find a problem with *everything*.

"What do you mean, Bronte?" Kenric asked.

"I mean that we've spent so long operating under the knowledge that we *can't* fix broken minds that we've never had to consider whether we *should*."

"You would leave Alden trapped in madness?"

"No," Bronte admitted quietly. "His recovery would be a tremendous gain. But where do we go from there? How do we decide who to heal and who not to heal?"

"How about the ones who were innocent—like Prentice?" Sophie suggested.

"Was Prentice innocent?" Bronte countered. "Regardless of whether he was working for good or ill, he was still violating our fundamental laws. Is that worthy of redemption?"

"Yes," Sophie answered, expecting the others to echo her. But the Councillors stayed silent.

"Okay, what about someone like Brant?" Sophie tried. Grady and Edaline gasped, like they hadn't considered the idea. "His mind was broken by accident."

"I would still fear a slippery slope with that precedent," Bronte replied.

"So what are you saying?" Councillor Emery asked him.

"Only that if this ability exists, it will need to be regulated and sanctioned—just like the breaks themselves. Careful thought and consideration will need to be given before each time it is used, and a unanimous vote should be required."

"Unanimous?" Terik asked. "You realize how rarely we come to those?"

"Exactly why it should be a requirement."

They argued back and forth and the others chimed in, some raising new points, others choosing sides. Sophie tried to keep up with it all but it got so complicated, and her body was so sore and tired, that she finally raised her hands and called out, "Excuse me!"

Her mouth went dry as all eyes returned to her. She cleared her throat. "Sorry. It's just . . . Don't you think we should wait until we find out if I can even do this before we start piling a mess of rules on it? And as the one who has the ability—don't I get any say in when I will and won't use it?"

"Yes to your first question," Bronte conceded. "No to your second."

Sophie opened her mouth to argue, but she caught Councillor Terik shaking his head and decided to refrain.

Councillor Emery rubbed his temples again. "Clearly, we need to explore the realms of possibility before we discuss the complexities of the reality. So how about we convene at Everglen an hour after sunset and see what happens? We can debate further from there."

The others agreed, and Grady promised to arrange everything with the Vackers. Everyone flashed away, and only then did Sophie realize she'd agreed to try healing her first mind in front of an audience.

"I get to go too, right?" Keefe asked.

"Of course," Grady promised, and Sophie was relieved.

Keefe deserved to be there—though she had no idea if she was really going to be able to fix anything.

"Good." Keefe met her eyes, and his face turned serious. "It's going to *work*, Sophie."

"I hope so."

"I know so. Which means you need to get some sleep. You have to be well rested for tomorrow's celebration of epic proportions. And I guess I should probably go home too."

"Will you be okay?"

"Yeah, I'll live." He dusted himself off as he stood. "Try not to die while I'm gone, okay? And no 'almost deaths' either."

"I'll do my best."

He winked as he held his home crystal to the predawn sunlight and slowly glittered away.

"I can't believe I'm saying this, but I think Keefe's growing on me," Grady mumbled.

"Me too," Sandor agreed. "Though I'd prefer he stop calling me Gigantor."

Everyone laughed. But then Grady's smile faded. "I'd better help the gnomes get Silveny somewhere safe, and you need to rally the other goblins, Sandor." He glanced at Sophie. "Think you'll be able to get some sleep, even with the pain?"

"I've had worse," she promised, wishing it weren't true.

Grady sighed and turned to leave.

"Are you going to tell the Vackers what I'm trying to do?" she called after him.

"I think I have to. I hate to get their hopes up, but they'll wonder what's going on when all the Councillors show up."

"I guess."

She let him walk a few more steps before she asked, "What if I can't do it?"

Grady walked back and took her hands. "Then they'll appreciate how hard you tried—and you'll know you did *everything* you could, and we'll all find a way to let him go for good. Okay?"

Sophie nodded.

He gave her another hug and wiped away the tears she hadn't even noticed she was shedding.

"Come on, Sophie," Edaline said, gently draping an arm across her shoulder. "Let's get you cleaned up as much as we can, and then you need to rest. You have a big day ahead of you."

SIXTY-ONE

SOPHIE STARED AT THE GLITTERING mansion of Everglen, trying to force her legs to move. She couldn't believe it'd only been two weeks since the day when everything fell apart.

She had to make things right today.

When the sun had set, Elwin made her guzzle so many elixirs and serums that she still felt light-headed as she made her way up the glittering steps. Or maybe that was nerves. Either way, she was glad she hadn't eaten anything, because there was no way she would've kept it down.

Grady and Edaline walked on each side of her, and they squeezed her hands as she stumbled forward.

"Remember," Grady said quietly, "all you can do is try your best."

She repeated those words as Della opened the door to greet them.

She looked like *Della* again, her piercing eyes sharp and clear and a hint of color in her cheeks. Fitz and Biana flanked each side of her, but Sophie didn't let herself look at them. She focused on the rainbow flecks of light on the floor, relieved she felt no reaction to them.

"Thank you, Sophie," Della said, throwing her arms around her in a tight embrace. Sophie tried not to think about how frail Della felt, or how much they all were counting on her to do this, but the pressure piled on top of her anyway. Especially when Biana joined the hug.

"I'm sorry, Sophie," Biana whispered, starting to cry. "I know I've been awful and I don't blame you if you hate me. It's just been so hard."

"I know," Sophie told her. "It's okay."

A tiny part of her wondered if Fitz would chime in, but he stayed silent, standing just out of reach. So she was completely surprised when he said, "You can't hear me anymore, can you?"

Sophie turned to face him, staring at his chin instead of his eyes. "Were you trying to transmit?"

He nodded—or she assumed he did because his chin bobbed up and down.

"I guess that means he fixed me, then." Which was a relief. But it made her sad, too—not that she expected Fitz to be having any more secret conversations with her.

"Can I um . . . talk to you for a minute?" he asked quietly.

"Uh, yeah. Sure. Um . . ." She looked around, trying to figure out where to go.

"Let's go outside." He offered her his hand, and several seconds passed before Sophie worked up the courage to take it.

She pleaded with her palm not to sweat as he led her to the shade of a nearby tree.

"The bruise is still there." Fitz pointed to the dark purple spot on the back of her hand, in the center—all that was left after Elwin finished treating her. Elwin had promised he'd make a balm that would get rid of it, but Sophie had a feeling it was one scar that would stay.

"It doesn't hurt." She pressed it a few times, until Fitz grabbed her other hand to stop her.

He waited for her to meet his eyes before he said, "Keefe told me what you went through yesterday—and what you've been going through ever since . . . well, you know. And I just . . . I . . ." He dropped her hands and looked at the ground. "Ugh, how do I apologize for being the hugest jerk ever?"

Sophie smiled sadly. "You weren't *that* big of a jerk."

"Yeah I was." He walked a few steps away, kicking the grass. "I was just so angry. All I could do was scream and break things. Half my stuff is trashed now." He turned back to her, but he kept his eyes down. "But . . . I'm so sorry, Sophie—for everything. And I wanted you to know that before you try to fix my dad, because if it works, I don't want you to think that's the only reason I'm saying it."

His words felt warmer than the sunshine peeking through the branches. "It's okay, Fitz. I'm not mad at you. I don't think I ever was."

He looked at her then, his brows scrunched together. "Why not?"

Sophie shrugged. "You thought you'd lost your dad. You had a right to freak out. But . . ." It was her turn to look away. "You really don't blame me anymore?"

Fitz stepped closer. "I never *really* did. I was just . . . I don't know. I was being stupid."

"Boy is *that* an understatement," Alvar said, making them both jump as he appeared out of thin air. "And I gotta say, Sophie. I think you're letting him off too easy. At least make him buy you a present or something."

Sophie laughed as Fitz glared at his brother. "Maybe next time."

"There won't *be* a next time," Fitz said, and the look in his eyes made Sophie's heart flutter. She'd almost forgotten what that felt like.

"Yeah, well, let's hope not," Alvar said, clapping Fitz on the back. "Anyway, sorry to interrupt, but the Council is obviously eager to get started."

Sophie sighed, wishing she could feel the same way. But there was a lot of pressure riding on this.

They walked in silence back to the front door, but before

Fitz followed Alvar inside, he whispered, "It's lame that we can't transmit anymore. I hope Tiergan still lets me be in your telepathy session."

She felt her cheeks flame. "Me too."

"And remember," he told her as they started up the stairs. "No matter what happens now, we're still friends, right?"

Sophie smiled. "Still friends."

"Whenever you're ready," Grady told Sophie as she slowly approached Alden's bed.

They'd moved him back to his bedroom, and all twelve Councillors had lined up against the curved walls, along with Keefe, Della, Fitz, Biana, and Alvar. Tiergan and Elwin were also there, in case anything went wrong and they needed either a Telepath or a physician to help—but Sophie was really hoping it wouldn't come to that.

It felt *right* this time.

Maybe it was just her rushing high from mending things with Fitz and Biana, but she couldn't help feeling like something really good was about to happen. She just had to trust, and try.

The room fell silent as she placed her hands against Alden's temples and closed her eyes. She waited until she felt calm and in control. Then she took one last breath and opened her mind to Alden's.

His mind was cold and thick and sharp, like swimming

through a raging river filled with jagged rocks. But no matter how hard the forces battered her, nothing broke through her mental barriers this time. No crazy memories or madness. No images at all. Just cold, quiet darkness that she sank deeper into—and then deeper still—trying to feel for warmth to guide her to the nook, like she'd done the last time.

Alden? she transmitted, filling his mind with the sound of her call. *It's Sophie. I'm here to help you.*

Please be here. Please have enough left for me to rescue you.

She repeated the call over and over until his mind was nothing but a series of echoes. It didn't seem to help, but she wasn't giving up. She filled his head with happy memories, faces, places, sounds—anything she could think of.

At first they were swallowed by the darkness, but the more she transmitted, the longer they lingered, and slowly they gathered around her, a safe nest of precious things. And as she concentrated on them, she felt the tiniest spark of warmth.

It was far away—almost out of her reach—but she followed it through the murk and it led her to the nook.

It was empty.

Alden! she transmitted over and over, begging him to respond. He couldn't be gone. She wouldn't give up. There had to be something else she could say, do, try.

She was *made* for this.

Her mind ran through the things Mr. Forkle had told her about the way he'd designed her, and as she repeated their conversation, she realized she'd missed one crucial step.

Inflicting.

She'd learned nothing from her one, lonely inflicting session except how to endure pain—but Silveny had sent her blasts of emotion all the time. Only problem was, she had no idea how Silveny did what she did. But maybe her instincts knew what to do—just like when she teleported.

She focused on love, the most powerful emotion of all, thinking about all the different people she cared about. Her family. Her friends. Iggy and Silveny. Even Sandor in all his gobliny glory. She was surprised by some of the faces that filled her mind, but she loved so many people in so many different ways. And as she thought about all the things they'd done for her, a buzz of warmth and happiness and energy swelled around her mind. Just a trickle at first, but the more she fed it, the more it turned into a raging surge.

She focused on the rush, and imagined her concentration wrapping around the flow and shooting it into Alden's mind.

Nothing happened.

She concentrated harder, transmitting images of Alden's family and friends and sending them along with the rush as she told him, *People love you, Alden. People need you.*

Come back for them.

She repeated the call over and over and over, and with each repetition the warmth rose.

Feeding it.

Fueling it.

She was close.

He was close.

But she needed something else to push him that last little bit, something to convince him he *had* to come back. And that's when she realized what was missing.

I can fix Prentice.

The words had barely entered Alden's mind when the warmth exploded around her in a geyser of heat and sparks, launching her consciousness up up up, blasting away the darkness and the cold and uncovering fragments of memories that slowly started piecing themselves together.

Alden? Sophie called, trying not to panic in the endless second that followed.

Then Alden's weak voice transmitted, *I'm back.*

SIXTY-TWO

THE MINUTES AFTER ALDEN OPENED his eyes were such an overwhelming flurry of laughter and tears that all Sophie could do was hold on and soak it up as everyone cheered and sobbed and crushed them both with hugs and kisses.

Then Elwin stepped in, made sure Sophie was okay, and herded everyone except family out so he could check Alden over.

As soon as they were downstairs, the Councillors started an intense debate over what to do now, and soon Grady, Edaline, and Tiergan had all joined in. But Sophie couldn't think coherently enough to participate. She was too stuck on the fact that Alden was back.

He'd looked at her and smiled as she left the room.

A real smile. An *Alden* smile.

"We did it," Keefe said, wrapping an arm around her and fist pumping the air. "Team Foster-Keefe triumphed! Clearly this is proof that we should work together more often. I'm sure Glitter Butt would agree." His smile faded. "How's she doing, by the way?"

"Her bones haven't responded to any of our healing elixirs. We'll have to wait for her to heal on her own. And she can't move her wing right now because of the splint, so we won't be able to tell if she can fly until it's removed. But she was able to walk, eat, and drink this morning—and she's still transmitting like crazy."

"Wow, really? I figured that would've stopped."

"Yeah, me too."

She tried to keep her emotions even so he wouldn't guess that she had anything to hide, but she could still feel him staring at her as she reached up to tug out an itchy eyelash.

Fortunately, Elwin came to the rescue.

"Sorry to interrupt," he said as everyone fell silent. "Alden would like to have a word with Sophie."

"It's strange how much has changed in two weeks," Alden whispered, after he'd asked her a billion questions about what had gone on while he was out of commission. "I feel like I've missed everything."

"Don't worry. With the way things go around here, I'm sure there's plenty more excitement to come."

"I'm afraid you might be right."

So was she—though after facing all of this, she felt like she could handle *anything*.

"I'm just glad it worked," she said quietly. "I wasn't sure if it would, since you hadn't been trained to retreat to the nook or save any part of yourself. How did you know?"

"I don't think I did." Alden stared out the window. "I'd been fighting the break day by day. Minute by minute. The only thing that kept me going was my family. I knew it would destroy them if I shattered, and I tried to hold on for them. But when I saw Prentice in Exile, I thought I was done. I felt the cracks form, felt myself fall through, and I thought, *I've failed.*"

"That was a break?"

Alden nodded. "I didn't tell anyone because I came back, and I thought that meant I'd fought to stay with my family. That I was strong enough to keep fighting. That I was safe. But then I saw Wylie and I thought about him growing up without a family—because of *me*, and—"

His voice broke and he wiped away a tear. "I think you must've pulled me back that first time in Exile—maybe my mind was so newly cracked that your ability could still work, I don't know. But it had nothing to do with me. I was weak. And the second time, the cracks were too big, too deep. I sank into them and everything collapsed."

"You must've held on somehow. Otherwise you wouldn't be here."

"Maybe. I do remember thinking about my family as I shattered, so it's possible some small part of me held on. But if it hadn't been for you . . ." He took her hand, staring at the star-shaped bruise. "I don't know how to thank you for everything you've done for me, Sophie—and for my family."

"You're back. That's all the thanks I need. Just, take care of yourself, get stronger, and if you start to feel any more guilt, remind yourself that I *will* fix Prentice. As soon as the Council lets me."

And if they wouldn't let her, she'd find a way to do it anyway. She could teleport now. She didn't need their permission to get to Exile.

"Leave that up to me," Alden said, interrupting her scheming. "The Council and I will be having a very long talk about— well, a lot of things."

"Are you up to that?"

"I will be soon. No reason to worry."

She smiled at the familiar words, relieved when Alden smiled too. And for the first time in a long time, she actually believed them.

"We still have to discuss the matter of the alicorn," Bronte announced as Sophie joined the Councillors outside. Elwin and Tiergan were inside, helping the Vackers, but Keefe had stayed with Grady and Edaline.

Sophie had to bite back her groan. "You can't be serious, Bronte."

"Oh, but I am. Treason is a very serious matter."

"Treason?" she repeated.

"Bronte, we are not going to discuss exiling this family after everything they've done today," Councillor Emery said firmly.

"Everything *Sophie* has done today," Bronte corrected. "And while *I* don't personally subscribe to the notion that a good deed can erase a bad, I'm not a fool. I know I'll be overruled on that."

Kenric, Oralie, Emery, Terik, and two Councillors that Sophie didn't know all nodded. She made a mental note of her supporters.

"I do, however, remember that Grady admitted to granting permission for this treasonous act—and before you go arguing that he was trying to help 'fix' his daughter, need I remind you that when he was reinstated as an Emissary, he swore an oath to put the good of our world above his own life? It's the same oath we've *all* sworn and *all* made tremendous sacrifices to uphold. Are we going to allow Grady to subvert it with no consequences, especially given that his actions led to the likely crippling of the most important creature in our world?"

"Hey—it's just a broken wing," Keefe argued, backing up when Bronte reeled on him.

"*Just* a broken wing? That wing is the primary method of transportation for this creature—not to mention there will surely be psychological effects as well. Animals lose their instinct to breed—even, at times, their will to live—when they suffer so serious an injury. And I doubt I need to remind any of you how vital it is that Silveny thrive."

"You want to blame someone, track down our attackers," Sophie snapped. "*They're* the ones who hurt her."

"Oh, we intend to," Bronte told her. "But Grady still allowed her to be in harm's way."

Sophie rolled her eyes. "Please, she was in harm's way in our pastures! The attackers have clearly been watching and planning. Sooner or later they would have found an opportunity."

"But they didn't need one, because Grady handed it to them on a silver platter."

Edaline reached for Grady's hand as several of the Councillors murmured among themselves.

"Even if we do concede to your point—which has *not* been decided," Councillor Emery said after a second, "I hardly feel such an offense merits exile. Especially considering the alicorn may very well recover."

"'May very well' and 'will' are not the same. And the timing must also be considered." Bronte had the gall to smile as he folded his hands and said, "Grady gave his word that he would have the alicorn ready to present to the Sanctuary during the Celestial Festival amid great fanfare and spectacle. In light of that promise, we announced a tremendous celebration. It was partially to repair the rift caused by Alden's loss—which is obviously no longer needed. But we also aimed to prove to the people of our world that they should have hope and trust and faith in their Council. What message will it send now when we not only cannot deliver—but present them with a wounded alicorn who could very easily never recover?"

No one seemed to have an answer, and each second of silence felt heavier as it passed.

"Silveny might still be able to fly," Sophie mumbled, knowing even as she said it that the chances were slim. The Celestial Festival was only four days away.

"Might, Miss Foster? You expect us to hang our hopes on *might*?"

"He's right," Councillor Emery said—though he didn't look happy about it. "We'll need to cover with an alternate spectacle, *and* find a way to make it clear to the people that the change is not a sign of our incompetence."

"And the best way to do that is to be able to inform them that the person responsible is being punished to the fullest extent of our laws. It'll send a message to the attackers, too, hopefully deterring any further attempt."

Kenric stepped forward when no one else did. "I will not concede to a Tribunal, Bronte. No matter how you try to twist it, there's nothing about what happened that would merit us locking Grady away in Exile like a murderer." He turned to the other Councillors. "That's not justice. That makes us just as cruel and reckless as the rebels we're trying to prevent. And if that's the kind of action we would consider to try and prove our worthiness, then we deserve every bit of criticism we're getting."

A stunned silence followed, until Oralie moved beside him. "I agree."

"As do I," Councillor Emery said before closing his eyes. "And it appears all the others agree as well."

Bronte's frown looked more like a snarl. "So we're just going to let him go unpunished? *That's* the precedent we're going to set?"

Councillor Terik sighed. "Perhaps we can come up with an alternative punishment."

That sparked an enormous debate, where the Councillors suggested everything from a public scolding, to relocating Grady to a permanent position at the Sanctuary, and everything in between.

"Can I say something?" Sophie asked when she couldn't stand it anymore.

She took a deep breath as everyone fell silent, letting the idea settle in so she could accept it.

"We're waiting, Miss Foster," Bronte snapped.

She glanced at Grady, reminding herself why she was doing this as she said, "I can make sure that Silveny still makes a dramatic appearance during the festival."

"How?" Bronte demanded. "Light leaping doesn't count, and last I checked, flight was a key element to her teleporting."

She'd thought so too. But she'd realized why the sensation

felt familiar as she teleported them away from their attackers. She'd done it before—when she made that impossible jump during base quest.

She wasn't blinking. She was making tiny, unplanned "slips."

Which meant she didn't have to fly.

She just had to *fall*.

"I can give you guys a far bigger 'spectacle' than you ever imagined," she said, hoping she sounded more confident than she felt. "And if I do, everything will be exactly the way we promised it would be, so no punishment would be needed."

"And what is this alleged spectacle?" Bronte demanded.

"It's . . . a surprise," Sophie stalled, not ready to reveal her secret. She'd have to now—and she would. But she would take any extra time she could get.

Bronte snorted. "You expect us to just blindly trust you to surprise us with some phenomenal thing—"

"Yes. I do. I think what I've done today more than proves that I can do things everyone thinks are impossible."

Several of the Councillors murmured in agreement. Bronte rolled his eyes.

Sophie turned to Councillor Emery. "But I'd need your word that there will be no more discussion of punishment—for any of us. Grady. Edaline. Keefe. Sandor. Me. We're all safe or no deal."

"And why do we need *your* spectacle?" Bronte snapped. "We're perfectly capable of making one on our own."

"Maybe. But mine will deliver on the promises you made and save you from looking bad—which I thought was the whole point."

"It is," Kenric agreed. "I say, deal."

"Deal," Councillor Terik agreed, along with several others.

Bronte's scowl was so deep it looked like his face had sunken in. But he knew he was trapped. "Fine, I'll agree to this *deal*—for now. But if anything goes wrong . . ."

He didn't finish the threat, but it wouldn't have mattered.

Sophie was afraid of many, many things.

But she wasn't afraid of herself anymore.

She could do this.

She just had to trust. And be willing to take the first leap.

SIXTY-THREE

ARE YOU READY FOR THIS? SOPHIE transmitted as she stroked Silveny's shimmering nose.

The earth's shadow had just started its slow path across the moon, making a red-orange eclipse in the starry sky. The Celestial Festival would be well under way, which meant she and Silveny were almost to their cue.

They were the finale.

Ready, Silveny transmitted, but without her usual enthusiasm.

Sophie had spent the last three days using every non-school-related second preparing Silveny for the night's big move. All the gentle medical care had helped Silveny stop panicking around other elves and animals, and Sophie had spent hours explaining every detail about what would happen and why and what they needed to do. Silveny was as ready as she'd ever be.

But now that the moment had come, Sophie wasn't ready to say goodbye.

Friend, Silveny said, nuzzling Sophie's neck and filling her mind with a lonely ache. *Come.*

"I can't," Sophie whispered. *You know I can't.*

Stay, Silveny tried.

You can't do that either.

Silveny hung her head, and Sophie felt her eyes get watery.

She'd only spent five weeks with the strong-willed alicorn—most of which had been filled with more headaches and glittery poop than she would've liked. But Sophie couldn't imagine looking out in the pastures and not seeing her fluttering around. Or sleeping without Silveny's warm calm filling her mind.

Silveny didn't want to go either. *Friend. Stay. Home.*

"It's not safe here, anymore," Sophie told her. "Look what happened to your beautiful wing."

She'd removed the bandage a few minutes before—the Council didn't want the public to see it—and there was a dark scar among the feathers. Sophie stared at the star-shaped bruise on her own hand as she traced the thin red line on Silveny's skin.

Another thing they had in common.

Another reason this had to be done.

The Sanctuary was hidden inside the Himalayas. The dwarves had secretly hollowed out the enormous mountains centuries before, and the gnomes and elves had converted the space to a lush paradise with every possible climate, comfort, and care. Access was restricted and regulated, and the Council had amped up security even more for Silveny's arrival to make sure that no one would be able to hurt her there. And Silveny would finally be able to meet the other alicorn, and hopefully with time they would breed. Ensure the existence of their species.

I'll come visit, Sophie promised, which perked Silveny up enough to fill Sophie's head with *Visit! Visit! Visit!* mixed with the occasional *Keefe!*

Yes, I'm sure Keefe will come too.

She reached up and ran her fingers through Silveny's icy mane, meeting her deep brown eyes. *But I'll miss you.*

Miss, Silveny repeated, transmitting the ancient ache she'd sent Sophie before. *Friend.*

Tears slipped down Sophie's cheeks, and she wrapped her arms around Silveny's neck. *What matters is keeping you safe,* she told her, repeating the words until Silveny finally accepted them.

Sophie tried to accept them too as Silveny lowered her shimmering head and let Sophie climb on her back.

"You don't have to do this, Sophie," Grady said, startling them both.

Sophie turned around and found Grady and Edaline watching her. It was strange to see them in their long silver capes embroidered with the Council's seal. But they were both officially part of the nobility again, assigned to assist with the search for the kidnappers and the Black Swan.

Assuming Sophie pulled this off without a hitch . . .

"I thought you guys were at the festival already," she said as she adjusted her heavy cape. The Celestial Festival was being held at the base of Mount Everest, so everyone had to wear thick clothes and clunky boots to stay warm.

"We were," Edaline said, stepping close enough to inspect Silveny's wing. "But I wanted to check Silveny's wound." She frowned at the dark red scar.

"And I wanted to tell you one more time that you don't have to do this," Grady added.

They'd both insisted on knowing what Sophie was planning, and she'd finally caved and told them everything: how Mr. Forkle modeled her DNA on alicorns, how she'd figured out how to teleport—in theory, at least—and how she was planning to test that theory for her *spectacle*. They'd been trying to talk her out of it ever since. Once she did this, the Council would know she could teleport, and they didn't want Sophie to feel forced to expose her secrets. Especially since they kept saying they were sure the Council would only give Grady a minor punishment.

Sophie gave them the same answer she'd given them every time. "I know I don't have to. I want to."

Edaline gave Sophie a hug.

Grady sighed. "Letting you go never gets any easier, does it? Though it might help if you weren't always doing such dangerous things."

Sophie smiled. "It's going to be okay. And hey, we've fixed everything else. We just need to solve this last thing."

Grady nodded. "I trust you."

"Me too," Edaline agreed.

"I suppose that means I should as well," Sandor grumbled as he stepped from the shadows. "But I still prefer when you stay by my side, Miss Foster."

Sophie smiled. "I know. And I promise I will *try* to be better about that." The kidnappers were still out there—and there were even more of them than she'd realized—so she was going to have to keep her burly bodyguard around for a while. "But I have to do this first."

Sandor reluctantly nodded. "I'll be waiting for you when you arrive."

Edaline wiped her eyes and took Grady's hand as he raised his pathfinder.

"I guess we'll see you soon," Edaline whispered.

"I'll be there in a minute."

Sophie watched the three of them glitter away and tightened her grip on Silveny's neck.

Silveny raised her glittering wings.

No. We're not going to fly, remember?

She was glad Silveny could move without any pain. But she had no idea if the wing could really support any weight, and she wasn't going to let Silveny hinder her recovery by trying to fly too soon.

Silveny tensed as they trotted toward the edge of the cliffs, and Sophie was nervous too. But if the last few weeks had taught her anything, it was that sometimes there was no guarantee. Sometimes she just had to trust herself and believe that if she put her mind to it, she was strong enough to pull through.

It always came down to trust.

No flying. Sophie repeated the command until Silveny tucked her wings. *Trust?*

Trust.

Sophie closed her eyes, taking a deep breath and rallying her concentration before she transmitted, *Run!*

Silveny whinnied and galloped forward, bounding across the last stretch of grass before she leaped off the edge of the cliff.

Calm! Sophie transmitted as they fell down down down, and she filled Silveny's mind with warmth as she repeated, *Don't you dare try to fly.*

Miraculously, Silveny obeyed, and Sophie forced her eyes open and focused on the dark rocks and shallow waves they were hurtling toward. They hadn't been able to practice this part—it was too dangerous to try more than once—but she knew she could do it. She embraced the fear and adrenaline pumping through her veins, gathered it all together until it was a giant ball of force, and shoved it out of her mind.

A thunderous crack split the space in front of them, and they slipped into the void.

Sophie concentrated on a mental image of the Sanctuary, and as she did, her instincts told her how to weave through the gray mist. More thunder crashed as the space parted and they raced through the split, onto the icy ground at the base of the towering mountain, amid a shower of sparkle and hundreds of twisting beams of colored light.

A flash of blue light painted across the sky, illuminating the thousands of wide-eyed spectators gaping at them in stunned silence as Silveny slowed to a stop.

Good girl, Sophie told her as Silveny dipped her head in the bow they'd rehearsed.

The crowd went wild.

Silveny whinnied, her silvery body quivering with excitement. Sophie tried to calm her, but Silveny was too caught up in the frenzy, and before Sophie could stop her, Silveny raised her shimmering wings and . . .

Launched them into the sky.

"You can fly!" Sophie screamed, even though they only made it a few feet off the ground before Silveny set them back down.

Fly! the giddy alicorn transmitted as Sophie strangled her with a hug. *Safe!*

Yes, Sophie told her, blinking back tears. *You're safe.*

Several of the Councillors—along with a fleet of goblins—rushed Silveny to the Sanctuary as soon as Sophie dismounted. She barely managed to transmit, *I'll see you soon,* as Silveny trotted away. But before the alicorn disappeared through the gates, Silveny filled Sophie's mind with warmth and told her, *Friend! Visit.*

Sophie wiped her eyes and promised, *I will.*

"You weren't kidding about the spectacle," Councillor Terik said, startling her as he approached from behind. "An elf who teleports? Definitely one for the history books."

"Great," Sophie mumbled.

He laughed. "You'll get used to your fame eventually, Sophie."

Somehow she doubted that. But at least she wasn't hearing whispers about "the girl who was taken" from the crowd.

Yet . . .

"In the meantime," Councillor Terik said, dragging her out of her worries. "I thought you would want to know that the Councillors are more than satisfied with what you've done here tonight. We can already feel the unrest easing."

She watched the families of elves laugh and smile as the lights danced in the sky. "I hope it lasts," she whispered.

"Me too."

The worry woven into his tone made Sophie wonder if he was thinking the same thing she was.

The rebels *would* strike again.

But Sophie planned to be ready this time.

Councillor Terik cleared his throat. "Now that Alden's back, I know you probably won't need my help. But you still have your Imparter. Hail me anytime."

"Thanks."

She hoped she wouldn't have to take him up on that, but with the way her life seemed to go, it was good to know she had at least one Councillor on her side.

"There you are, Miss Foster," Bronte said, stepping from the shadows. He eyed Councillor Terik as he said, "Am I interrupting something?"

"Yes, Sophie and I were having a pleasant conversation. So I'm sure this is your cue to ruin it."

Bronte scowled and folded his arms. "Actually, I do need to have a word with Miss Foster. *Alone*."

Sophie sighed. Of *course* he did.

Councillor Terik gave her an apologetic smile as he left her with her pointy-eared nemesis. But Sophie held Bronte's icy glare, surprised at how easy it was to face him.

"You really can't feel that?" he asked after a minute.

"Feel what?"

"Apparently your mind is impenetrable to inflicting now."

"*You tried to inflict on me?*"

"Oh, relax. It didn't work, did it?"

"No," Sophie grumbled, wishing she could fling something at his head. "Was that all you needed?"

He released an epic-length sigh. "No. I also wondered . . . is it true that you can inflict positive emotions?"

"I think so. Why?"

His eyes dropped to his hands. "Well, then. Perhaps we'll have something to teach each other."

His voice was barely a whisper, and Sophie wondered if she'd heard him right.

Did Bronte just admit that *he* had something to learn from *her*?

"Anyway," he said, the edge returning to his features. "I suggest you prepare for your next session. I will *not* be holding back."

Sophie doubted he had the first time. But she'd already faced her deepest fears. How much worse could it be?

She flashed her most confident smile, which felt more like a smirk, as she told him, "Bring it on."

Sophie sat alone on the cold ground in a shadowy corner of the valley, watching the beams of light twist and spin above the snowcapped mountains. She could definitely understand why the elves had turned Orem Vacker's flashing into such a celebration. It looked like fireworks and lasers and the aurora borealis had all been choreographed to dance around the eerie red moon.

But she hadn't felt like joining the festivities.

"So, I think I speak for everyone when I say, *You can teleport?*"

Sophie turned around, surprised to see Dex standing with Fitz, Keefe, and Biana—especially since he didn't even look annoyed about it.

"Oh, you figured that out, huh?" She'd been hoping it would take them a few days.

"Keefe told us."

"Yeah. I knew the moment you brought us home. Seriously, Foster, when are you going to realize you can't lie to an Empath?"

"I think I'm finally figuring that out. Not that it matters. You guys know all my darkest secrets now, don't you?"

"If you mean that you're secretly in love with me," Keefe said, plopping down beside her, "then yeah, everyone is *well* aware. And if you mean the stuff about your DNA, well . . . we heard Grady explaining that to Alden."

"Oh." She didn't have much more to say than that. Except, "Well, now you know how weird I am."

"Uh, I've always known that," Dex said, sitting on her other side. "But remember? I like weird."

"Me too," Biana chimed in.

"Me three," Fitz added, smiling so wide when she met his eyes that her heart fluttered. "We could all use a little more weird in our lives."

Sophie wasn't so sure she agreed. With how crazy everything had been, and all the things she still had to figure out, she wouldn't have minded if life got a little more normal for a while.

But maybe weird was okay too.

Especially if her friends were willing to accept it.

"Whoa, are you crying?" Keefe asked, and she blushed as she tried to smear away her tears. "You're supposed to cry when bad things happen, Foster, not good things."

"I know. I'm sorry. I don't know what's wrong with me."

"I do," Keefe said, taking her hand as Dex grabbed the other and Fitz and Biana each squeezed her shoulders. "Absolutely nothing."

Sophie smiled as she glanced up at the flickering lights in the sky, feeling nothing but calm and happiness as they flashed in her eyes. "I hate to say this, Keefe, but I think you might be right."

ACKNOWLEDGMENTS

Writing this book broke my brain into a million tiny pieces, and I never would've been able to put them back together without the help of many incredible people.

To my amazing husband, Miles: Thank you for putting up with all the late nights and travel days, for always making sure I have a steady supply of Pepsi, and for letting me steal your favorite Batman shirts for my glamorous writing attire.

To Mom and Dad: Thank you for your tireless efforts to get *Keeper* into the hands of kids, and for not being *too* scared of my imagination when you discovered the rather dark places my mind can go.

To Laura Rennert: Thank you for being the constant I can turn to in this ever-changing business. It's probably not part of your job description to be the Keeper of my Sanity, but you have risen to the task perfectly.

I also must thank Lara Perkins for being the Sender of Happy E-mails, the rest of the Andrea Brown Literary team for their ever-present support, Taryn Fagerness for her tireless efforts to share my stories with the world, and Sean Daily for navigating the chaos of Hollywood.

To Liesa Abrams: Thank you for the advice that helped me realize which stories I needed to tell, for trusting me when I basically abandoned the synopsis I'd given you, and for the notes that guided me out of the mess of that first draft.

I also want to thank everyone—and I really do mean everyone—at my incredible publisher, Simon & Schuster, especially Bethany Buck, Mara Anastas, Lauren Forte, Alyson Heller, Fiona Simpson, Anna McKean, Siena Koncsol, Carolyn Swerdloff, Julie Christopher, Emma Sector, Lucille Rettino, Paul Crichton, Michelle Fadlalla, Venessa Carson, Anthony Parisi, Ebony LaDelle, Matt Pantoliano, Michael Strother, Amy Bartram, Jeanine Henderson, Mike Rosamilia, and Mary Marotta, and the entire sales team. Plus a special thank you to Karin Paprocki for once again designing a breathtakingly beautiful cover, and Jason Chan for finding a way to top the *Keeper* artwork—something I didn't know was possible.

To Sara McClung: Thank you for the hours and hours and HOURS we spent brainstorming (I'm pretty sure my brain is still recovering from those), and for always asking the questions that lead me to the "Yay—I know how to fix the problem!!!" moment.

To Sarah Wylie: Thank you for always knowing how to pull me out of my deepest fears and doubts. I'm also pretty sure there wouldn't be a *Keeper* book with Keefe on the cover if it weren't for all of your rather, um . . . enthusiastic fangirling.

I also need to thank C. J. Redwine for always pushing me to be brave with my writing, Kiersten White for giving me an excuse to escape the deadline cave (especially since there's generally pizza involved), and Faith Hochhalter for constantly finding new ways to prove to me that I need to "trust the Book Babe." Huge thanks also go to the amazing ladies of Friday the Thirteeners, who are always available to cheerlead or commiserate, and all the awesome local SoCal writers for loyally attending my signings so I didn't have to worry about being there alone.

I wish I had space to thank by name all of the amazing teachers, booksellers, and librarians who have gone so above and beyond to share *Keeper* with their readers—but this book is pretty epic-length as it is. So just let me say to all of you: I know there are many books you could lend your support and energy to, and I will never be able to express how grateful I am that you've given it to mine. Thank you for everything you do. You are wonderful, wonderful people.

Thank you, Katie Bartow, for the fabulous blog tours and the many other ways you've helped me. And to the incredible people at SCIBA, thank you for the years of support and for always hosting my favorite events. I also have to thank Alyson Beecher, M. G. Buehrlen, Shannon O'Donnell, Kari Olson, Matthew Rush, and Courtney Stallings-Barr for their incredible encouragement, both online and off. And to all of my blog/

Twitter/Facebook/Tumblr/Instagram/Pinterest followers (man, I think I spend too much time online), thank you for connecting with me through these crazy social networks and braving my shenanigans.

And last—but definitely not least—I want to thank you (yes, YOU), my loyal, awesome readers! (I have to assume you're awesome if you've read this far, right?) An author can write a book and a publisher can print it and a bookstore or library can put it on their shelves—but it would still be nothing if no one ever picked it up and read it. Thank you for giving my stories a chance, for telling your friends and family to read them, for all the amazing e-mails you send me (even though it takes me forever to reply), for the incredible photos and fan art you send, and the adorable debates I see you have online about Dex, Fitz, or Keefe. I truly wrote these stories for you. Thank you for reading, and I hope you enjoy all of the adventures still to come!